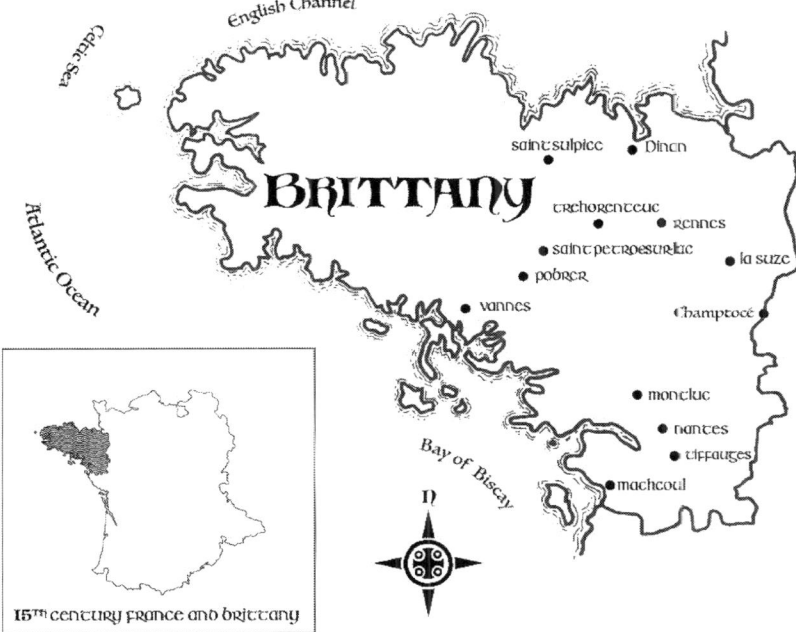

Celtic Sea

English Channel

saint sulpice
● Dinen ●

BRITTANY

trehorenteuc
● rennes ●
● saint petroesurlac
● la suze ●
● pobrer
Atlantic Ocean
● vannes
Champtocé ●

● moncluc

● nantes

● tiffauges
Bay of Biscay
● machcoul

N

15ᵀᴴ century France and Brittany

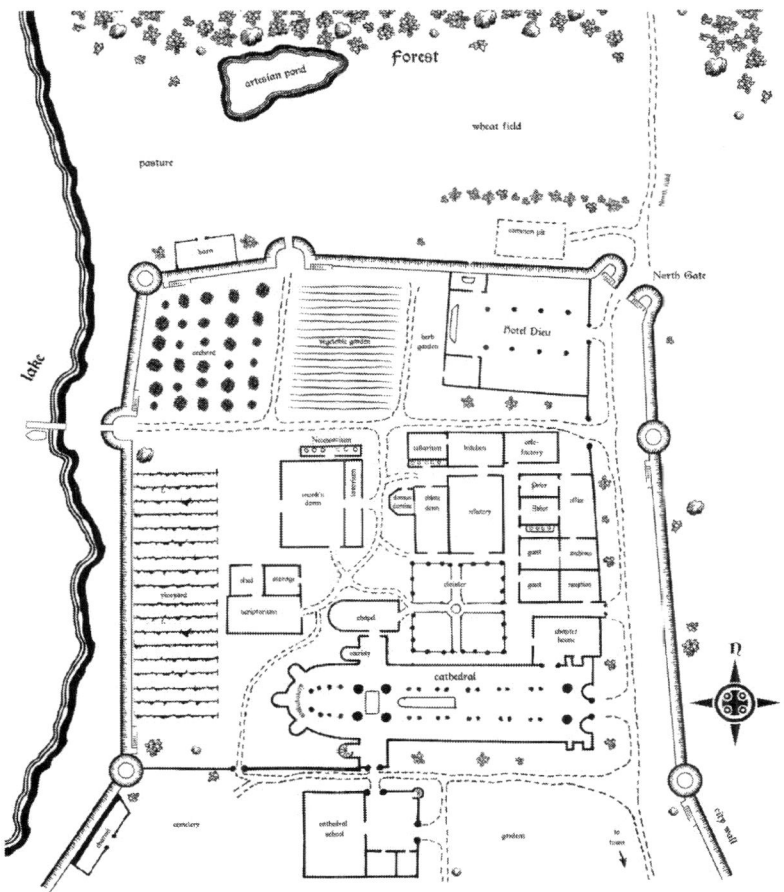

Abbey of Saint Benedict - Saint Petroc-sur-lac

The Oblate

P.A. Colón

To dear Anne and Dick, with
great affection and regard.
Pat Colón
March. 2021

Published by Amazon KDP.com

ISBN: 978-1-64970-194-7

Cover design by St. John Colón.

Cover: An Oblation from *Decretum* (MS 103) of Gratianus
(?-1160), courtesy of Médiathèque de Troyes Champagne, used by permission.

Also by P.A. Colón

Nurturing Children: A History of Pediatrics
A History of Children: A Socio-Cultural Survey
Tincture of Time: A Concise History of Medicine
Iconography: An Irreverent Introduction
Zeus in Art: A Survey of a Serial Seducer

For Billy

I, a mere boy, did not presume to oppose my father's wishes, but obeyed him in all things, for he promised me for his part, that if I became a monk I should taste of the joys of Heaven with the Innocents after my death.... And so a boy of ten, my father gave me, a weeping child, into the care of the monk, Reginald, and sent me away into exile for love of Thee, and never saw me again.

Orderic Vitalis, *Ecclesiastical History*
(c. 1138)

Yannnette, wife of Guillaume Sergent, living in the parish of Sainte Croix in Machecoul, in the village called Boucardière, says that around Pentecost a year ago her husband and she left their house and went to dig in a field so that he could plant some hemp, and they left their son, who was eight years old, at home so that he could watch their little daughter, a year and half old. Upon their return, they did not find their eight-year-old child, for reason of which they were very surprised and grieved. They went to the parishes of Machecoul and elsewhere to ask about him, but they have not since had any news of him, nor has he been seen by anyone.

Inquiry of 29 September 1440.
Canonical Trial Nantes, Brittany

PART ONE

1

ABDUCTION

Yann Dunard sold the finely fashioned armchair he had carved as a gift for Marie at a good price. It would provide food for a month. With the payment made to him secure in his pouch, he and Marie nudged their way through the bustling stream of shoppers and noisy vendors at the Saint Hélène market in Saint Petroc-sur-lac, oblivious to the smelly detritus of spoiling vegetables, animal dung, and steaming offal.

They reached the southern edge of the market when a chilling howl muffled the din and stilled movement except for heads that turned towards the source of the pitiful cry. People collected around a distraught woman in the arms of a man who made futile attempts to soothe her.

Muttering accounts of what had happened coursed through the crowd. 'Her daughter's gone missing . . . ,' '. . . fourth child to disappear this month,' '. . . six disappeared in six weeks.' Anxiety registered on dazed faces and shocked rumblings filled the square. 'The sheriff!' someone shouted. 'Go to the sheriff.' General acclamation pressed the man and woman forwards accompanied by a sympathetic few.

Shaken, Marie blurted, 'Yann! They are Megen and Benabic Redon, from our parish! It's their daughter Rozenn who is missing.'

'Holy mother of God. Yea. I've seen them at Mass.' They made the sign of the cross and stood numbly amongst those who frequented the market that boasted colourful wooden stalls with neatly arrayed shelves laden with goods that catered to the rich, and stalls of weathered wood in want of fresh paint and repair that sold wares to the humble. Unremarkable, except that amidst hundreds of people, a child who had accompanied her mother and father to buy household provisions on a mild sunny day in May 1434 had been kidnapped.

'Michel!' Marie exclaimed.

Yann's reassuring hand on his wife's shoulder calmed her. 'He is safe at school . . . but I shall only rest easy once our son is with us.' Wordlessly they walked, work cart in tow, towards Pobrér, south from the city in the region of Brittany close to the Broceliande forest. They passed parched and fissured leas, a wasteland that reflected the four years of drought that augured nothing but starvation and death.

The blighted landscape mirrored Yann's despair. His land was also barren, and he could no longer provide for his family. The pair hurried, each with their own thoughts. Marie longed for the time when Yann's toil was rewarded with marketable crops that allowed a modest surplus as well as sustenance. The security they had known and a happy family life had been riches enough – and would be still, if only it would rain.

Yann grappled with the heartache and guilt he felt regarding his decision to oblate Michel to the Church. For months he had concluded their circumstances left no alternative. It would save his boy's life, and he rationalised it was after all a common custom throughout Europe. Remorse, nevertheless, was the lingering consequence of his resolve.

The diminished population, by flight and starvation was but one aspect of the severity of the crisis. Multitudes had been afflicted with lethal contagious diseases and wasted by periodic raids of the infamous *écorcheurs* – deserters from the French army of the on-going One Hundred Years' War.

Kidnappings of children were but the latest misfortune that struck the community, intensifying the community's terror. Faith in God's providence was severely tested, but supplications to the Church and its saints never wavered, echoing throughout Saint Petroc's cathedral and in every church in the province.

Interlaced with pious appeals and the fear that prompted them were the infinite number of superstitious rituals commonly observed and trusted – universal beliefs rooted in faith their delusions would rescue them should all else fail.

Not all, but many in the Christian community, imbued with a millennia old mythos, deemed God's wrath the cause of their misery, and begged mercy and forgiveness for their sins. Droves of supplicants made offerings to the Church to gain God's favour. Those who had the means gave coins to the cathedral fund or to the abbey. The poor proffered a small quantity of grain or a pigeon in exchange for monks' prayers in their behalf. With hope penance for sins and God's forgiveness would bring them better fortune, folk slogged on macerated knees the length of the cathedral's nave to prostrate at the front altar in atonement.

Those who offered their children as oblates to God and to the Church supposed this was a particularly wondrous means to curry divine favour. Only the cynical scoffed it relieved a family of a mouth to feed, preserved whatever remained of an estate to bequeath, or rid a family of a deformed child whilst endowing a monastery additional labour to serve the religious community.

Yann and Marie Dunard were amongst those trapped in the vortex of social disintegration and the hopelessness it spawned. Their once deeply rooted happiness had long been displaced by desolation, but their love for each other and for their son – the joy that gave meaning to their lives – never waned. For Michel's sake, they forced cheerful demeanours to sustain the impression of a trouble-free household. The harmony of the past when evenings were spent with pleasing diversions after one of Marie's delectable meals was memory, of Yann entertaining the family on his double reed *bombard* whilst Marie and Michel tapped, clapped and sang merry tunes, dancing around Yann's hand-hewn table and benches in their one room cottage; the shrill sound of the *biniou* – a cherished part of Brittany's heritage and Yann's legacy bagpipe from his grandfather – often entertained them outdoors in fine weather after an arduous day in the fields and garden.

In those days, when crops grew plentifully, a five-year old Michel cheerily worked alongside Yann, jerking weeds out of the ground, careful not to disturb the vegetables taking root there. Marie tutoured her boy on botanical marvels that filled his mind with wonder as he watched her expertly season stews in the kitchen or prepare herbs to use for common ailments. Nightly rituals ended with prayer and bedtimes stories of the region's history and legends until, with a kiss, a drowsy Michel would turn on his side, ready for restful slumber.

The drought shattered those untroubled days, and as crops no longer grew, a blistering sense of looming disaster for the family consumed Yann's thoughts. Bereft of a means of sustenance, one by one he sold hand-crafted furniture and his beloved *bombard* and *biniou* to buy food. As their circumstances deteriorated, Yann finally dared to propose to Marie that Michel be given to the monastery. She rejected the proposition with all the power a threatened maternal devotion could marshal. Endless discussions met with resistance. Yann told her they were doomed. Marie argued spring would bring rain and new growth. Spring arrived. The drought persisted. There would be no crops, and Marie conceded they faced starvation.

The unprecedented kidnappings that had begun in April aroused in her the same degree of trepidation that assailed Yann. His pleas to oblate Michel began to have sway, especially when Yann appealed to her devout nature, persuading her God would pity them and bestow blessings as recompense for the sacrifice of the gift of their beloved son. This assertion crooked her thinking to believe the commitment of Michel to the monastery was God's Will and, in a monastery, he would be nurtured by good men and protected from the evil caitiffs lurking in the province.

Grim, on a dank mid-May night, Marie and Yann whispered outside the door of their cottage lest Michel be roused from sleep. Marie's somber face in the glow of a full moon illuminated the years of deprivation and want that had etched away a once winning countenance and dulled her once luminous green eyes. Yann's craggy features reflected the failure of his struggle to protect his family from the disaster that now threatened their lives. Both, still short of thirty-two years old, looked gaunt and worn, all passion spent.

Marie winced, shaking her head. Yann ignored her stubborn resistance and insisted, with agitation in his voice, 'We must tell Michel, then take him. Marie, you agreed!' Their fraught murmurs awakened Michel. He sensed tension and strained to decipher the discourse outside. When he heard his name mentioned, he vaulted to the shuttered window. 'The arrangement has been made. I have the required papers. The abbey has agreed to take him. We've hesitated too long in this. We must not wait longer.'

Marie keened, 'I cannot think to part with him. There *must* be another way.

'There is no other way,' Yann said curtly. He looked towards the cottage. 'Hush my love, Michel will hear us.' With weathered hands, Yann stroked Marie's dark hair, prematurely streaked with grey, and sheathed her close to his body. He rocked her soothingly with feigned optimism. 'Be not disconsolate. It will be alright.' He felt the sting of his lie. With Marie's face in his hands, he pleaded, 'For Michel's sake we must keep to our intent. You agreed a month ago . . . we *both* agreed it's the right thing to do,' he added impatiently. 'We shall give him life! A good life where he will be well cared for, be with those who love and serve God and who will love him. It is everything we could wish.'

Bitter thoughts of past and current hardship and the recent kidnappings ignited the foreboding that amplified with each passing day. 'I'm sore afraid for our son. That Redon girl. Just this morning. So many children disappeared in a matter of weeks! I fear for Michel, I tell you!' He added sourly, 'And must wonder where a meal will come from once this food is gone. I don't want him here when that time comes.'

'I can't endure the loss. Oh, Blessed Mary, help us.'

Yann sighed. 'Marie. My dearest love. I too am sick unto death.' He pulled Marie close to him as she relapsed into muzzled moans.

Aghast by what he had heard, Michel shuddered as he watched Marie and Yann slowly move away from the cottage into mist that now crowned the sky. The silky whistle of a springtime breeze became more audible than their distressed voices. There was no need to hear more. Michel understood their intention to forsake him. He shivered, ran to his bed, wrapped himself in a blanket and cried. Sleep that would ease his mind eluded him for a long time until, despite tears, a thumping heart, turmoil in his head and attempts to resist drowsiness, he lapsed into a fitful, agitated state, punctuated by ill-defined, but disturbing dreams.

Rivulets of sunlight filtering through the chinks of the cottage stirred Michel. He ran fingers through sweat-matted hair as currents of chill morning air coursed through the unevenly caulked wattle of the wall. Awake now, he saw that his parents' bed, not six paces away, was empty. *I've overslept. I'm late for school.* Then it came to him – the shattering pronouncement in the darkness of the night before his parents evaporated into a void. He ran to the door and flung it open, expecting to see them working in the field. The sunlight glowered straight on into his eyes. Squinting into the brightness, he scanned the mist that hovered over shriveled clods of desiccated earth. It was quiet and still. Not even a carrion crow disturbed the air. His mother and father were nowhere in sight. The sounds of horses' hoofs caught his attention. He looked south to see two men on horseback trotting, then galloping, towards him until he heard the welcome timbre of his mother's voice calling his name. He swiveled around and watched as, burdened by yokes on their shoulders, Marie and Yann lumbered towards the cottage. *They've been to the well is all,* and he ran happily towards them, eager to embrace them.

The men on horseback were nearly upon them. Yann noticed their fine clothes and wondered why gentlemen would approach at such a hurtling gait. It aroused his natural peasant's wariness. He hurried to Michel's side and cut short the boy's greeting, quietly ordering him to take the yoke and go with his mother to the cottage. Marie silently motioned her son to follow her.

Michel and his mother silently peeked through gaps in the shutters as the men talked to Yann. They appeared menacing. 'Mama, I should go and be with Papa.'

'No! Your father told you to stay with me,' she snapped. She smiled and drew him close to her. 'He will be alright, my brave knight.' Kissing his forehead, she laughed, 'So like your patron, Saint Michel l'Archange. Always ready to do battle with the devil!'

Some minutes passed before the men spurred on and Yann walked to the cottage, his face etched with sadness. Marie and Michel dashed towards him, curious and uneasy. 'Who were they Papa?'

'No matter. They are gone.' Yann looked at Marie and said unhappily, 'It is time. It must be now.' Marie flinched. Yan said quietly, 'Michel, go. Water the garden. Then I want to talk to you.'

Without a word, Michel headed towards the garden patch, disquieted to see the red and puffy eyes that disfigured his mother's face.

Yann told Marie he could of course not be certain, but he sensed wickedness. 'They said they wanted him as a page for a lord. They offered me money. Do they take me for a fool?' He took Marie by her hands and said tremulously, 'I think they have something to do with the children who have been seized.'

Marie nodded. 'The way they stared at Michel as they approached. It was . . . unclean.'

'We must take him to the monastery now.'

'Tomorrow, Yann. Please. It is Michel's birthday.'

'I had forgot that,' Yann said sadly. 'A babe born on the feast of Saint Isidore, patron saint of farmers. A cruel joke. The saint has failed us, and now we lose our son.' He brushed away tears and shook his head. 'No, Marie. We must go today. Through the woods. I do not want to come upon those men.'

When Michel returned, Marie sighed and said flatly, 'I love you, my sweet boy.' He stared at her dumbly. The assertion sounded like a death knell. Yann hugged him gently and carried him to a bench. Michel's nightmare was evolving into reality.

Tears fell as Michel listened to his father say he was to be an oblate in the monastery. The prospect depressed him. *Live like a hermit? Beg on the street? Be a servant?* He loathed every aspect of monastery life as he imagined it. 'I do not want to go, Papa,' he said with a break in his voice.

Yann strained to keep his composure. 'We are heart sore to have you go . . . but the good monks will take care of you. He added, hoping to appeal to Michel's love of learning, 'You're a clever boy. You'll be able to go to the cathedral school.'

'Listen to your Papa. Indeed, you have told me you want to study at a university one day. Pray think how wonderful that would be for you.' Marie's attempted enthusiasm sounded limp, her voice hollow, despite the hopes she harboured for her gifted son.

It was she who had insisted Michel attend school, just as she had studied at the Abbey of Le Pallet founded by the great Heloise until she was called home to help work the family homestead. Her passion for poetry and history persisted, and she often went to the abbey to sit at the feet of her beloved Soeur Deirdre, who taught her French, the history of Brittany and France, and read poems written by Master Pierre Abelard, the beauty of which made the soul soar.

The family lapsed into silence as they sat at the table Michel had helped his father build. *The hand carved armchair.* Its absence and the empty space amplified Michel's sense he too was disposable. Marie rose and went to the hearth for the pot of fortifying *blé noir* she had prepared for the long walk to the abbey and served it. She sidled back on to the bench beside Michel. They ate the gruel without appetite.

Giggles and squeals permeate the otherwise quiet surroundings as three children play a game of chase and tag on a dusty road. Aedden, a fourteen-year old, charged to mind them whilst their parents took their last pig to the slaughterhouse, sits at the entrance to their cottage bored and barely attentive to the antics of his siblings. Eight-year old Dilwyn is fast on his feet and easily wins out over his younger brother and sisters. Winoc and Katerine are accustomed, unbothered, to losing games. It's great sport to play, and who wins doesn't matter.

The children pause and fall silent as hoof beats distract them. They move to the side of the road and stare as four horsemen on elegant horses ride towards them. When the men, richly attired, draw near, they rein in their horses and dismount. Aedden leaps to his feet, eyeing them suspiciously.

'Good day to ye. Where is your father, child?'

Dilwyn tells him he is not at home. 'And your mother?'

All three shake their heads.

One man smiles and asks, 'Do you like horses, little girl?'

Katerine answers, excitement in her voice. 'Oh indeed, sir.' She turns to her brothers for confirmation.

'Would you like to ride on one?'

The children barely contain their exhilaration.

Aedden is upon them and snaps heatedly. 'Look you. They go nowhere with you. We do not know who you be. Why pose this? You be but strangers.'

'Good day to you lad. We mean no harm. We thought only to amuse the children – and you if you like. We might ride to a place we know that has sweets and other treats.'

'No! I'll not allow that. Be on your way – now!' Aedden turns to his brothers and sister and orders them inside. The children, disappointed but obedient, turn towards the cottage just as one of the strangers, sneering, clouts Aedden with force enough to fell him to the ground. The children recoil and, screaming, begin to run, but the men easily take hold of them as they kick and shriek. One of the men takes opium and mandragora soaked sponges from his backpack and watches as his fellow lowlife thrust the soporific into each child's nostril. It takes little time for them to go limp. Holding fast to each hostage, the men adroitly mount. The lead horseman deftly lifts the unconscious Aedden onto his horse. The band with their victims take off in a canter into a forested road north. The kidnappings took no more than five minutes.

'Michel, are you ready?' Marie fondly stroked his hair. She arranged her head scarf and patched shawl around her shoulders and took hold of a small bundle. We leave now.' She turned away, biting her lip. 'Yann, have you the petition?'

'Yes, Marie.' He glumly showed her the small *palimpsest* made from well used parchment on which the village scribe had written for him the promise to oblate Michel to the monastery.

Michel paused at the door to commit to memory each feature of his home. He turned abruptly and walked into the late morning light. At the sound of the door closing, his spirits sagged, but he did not look back as they walked towards Saint Petroc sur-lac and the abbey, heavyhearted but resigned to life in a monastery.

As they trudged through woodland hills into glens, none were heartened by the occasional twitter of birds that vainly foraged for berries. The clear sky and hot sun gave no comfort as they passed clearings of dehydrated earth and dried up streams and ponds. All the sights and sounds betokened the drought that had determined their fate, evoking embittered thoughts. Above them, gliding vultures hovered. Apt symbols of the decay of the blighted region.

On the main road within sight of the walled city of Saint Petroc-sur-lac and Lac Gwencallon, Michel's mood lifted. He skittered ahead towards its edge. His hopes to skip stones were dashed as he surveyed the dry lakebed, and he looked for other diversions.

Several roads swarmed with people on their way to town. At one lonely fork from the southeast a man unsettlingly stumbled forwards, breathless, haggard, and alone. People on the main road warily distanced themselves from him. Yann and Marie felt uncomfortably close to him and followed suit. The stranger called out to them, and Yann succumbed to courtesy. Despite misgivings, he retraced his steps, reluctantly followed by Marie.

The man's face had the growth of several unshaven days. His clothes were those of a gentleman but were wrinkled and stained. A red-enameled cross intersected with four small crosses hung from a chain.

‡

'*Monsieur, Madame* – good day to you.' He wiped his brow with a cloth. His shortness of breath was pronounced. Yann haltingly tipped his hat. Marie smiled faintly, but tugged at Yann, silently urging him to walk on. The man posed a question that stalled them. He spoke in French and Yann understood at best only the gist of what the stranger gravelly had spoken. Yann thought it sounded like his father's voice just before he died.

'This path, you say? It leads directly to the gate into town.'

'Do you know of an inn therein?'

Yann deferred to Marie's comprehending ears and she hurriedly answered, hoping to be clear of him. 'Go to the main square. The best inn is the Herblain.'

Yann hesitated. 'May I assist you, sir?' Marie agitatedly pulled at his shirt again, but repeated the question in French.

'Oh, no need. I am merely tired from a long journey. I shall welcome rest at the inn. Do continue on your way.' He beckoned a farewell. Marie and Yann scurried away from the unknown traveller. They returned the wave Michel, some distance ahead, had conferred.

The old man took not more than ten steps when he staggered and fell to the ground, emitting a piercing cry of pain. Yann and Marie spun around with a start and, despite qualms, went to him. They helped him to his feet, supporting him as he stood on unsteady legs. Marie noted people going to town consciously kept their distance. She yearned to be amongst them. The man coughed repeatedly, huffing for breath. Yann and Marie looked at each other with alarm.

Michel had seen the man fall and his parents go to his rescue, and darted towards them. Marie saw him approaching and shouted shrilly. 'No. Stay there.' Michel instantly stopped and regarded the bewildering scene from afar.

The stranger forced a deep breath. 'I am better now.'

'*Pas de tout, Monsieur.*' Marie insisted.

'Oh yes, quite alright. Please, go on. I am fine.'

With mounting anxiety, Yann and Marie turned, eager to absent themselves and meet up with Michel. Relief and a hug momentarily eased Marie's mind when they reached their son. As they continued towards the town, Marie looked back and watched as the stranger progressed slowly and with difficulty. She saw him go off the road and lie down under a tree. She said nothing, but unease shifted to foreboding.

Marc Gervais awoke with a start, with perturbed thoughts about the day's challenges. He dressed quickly and, as per his habit, flung the chain of office of the Sheriff of Saint Petroc-sur-lac over his well-worn leather knee length coat, well-aware the medallion inspired confidence and respect in others.

He had an intelligent face, with penetrating blue eyes that denoted a man of serious intent. Tall and firmly muscled, with a large head covered in a mane of coarse blond hair, he was a youthful thirty-four. The small scars on his chin and over his left eye were the badges he had brought back from battles in Normandy. He still carried himself like a soldier.

Anxiety gnawed at him. The celebration of the feast of Saint Isidore together with the procession of the Baron Gilles de Rais through the city guaranteed chaos. The arrival of the baron in Saint Petroc-sur-lac, always orchestrated by him as a spectacle, was a disruptive force that lured sneak thieves to prey on distracted onlookers. Marc and his deputies would be rigourously tested to maintain order.

Despite the stratagems Marc and the commandant of the civic guards had meticulously crafted and the drills he had rehearsed repeatedly with his own men, at best Marc predicted disorderly conduct throughout the town and the necessity for exhaustive surveillance of known and suspected mischief makers.

It was the worst of the possibilities that caused him anguish. The revels and the size of the crowd they attracted would make the detection of scoundrels difficult, even impossible. Abduction of another child was an easily imagined possibility, and the thought sickened him. Marc laboured to concentrate on his responsibilities for the day –

a review with his well-trained men and a meeting with the mayor late afternoon to report on the missing children. Why such a day had been chosen by the mayor was beyond Marc's grasp.

'Churlish fool,' he muttered. He massaged throbbing temples. His investigation of the six children who had disappeared had been thus far fruitless, and he dared not imagine having to cope with another kidnapping. With no progress made in his investigation and scant information to convey, he faced a disagreeable encounter that would amount to nothing more than an opportunity for Gondore Serrigond to launch a torrent of verbal abuse.

Marc despised the mayor. He sensed the man had no honest concern about the kidnapped children or any interest in any aspect of civic life for that matter. Political advancement was what he was after, and any municipal failure blighted his reputation and threatened his ambitions. Marc thought the mayor vainglorious and totally devoid of principle. In his view, he was contemptible.

Marc shrugged off his thoughts and steeled himself to the primary task of the day – rely on his deputies and keep the people of Saint Petroc-sur-lac safe. He left his house with one thought in mind: it was in God's hands now.

Sentinels with halberds stood on the turrets that capped the seemingly impenetrable ten-metre high wall that sur-rounded the city. The broad portcullises at the entrances to the once ancient stone citadel were raised in an invitation to throngs of folk from the surrounding countryside come to attend the festival and see the baron. With experienced eyes, guards, arrayed in the colourful green and yellow of the city's standard, speedily assessed those who entered with an aim to ferret out deviant looking characters.

At the south gate, Michel and his parents were pressed forwards by the exuberant crowd. Michel sensed an occasion and suppressed all thought of the providence the day held for him. 'There is a fête. Surely so.' He pleaded,

'Can we go to the town square? There will be mimes and jugglers.'

'All kinds of merriment,' Marie said imploringly.

Yann feigned good humour and smiled assent. 'Saint Isidore's Day and Michel's tenth birthday as well. Indeed, a day for celebration.' They inched their way through the pack of high-spirited revelers on a winding street until all spilled into the Place d'Aszhur, named for the king of the Arthurian legend rooted in the region.

The square had been transformed for the occasion. Colourful banners festooned the half-timbered town houses around the square, gamboling in the wind in harmony with the mood of euphoric revelers. The crush of the roisterers swept the Dunard family to the centre of the square. All jockeyed for position to best view the larkings of troubadours, jugglers, acrobats, magicians and puppeteers, there to entertain and earn a *sou* or more.

The raucous sounds and the holiday atmosphere enthralled Michel. 'Look. A bear!' Before Yann could restrain him, the boy jostled through the pack until he was but feet away from the impressively fearsome looking animal. Marie and Yann squeezed through the crowd as they vainly tried to reach his side. They contented themselves to stand, with a watchful eye, a short distance from their errant son.

The size of the great brown bear was astounding. When the trainer coaxed it to stand and prance on two feet, doubling its height, the spectators screeched. The bear threateningly swaggered close to the crowd, initiating a scampered, howling retreat.

Michel stood unmoved, transfixed. A mild sense of intimidation was countered by exhilaration as the formidable beast approached and stopped directly in front of him. Michel stood his ground even when the bear raised a paw and growled menacingly. The trainer quickly tightened his hold on the animal's chain and yanked him back from the crowd. With an admiring backward glance, he called out to Michel, *'Tu as beaucoup de courage, mon petit homme.'*

Marie and Yann edged their way to Michel's side as the bear performed additional sportive tricks at a safe distance from the onlookers. Their expressions reflected relief. Michel's was full of wonder.

They moved on, enticed by entertaining feats by jugglers and sword swallowers, and paused to laugh at clowns' capers, watch strident puppets, and be suitably dumbfounded by a conjurer's tricks.

Yann touched Michel's shoulders and said, 'Come. I have been told there is to be a grand spectacle. We should look for a good place to watch.'

As guards resolutely forced back the mob to form a broad channel to and from the square, Michel and his parents found themselves in a prized position near the steps of the town's municipal centre, with none to obstruct their view. The bishop, mayor, members of the city council and other dignitaries, flanked by guards, stood fashioned as a welcoming tableau.

A resounding fanfare charged the air. Startled pigeons flitted from the complacency of their roosts into the sky in all directions. Thunderous cheers greeted scores of richly appareled noblemen trotting on horseback into the Place d'Aszhur. The sartorial beauty astonished Michel.

Subdued, honeyed voices drew his attention away from the equine parade to a procession of young boys dressed in white. A musician played a portable organ carried by several men. The children chanted melodic encomiums about their benefactor. The sweet harmony hushed the onlookers as the choir processed to the steps of the town hall, where they formed rows on both sides of the rostrum.

An eruption of tumultuous cheers doused the choral voices as the luminary responsible for generating the frenzy theatrically materialised. He was astride a great stallion, satin black and bedecked in a caparison adorned with ornaments and jewels fashioned from pale blue silk and decorated with fleurs-de-lys and a coat of arms dominated by a swan with a spread wings argent. He rode at a restrained gait into the square as universal gasps of approval intermittently vied with uproarious acclaim that surged to a deafening pitch.

Michel, spellbound by the grandeur, scrutinised the handsome man, who had a neatly trimmed bluish-black beard and thick dark shoulder length hair. He sported an elegant, plumed, broad brimmed hat, and his lush garments of velvet and silk were complemented by a satin tunic set with precious gems emblazoned with a large gold-threaded embroidered fleur-de-lys.

Dashing and imperious, with an air of one accustomed to admiration and deference, he drew on his horse's reins so that it reared and pawed the air dramatically. He resumed a dawdling step as he acknowledged the adulation of the cheering onlookers.

Abruptly and expertly he halted his mount at the steps of the town hall. The obsequious welcoming congregation reverentially bowed as he alighted from his horse. The mayor advanced forwards. The boisterous assembly respectfully fell attentively silent as the mayor delivered what to a few was an unctuous message regarding the deemed honour the illustrious visitor bestowed.

With a practiced aura of modesty that cloaked a faintly disguised *hauteur*, the recipient of the effusive banalities bowed a salute and smiled cordially and feigned a blended expression of interest and humility. Smiling engagingly, he nimbly returned the accolade with excessive pronounce-ments of his own that charmed everyone.

The Bishop of Saint Petroc-sur-lac, Bernard du Loi, raised his right hand and imperiously stood apart from the others. With lightening agility that startled Michel, the nobleman removed his hat, vaulted towards the bishop, and fell to his knees to receive a blessing. The crowd responded with a buzz of approval as the bishop awarded him the Church's holy graces.

Turning to the crowd, the dashing figure briefly addressed the awed assembly before adroitly mounting his horse. He coerced it to pirouette in place several times. A deafening ovation ensued, and once more agitated birds rocketed in confused flight. With raffish waves of his hat and dashing flashes of a charismatic, if studied, smile, the prestigious celebrity accepted the crowd's acclamation with what could be considered condescending nods of appreciation. A flamboyant wave of his hat excited even greater clamour as, at an exaggeratedly leisured pace, he exited the square and headed towards the north gate of Saint Petroc, followed by his flashy entourage. The roars, in diminishing waves of timbre, faded away as did the apparition that had dazzled them.

The town's public figures disbanded, and the assembled masses disbursed in pursuit of festival diversions as Michel, transfixed by the majesty of what he had seen, stood stock-still. He turned to his father and said wistfully, 'I shall never see anything so grand again.' Yann's expression bared the guilt he felt, until Michel plied him with enthused questions that established the bliss, not lament, he in fact felt. 'Papa, who is he? He must be very famous. Is he the king?'

Yann laughed. 'No, not the king, but you're right. He is famous. He is Baron Gilles de Rais of Brittany, a Marshal of the Army of France and known throughout the land as the man who fought at Orléans with Jeanne d'Arc. The king proclaimed him worthy to wear the royal fleur-de-lys. A very special honour. He has many castles in Brittany, and I suppose he is going to one of them now, near Tréhorenteuc. I know little else; except he is highly esteemed and exceedingly rich.'

'I think he must be very nice,' Michel said and added diffidently, 'He looked directly at me and smiled.'

'Indeed. They say he's very devout.' Marie remarked, 'He smiled at you, you say?'

'Oh yes. I am sure of it.'

'Well,' said his father. 'That is something to remember.'

Michel fantasised that to be a page in the baron's household would please him more.

Of a sudden, Marie gripped Yann's arm. 'Those men,' she whispered with alarm.

Yann caught her eye and turned in the direction of her gaze. He nodded. 'The same. We must go. Now!' He took a confused Michel by hand in a tight grasp and dragged him along with Marie just behind. Once out of the square amongst a group of people enlisted as unwitting security for them from any menace, Michel sensed his mother and father relax, and he silently relived the marvels he had seen. He kissed his mother and father and blurted, 'This has been the most wonderful day I ever had!' Yann and Marie exchanged plaintive glances but forced smiles as they meandered on a quiet lane that would direct them to the main road that led to the abbey's monastery. Michel inhaled the tantalising aromas as they passed houses along the way that fueled his appetite. Residential life never seemed so appealing and a monastery so abjectly alien.

2

THE ABBEY

The Abbey of Saint Benedict towered over the town and the landscape beyond. Built in the eighth century as a lowly monastery to house nine monks, it now accommodated more than forty monks, fifty lay brothers and twenty-four oblates. Within its confines were a cathedral and its school, a scriptorium, and a hospital, and a charnel house.

The seven-hundred-year old monastery preserved much of its original facade. In contrast, several architectural imprints had transformed the original tenth century cathedral. The Romanesque features of thick buttresses, massive columns and ponderous arches had been replaced through the centuries with graceful gothic architectural features of incomparable beauty.

'First a visit to the cathedral and then we shall have the feast I prepared.' Michel hugged Marie. She laughed. 'Yes, my dearest boy, we have time.' She put her arm around his shoulder and, with effort, wanting to believe it herself, continued, 'Your Papa and I will come to the cathedral every holy day when the monks and oblates join the community in worship. We'll be able to see you then. What joy that will be for us.'

'So! We can have visits then?' Michel asked hopefully.

With a bowed head, Yann responded. 'We're not sure, my little one. Perhaps.'

Yann, Marie, and Michel entered the cathedral with the reverence the space inspired. They gazed at the recently painted azure ceiling adorned with bright stars. It seemed they had entered a celestial world in which the presence of God was corporeal. They wafted down the long nave, marvelling at the towering stained-glass windows and murals on the walls that depicted bible stories, the life of Christ, and the lives of saints. The cathedral's ribbed arches that extended to a lofty ceiling were a giddying height and seemed exalted enough to touch paradise itself. Michel thought a bird would be lost in such a place, unable to find its way into nature.

At the main altar, they knelt and bowed their heads in prayer. Each prayed with special zeal, and especially to Jesus' Holy Mother. They recited together the venerated *Ave Maria* known to all the faithful who, with this prayer appealed intervention of God for blessings. Marie and Yann Dunard prayed for the happiness and welfare of their beloved Michel. He pleaded for rescue from the austere monastic life to which he felt condemned.

Marie and Yann rose to their feet, smiling to cloak their misery. Michel followed them as they moved down the nave towards the cathedral's doors. For them and for all the genuinely devout, the cathedral was a symbol of an all-powerful and loving God. It was a sanctuary for all, a place for prayer and worship, for comfort, shelter, and escape from worldly woes. For all of those who lived lives that were harsh, mired in despair, and shorn of hope, the cathedral was heaven on earth.

Once outdoors, they strolled to the cathedral garden, now in full bloom with a myriad variety of flowers. 'Look. Over there, with some monks,' Michel cried out. 'Paol Eric – from my school.'

Marie was quick to distract his attention. 'Come sit beside me on the grass and taste the delicious *tortierre* I made especially for you.'

Yann sighed and said simply, 'You'll see him later. It will be good to be with your friend. I'm happy for you.' Reaching for a leather pouch, he affected good cheer. 'Ah, cider!' That proved an effective distraction, and Michel turned hungrily to the food. He ate greedily, savouring wonderful flavours. It had been a long time since he had tasted meat.

He and his parents chatted and laughed about the wonders of the day. It was a happy time, like those he had known throughout his life until . . . until now. He gazed at his mother as she finished her meal, and a pervasive unhappiness overcame him.

Yann stood, extended his hand to Michel, and said, with woe in his expression and in his voice, 'We must go to the monastery my son.' In a brighter tone, he said playfully, 'Come, hold my hand. You are not too old for that!'

Michel obediently stood and tightly latched on to his father's hand as tension rose within him. Marie also clutched her son's hand firmly and forced a reassuring smile as they walked to the front entrance of the monastery.

The faithful of the Saint Petroc-sur-lac region were indebted to the dedicated monks of Saint Benedict for their unstinting service to the community's spiritual and material needs. Believing them to be virtuous men who lived Christ's dictum to love one another had given Marie and Yann courage to entrust their son to these good souls. To Michel, the abbey and those in it appeared threatening – austere and unfriendly. As they approached the gate, Michel slackened his pace. 'It is not beautiful like the cathedral.'

With forced cheerfulness, Yann told him, 'It will be wonderful to live in such a place. It's quite comely, I'm sure of it.' Michel was skeptical.

They arrived at the great door of the monastery in stressed silence. Yann yanked on a rope that triggered cantilevered bells to ring. Marie knelt in front of Michel and said, 'I must leave you here.'

Michel panicked and clung to her. 'Why can't you come with me?'

Marie shook her head sadly. 'It is not permitted.' She clasped him tightly to her bosom and kissed him. 'I give you my blessing, my little one. I know you will make me proud of you every day in everything you do. Remember this. I shall always walk beside you with love to guide you.' She forced loose her son's hold on her, turned and ran off, repressing howls. She headed towards the cathedral to seek whatever solace she might find there. She heard Michel cry for her, and she stifled screams.

Michel's futile appeals to his mother were muted by the yowl of the entrance gate as it swung opened. He spun about in a paroxysm of fear to see the porter, an old, bent monk dressed in a coarse black robe. With dismay, he noted the monk had a tonsure. *All monks have tonsures.* Sullenly, he worried they would shear the crown of his head too.

'Good day, Brother.' I am Yann Dunard. This is my son, Michel. I have come to offer him to Holy Mother Church.' Michel reeled as the finality of the intention intensified his wretchedness. He choked back tears.

'Come in,' said the monk pleasantly, with a smile directed at Michel. 'I am Brother Alaric. The abbot has been awaiting you for some time.' He admitted them into the monastery reception room, and bowed a farewell.

Yann sat nervously and Michel paced. He dared not look at his father lest he cry. Suddenly, he called out, 'Papa, I am afraid.'

Yann saw his agitated face and, supposing he knew the cause, unleashed remorseful guilt feelings. 'I am so, so sorry. Please, child. We would give our lives to keep you with us if we could.' He bowed his head. 'Michel, forgive me.'

Michel's consternation deafened Yann's lamentation as he bounded to his father's side and pulled on his sleeve.

'Come. Quickly. Come see. Demons and devils. They are horrifying.'

Yann and Michel, repulsed by a painting with dreadful images, stared at a decomposing, nearly skeletal body with snakes, lizards, and toads emerging from a disemboweled abdomen. A laughing, hideous creature held the hand of a richly dressed prelate – a pope, perhaps. An equally grisly, wasted being, also laughing and dancing, traversed a field with what appeared to be from the cut of their apparel, a king, a cardinal, a bishop, a monk, and men of high rank. Yann squirmed when he saw a humble tradesman and a peasant woman in the group. The inference was clear – they all were going to hell.

Yann put his arms around Michel to shield him from the hideous figures just as three monks crossed the threshold. Assessing their state and the cause of it, one approached them and smiled reassuringly. 'Peace be onto you, my sons. I am William, Abbot of the Abbey of Saint Benedict.'

To Michel he said, 'Do not be troubled. In time our monastery will become a familiar and, I have no doubt, an agreeable place to you.' He motioned towards the offending painting with a brush of his hand. 'This theme has been called a *Danse Macabré* since the late 1300s. In the fullness of time, my son, you will understand it represents those whose lives offended God. You are but a child and cannot yet understand the wickedness of the world this scene signifies. Be assured our existence here is to gain God's favour by leading lives of goodness through charity and prayer.' He peered into the frightened child's eyes. 'We are here to protect you and guide you to grace and virtue, and shall do so with love and kindness. Be not afraid. You come to God and will do here his work on earth.'

Michel inspected Abbot William. He was tall, much taller than his father, and trim, with ginger hair and blue eyes. He noticed his spotless black habit was too short, well above his bony ankles, and his sandals appeared much too big for his feet. He smothered a nervous titter as they squeaked when he walked.

The abbot noted the boy's lively brown eyes were inflamed from crying, and he ruffled his shiny brown hair good-naturedly. His facial expression was warm, reassuring. 'Michel - after the archangel who courageously fought and triumphed over the devil?'

Yann murmured, 'Indeed, my Lord, the saint is his patron.'

The abbot said amiably. 'You must have great aspirations for him.'

'Michel has honoured us in every respect, my Lord, and I believe you will not find him wanting in any way.'

The abbot turned to Michel and told him, 'Fear not, Michel. We have no devils here for you to vanquish, but here you will be able to do Saint Michael's work by leading souls, as he does, to God.'

William looked admiringly at the boy, thinking the child would do well. There seemed something exceptional about him. He was sure of it, and he considered his judgement in such matters rarely flawed.

Abbot William motioned to proceed. Yann gave him the petition. 'Brother Julien and Brother Brien will witness the oblation.' The abbot looked at Yann and Michel sympathetically and asked: 'Do you both understand this decision is binding until well beyond puberty?' His voice was kindly, but authoritative.

Michel and Yann looked at each other glumly. Neither one knew what puberty meant. It sounded ominous. There was a suspended pause. Finally, both muttered simultaneously, 'I understand.'

'Michel, we shall clothe you, feed you, and educate you. In our care, through prayer and good works, you will find comfort and strength and learn to accept God's will in all things. Will you promise to live by the rules as set down by Saint Benedict and followed here? What say you to this?'

'I do so promise, my Lord,' he said, dejection in his voice and ignorant of what the rules were.

'Yann Dunard, please sign the petition to be witnessed and made irrevocable until the boy's twenty-fifth year. This is our abbey's rule.'

Yann took the quill offered him, his hand shaking. With one fist clenched, he began to trace each letter of his name, much as he had rehearsed doing in Marie's presence. Brothers Julien and Brien each took a quill and added their names to the document with facility. Yann Dunard sighed with resignation.

'Come follow me,' the abbot said. They walked to an altar above which hung a painting of the mother of Christ cloaked in a great blue cape spread open to display the multitude of humankind she protected. Michel felt weak, but stood quietly, exerting to steady himself.

'Yann, place your hand on your Michel's shoulder,' Abbot William said with a sympathetic voice.

Yann kissed Michel's head and whispered, 'I love you.'

Abbot William intoned the traditional proclamation of oblation: '*Almighty God, we humbly ask that, through the intercession of Saint Benedict, you bless this child who enters our abbey as an oblate. Grant him your grace to do good works and true charity and guide him with your love for the goodness of his soul and salvation. This we ask through Christ our Lord. Amen.*

So. It is done,' the abbot murmured. Turning to the child he sympathetically said, 'Henceforth you will be called by your locative name: Michel de Pobrér. And now you must now bid farewell to Yann Dunard.'

The abbot's pronouncement smarted like a lethal wound. Yann stiffened, embraced Michel, gave him his blessing, and wrested himself free from the boy's unyielding grip. As he swung around, he nodded to the abbot and tore out of the room and from the abbey to join Marie in grief.

Michel stood with tears streaming down his face. The abbot gestured to Brother Brien, and said to Michel, 'You will now meet the *Domus Magisterium*, Prior Fidelis, who will guide you in all things and will help you to become accustomed to monastery life.'

Brother Brien smiled. 'Welcome to the Monastery of Saint Benedict. Follow me, Michel de Pobrér.' Silent and wooden, the child trailed the monk past the cloister, frightened, but inquisitive. He scrutinised every building as they passed by.

'Prior Fidelis eagerly awaits you. He will be your teacher. He is to be addressed – as are all teachers – as

Magister.' The monk smiled. You are going to like him very much!'

'Prior Fidelis, this is Michel de Pobrér, our new oblate.' They were in the abbey's vegetable garden. Michel glanced at several oblates tilling the soil but focused on Fidelis. He knelt at the border of an herbal bed and grimaced from stiffened knees as he rose. 'Ah, at last! I have been told about you.' He greeted Michel jovially and with the sign of the cross as a blessing. 'Welcome to our humble monastery.'

Fidelis had a kind face. Michel studied his short, mostly white beard and his unruly hair which seemed to spring in all directions from the tonsure at the top of his head. Short and endowed with a rotund figure that filled his habit, he had a pleasing countenance, one that appeared to smile with perpetual geniality. The tension Michel felt lessened in the amiable glow of Fidelis' presence.

'Come meet your companions.'

Michel took note the oblates appeared pleased as Fidelis approached them. There were five oblates, and all inspected him thoroughly, as he did them. He seemed to be the youngest of the group. The tallest appeared to be no more than fourteen. One boy had a crooked back. Another, a club foot.

'Continue your work, lads. I want to show Michel the *dormitorium.'*

Michel followed Fidelis from the garden past the kitchen to a funereal room with a large fireplace in the middle. With a sweeping gesture, Fidelis told him, 'This is where oblates sleep and spend recreation time. In winter, a fire burns from Vespers to Matins.' Michel looked confused. *Vespers. Matins. What are they?* 'You will appreciate the warmth, I warrant you!'

Michel thought the unadorned room dreary and unwelcoming, despite the promise of a winter fire. There were straw filled mats on wooden frames, not unlike the cot in Michel's cottage, and several small tables and benches. Fidelis led him to one in the corner of the room. Thoughts of home provoked tears. Brother Fidelis chose to ignore them.

The monk deduced the Dunard family to be extremely poor, but proud and loving, judging by the worn, but clean rags the child wore. The boy was scrawny – under-nourished. Whenever Fidelis thought about the desperation parents felt that induced them to part with their children, he imagined the sorrow he was certain such decisions exacted. He prayed to God for guidance and understanding, for the world's harshness was extremely hard to accept.

Fidelis felt an obligation to help oblates adjust to what assuredly for them was a strange way of life. He had a gift that could judge when bleak clouds lifted displaced by confidence, optimism, and resilience. To encourage that end, Fidelis spent a part of the day working side by side with novitiates in his beloved garden, and he designated older, seasoned, oblates to guide new boys in the routine and rhythm of monastery life. His good humour cheered all the oblates, and he often entertained them as they worked the soil with adventuresome tales – true and invented.

Fidelis showed the boy a neat pile of clothing. 'This shirt – a *camisa* – is worn under the black gown – a *froccus.* Monks wear a *scapulare propter opera,* a tunic to protect monastic robes whilst we work. We have designed a simple pectoral for oblates to wear around the neck. It is modeled after the scapular miraculously given to a Carmelite monk in England – Saint Simon Stock – in 1251. There is a special grace in wearing it as a reminder to seek indulgences for salvation through prayer. It is to be worn always, removed only for cleansing.'

Michel examined the strange looking two rectan-gular patches made of coarse brown wool attached to strings of twine. There were images on both sides: Mary, a Greek symbol of Christ, an image of Saint Benedict, and of Christ crucified. Fidelis put the scapular over Michel's head. One patch lay on his back, the other on his chest. It made his skin itch.

'We look to the Rule of Saint Benedict to guide us. Before and above all things, care must be taken of the sick and the poor, that they be served, in very truth, as Christ is served.' Fidelis exclaimed, 'Benedict's very words, Michel, more than nine hundred years ago! He asks us to serve people in God's name, obey the abbot in all things, to own nothing, and to live a chaste life.'

Michel weakly nodded. Fidelis noted how forlorn he seemed and smiled sympathetically. 'Dear boy, be not troubled. I have assigned two kind lads to guide and help you adapt to our ways here.' He added amiably, 'Tomorrow after breakfast, you and I shall have a chat about monastery life in the abbey. Mark me. Many things will please you!

Michel was unconvinced.

Fidelis continued, 'All is strange to you now, but in time you will feel happy here. I am very sure of that. Now rest awhile. A senior oblate will come anon.'

Alone in the dormitory, Michel felt oppressed by the dour silence of the unfamiliar, cavernous room. A single candle provided an unwelcoming somber glow.

He lay on his cot face down on the coarse linen as thoughts drifted to Yann and Marie. His eyes blurred with tears that spilled over and dribbled down his cheeks. He swiped a hand across his runny nose, smearing mucous along his upper lip. At the sound of footsteps, he wiped his eyes and sat up.

'Welcome to Saint Benedict, Michel. I am Ioseph – the senior oblate.' Michel stood to greet him. 'In the coming days – weeks should you need them – I shall help you adapt to our life here, and I urge you to come to me with any concerns. You'll find this is a loving abbey. The rules aren't hard to learn, and mostly all the monks are kind. Magister Fidelis is our favourite.'

Ioseph spoke in Latin, the language of the monastery.' Michel winced. Latin had been a subject in his village school, but the sound of the mostly unfamiliar words reinforced in his mind how deeply he had been plunged into an abyss.

Ioseph handed him a slate. 'These are the names of the eight hours of Compline – the Divine Office. You should know them because the hours, announced by the chapel bells, mark the times to assemble in the chapel for prayer and signal specific monastic duties. Oblates heed the bells six times a day and only go to the chapel four times. I have underlined those times for you.'

Michel looked at the incomprehensible words. 'I don't understand.'

Joseph laughed. 'I know. It's a foreign language. For now, just do what the other oblates do when you hear the bells and you'll be fine.'

Michel studied the slate and the underlined words. 'Only six are underlined.'

'Matins and Lauds are in the middle of the night. We don't have to attend. The abbot wants us to be well rested.'

Michel jolted as the chapel bells began to ring.

'Vespers. All are beckoned to the chapel now for prayers and chants. Afterwards there is supper in the refectory. Brother Pierre – we call him Brother Cook – always makes delicious meals. Next we have two hours of recreation when we can talk and play games before Compline. Then it's to bed and silence!'

Michel followed Ioseph and joined the oblates who were assembling. They formed a queue, two abreast. 'Keep your eye on what the other oblates do.' Ioseph whispered. He looked at Michel and told him, 'Tuck your hands in your sleeves and keep your eyes down.'

Michel survived the unfamiliar service in the chapel, but struggled to quell the tension he felt as he aped his way through the prayers and antiphonic chants, and was glad when the ordeal ended and the oblates and monks retired to the refectory for the evening meal. There was an abundance of food that left Michel with pangs of guilt, painfully mindful his parents would as usual go hungry, portioning out the food they had on hand to make it last, with little hope of replenishing it once it was gone.

Back in the dormitory, the oblates were chatty and animated, speaking Gallo, the *patois* of the region. It was a welcome reprieve for Michel after the strain of the afternoon. Some played chess or knuckles. Others shared gossip with subdued laughter that rebounded off the walls. Ioseph formally presented him to the oblates. Paol Eric broke ranks and hugged Michel, a gesture that uplifted his spirits beyond measure. Ioseph smiled and said to Michel, 'Come with me. I want to show you two important places.'

As they walked, Ioseph spoke further about monastery routine and how each oblate had apprenticeships. 'There are many trades. Magister Fidelis will assign you to one of them. He paused and said, 'You look worried. Don't be. We're all are here to help you.'

They arrived at a long narrow room adjacent to the dormitory. 'This is the *necessarium*. There are several others in the monastery and one in the cathedral school.' Michel looked puzzled by the lengthy raised stone platform covered by a plank of wood along the wall that had ten round hewn openings evenly spaced a metre apart. 'The stone is hollowed through, and a trough at the base has water flowing the length of the room that carries the turds to a conduit that empties into a cesspool.' Ioseph smiled. 'You are impressed, I see. Nothing like that in the countryside, eh? Come See this!'

Ioseph took him to a room that astonished Michel. Along the length of the ceiling were pipes with shower heads from which water flowed into a two-foot wide trough. 'This the *lavorium*. Water only flows through the pipes when the tap is opened for bathing. There are thick cloths for drying. That stone basin in the center also has running water for washing hands and face and cleaning teeth. The Abbey at Cluny devised this system centuries ago, and the Arabs centuries before Cluny. Another day I am sure Magister Fidelis will tell you the history of these wonders. It is an interesting tale, and he loves to recount it.'

They returned to the dormitory, and Ioseph said pleasantly, 'I shall leave you to your friend. You will have much to tell each other, and, as you will learn, all the oblates are the ultimate authority on monastery rules!' Michel bowed and rushed to Paol Eric, who introduced him to the oblates Christopher, Adrian, Henri and Christian.' Their cheerful banter and the newfound camaraderie buoyed Michel's mood. The boys assured him monastery life was pleasant enough, if confining and isolated. 'Sometimes we hear town tidings from the monks or almoners, but not oft enough,' Christian said.

'The monks are all good to us . . .'

'*Mostly* good, you mean,' Paol Eric snuffed. 'Take care of Brother Garnier and Brother Huguet when they're in a temper!'

'And not all the monks like each other. You can tell by the way they look at each other, Henri interjected.

'No one beats us if we break a rule,' Christopher assured him.

Michel's eyes widened. 'What punishments are there?'

'Nothing awful. Miss chapel and stay in the dormitory. We all like that one. We can play. The favoured punishment the monks give us is to walk the labyrinth.'

'What's a labyrinth?'

'It's a big circle with narrow winding paths that lead to a big centre space. You're supposed to meditate as if you're walking towards God and come out holier, Christian explained.'

'Have you had to walk it?'

'Yes. It's fun, really, the way it loops and turns, but we don't tell that to Magister Fidelis. It's supposed to be a penance. Actually, the only real penance is to miss a meal.'

Adrian told him, 'Monks and lay brothers are punished as well. We don't know what they do wrong, but sometimes one will be prostrated in front of the altar when we enter for prayer.'

Christian said, 'Just yesterday I saw two monks arguing with each other! But I don't think they got caught.'

'Look you,' Paol Eric said as a word of warning. Stay away from Devi and Samzun.'

'Who are they?'

'Oblates. They're always breaking the rules and it pleasures them to taunt us. They'll trip you up or whack you, and then feign innocence. Once they put red ants in my bed! But I didn't tell anyone. No one would ever do that.'

'Which ones are they?' Michel asked. 'Truly, I shall shun them.'

In the chapel for Compline, Michel fought exhaustion as prayers and chanting droned on. He was grateful to crumble into bed when they returned to the dormitory, but sleep refused to ease his troubled soul. Images of his mother and father nagged his unhappy mind. Efforts to suppress his thoughts to encourage needed rest finally triumphed, and, despite the despondency he felt, sleep obliterated troubled consciousness.

3

AN OMINOUS DEATH

The Herblain Inn, on the north side of the Place D'Arzhur, catered to a modest number of customers for a noonday meal and an evening of drinking. On festival days there were crowds of hungry customers all day until late into the night. The innkeeper, Aubert, was high-spirited on such occasions, for there was good money to be made, and he welcomed the ruckus that vibrated throughout, despite its deadening any hope of genuine discourse.

Aubert was his own best endorsement of the quality of the inn's food. He was rotund and burly. Of medium height, he was bearded and middle aged. Although confident his staff was efficient and reliable, he kept a watchful eye as he and they bustled about, serving stews, ciders, and ales. It was the finest and largest inn in town with several large windows with a southern exposure overlooking the square.

Abundant light guaranteed a bright, cheerful, and welcoming dining area, especially during winter days. A half-timbered structure, it had an overhang that in summer kept patrons dry when it rained and relieved them from the heat of direct sunlight. The interior was large and plain enough to facilitate a thorough scrubbing, and Aubert ensured the inn was always clean and inviting. In the expansive dining area, there were rustic trestle tables, oil lamps, and wooden benches that scraped across uneven floorboards when people sat or prepared to leave.

The room had a large hearth and a welcoming fire on damp, chilly days. There was an entrance to a pantry and the kitchen, and steps leading up to several rooms that accommodated overnight travellers – rooms that were fresh and bright as well as comfortable, if somewhat overcrowded at times. The innkeeper often could be found behind a long-raised counter against the wall, the place where he kept his money and where he sometimes added a finishing touch to a platter ready to be served.

It was late, and most revelers had left the town. Three laggards settled their bill and left the inn, and Aubert and his charges methodically busied themselves with a clean-up.

In the far corner, a man who wore a chain with a cross around his neck appeared muddled and confused. He sat with his head drooped against the wall. He perspired profusely and made strained, rattled attempts to breathe. His eyes were closed with crusted detritus clinging to the lashes. His expression suggested he was experiencing great pain.

A boney youth apprenticed to Aubert approached to clear the table. He stopped short, startled by the man's appearance, and cringed at the sight of the inky colour of his lips and the froth that lathered about his mouth. He said nothing, but stealthily backed away and rushed to the counter where the innkeeper was slicing himself a thick chunk of now somewhat shriveled beef.

'Master Aubert!'

The innkeeper noted alarm in the voice. 'What is awry Melor?'

'He is very sick, Master – soaked in sweat and straining for air, and his mouth is all blue and frothing!'

With raised eyebrows, Aubert set a long knife on the counter and wiped his hands on his soiled apron. Squinting across the room, his mouth dropped, and his eyes widened. His eyes scanned the room to verify all customers had left the inn. 'Melor. Run to the Hôtel Dieu and bid Brother Lucien come – now!'

The lad ran through narrow lanes, careful not to trip in cart-wheel ruts. He dodged pedestrians, wagons, animal dung and puddles of organic fluids as he raced towards the hospital. When he arrived at the entrance, breathless, he pulled impatiently on the bell's rope. An annoyed brother opened the squealing door, but when the young man delivered the details of the sick man at the inn, the friar paled and told the boy to wait but a moment for the physician. He left the lad nervously pacing. Melor was visibly relieved when Brother Lucien opened the door carrying his medical pouch.

'Tell me what has happened, lad,' Lucien demanded as the pair quickly made their way back to the main square. He listened as Melor, panting, described the situation at the inn. On the way, they passed the sheriff's townhouse. The door was open and inside was a small, agitated gathering, shouting, and wailing. Lucien caught snippets of the words exchanged.

No, no. I told you. North . . . on the way towards Dinan.'

Another child disappeared, Lucien thought, but there was no time to dawdle to learn more, given Melor's story.

The imposing figure of Aubert stood at the threshold to the inn as Melor and Lucien arrived. Aubert admitted them and bolted the door. He whispered, 'No hurry now, Brother. The man is dead.'

Lucien looked squarely at the innkeeper and raised his eyebrows in a question. 'Yes, I am sure,' said the innkeeper. 'He has all the markings.' He nodded his head to the place where the stranger slumped against the wall.

Wordlessly, Lucien walked over to the body. Alarmed, Aubert called out, 'Brother. Don't. You wear no protection.'

'No fear, Aubert. I have survived the pestilence. It will not sicken me more.' Lucien carefully lifted the man's head, pressed it gently back against the corner wall and studied his face. 'Near to death, Aubert. Not yet dead. He is unconscious.'

He had a bluish hue. The lips were parched and cracked from hours of forced mouth-breathing. The semi-protruding tongue had papillae like coarse sandpaper. Dried spume encircled his mouth. Crusts of pus covered the corners and lashes of his eyes. Lucien lifted one arm that had dark stains on the cloth that covered his armpit. He recoiled from the putrid smell that emanated from it. 'Who has been near this man?' Lucien asked sharply.

The innkeeper motioned towards the lad, who stood, visibly shaking with fear, the blood drained from his face leaving a chalky pallor. Melor protested that he never touched the man or his plate or goblet once he placed them on the table. He had kept a careful distance from him when he realised the man was ill.

'He came in late,' Aubert commented. 'Lumbered in, I should say. Never saw him before. I thought him drunk as a weasel, so I waved him to the far corner. I did not want a nuisance. He were alone there. Of that I am assured. He were near no one. I take an oath on it.'

'Good,' said the monk. He turned to Melor, 'Go to the infirmary and ask for Brother Laurentius and Quimper. On my order, ask only for them. They are to bring a litter here and quickly. Tell the usher to guide you to my dispensary. Await my return there. You are not to go home – or elsewhere. Do you understand me?' He admonished him forcefully, 'Hear me, boy. You are not to tell anyone of this – not ever.' Lucien had the youngster repeat the instructions to assure his words had been understood.

The servant was near faint, and Brother Lucien addressed him kindlier. 'Be not fearful, lad. I have a potion for you. It will protect you from the pestilence. I promise you that. Go, now, go! Tell Laurentius and Quimper to hasten! And remember – not a word. We do not want panic in the town.'

Lucien turned to face the proprietor. 'Were you near him?'

He shrugged his shoulders. 'I was behind the counter, and he was over there by the door. Far enough away, I'd say.'

Lucien nodded agreement. 'As a caution, I'll give you both doses of the black potion.'

Auber nodded thanks. 'When I sent Melor to find you, I closed my doors and sent my workers home. None but the lad has been near that table since that man sat down.'

Lucien thought for a moment and then said, 'Do not touch the dish or spoon. Put on gloves. Burn them, the bench, table, and everything on it. Tomorrow I'll report the death to the magistrate. Those people outside. I would have them gone.' Lucien opened the door to the inn and shouted, 'Go home. A man has died of the dropsy. A stranger. He will be taken for burial to the common pit. Go home, I say.'

The innkeeper's disquiet was assuaged. He knew the survival of his inn depended on having all believe the man had died from a familiar and non-contagious illness. They would thank him for the lie that safeguarded them from needless terror.

Brother Iohannes admitted Melor to the Hôtel Dieu. Informed of Lucien's directives and the reason for them, the monk blanched. He left the lad standing and went to summon Laurentius and Quimper. Soon thereafter, the two monks dashed by, a litter in hand. Iohannes summoned Melor inside. 'Brother Lucien's dispensary is in the far corner.' Melor followed the monk, fretful, but curious.

Lit by torches fixed to the wall, the hospital had a towering barrel-vaulted ceiling supported by thick evenly spaced stone arched pillars. The hall was immense. There was room for more than a hundred and fifty of the sick and triple that in an epidemic. There were alcoves on both sides of the great hall, framed by elaborately carved wooden partitions. Melor peeked into one that had a candle to light the space, and, to his dismay, he saw a priest anointing the head of on old man lying on one of six cots. The boy made the sign of the cross and quickened his pace. In the vast middle of the hall between the soaring pillars, were long trestle tables laden with curative aids.

The boy gawked at tools on a particularly large table and wondered what they were. Brother Iohannes glanced at the lancets, probes, saws, trocars, and other instruments of surgery and said nothing for a moment. Finally, he said noncommittally, 'They belong to Brother Lucien,' thereby evading the disclosure that Lucien performed surgeries in violation of Church law that forbade the clergy to do so.

They reached the end of the hall. In the middle of the wall, adjacent to two rooms, was a marble altar. A monumentally sized crucifix hung on the wall, and a flickering candle within a red lantern, a sign of consecrated hosts inside the tabernacle, was suspended by a thin wire next to it. Brother Lucien's dispensary was the room to the left of the altar. Opening its door, Brother Iohannes beckoned the lad enter. Melor was impressed by its size.

The room was lined on two sides with shelves that held neatly stacked and labeled crocks. A wide, long table flanked by benches was in the middle of the room with bowls, mortars, and pestles on it, and over it hung a canopy of herbal bouquets. 'Await Brother Lucien here,' Brother Iohannes told him as he set a candle on the table. Melor meekly sat down on a bench, uncertain and afraid.

When Brother Lucien arrived at the dispensary with Aubert, he gave him and Melor a remedy known to prevent the plague. 'Mix this vial with equal parts water and take a spoonful for seven days.'

Aubert asked about the stranger.

Lucien shook his head. 'He will not last the night. Now go, both of you, and be silent on this matter. Swear to it!'

Having witnessed and participated in the slaughter at Orléans, Lucien abhorred violence and desired only to make atonement for the part he had played in inflicting harm on his fellow human beings. A man of wit and even temper, he had sought a haven where peace and order prevailed in which he could lead a meaningful life that was useful to others, and fulfill spiritual longings.

In 1429, at the age of fort-two, those longings had directed him to the Abbey of Saint Benedict, where his spiritual and corporal needs had been well satisfied. Eluding the tragedies of the world, he had quickly realised, had been a fantasy.

Lucien's experience in battle, especially the care of the wounded, and his immunity from smallpox and the plague, served him well in the treatment of all kinds of noxious diseases in the Hôtel Dieu. He applied his expertise effectively to the most challenging of the many stricken who frequented the Hôtel Dieu. If not always successful medically, giving comfort and consolation were always within his grasp. His energy and endurance, applied to an exhaustive schedule of medical care and botanical experiments even as he attended to his spiritual needs and monastic obligations, provided a fulfilled and contented life.

He sat in his infirmary, concerned about the consequences of a death from the plague. Educated in theology, law and medicine, his erudition was of no use to him under such circumstances. It was crucial to determine if this was an isolated incident that posed no risk to others, in which case it was critical the stranger's death be kept secret lest there be general pandemonium. Were there to be more deaths, an avalanche of issues would have to be addressed. He sighed as he considered that yet again he had to grapple with a crisis that affected the community, and the world he had sought to escape once more invaded his sanctuary.

A knock on the door interrupted his thoughts. Quimper entered to announce the stranger had died. Lucien nodded. 'I shall have the abbot informed, Brother.' He sighed and dallied no longer with his thoughts.

He wiped his clean-shaven face, compromised by indicative, but not disfiguring, marks of smallpox, smoothed his honey blond hair, stood, and walked from his dispensary. He instructed Iohannes to send for the abbot before entering the room where bodies of the dead were prepared for burial.

Brothers Laurentius and Quimper, like Lucien, had survived the pestilence and smallpox, and were immune to both, enabling them to attend to those afflicted with such communicable corruptions without fear of infection. They were also well practiced in preparing the dead for burial. When Lucien arrived, the brothers had disrobed the dead man and had placed him in the *lavabo* – a shallow man-sized basin chiseled out of the stone floor. A barrel filled with water, two wooden buckets and sponges were adjacent to the basin. Lucien watched as the bothers ritually washed the lifeless form with the water from the bucket that flowed down a grooved sluice on the north side of the abbey to spongy earth that would absorb the water, blood and other body liquids, gradually neutralizing all contaminates. The site was close to the common burial pit, unsanctified ground that received the anonymous dead, the un-baptised, paupers, and unfortunates who died from contagious diseases.

In the name of Christ, Laurentius anointed the man's body with oil in the same manner as had done the ancients to those who set upon their long journey in Charon's vessel that crossed the river Styx. Involuntary flatulence escaped from the dead man's torso, emitting a foul odour that pooled with the stench of ruptured buboes on pus-laden lymph nodes in the armpits and groin. The monks, Lucien included, flinched with aversion and, in the already fetid air, felt nauseated.

On a wooden table lay a stack of folded body-sized rectangle white sack cloths, a supply of thick needles and long cords of rope. Quimper took one of the cloths and spread it on the floor. He and Laurentius dried the body and placed it on the fabric. Laurentius reached for two threaded needles and handed one to Quimper and both began to sew the edges of the cloth tightly together to enshroud the corpse.

Abbot William arrived and stood at a cautious distance from the entrance. The monks respectfully stood and pulled back the stitches they had begun in order to expose the body to full view. The abbot studied it from afar, and enquired, 'His identity is still a mystery? Had he no rings, no seals?'

'No, my Lord Abbot. Only a purse with a few gold florins, French sous and deniers, and some Italian coins,' Lucien told him. 'Surely an honest and prudent man, the innkeeper, to have left them undisturbed.' Gesturing towards the body, he continued, 'This poor wretch was a man of substance.' With a side glance at the man's clothing and boots that lay neatly on the table, he nodded the abbot's attention to them. 'They are all of excellent quality, and the boots were crafted with the finest leather.'

Lucien retrieved a chain of office from a small table. 'He was wearing this around his neck.' Without touching it, the abbot studied the cross and raised his eyebrows in recognition of the Cross of Jerusalem of the Holy Sepulchre of the Knights Templar. He surmised the man who had been wearing it had come from afar. Brindisi came to mind. He wondered how and why this stranger had travelled to Saint Petroc. 'You are certain it is the blue sickness?'

'Aye. The hands and feet are swollen; there are blackened swellings under his arms and between his legs. He has fullness of spleen. Whilst yet alive he breathed heavily; his lips were blue, and froth spewed from his mouth.'

'Who told you this? Who has been with him?'

'Only the innkeeper's boy. As surety, I gave him and the innkeeper the black potion.' Lucien added a footnote. 'And swore them to secrecy.'

Abbot William nodded approval. 'Assure that only Laurentius and Quimper shroud and bury him.'

Laurentius said, 'We will cover him with lime and a heavy layer of earth in the burial pit, my Lord.'

Lucien told the abbot that when the litter arrived at the inn, gossip about a sick man inside attracted several people who milled around the entrance, and that he had told them the man had died of the dropsy and urged them to return to their homes.

'You have done well – all of you,' the abbot told them and reflexively admonished all three to tell no one of this night's tragedy. 'It suffices that people believe he died of dropsy. Better they know nothing more.' He turned to leave and hesitated. Turning around, he told the monks, 'I absolve you from attendance at Matins and Lauds. You will need rest once you have finished your work.' He blessed them all and retreated from the Hôtel Dieu.

Lucien accompanied the abbot as far as the altar, where he sank to his knees to pray for the soul of the unidentified stranger. He also prayed fervently to God to spare the community from another devastating epidemic of plague and to Saint Benedict to intercede with God to save them all – heedless in his distress of his oft avowed rejection of the universal belief in divine intervention.

Abbot William left the Hôtel Dieu with a whirlwind of anxious thoughts, amongst them the recollection Saint Petroc-sur-lac had lost more than two-thirds its population in a prior occurrence of the *Great Morality*.

The majority had died from the sickness, but a considerable number had died in flight and from other diseases, accidents, and skullduggery. It was a stunning and sobering irony. His apprehension mounted as he considered the mere rumour of a victim of plague would spark wide-scale alarm, panic, and even an irrational exodus. He had to attend to the disconcerting but obligatory responsibility of informing the bishop and the mayor of the stranger's death and its cause in the morning, and would confer with Lucien to discuss protocols he and his assistants had devised should there be more who had been infected. *Not tonight. In the morning.*

With luck and God's grace no one else had been contaminated, in which case there would be no need to implement emergency procedures. He distractedly pulled his cowl over his head and went to the chapel. Kneeling on the stone floor, he prayed the community be spared, and prayed for the poor wretch who had died. He petitioned God and his Holy Mother for fortitude and wisdom to deal with what could evolve into a major disaster.

4

CALAMITY

The seething anger generated by Marc's meeting with the mayor dispelled as he dealt with the mayhem that had ensued in the town despite the inestimable number of containable strategies and preemptive maneuvers he had devised and implemented. There were complaints from dozens of people of picked pockets and other petty thefts that required police action and time-consuming written reports that guzzled strained hours. The number of arrests of rowdy, sodden drunks, attempts to contain disorderly commotions and unremitting incidences of criminal behaviour – all foreseen by Marc – commanded his attention.

Frustration and exhaustion gave way to anguish when a deputy reported a four-year-old had been kidnapped. Their mother, a local laundress, had been working at a nearby stream. She had admitted to being distracted by her work but avowed she had kept her child away from the water's edge. She had checked on her child every ten minutes, or perhaps twenty. She had no inkling of the exact time she realised he was gone. Shaken, Marc had feigned composure and had issued orders to his men with contrived aplomb.

Having formed a delegation to deal with miscreant behaviour in the town whilst he and several of his men set out to search the area, several fruitless hours later he had dully relieved his troops with instructions to rest and prepare for the following morning when they would receive their assignments.

It was after midnight when he finally arrived home, listless and depressed. His domicile was both home and office for him. Not a perfect arrangement, for he was never able to escape the encumbrances of his occupation. He struggled to put aside stressful thoughts in hopes of restorative rest.

Marc lived alone and preferred it that way. His wife had died birthing their only child who had died as well, and he had no desire to endure such grief ever again. Still, he was young, tall, and handsome, and his moustache was the touch that gave him the *élan* that attracted women's attention. He was characteristically unaware of his appeal, indifferent to unwanted attentions, and his manner successfully deflected women's pursuits.

The loss of his wife and the hope of children had made him grave and somber. His profession as sheriff, dealing with inconsequential infractions of the law as well as coping with serious and sometimes terrible offences reinforced these traits. The community nevertheless respected him, for, contrary to his self-appraisal, he was good at his work, and everyone who knew him thought him kind and generous. On occasion, some had even noticed a trace of humour in him.

He staggered into a chair, his body as devoid of strength as was his mind bankrupt of ideas, feeling physically and psychically ill, and troubled by the realisation that, despite all the efforts of his team and himself, he had no further insights about the children kidnapped since April than he did about the abduction that morning. He fretted about how his day had ended with only the report of a small boy who had disappeared and a disappointingly blank report from his under-sheriff, Donan Cadoret, of enquiries he had made regarding the Redon and Alenard kidnappings.

Head in his hands, elbows on the table, Marc felt completely baffled and useless to his task, with no plan and no hope of one. He angrily swiped a goblet from the table, sending it flying. He leaped up and paced aimlessly, exasperated and distraught. He feared he would never apprehend the criminals and feared more children would go missing. Those thoughts gave rise to panic as he ruminated he was helpless to prevent such offences. Immersed in self-pity, he sulked with a niggling sense of incompetence, berated himself for his inadequacies and punished himself with self-loathing.

Sudden, incessant thumps on the door mixed with vocal clamour warned him of woe to come. He dashed to the door and, upon opening it, was beset by six frenzied men and women who shoved their way into his home with distraught outpourings.

'I pray you . . . calm down! I cannot understand what you say. Quiet I tell you! Explain what is wrong. You, sir, what has happened.'

The man, frantic, described how, amongst the crowds departing the city not a league north of Saint Petroc, his daughter had been walking beside him and had suddenly vanished. 'She had lagged a bit behind, it is true . . . but she was quite near to us. And then, gone!' He said he and his wife had retraced their steps to the town, with no sign of her since sunset.

'In the main square, you say.' Marc interjected.

'No, no. I told you. North . . . on the way towards Dinan.'

A couple wailed their four children were missing. 'Our oldest boy had been left to look after the others. When we arrived at our cottage after a trip to the slaughterhouse, they were nowhere to be found.'

Marc Gervais replied in frustrated fury. 'It is late! Why do you come to me only now?'

A woman babbled through tears, 'We have searched all afternoon and this night. My husband and I cannot find our son.' Pointing to the others, she said, 'We came together just a while ago in the square and shared our stories. Only then did it come to us you could help.'

Marc felt chastened and moved to sympathy for the inconsolable group. As his mind grappled with the cataclysmic news delivered to him, nausea swelled within him, threatening to overtake him. *Seven children gone in one day. Six prior unresolved disappearances. In less than two months!* He thought he would go mad.

48

5

OBLATES

The bells jostled the community from their beds at six the following morning. As custodian of the clock, Brother Simeon rang the bells for each of the canonical hours, repeated seven additional times a day, a ritual that beckoned the monastic congregation to the chapel to turn monks' thoughts to God with prayers and antiphonic chants.

At the sound of the bells, Michel stirred, groggy and disoriented. In the dim, unfamiliar room lined with beds he saw several boys alighting from their beds. Oblates – and he was one of them. His heart sank. Although he had been pleased to meet several boys and reunite with Paol Eric the night before, Michel yearned for the security of his home. For his parents.

Now awake and focused, Michel saw Ioseph approach. As the oldest oblate, Michel had been told Ioseph enjoyed some privileges of rank. He was a mature and studious lad, destined for theological studies in the university. His soft-spoken kindness had reduced Michel's trepidations, and his presence now was reassuring. 'Prime, Michel. We cannot be late,' he said gently. He turned and gestured to one of the oblates edging towards them. 'This is Padraig. He will stay with you throughout the day and help you *carpe diem*.' He and Padraig smiled.

'Indeed, Michel, I shall be with you for as long a time as it takes for you to master our routine and learn proper comportment. I am ever at your service should you be uncertain about your duties.'

Ioseph echoed the sentiments and said, 'Do remember, we all have had to learn these things at one time. I am sure you will do well, Michel, and I wish you God's grace.'

As Ioseph walked away, Padraig told him. 'It's just like last evening. After Mass and the Eucharist, we proceed to the alcove of the refectory for breakfast. Remember. Silence, hands in sleeves, eyes down.' He paused. 'Magister Fidelis bids you meet him in the cloister after our morning meal. I shall come for you once he dismisses you.' Padraig signaled Michel with a nod of his head and together they joined the other oblates. Much like the students in Michel's village school, they marched in formation. The familiarity of the exercise gave Michel confidence as the oblates and he walked to the chapel.

Michel stood in the cloister on the side nearest the refectory, waiting for Magister Fidelis. He looked around appreciatively. It was a beautiful place, and still. Built in the twelfth century, it was typical of cloisters, except for a column that faced the inner door of the abbey's entrance that had an impressive, almost life size stone carving of the four evangelists. The peristyle had double-columned pillars that formed graceful arches that supported the corbelled interior roof. The sheltered walkway was paved with smooth river stones, and there was a stone bench that spanned the length of the wall that abutted the cathedral. Each pillar had extravagantly carved capitals with biblical scenes or exotic animals. One of the capitals depicted a clergyman – perhaps Saint Benedict.

Michel gazed at the cloister's courtyard. Open to the sky, its grass had pebbled walkways bordered with flowerbeds that intersected in the form of a cross. In the center of the square was a decorative fountain with water that playfully spattered into a large font.

'Is this not a pretty place?' called out Magister Fidelis. Michel whipped around and watched Fidelis bustle towards him and repressed a giggle, entertained by the monk's quiet, waddling gait. Michel was to discover that Fidelis' steps produced little sound, and he often was upon you when you least expected – or desired – his company. '*Dominus vobiscum*,' he said jovially.

Michel thought but a moment before returning the salutation. '*Et cum spiritu tu tuo*, Magister.'

'Tell me how you fare.' Cheered by his warmth, Michel smiled as Fidelis touched the boy's shoulder, gently urging him forward. 'Come. Sit with me over here. The monks and lay brothers, and, yes, oblates too, come here to pray and meditate. I trust in time you will do the same.' Once seated, Fidelis said, I have many things to tell you about the monastery. As you know, I am the prior of the abbey as well as a teacher. But first and foremost, I am a priest and your spiritual guide, and I want you to confide in me whenever you are distressed.'

Michel longed to tell him just how distressed he was.

'We follow the Rule of Saint Benedict of our own will in hopes of doing God's work on earth.'

Not my will, Michel thought bitterly.

'Everything we do in the monastery is to that purpose.' Fidelis chuckled and added mischievously, 'There *are* punishments when rules are broken.' Michel looked alarmed, but was quickly reassured. 'Ah, but not until you know what the rules are and have learned to skirt around them!' Fidelis laughed good-naturedly and overlooked Michel's brooding. 'It is a good and happy life we have here, my child, as you will learn in short order.'

Michel affected a smile.

'Hmm. Where to begin? I have a letter from your parish priest that avows you have been an accomplished pupil.'

Michel shyly lowered his head.

'Now, now. No modesty. We are pleased by scholarship,' he said in the Gallo language. 'Hereafter, we can speak in Latin. I understand you know your grammar well. A good beginning, Michel. I teach Latin and am sure you will speak it perfectly right soon.'

'*Spero ita,* Magister.'

Fidelis looked elated by the Latin response. 'In the cathedral school, there are many subjects that will interest you.'

Michel glowed with interest.

'Ah, you are pleased. I am glad.' Fidelis smiled pleasantly and continued, 'Weekly, Magister Gilles teaches church history, theology and scripture in the monastery.'

Michel meekly asked, 'But where? I don't know where to go, Magister.'

'Padraig will accompany you everywhere until "where to go" is second nature. Do not worry so. Mind, I rely on you to apply yourself to your studies earnestly.'

'Oh, yes, Magister. 'I am eager to learn.'

'Good! You also will be pleased to know that I have chosen, for the present time at least, to appoint you to the scriptorium. Brother Rafe will be your magister there.'

'Please, sir. I don't know what a scriptorium is.'

'It's where monks fashion books of singular beauty. Each day after the meal that follows Sext, you will work there until None.' Michel tried to remember what times they were and became uneasy.

' If Magister Rafe deems you are worthy – and I have little doubt but that he will – he will accept you as an apprentice.'

Fidelis hesitated, lost in thought. 'Let me see . . . chapel, meals, school, scriptorium. You know about the bells. What else? Ah. Daily tasks – from None until Vespers. Four days a week you will work with me in the garden. On Fridays you will help our fishermen with the catch. Oblates take turns barreling the fish and storing them in the cellarium. Our pond supplies enough fish for the monastery with a plentiful quantity to distribute to the poor.'

'There is water in the pond, Magister?'

'Yes. It is an artesian pond, Michel. Not even a drought can stop the water from rising from under the ground. Now, where was I? . . . . On Saturday mornings you will assist the almoners portion food, money, and clothing to the needy. Then, of course there are the cows....' He thought for a moment before going on. 'During school holidays and in winter you will work in the cellarium with the cellarer to the kitchen – he oversees all stored provisions – and in the stables. There are other incidental tasks. Some of them will not be much to your liking I warrant!'

Michel felt giddy. He didn't know what a cellarium or a cellarer were, and he doubted he could remember all the details with which he felt bombarded. Characteristically, Fidelis laughed. He studied the boy and saw both pleasure and bewilderment. He reminded himself there was only so much a young mind could absorb at one time. 'Oh, do not scowl so, Michel. All in good time. All in good time. Everyone will help keep you on course. Today after school, come to me. I want to present you to Magister Rafe. Ah, *bonum*! Here is Padraig. He is several grades ahead of you in school. Go along with him now to your class.'

In a classroom with children his age, Padraig presented Michel to Magister Alexander, who welcomed him briefly and directed him to a bench. Michel was surprised to see students from the town and astonished one of them was a girl. Michel felt awkward, but the presence of oblates made him feel less ill at ease. He strove to calm himself, and welcomed the prospect of continuing with his studies. After just one session in class it was clear the cathedral school would be a challenge. The prospect lifted his spirits considerably.

He told Padraig he was surprised to see a girl in a school.

'Hmm. There are two in my class – Aisling and Jacqueline. Aisling is truly kind, and sings like a nightingale. Jacqueline is a wonderful artist. In your class I only know the girl's name: Claire. All the girls are very quick!'

I didn't know girls went to school.'

'It is rare, although I've been told there are several educated girls who are saints and scholars. I don't know why girls usually can't go to school, especially when they are as able as boys.'

Michel quickened his step to keep pace with Fidelis on their way to the scriptorium. They entered a dark paneled, high ceilinged chamber with narrow, elongated windows on the north side that admitted the best light. The south wall had rows of shelves on which were neatly aligned large volumes of books and manuscripts. Double rows of desks and trestle tables with raised surfaces on which to write filled the room. A monk sat at each desk, silently focused on copying script from a completed text. The air was full of incongruent, unfamiliar aromas and a mild, musty odour.

Fidelis cordially presented the boy to Magister Rafe, exchanged a few pleasantries with him, and took his leave.

Magister Rafe was slender, and in constant motion, with graceful fingers flexed in midair as if grabbing an unseen baton with which to conduct his voice. His voice was in fact melodic, and the sounds he emitted were lyrical and full of enthusiasm when the topic was of books. He was pale, as were all the monks in the scriptorium, whose daylight hours were confined to desks illuminated by mere slivers of light from the windows. Except for the canonical hours and meals, Rafe and the scribes rarely were seen.

The monks appreciated Rafe's even temper and, most characteristically, his passion for books fiery as the sun. Rafe's heaven was the scriptorium. He projected an aura of authority and ensured his scribes met his exacting expectations to give unwavering attention to the manifold details of the art of scripting manuscripts. Illumination took especial care and was a process that took years to learn and a lifetime to master. Rafe worked his apprentices hard, as Michel would come to know, but fairly, hoping for a corresponding zeal.

In 1423, when a visiting priest showed him an image of Saint Christopher carrying the Christ child created from a wood block printed on paper, Rafe was stunned to learn multiple copies had been made from the original woodcut. At first Rafe speculated with a mild panic *sacra scriptura* and illumination could in time become outmoded. But as he studied the image he realised that, although pleasing, it hardly compared with the majesty and beauty of the illuminated manuscripts produced manually by scribes. Inwardly he scoffed at the new process. *A carving in word coloured by hand, copied mechanically and repeatedly. Dreadful.*

Rafe studied Michel, attempting to assess his potential as he introduced him to what was for him a *sanctum sanctorum*. He guided the boy past desks of pallid monks as Michel scrutinised the monks who, with intense concentration as well as adept calligraphic precision, formed painstakingly neat rows of decorative lettering. A few were engaged in fashioning astonishingly elaborate gilded and vibrantly coloured images on large pieces of a much finer quality of parchment than his father had given to the abbot. Rafe noticed Michel's interest and, waving a hand in the direction of the gifted illustrators, he said, 'It is a labourious process that brings one to these stalls as an illuminator of manuscripts on velum. There is an old saying among scribes, "The fingers write but the whole body suffers." It is an arduous endeavour, but well worth the effort. Come and see an especially beautiful example of their work.' Michel gawped at the illustrated manuscript Rafe set before him. The intricacies of design and colours were resplendent.

Rafe remarked, 'Ah, my lad, one must begin at the beginning – learn how to prepare the parchment and then the vellum. No easy tasks, but fundamental ones. Come with me.' He led the way into a large shed. Michel flinched at the unpleasant odour. There was a pile of untreated animal skins and wooden frames with tautly stretched skins. Christopher stood with a long wooden rod next to a large vat filled with sheep skin covered in water. Paol Eric stood beside a vat busily stirring as well. Rafe introduced Michel to a sharp-eyed monk. 'Magister Timothy is most proficient in preparing parchment and velum for use in the scriptorium. He will be your task master.' Timothy greeted him with a nod as Rafe took his leave.

Brother Timothy apathetically told Michel, 'The oblates clean raw sheep skins first in water, then in a solution of lime and water that loosens whatever wool remains on the skin. They then are left to dry, and then scraped with this.' He showed the boy a semi-lunar knife. 'Finally, once smooth with no hair residue, the skins are rinsed in water of all lime deposit and set to dry before being stretched on racks. It is a very time-consuming process.'

Michel thought the diligence and concentration given to the work impressive, if tedious, but he was disenchanted, realising only lowly chores were to be his lot before he advanced to more creative endeavours. The insight collided with his fantasies about learning calligraphy and applying ink to parchment, with years to pass before he could claim the prize of a quill.

Bells sounded. *What bells are they? What's the time?* Michel anxiously looked about him. Christopher and Paol Eric passed him with a nudge, and all three headed for the door after a bow to Magister Timothy.

Padraig awaited them outside the annex. With a reminder to Michel to tuck his hands in his sleeves, he and the other oblates scampered towards the chapel for None.

Marc Gervais awoke with a start as the memory of the catastrophe of the night before recharged his mind into wakefulness. The nightmare of the harrowing time spent taken depositions from distraught parents seared his brain, and he damned himself for lamenting the precious time consumed with reassurances and condolences given to the grieving parents, and the reports he had to write. He had been impatient to initiate the hunt, but much needed rest for himself and his deputies had restrained him from giving immediate chase. Resolved to muster a search party at dawn, exhausted, he had lunged for his bed.

As morning light illuminated the room, Marc collected his scattered thoughts with a regimented determination to subdue his anxieties and collect his wits to formulate a coherent plan. *Donan,* he thought. *Donan's judgement is paramount.* He hurried from his house in search of his under-sheriff, whose wisdom he hoped would serve him yet another time. He took to his horse and within a half hour he arrived at Donan's home.

Donan had just begun to breakfast and was alone when Marc burst into his cottage and broke the news of the debacle of the night before. Donan listened with stony incredulity. 'So many. How could this be so?' He whispered. 'And where was I last night when you needed me?'

'You were with me until the last. I dismissed you with high hopes we had seen the worst of the day's misfortunes.' He guffawed. 'You, my friend, were having sweet dreams as hell opened its gates to me.'

Marc recounted the events of the night before and his plan to take to the field. 'I have no illusions about this endeavour. We've had nothing but failure thus far.'

Donan, having absorbed the sordid details Marc had described of the prior day's kidnappings said quietly, his face stricken with gloom, 'So it's not a solitary demon we seek.'

'Precisely. You see that. A band of them. How many could there be? Think on it – a child by the river. One on the way north. Four from their own home also on the north thoroughfare. One in the city – only one – snatched under the very eyes of his parents.' Marc shook his head, agitation in every fiber of his mien. 'Surely we have been simple minded in our thinking.'

'Come. How could we have guessed? In the past the seizures were irregular, but one at a time. Our conclusion there was but one malefactor was logical.'

'You forget. The Alenard children. Two of them. It didn't occur to us . . .'

Donan shrugged. His face sagged.

Marc methodically attempted a mathematical prob-ability. 'Five caitiffs at least. Probably several more.' He looked forlornly into space. 'I do not know how to judge this or act on it. We have not been able to capture one adversary, and now we face the possibility of a half dozen. A dozen?' He sat down, dejected, his eyes closed as his mind swirled with the complexities of the deduction.

'Marc, there's nothing for it except to continue as before, with new understanding and, God forefend, with fearsome expectations.'

Marc stood and looked at Donan with consternation and presentiment. 'By God's bones, you're surely right. I quake at the thought.' They stared at each other, their thoughts jumbled in a muddle of anxious uncertainty, paralysed with dread of what they feared would follow. They perfunctorily took their leave of Donan's wife with no attempt to masque their dismay.

News of the kidnappings reached the inhabitants of Saint Petroc-sur-lac, plunging all into terror. Marc relegated a deputy to inform the monks who, deeply perturbed, discussed the matter in the Chapter House with the duly alarmed community. A decision was reached to establish a guard comprised of lay brothers to accompany the oblates to and from the cathedral school.

In the stable, two lay brothers complained about the additional duty – 'As if we hadn't enough to do' – unaware that Paol Eric, there to groom a mare, crouched undetected in a stall, stunned to hear what had occurred.

He had his opportunity to communicate the unsettling news after Vespers in the dormitory. 'Seven, you say?' Christopher gulped incredulously. Michel cringed. He now understood more fully the sense of danger that plagued his parents. All the oblates were upset, barely able to comprehend the fact so many children had gone missing in one day.

Christian exclaimed, 'How could that happen? 'Any one of us could be stolen,' Adrian blubbered. Henri began to cry as Magister Fidelis entered the dormitory. He soothed Henri before he addressed the anxious oblates to assuage their fears with a reassuring message.

'You are well protected here in the monastery, and, as an extra caution, there will be lay brothers with you when you are without the monastery walls. You can be sure no harm will fall on any of you. Now let us pray for those families and children who are burdened this night, that God will deliver all the children safely to their loved ones.'

6

TRAGEDY

In the three days following Michel's oblation, Marie and Yann mechanically and silently followed a familiar routine lest the depressior from the loss of their son overpower them. Yann hurled stones into useless heaps or stalked off to the well as he tr:ed to unshackle a fragment of anger and bitterness.

Marie thrashed about in the garden where she had coaxed a few tubers to grow, stifling her rage. Impassive focus on household chores released some anger, but, unable to contain her wrath, she tramped down repeatedly th= already heavily packed earthen floor, and obsessively scrubbed the tabie and the benches, ridding herself of a mere splinter of despondency, leaving a substantial residt= for another hour, another day.

When together for meals or rest, neither felt inclined ω break the silence, although even in their individual heartbreak concern for the other surfaced from time to tir_e as laconic dialogue. Despite consciously shirking talk abc1t Michel, inevitably he became the subject of their sporadic communiqués. Each made vapid statements that were more justification for having oblated Michel to the monastery than discourse.

'He will be eating well, now,' Marie said.

'The abbot told me the oblates eat meat as well as fowl; and in winter, they have heat in their dormers. He will be warm.'

'He will be at the cathedral school every day.'

'He will master the bible. He will pray for us,' Yann whispered.

That comment ignited fury in Marie. 'He best pray for me long and hard, husband, because my bitterness consumes me.'

Yann bowed his head and said nothing. He longed to tell Marie how much he too missed his son, how pained and miserable he felt, how he yearned to comfort her, but he feared intensifying his wife's ire. It did not occur to him that, were he to tell her his thoughts, much of Marie's sorrow would be defused, enabling them to grieve together.

The next morning, Marie noticed Yann's gaunt and apathetic appearance. He shook his head when she offered him bread and broth. 'I am without appetite.' Queasy, Marie also spurned food. She felt languor and ascribed it to the void of a home without Michel's presence. When a piercing headache assailed her, Marie sensed more miseries would follow. She supposed it was the influenza. She could minister to that with herbal remedies. Both rested fitfully that night, their sleep disrupted by persistent and excruciating headaches, cough, and chest pain.

Upon rising the following morning, Marie fetched dry willow leaves from a shelf over the hearth and ground them, then boiled them until satisfied the potion was strong. She and Yann drank the bitter tea that somewhat reduced their fevers. The next day fevers spiked. When malaise, nausea and heightened pain were accompanied by unrelenting coughs with expectorated bloody mucous, concern transmuted to terror. Marie, her voice tremulous, said, 'The traveller on the road. I am sure of it.' Horror registered on both their faces as perception took shape of the nature of their illness. 'We touched him – took him by the arms and raised him to his feet – oh, God. We were at his side as he coughed! *Sweet Jesú.* No. Please, God, no!' She fell weeping into Yann's arms in a despairing dirge.

Yann, immobile and dazed, pressed her to him, unwilling to let go his hold lest they both be lost to each other forever. He hawked with escalating force as foul smelling and bloody mucous filled his mouth. Marie fetched a cloth and then another as Yann visibly grew weaker. 'Lie down, my love and rest. I go to the garden for herbs to mix a remedy that will ease you.' Short-breathed as she left the cottage, Marie began to cough blood.

Marie was well tutored in the medical arts all peasant women knew, handed down through generations. A thorough knowledge of herbals and the production of therapeutic elixirs and salves were vital allies against minor and major sicknesses, and all were schooled in them. Marie was expert in concocting herbal tonics that treated simple colds and complex chest ailments, headaches, an influx of intestinal worms and digestive upsets. She knew the recipe other women used to induce an abortion. For herself, she had prepared the brew that had eased her labour pains when Michel was born.

She also had a prescription for a drink that induced a quiet death, and gloomily but stoically, she set about to formulate the draft whilst her wits and strength remained. She hastily collected ingredients from the garden and limped into the cottage, coercing a wan smile. Yann coughed uncontrollably. Marie fought to disregard the pain, debilitating chills, and her hammering headache, and prepared the recipe that would mercifully release them from even worse torment. She milled the deadly desiccated herbs in a wooden mortar until they were a well-blended powder, uttering phrases of optimism and comfort to Yann, who lay close by. She pooled the mixture with wine to obfuscate the bitter taste of the hemlock, the mandragora that would still the heart, and the poppy that would be anesthetising. Surety their lives would end in an untroubled sleep.

Girding her fortitude, exerting to breathe, she poured two equal portions into goblets and studied the lethal concoction she had made. Momentarily immobile, she agonised about her purpose. She considered the grave lie she was about to pronounce to Yann, and sorrowfully reflected that never in their lives had a falsehood been exchanged between them. She winced with moral uncertainty, agitated and disturbed by thoughts of the consequence to her soul in committing what was a grave transgression in the eyes of the Church.

Coughing, and weaker with each passing minute, she ruminated about fate, suffering and pain. *Surely it cannot be part of God's divine plan to inflict such suffering. Surely the good God would want us to go to him in a painless sleep with welcome visions of his eternal kingdom, not in embittered torment, terror, and indescribable anguish.*

Yann's coughs spurred her to action. More blood poured from his mouth. He was writhing now, and he struggled for air between coughs. She, too, could feel mortality skulking upon her. Mutely she appealed to God to help her, and wondered where Mary was in this hour of need. *Where were both their graces?* A sudden panic engulfed her. Michel! She feared he might also be polluted. She revisited each minute of their encounter with that sick man. As she recalled the force with which she had ordered Michel to stay away, she thought him safe from harm, certain he had escaped being exposed to the pestilence.

Through blurred eyes, Yann, his body failing as each moment passed, detected the agitation in the room. It intensified his growing panic. In a faint voice he wheezed, 'Marie. I can barely see you.' She stumbled to the bed, cleansed his mouth, and patted his head. She coerced a reassuring smile on her lips, heedless of the tears that filled her eyes. 'Can you see me now?' she whispered, even as a veiled storm of bitter rage con-sumed her that intensified her resolve to administer the potion to Yann and then herself.

She murmured soothingly that she wanted him to drink a wine mixed with herbs that would reduce his pain and bring on restful sleep. With shaking hands, she kneeled by his side. 'Dearest Yann, let me help you lift your head.' Yann obliged her, barely able to prop his torso on one elbow. Shakily, with Marie guiding the cup, he brought the goblet to his lips and resolutely forced the potion down his throat before collapsing onto his back. Marie caressed him.

'Good. You will soon sleep, my dearest Yann.'

Yann faintly smiled and feebly reached out to her with his hand. 'I am certain of it, my love. Now, quaff the drink and lie with me so that we can both sleep in peace. Hold my hand, Marie,' he said in a whispered rasp, 'and think of how much we have loved each other all these years.'

Merciful God, Yann knows my mind. She stroked his face and weakly reached for the goblet, drained its contents, and set the empty vessel on the floor as she, incalculably weak, slipped slowly into the bed. They interlocked hands, and Marie rested her head on his chest. The brew combated the intensifying pain but could not intrude on thoughts. She wished happiness, not grief, for Michel. She hoped he would pray for their souls. She moaned as she wondered if he would ever even know what happened to them. She prayed God would purify their souls in these, their final moments, and begged forgiveness for the bitterness and mistrust of God's mercy she had harboured. She prayed to Mary to intercede to God for his loving grace.

Drowsiness and, finally, sleep compassionately took Marie and Yann from this world.

64

7

THE WILL OF GOD

Michel, as did the other oblates in his class, kept to himself
at the cathedral school. His studies interested him, and he
worked hard to excel, but he felt timid and self-conscious
in his oblate's robes. They were a visual reminder of the
social breech between him and his classmates who were all
from the town's most prominent families. Claire, Michel
had discovered, was exceptionally bright, superior in
intelligence to her male counterparts. She too, was excluded
from interaction with the tight, impenetrable faction of boys
unwilling to admit into their company anyone judged social
inferiors. In any case, the rigid scholastic routine did not
allow much time for the students to intermingle, unless one
considered the brief time before the school day began or at
the end of the school day as students organised their school
materials before leaving the classroom.

On this, his fifth day of classes, Michel sensed the boys
were distracted and inattentive. They whispered covert
exchanges. He was curious about the atypical murmurs in
the classroom that abruptly ceased when an irritated
Magister Alexander called the students to attention and
chastised them for their boldness. Silent thereafter,
Michel's classmates sustained a palpable tension
throughout the day. Michel exerted much effort to

concentrate, but he was unsettled by the snippets of gossip he could not decipher, and his attention ebbed frequently.

When the school day ended, Michel approached Claire to ask if she knew why the students were so rattled. She told him that everybody was talking about a stranger who had died at one of the local inns the prior week. She told him there had been an investigation by a special council that had ended the day before. 'They said the man died of dropsy, but no one believes it.'

Michel asked with formless unease. 'Why does no one believe the council's finding?'

'Well . . .' She hesitated. 'The curious mystery after the man died! The doctor from the Hôtel Dieu told people he had the dropsy. The innkeeper closed the inn. People saw flames from the garden behind the inn. The lane to the abbey was closed after a litter carried the man to the Hôtel Dieu. The inn has been closed all week and guards have been posted nearby as a hindrance to approach the place They say the stranger was buried immediately, and rumours began straight away that the man died of the blue sickness. So, everyone is troubled that may be true, and terrified they will get sick and die. Many families have left town. Brion's father was the chief inquisitor of the enquiry and he told Brion he thinks the man died of the pestilence, but there is no proof. Brion was not supposed to tell anyone.'

'When did the man die? Last week, you say?' There was a frenzied tone to Michel's queries.

'Yes. On the feast of Saint Isidore – the day the Baron de Rais passed through the town.'

'Do they know who the man was?' Michel asked, fearing he knew the answer.

'No. That is, I don't think so. They say he was a stranger to Saint Petroc – a foreigner. They say he only arrived in town on the feast day. Why do you ask? Michel. Why do you look so distressed?'

A stranger. It had to be the traveller his parents helped on the way into Saint Petroc. Michel was sure of it. The man had fallen. His mother and father helped him to his feet. It had seemed he was weak, surely sick and, even from afar, Michel could see he coughed uncontrollably. Frantic, Michel muttered abruptly, 'I must go.' He darted from the school room, leaving a perplexed Claire to wonder about his strange behaviour.

Michel rushed to the monastery's unlocked side gate and, panic stricken, sought out Fidelis. The chapel had only two brothers readying the altar for Sext. He darted to the cloister and spied Fidelis in the shadows, sitting contemplatively on a stone bench, fiddling a rosary.

'Fidelis! Fidelis!' The monk was startled by the form of address and Michel's visible agitation. He responded in the Breton patois, 'Hush child. Calm yourself. What is the matter?'

Breathless, Michel asked, 'The stranger who died last week – did he – was he – was it the pestilence?'

Fidelis looked intently at Michel, trying to interpret the motive behind the question. *Who had told him about the stranger? Who had mentioned the pestilence? Why did Michel seem so afraid?* Composed, Fidelis calmly, but warily, questioned the boy, 'Why do you ask, Michel? Child. Why are you troubled?'

Michel described in detail the meeting with the traveller on the feast of Saint Isidore, and how his parents had aided him. 'The man who died. I'm certain it was the same man. Quickly! My mother and father are in danger. Please. Please, help them.' His face was flushed, his heart pounded, his body was shaking.

Fidelis held the boy's arms and soothingly implored him to compose himself. Michel sat on the bench with unfocused eyes, numbed with psychic exhaustion. 'Michel,' Fidelis asked with trepidation, 'did you also help this stranger?'

Michel shook his head vigorously. 'I had walked ahead of my mother and father before they met the stranger and waited for them at the lake.' He began to cry. 'I am sore uneasy. My mother. My father. I fear for them. Oh, please, sir, will you help?'

Fidelis rubbed his chin apprehensively but concealed his concern to spare Michel further anxiety. He tenderly patted the child's head, hoping to pacify him, and said quietly, 'Surely nothing is amiss. To be positive, I shall send Brother Laurentius by horse to Pobrér. Now, look at me. Look at me, Michel. You must give heed to your stewardship with faith all is well. We shall know soon enough how your parents fare. Until we know more, you must attend to your tasks. Do you think you can do that?'

Michel nodded weakly, as the monk uttered reassurances and gave him his blessing. Once Michel described the location of his family home, Fidelis said, 'Now go with God, and leave me to send Brother Laurentius to your parents' cottage.'

Fidelis hoped Michel had not noticed that his questions about the stranger and the plague had gone unanswered.

Fidelis' prayers were particularly impassioned that day. Unmanageable civic disorder would erupt should news of two additional deaths from plague become known. He gravely discussed his anxiety with Abbot William and Lucien, and was relieved to receive reassurance that tactics to deal with a potential crisis had already been formulated. Satisfied, Fidelis voiced his concern for Michel. 'Until Laurentius has returned there is naught to do except to charge senior oblates to keep take heed all is well with the child.'

Michel, apprehensive and fretful, carried on with the monastic routine when every instinct urged him to flee the abbey and race to his home. He had no appetite, and welcomed his garden chores that allowed him to expend tension and fear with frenzied jabs into the earth with a spade.

After the midday meal, Brother Laurentius rode fast to Pobrér and arrived within the hour. Having been told specific, identifying characteristics of Michel's family dwelling, he felt sure he had identified the Dunard cottage that stood alone surrounded by barren fields.

Laurentius hoped the pervading quiet did not portend ill. He braced himself as he knocked, and there being no response, slowly opened the door. The foul odour of disease and death overwhelmed him. Holding a cloth to his nose, he approached the bed and made a perfunctory examination of the bodies that lay on it to confirm what he suspected was the cause of death before he rushed outside from the stench. Unnerved by his discovery, he thought to bolt the house to dissuade intruders, an illogical idea considering the isolated location, but one that fulfilled his sense of mission. Reluctantly, he took a deep breath and reentered the cottage. He surveyed the room and spied a broom in the corner. Assessing its usefulness, he concluded it would serve. He took the broom outside and wedged the stick through the handle of the wooden door diagonally against its frame. Turning away, he retched uncontrollably.

Laurentius described his finding to the Magister of Oblates as Fidelis listened with silent perturbation. He made the sign of the cross with heartache in the gesture. 'I thank you, Laurentius, and, yes, give your account to Brother Lucien.' He spoke with a wavering voice, inclined his head, rose, and walked to the abbot's office. He sighed heavily, knocked, and entered.

'In truth, I am as loathe to rupture the state of ease Michel has exhibited after just a week in the monastery as much as I am to deliver him this sorrow.'

'It is a sad business. I am dismayed for the boy.' William paused and announced, 'I shall have his parents interred in our cemetery with a solemn burial ritual and celebrate Mass in the cathedral with all our community present. It will be a comfort for the child.

'William. So good of you. It will be a blessing for him to have his parents' grave close by.'

William nodded. 'To our advantage, it will dull speculation about the cause of their deaths should the news become known. A much-desired ruse, now that we know our fable about the foreigner's death deceived no one.' He sighed. 'There is much to be done. I shall beckon Lucien to inform the bishop and the mayor of what has befallen. The magistrate of Pobré: must also be told. The *post factum* consequences of an account of two more deaths from the Great Mortality are calamitous, and the officials are sure to quake. Fear of the pestilence in the course of an instant will be the foremost talk on all tongues, attenuating in magnitude all other anxieties. My hope is to conceal the cause of these deaths. Now you must go to speak to the boy. I bid you Godspeed, my friend. I do not envy you your undertaking.'

Upon taking his leave of the abbot, Fidelis pondered how he might best posit the delicate and grave obligation to announce the tragedy to Michel, and realised there was no softening approach to the matter. He elected to tell him bluntly.

Apprehension swamped Michel when summoned to report to Magister Fidelis in the cloister. He felt faint. With foreboding, he slowly made his way to the cloister and stood, looking vulnerable and limp, in front of Fidelis.

Certain a benevolent directness with the boy was best, Fidelis told him, just as the Vespers bells tolled six, 'I am grieved to tell you your parents are dead.'

His face a stricken mask, Michel laboured to absorb Fidelis' pronouncement. He stared at Fidelis as the monk described the circumstances of the discovery of their remains. He saw lips moving, but his ears registered only the droning sequence of bells that, to his ears, pealed in escalating volume with each knell. Then he fainted.

Fidelis' message resounded in his head when Michel awoke in his cot, and he lay there, crying. The finality of death and the lingering grief it conferred pressed despair on his psyche that stifles breathing and sorrow so painful that only one's own death would relieve it. He had entered a place where surcease from heartache would never be absolute. A state of mind in which, even years on, a sound, a taste, a smell, a sight – would stingingly re-inflict a fresh lesion of sorrow, even if only fleetingly.

Michel turned on his side and continued to cry. Fidelis stood over him, poised to offer consolation, and felt entirely inadequate to the task. He prayed for wisdom to help the boy, and sadly concluded he had only the promise of God's peace and love to recommend to him. He sighed, realising how inadequate that would seem to a lad who measured life by the world's standards and conduct – a world in which God's role was important, but took a decided second place.

At length Michel wanted to know every detail of what had happened. Fidelis related what he knew, and confessed it was not much. When a cascade of tears ceased, Fidelis, sympathetically aware a replenished reservoir would again spill over, decided it was time to help the boy cope with the turmoil in his soul. 'Come with me to the cathedral, Michel. You will find comfort there.'

They passed the sacristy into the north transept of the cathedral to the oblates' chapel that had a beautiful statue of Mary with the child Jesus which Michel had seen with his mother and father the week before. Tears filled his eyes. Fidelis guided him to a bench along the wall and sat beside him. Fidelis said quietly, 'Let us pray for your mother and father. God's goodness and mercy are as infinite as is his love. He and his Blessed Mother will listen to our prayers. They will grant salvation and eternal peace to your beloved parents. I shall pray for you as well, that God grant you peace to ease your sorrow and comfort your soul.'

Fire in his eyes, Michel dared to blurt out, 'Comfort? How so? *He* let them die. My mother and father were kind and good. How could God let them die?' Enraged, he said, 'It was the blue sickness, wasn't it? The pestilence. Wasn't it? Wasn't it?'

Fidelis answered fretfully, 'Yes, my son. I fear it was.' He added, 'I cannot pretend to understand God's design for us all, but I do believe we must strive to accept God's will, for I have learned in my life that acceptance brings peace.'

Michel lashed out, hysteria in his voice. 'God's will? To be on that path and meet that stranger? God's will to make my mother and father die? If that was God's will, then I hate God. I tell you I hate him!' His voice faltered, displaced by uncontrolled sobs.

Shocked by Michel's brazen outburst, Fidelis said nothing. He felt pity for the hapless boy, and was at a loss to rebut his blasphemy. He waited until Michel was calmer before he spoke, 'There are many mysteries in life, Michel, and many times I too am at a loss to comprehend them. I understand your anger and I know God does too. Your parents' death is tragic, and you are anguished. I and all in the monastery grieve for your loss.'

He paused, praying useful counsel might emerge. 'Michel . . . when our hearts can no longer bear the sorrow – I am sure of this – it is essential to look to God for solace and consolation. God nourishes our souls and minds with fortitude to endure the tribulations that befall us in this world and gives the grace to endure until we finally find peace. That makes life's vicissitudes bearable and gives the courage to go on. I think God's will is that we become more perfect beings in this life in preparation for immortality. Know this – I feel certain of this as well – that peace does come, and it comes through God's benevolence. It may take you much time to accept that, but I hope you come to believe it, for I think it will give you much consolation and wisdom. For now, it suffices to simply mourn. The love you have for your parents merits the grief you feel now. You need not pray. God knows your presence in this quiet place. Peace will come to you if you be patient. It may not come for a very long time, but in time it will be given to you.'

Michel, his eyes red and swollen, regarded Fidelis with affection, grateful for his kindness. But his mind was battered, and he reasoned that if he dwelled on thoughts of his parents and how they died, the fury he felt would overpower him, corrupting the love for them he prized. He moaned. The turmoil and agony were unbearable. Better not to think at all, he decided.

He gazed blankly around at the chapel walls, unmoved by the stained-glass windows that, with their cobalt blues and ruby reds, sparkled like jewels. He shifted his attention to the small alabaster figures of Mary with the Christ child in her arms. It was such a happy statue. Mary wore a blue mantle with a gold fringe speckled with gold stars and a red gown that fell in folds like a Greek *himation*. Mary's slender body was sculpted in a graceful curve. She cradled the child Jesus in her left arm on her hip. Jesus held a ball in one of his hands. They faced each other, exchanging loving smiles. Michel cocked his head slightly and looked closely at the Virgin's sweet face. It reminded him of his mother and her devotion to the Mother of God. Tears suspended the thought.

Fidelis stepped forwards and quietly guided Michel out of the cathedral. 'I want you to rest. Father Abbot will preside at a Christian burial of your parents in our cemetery later this night.' Worn and wasted, Michel followed Fidelis meekly to the Hôtel Dieu.

Michel listlessly sat on a cot in one of the infirmary stalls. Fidelis was in Lucien's dispensary. He requested Brother Iohannes give him a sleeping potion. 'Alter it to half strength, Brother.'

Iohannes retrieved a sealed vessel from a shelf and poured a mixture of hyoscyamus, mulberry juice, poppy, and wine into a vial with water. 'If Michel drinks it all he will sleep profoundly. Use your judgment, Fidelis. Stay with him a while. Should his sleep be too deep, place drops of fennel in his nostrils.'

Fidelis nodded. 'I shall keep the watch.' Fidelis placed the vessel in a deep pocket and hurried back to Michel. He mustered a smile and offered the sleeping draught to Michel. 'Drink but half of this child. It will help you sleep.'

Michel obediently drank half the vial, removed his sandals and lay on the bed, silently beseeching the comfort of Fidelis' presence. The monk told him reassuringly.' Fear not. I shall stay with you.'

With Fidelis at his side, Michel felt safe to close his eyes. Asleep, he dreamt he was working in the field alongside his mother sowing seeds as they followed his father and an iron-tipped plow grudgingly pulled by an ox. His father turned around and his face was that of the hideous decaying head Michel had seen in the painting his first day at the abbey. He woke up in a start, dripping with sweat. Shuddering, he sat up.

Fidelis, by his side, soothed him. 'A dream, Michel, and a bad one. Try to rest more.' Fidelis stroked his back soothingly, and Michel became drowsy. Reveries of his mother and father in happy times came to him. It was his saint's day, and his mother and father laughed and hugged him. A special meal his mother had prepared lay on the table. His father presented him with a fine carving he had made of a horse and cart. It seemed they were touchable, and he extended his arms, but the harder he tried, the further they drifted away from him. The drowsiness deepened as, without success, he continued to reach out to embrace them. He did not remember falling asleep.

Lucien rode slowly on his way to Pobrér and the Dunard cottage, keeping pace beside the horse driven cart in which Quimper and Laurentius sat, Laurentius at the reins.

At the cottage, the silence seemed menacing. Lucien admonished the monks to wait outside. Pausing to light a candle and inhaling deeply, he opened the door to the cottage, dim, save for the candle in his hand and the waning light of dusk that directed his gaze to a bed on which lay two bodies. Suppressing the nausea generated by a putrid odour, he approached the bed, and with professional detachment ran candlelight over the corpses. He shook his head, dismissing any doubt about the cause of their deaths. He saw two goblets on the floor. He lifted one to his nose and detected a faint fusty residue clinging to the wood – a substance well known to him.

He inwardly moaned as he realised that, although Michel's parents had been afflicted with the plague, it was the substance they drank from the goblets that killed them. 'Heavenly father forgive them,' he muttered. He decided instantly this was no suicide. Lucien would not deny them Christian burial. He picked up the goblets and put them on a shelf. Facing the bodies of Yann and Marie he whispered, 'Rest easy in your eternal home in heaven.' He blessed their bodies and hurried into the cool of evening and the recuperative fresh air.

Lucien stood watch as brothers Laurentius and Quimper transferred the bodies to the cart and covered them with straw just as Marc Gervais, like a phantom, appeared from the ink of night. 'I made haste once Abbot William sent word of what happened. I stopped at each domicile on the way to make discreet inquiries. None saw two travellers pass them by for more than a week.'

'That is encouraging. When did you get back to town? I was told you and your company had gone north to scout.'

'True, and as usual, to no avail. We learned nothing. A week gone, and nothing to account for it.'

'But no more children taken.'

'No. Thank God. But I am disconsolate, Brother.' Lucien nodded but said nothing.

'What plan have you for the burial?'

'Abbot William hopes to assure their deaths and the cause be undisclosed. As it is, despite the pretense we put forth to stifle rumour, word is rife in the town that the stranger's death last week was caused by the pestilence. Should it be known two more have died, fear will mount, and further flight would be impossible to bridle. To that end, we take the bodies to the abbey where, should explication be unavoidable, it can be told that they died from starvation and, in consideration of the new oblate, his parents were buried in sanctified ground in the abbey cemetery. We trust it will not come to that and secrecy will prevail.' He sighed. 'More than all we pray no other deaths will come to pass, but we must fear disaster could be upon us.'

'I grasp the objective and think it prudent, Brother. I am bound to silence on the matter. You have my word on it.' He smiled mischievously and added, 'I am impressed with the inspired inventiveness of the story a man of the cloth proposes to tell the folk of Saint Petroc. Mark you, I doubt if I could do better.'

Lucien playfully cuffed him on the back and retorted, 'Oh, I am sure you could best me at the worst of times, my friend!'

Marc guffawed. He took a final look at the bleak dwelling. A grave expression returned. He sighed. 'I think it wise the cottage be set afire to ensure no one enters. Tomorrow at first light I'll return to notify the magistrate of Pobrér of what has happened and of our stratagem. I will certify from neighbours to the south the last time they last saw Marie and Yann Dunard. That would tell much as to whether or not anyone is in peril from the pestilence.' He was prepared to spin a tale about the abandonment of their home in search of work in Dinan or Rennes. 'Should it be needed, the foundation of my narrative will be that their son gone, and their house burned, the two left the province With luck, none will have been in contact with the Dunards and my story of their absence will appear reasonable.'

'Indeed, it would appear we both are great spinners of tales.' Lucien laughed. He looked at the cottage and sighed. 'And now, to the task!'

The dried-out thatch seized the fiery torch and rapaciously performed its destructive power. The small group waited until only embers remained. Silently they turned the cart towards Saint Petroc-sur-lac, walking the horse at a furtive pace.

It was a moonless night and still, with only the clout of hooves, rumbling of wheels, the croaking of frogs, and the occasional whoops of perturbed owls to intrude on the silence. A half league from the south gate of the town, the procession halted. The monks tied muffling rags around each hoof of the horse before resuming the funeral convoy. They avoided the south gate by skirting around the city wall to the north side that led to a door that gave access to the monastery.

Lucien sent Quimper to fetch a vial of the black potion to give the sheriff as a precautionary measure. With the remedy in hand, he instructed Marc on its use.

Marc embraced Lucien and said, 'I bid you farewell, Brother. I'll come to you tomorrow night with news of my day's adventures.' Sighing, his commission finished, he took his leave.

The monks cleansed and anointed the bodies in the *lavabo* in keeping with the obsequies associated with Christian burial. When shrouded, they placed them on wooden litters and carried them to the cemetery.

At the sanctified burial site, lay brothers had followed Lucien's instructions to dig a wide and particularly deep grave, and Laurentius and Quimper placed the bodies side by side and covered them with layers of lime and earth. As Laurentius left to inform the abbot all was ready for the funeral rite, Quimper remained at the grave site, leaning on a spade. He heard a faint rumble in the distance. It caught his attention, and surprised, he saw that, although only an hour until prime, the sky appeared to be darkening. In the distance, a portentous black veil was rushing towards him.

Abbot William, Prior Fidelis, Brothers Lucien, Laurentius, and a frail but resolute Michel walked from the monastery past the front of the cathedral to the cemetery. Black clouds now hovered overhead, and a startling explosion of thunder broke the silence. As the abbot dipped the *aspergium* into *aqua sancta* and misted the bodies with the holy water, a simultaneous sprinkling of rain dampened them all and moistened – barely – the dehydrated earth. The unexpected phenomenon was distracting, but Abbot William continued with the ritual. Michel was numbed by grief, and each mizzle of water from the sky intensified his bitterness. He nevertheless stood dry eyed and motionless with a soul full of anger, indifferent to the church's blessings Abbot William entreated.

The abbot signaled an end to the service with a final thrust of the *aspergium* over the graves whilst intoning a final supplication that was in concert with what was by now a cascade of surging rain:

> *Lux aeterna luceat eis, Domine,*
> *Cum sanctis tuis in eternum quia pius es.*
> *Requiem aeternam dona eis, Amen.*

The mourners departed, leaving Fidelis, Lucien and Michel to ladle now sodden soil onto the graves. Anguish that belied his stoic demeanour permeated Michel as the rain, a cruel quirk of fate, pooled on the mounting layers of earth that blanketed his parents' bodies. *Where had the rain come from, and why was it so long in coming? Too late to reverse any of our fates*, he thought morosely. The irony was not lost on Fidelis and Lucien, who placed sympathetic hands on Michel's shoulders and felt some of the tension leave the boy's body.

As the rain continued, they said additional prayers. Michel dashed to the garden and returned with two of his mother's favorite flower. Lucien and Fidelis shared amused expressions and disregarded Michel's failure to request permission to harvest them from the abbey garden.

As they walked back to the monastery, Fidelis said quietly, 'There will be no chapel this morning. The community will gather in the cathedral for High Mass and special prayers for the repose of the souls of your mother and father. And no school today. I want you to stay close to me.'

There were no further deaths from the Black Death in the days and weeks after the deaths of Marie and Yann Dunard. Michel visited their graves daily, spending as many melancholy moments as were permitted. He knelt, not in prayer, except for lip service to a recitation of an *Ave* or two. Mostly, vacuous in grief, unwilling to think, and indifferent to the dark clouds and continuous rain suited to his brooding, he grieved. Brother Lucien had made a wooden cross that marked the site where Marie and Yann lay, ever endearing him to Michel.

It rained steadily for weeks, and each day further stimulated the brown earth to generate a nascent mantle of green that promised nutrient growth throughout the surrounding region once again. Michel hated the sight of it.

8

HEALING GRACE

Weeks turned into months as Michel coped with his loss. The support of Fidelis and Lucien and his oblate friends chipped away the most desolate of Michel's sorrow. Fidelis, with other monks with whom the boy had contact, gauged his emotions, ever ready to offer comfort, and in time it became apparent that Michel had accepted his loss and had resumed normal boyhood activities.

Fidelis was pleased his focus on studies needed no prodding, and noted that he kept to his obligations diligently, bravely coping with forlorn spirits. Fidelis made efforts to lift his disposition, and on warm sunny days, equipped with worms, lines and hooks, he took Michel with him down the hill to the pond's shore to fish, philosophise, and entertain him with sagas of Breton lore related to the Arthurian legends embedded in the Broceliande forest close to Tréhorenteuc. He told him of Arthur, the Round Table and all of Arthur's knights. Sir Gawayne was Michel's favourite.

The monk was rewarded with wide eyed, uplifted spirits when he recounted the local legends, and especially when he related harrowing tales of evil spirits in the Valley of No Return.

'The wicked Vivien le Fey tricked the magician Merlin into confiding to her all his secrets, and she forever entombed him in an invisible bubble, where he remains.

She lives there still as well, and vile things happen near Tréhorenteuc to this day. It is a sinister place, with a giant who eats people, especially children. Promise me, Michel, you will ne'er go there.'
'Oh, I swear it, sir.'
Excited on such occasions. Michel could hardly wait to relate to his friends the chilling tales Fidelis told him about demons and sorcerers close by in Tréhorenteuc, and the heroic stories he had heard about King Arthur and Lancelot and Galahad and Percival and Kay.

Fidelis, delighted how easily the child's curiosity and interest were stirred, continued to divert Michel's mind from grief as they worked together in the herb garden.

Michel's mother had tutored the child on the use of botanicals' healing properties, but he was not privy to their centuries old use or the scope of their application for those afflicted with sickness.

Fidelis taught him in detail which herbs were used and blended and for which diseases. Fidelis was a natural born evangelist, and he imbued the herbs with miraculous properties, declaring them gifts from God. It pleased him to note that the instructions on the use of insects, animal waste and even odiferous flowers to protect plant growth from predators intrigued Michel. He made a mental note to discuss Michel with Lucien.

To further curtail the boy's mind from doleful thoughts, Fidelis proposed he help the lay brothers with a project to render the vineyard grapes impenetrable from Dionysian foragers. 'It is a time-consuming effort to make the netting and cover the vineyard, Michel. You can be a great help in the effort.'

At first, the hard work kept Michel's mind absorbed in the task and distanced from his sorrow, but he felt uneasy when he was with the lay brothers. They could be gruff and bad-tempered, and it soon became evident they stole from the cellarer. Michel felt miserable, trapped.

'Here, have some cheese, boy,' Beladore called out with a belch as he swigged stolen wine from a pouch. Michel blanched and shook his head.

'What troubles you, lad?' Condriti asked. Michel looked away and said nothing. 'You look bothered. Be ye so?'

Michel shook his head again - a little too vigorously.

'He be troubled about the *vitailles* and wine, me thinks,' Felix said. 'Look thee, boy. Why shouldn't we have some of their cheese and swill it down with wine? We grow the grapes and make the wine, and the monks sell it at great profit. It is owed to us to have our share.' He smirked. 'Come now. They don't miss it.'

Michel blinked and swallowed hard. His heart pounded. *They are stealing! I must tell Fidelis. No . . . no . . . I can't do that.'* He resisted the impulse to run away when he had a sudden inspiration. 'I am not well, Brother.' He had their full attention. The three looked at each other and at Michel.

'Well, best you go then to the infirmary to find out what ails you!' laughed Beladore.

Michel nodded and ran from the field, but not before he went deep into the vineyard to look for thorny vines he had seen there. He scraped his arms and hands until they bled. Satisfied, he went to talk to Fidelis with a concocted story of how he had often pricked himself. 'I have had fever, Magister.' He shifted his eyes. 'I don't think I am well suited to this task.'

Fidelis eyed him skeptically. *There's more to this than what he is telling me.* 'Michel is it that you want me to assign you a different chore?' he asked, hoping to glean some inkling of the child's mindset, for it seemed he was genuinely dismayed. Michel said nothing and lowered his head. 'Come lad, tell me. What is it?'

'Well, Magister, I miss working with botanicals and long to work with them.'

'Hmm. Quite so,' Fidelis studied the boy. *Is that all it is?* Whatever the issue, it was clear the boy would not divulge it. Fidelis considered the matter and said to him, 'I shall look into the matter. Now go to the infirmary and see to those wounds.'

Fidelis told Lucien of the boy's interest in the medicinal properties of herbs, his industry, and commitment to his work. Lucien observed, 'He is young still, but can be put to good use in my dispensary if you can schedule him time with me. I would like that Fidelis. Look to it, will you?'

Michel stifled exhilaration when Fidelis told him of the opportunity to work with Lucien. He would not have to work with the *vignerons* anymore. He would be liberated from the drudgery of preparing parchments in the scriptorium. 'You will have to give up the apprenticeship in the scriptorium, Michel. Will you not regret learning the art of calligraphy and illumination?'

Michel artfully told Fidelis, 'Serving Brother Lucien and helping the sick would be more meaningful. I know my parents would want that for me, Magister.' It was a true enough statement. Helping heal the sick and working in the herb garden and becoming proficient in mixing and brewing herbal remedies appealed to him.

Michel arrived at Lucien's dispensary with noticeable enthusiasm, much to his mentor's delight. His keen interest and aptitude were quickly apparent, and Lucien marvelled at the rate with which he mastered skills to prepare medicinal concoctions. He showed compassion for the sick, and no task was too menial for him as he was called upon to feed, bathe and even abide by the side of lonely ailing souls. He evolved into an able assistant on whom Lucien could rely. 'He is a treasure, Fidelis. It would please me greatly to have his presence in the Hôtel Dieu formally as an apprentice.'

He will be glad of it, Lucien. I do believe he should continue to tend the vegetable garden and the herbal beds as well. Would you agree?'

'Absolutely. I know he derives strength and a sense of purpose when he works the land. He mused, 'The work lessens the pain he sustains within.'

Inevitably Michel discussed with Lucien the heartbreak of his parents' death and the circumstances that resulted in the tragedy. Michel felt at ease expressing his sorrow and anger with an intuitive grasp Lucien would be sympathetic to his feelings.

'Bad things happen, Michel, and none of us really knows why. I believe it is the natural order of things – the bad and the good. I do think it important to pray for acceptance of whatever happens in life, and offer compassionate support when we can. Oh, I know most bless or blame God, depending on happy or lamentable circumstances. I don't think God has anything to do with any of it.' Michel was bewildered, and admitted he did blame God for his parents death.

'I tell you God had nothing to do with the tragedy.'

Michel was shocked and confused. 'Then what does God do? We're always praying to God and asking for something.'

'Yes. I find myself doing that sometimes, when I really think God has endowed us all with tools necessary to deal with life, and we can pray for spiritual guidance to tap the strength we have within us to cope with the trials and sorrows life invariably brings us. Saint Jerome's Vulgate Bible refers to this in The Book of Solomon. It is a template to follow – prudence to know right from wrong, a sense of justice, fortitude to face fear, and temperance to control the temptations of the flesh. Interestingly, the ancient Greeks valued these qualities. Saint Paul added the Christian virtues of faith, hope and charity – love. It is the greatest virtue. Jesus taught us that. All these attributes are what I most highly value and pray to receive so that I may do my best on earth.'

Michel thought about all the children who had disappeared, a subject that troubled him mightily. 'There is so much evil in the world. It distresses me so.'

'Indeed! But I think the world has more good in it than bad. Think on it! The sheriff and his deputies are relentless in pursuit to find the children and punish the evildoers Parents' grief at the loss of their children is a sign of their love. Many in the community feel much compassion for those who have suffered losses as well as worry about their own children. They offer condolences, deliver food, keep company with the bereaved. Yes. I do believe there are far more who are good in the world than there are evil. Mind, I think it difficult to live a virtuous life. Seven deadly sins there are that undermine our intentions. I have known many transgressors, and I am ashamed to say I too have too often been among them. Perhaps it is why I continually pray to cleanse my soul of sin.'

He looked at Michel. 'We are all of us flawed, but can all be redeemed.' He thought a moment. 'Mostly, I try to keep to what I must do each day in and out of the infirmary to ease the burdens of pain and sorrow of the truly afflicted. That is the mission I have. And I look to prayer and hope for moral integrity to do my job well.'

'But people say they are being punished by God when bad things happen.'

'Hogwash! The Church tells us God is directly involved in everything we do and all good things on earth come from God. But were that so, one must believe all bad things come from God. It is an absurdity, I tell you, and I deride the idea God punishes or rewards us on earth. What kind of God would that be? As for me, I settle for striving to live as virtuous a life as I can for my own soul's sake, not for any reward from God or fear of punishment. God help me Michel, what I believe, frankly, is heresy, so I keep my thoughts to myself.

I shall not speak to anyone about anything you tell me, Magister.'

Lucien laughed. 'That is very good of you, Michel. I thank you for your loyalty.' He paused and added, 'Mind you, although I do not think God is directly involved in our lives, I fervently believe prayer is the greatest means we have to guide us through life's turbulent seas. It is like an anchor that steadies us, or a fixed star in the firmament upon which we can rely for direction to a safe harbour. Prayer gives us strength to bear all things. I highly commend the practice.'

'Fidelis said something like that to me the night he told me my mother and father had died.'

'Did he? That is interesting. I must ask him more of his philosophy. And what think you about these ideas?'

'They seem wise,' Michel acknowledged.' But they confuse me. It's a new way to think about God – and so different from anything I've been taught. But what you say makes sense, sir. and I shall cogitate on it.'

Lucien suppressed an inclination to laugh at the child's *gravitas* and simply expressed his appreciation for his considered thought on the matter.

Michel's eyes filled with tears and sighed. 'Today is the feast of the Assumption of Mary into Heaven. My thoughts are of my mother, who was devoted to Mary, and I am downhearted anew. I need comfort.'

Lucien quietly said, 'It is good to relieve your sorrow, child.' Lucien fell silent, lost in thought. Inspired, he cupped Michel's face in his hands and looked deeply in his eyes. 'Pray *to* your mother and father, Michel. Pray *to* them. They will hear your supplications and give you the strength and consolation you seek.'

The nutrient rich loam, nourished with an unfailing supply of water, yielded crops effortlessly. It saddened Michel when thoughts came to him of his father's fruitless work on sterile land, and felt bitter when he thought of the drought that had begun his family's woes.

Yet, when he thought of how the steady rain since the night of his parents' burial had transformed the cracked, scorched earth of the entire valley into verdant, fertile, and productive farmland, he was glad for those who benefited by the resurgence of nutritious growth.

Vegetables grew, flowers blossomed, trees bore fruit, and people were no longer starving. He simply wished the rain had begun in time to save his family, and at times the irony of its arrival the night his parents were buried gave him more distress than he could at times endure. Incensed gashes into the ground with the spade, hoe and fork as he worked help fragment disturbing thoughts until, wet through with perspiration, his first glimpse of new shoots thrusting upwards from the soil that promised new growth and life sustaining vegetables invariably gladdened his heart.

Fidelis' and Lucien's attentiveness nudged Michel further from the abyss of bereavement, as did prayer and the routine of study and work. The time he spent in the dispensary was excitingly instructive. Lucien's skill in treating the sick edified and motivated the oblate to emulate him. He noted how the gentle and reassuring care given soothingly eroded fear and inspired hope.

Lucien directed musicians to play soft music daily, a pacifying complement to the treatment of afflicted bodies and troubled minds. Michel and lay brothers kept company with the sick and prayed with anxious patients, effacing much of their anxiety. Lucien's ministrations prompted trust, even serenity, and all were always healed by him, if not always physically, then spiritually.

As he withdrew from a patient's side Lucien always left behind a message of optimism and a blessing. They were lessons Michel took to heart, thankful for the healing grace he himself felt as a result of Lucien's nurturing attentions.

9

INCREASED WOES

Brother Alaric heaved open the weighty monastery portal as Brothers St. Jean and Becket, with bulging pouches of coins looped around their belts, greeted a multitude of people, there for the weekly distribution of alms and goods in a tradition that dated to Saint Benedict's time.

The almoners benevolently had the means to continue the saint's mission because of the large donations of money and clothing in exchange for monks' prayers for the donors' souls. It was an equitable bargain that enabled the monks to give the poor, along with their blessings, the necessities of life.

This week was much like any other. Oblates Michel, Christopher, Padraig and Ioseph stood behind the monks with laden carts. The people who gathered were humble, polite, and grateful, praising God and his earthly disciples.

Michel saw in their faces shadows of his parents' countenances. They were reminders that the poor were casualties through no imperfections or personal faults, just as the privileged few often were kept from destitution through providential chance rather than from merit.

Startled by a woman's cry and shrill laments, Michel watched as she shoved her way through the crowd to Brother St. Jean's side, knelt, and kissed the hem of his habit. She raised her hands entwined in supplication. 'Help me, I beg you, help me find my babes.'

Brother Becket gently lifted her to her feet and tried to pacify her, encouraging her to tell him calmly what had happened as Brother St. Jean entreated the agitated and curious onlookers to wait but a while. He closed the door and stood by as Brother Becket attended to the woman. 'I was waiting for your kind charity among the throng with my boys at my side. I never noticed their absence.'

'Perhaps they have but wandered off to play,' Brother Becket suggested. He glanced at Brother St. Jean with a furrowed brow that disclosed inner dread.

She shook her head. 'Nay. When I saw they were gone, I became frantic, and two women told me they saw two boys the ages of mine riding on men's horses heading north.'

'How so? Why did the guards not stop them?'

'I rushed to the gate to ask them that. They told me a horseman beseeched their help for his lame horse. They looked, but found nothing amiss. They noticed naught else. They saw no boys.'

The almoners tried to sooth the panic-stricken mother. Brother Becket said, 'We shall go to the sheriff for help. Have courage. And pray. It may be possible to save them.'

Brother St. Jean opened the gate for the woman and Becket, who ignored the anxious murmurs of the mendicants as they set off to report the incident. The distribution of goods began without comment until all had received an allotment and dispersed, exchanging agitated and fearful deductions about what had happened.

Michel, shaken and deeply saddened by the incident, remained at his post until dismissed by the almoner. He returned the cart to its storage space and fretfully ran to the chapel to pray for the woman and her children with newfound humility that recognised his grief was neither unique nor uncommon. He also understood why his parents had been afraid for his safety.

When Michel told his fellow oblates what had happened, they nervously discussed the abductions and rattled on about the two gone missing. 'I fear there will be more,' Henri said and blessed himself. Christian expressed relief they, at least, were protected by monastic walls.

In the ensuing days, Adrian heard a lay brother mention the sheriff's posse continued to search for the children. Michel prayed with greater fervour for the mother and her sorrowful loss, and continued to do so for a long while, although he heard no more about the matter, and would never know if the woman's children had been delivered back to her.

Summer had produced a profusion of crops and bountiful grass for grazing cows. The oblates helped work the fields, and farm work mushroomed as crops matured and wheat and grass grew taller, ready to be harvested. As the boys kept to their chores in the fields, they kept an eye on the cows, tethered to prevent them from eating crops, and known to break loose. One late afternoon when Michel was harvesting cabbages, he looked up to see two cows ambling towards the high grass close to the lake's shoreline, and he raced after them. He easily had them by their lead ropes as they chomped on the sweet grass, and he paused to gaze at the brilliant glint of the sun reflected in the smooth water of the lake, exulting in the heat of the unseasonably balmy September day.

His eye caught movement on the far western side of the lake. Three small figures – children surely – tended sheep on a gently sloping knoll too hilly for farming, but good grazing land. Michel smiled at the diminutive figures, and mused they seemed free and purposeful in their work. He indulged in a reverie in which he too was unbound from the monastery and able to lead a life of his choosing.

From that distance, he could not hear the noise of galloping horses, but he saw them, the dust they stirred, and the men who rode them as they spirited towards the children. He thought it a curious sight as they gained ground, sending sheep scampering. Just then the chapel bells sounded Vespers, and Michel realised that once again he was going to be late. He tightened his hold on the cows' leads and ran to a grassy area where they could graze, secured them, made sure they had water, and dashed to the back door of the monastery.

Several days later he heard the rumour that three shepherd boys had been abducted. The connection between what he had seen and the boys' disappearance was unmistakable, and he reported the incident to Fidelis.

Later in the day he was sent for by Abbot William. Sheriff Marc Gervais was with him. Marc greeted Michel warmly and, with a few words of banter, ingratiated himself with the boy before he quizzed him about what he had seen.

'Not very much, I fear, sir. They were far across the lake, too far to see well or comprehend what was about to happen. There were three men on horses, and they were by design racing towards the children. Then the chapel bells rang, and I dared not tarry to see more.'

Marc nodded but was disappointed not to have been given more clues. At least, he reasoned, he now knew approximately when and where the boys had been abducted, and that three men were involved – all useful information.

'My lord abbot, will you give permission for Michel to ride with me to find the site where the shepherd boys were last seen? Only he can identify the precise place for us.'

Michel's eyes betrayed the pleasure he strained to hide. The abbot nodded affirmation, and Michel remained placidly erect with no sign of the jubilation he felt. Marc took his leave and Michel with him.

When Michel saw the size of the sheriff's mount outside the monastery door, anxiety passed through him. 'Forgive me, sir . . . I have never ridden a horse.'

Marc roared with laughter. 'No fear. I'll make a horseman of you. Best you sit behind me and hold on tightly. You have given the general direction; now you must lead the way to the place.'

With hounds barking, eager for a hunt, Marc and his retinue broke into a gallop. With closed eyes, Michel clung to the sheriff, holding fast with his arms around Marc's waist. It seemed the horse tore over the land with the speed of an arrow. Once he dared open his eyes, he caught the cadence of the horse's movements and relaxed, letting his body glide with the animal's gait.

He luxuriated in the world's broad vista outside the monastery's walls. The once denuded landscape had been transformed into a verdant Eden, with a lavish array of late summer blooms with aromas that sweetened the air and attracted several species of birds, all in full song. Michel had little memory of summer landscapes before the drought. The view he had from the lakeside was but a glimpse of the vastness of nature's grandeur, and he wondered how he could ever be content within the confines of the abbey after this astonishing adventure.

When the sheriff jerked the horse's reins that forced an abrupt halt, Michel's sensibilities returned to his undertaking. He studied the area carefully to ascertain where he had been when he first noticed the shepherd boys and the direction from which the riders had approached them. 'Yea, Sheriff. I recognise this place. Go directly forward.'

Not long after, a few straggler sheep further established they were close to the site where the shepherds had gone missing. 'Down you go, Michel. We shall walk and examine the earth.'

Michel, full of his newly endowed purpose, guided the posse to a locale that tellingly showed signs of a struggle. He picked up a staff.

Marc told him, 'Give it to the hounds to sniff. Yes. Well done.' He smiled broadly. 'I should say that makes you a proper deputy sheriff, Michel!'

The dogs' keen noses guided the direction they should go, and barking, they went forward, once more on horseback. The sleuths followed the dogs north and east. When they arrived at a wide stream, the animals became confused, and bayed with frustration as they went pell-mell along the bank. Marc took them to the far bank, but it availed nothing.

There was a fork in the road ahead, and both paths led north. Marc and his men explored each of them. The hounds snuffled eagerly and thoroughly, but in time their bawls and yaps told the story. They were unable to pick up the lost scent. Discouraged, Marc and his men headed back to town. Most discouraged of all was Michel when Marc returned him to the monastery.

'We thank you, lad, for your efforts. Truly you have been helpful to us this day. Why look you melancholy? Chases that give no apparent reward always give further insight and hope. If we persist, and with luck and God's guidance, fear not, we shall find the fiends and the children.'

As he took his departure, Marc said teasingly, 'I trust we may call upon you for further service to us lad,' leaving a blushing and wistful Michel to his fantasies and an amazing escapade to relate.

As the weeks passed, the number of children reported missing increased – a girl gone to visit a grandmother, a beggar boy in the town, two children sent to fetch a monk to administer to their dying father.

Marc's anxiety engulfed him. Dreams of fists banging on his door fractured his sleep. He was edgy and agitated as he and Donan obsessively analysed the file of each kidnapping that had occurred, vainly hoping to eke information that would inspire them in their pursuit of the criminals.

Their lack of progress left them both demoralised with a crushing sense of failure. 'I see only shadows of evil faces and twisted brains but know not their purpose and have little hope of discovering who they are. I tell you I am sore sick of heart and weak with perturbation.' Marc groaned. 'The children! Dear God in heaven, the children. Not a sliver of evidence since April of who has them, where they are or if, God's blood, they are alive! I cannot bear the thought of even one more child's disappearance, yet I have no hope I can prevent another iniquity. I am at hell's gate from despair.'

'Hold on, Marc! By God's holy rood, take hold of yourself! I too am troubled, and my spleen is full of gall, but I won't give way to hopelessness. Nor must you. Rather we must bend our minds to plot deeds as terrible as those whoreson reprobates. Then we might gain insight into their thinking.'

'And? How will you do that?'

Deflated, Donan said lamely, 'I don't know.'

Baron Gilles de Rais had left the Château de Merlin for his castle in Fougères in September. His exodus to the east averted another grandiose and disruptive procession through town, enabling Marc to focus on matters pertaining to the diabolical disappearances of children. By late October, overall instances of crime in and around Saint Petroc-sur-lac had decreased. Marc surmised that, the drought ended, and bounty from now life-sustaining fields harvested, there was sustenance enough for all including the most wanting, rendering petty thievery less of an imperative.

Astonishingly, and to their inestimable relief, there had been no further reports of children missing. Marc and Donan were as bewildered as they were relieved, but each day passed with an undercurrent of apprehension. As weeks went by without incident, they dared to wonder if the horror had ended as mystifyingly as it had begun, and hoped that whatever nefarious aims that had instigated the abductions, the devils had moved on.

The strain on Marc, however, continued unabated as he answered to a contemptuous town council and endured the mayor's cantankerous wrath after he had read Marc's account of the unsolved kidnapping cases. The mayor ordered Marc to report to the bishop. The bishop's reaction, Marc mused, would be far more vitriolic than anything the mayor was capable of issuing to him.

He waited in the antechamber of the office of Bishop Bernard du Loi of Saint Petroc-sur-lac, reviewing the official list of missing children from the Saint Petroc region from April to September. Twenty-two children missing. It was a staggering number for any community let alone one that had always been mainly peaceful and law abiding. *No wonder officialdom is up in arms.*

Marc anticipated du Loi would be scathingly critical on several points. He would doubt the thoroughness of the investigations and declare them careless, inadequate; he would challenge Marc's dedication – or lack thereof – to his responsibilities, and scathingly question his competence and professionalism.

Marc was prepared for a barrage of belittling reprimands embellished with more than a few stinging invectives. It would be nothing he had not heard before, and he was resigned and inured to whatever insults the bishop might lob at him.

His thoughts transmuted to introspection as he waited in the bishop's anti-chamber. He scowled, mulling over the critical abuse to which he had been subjected from town officials and the mayor. *I can't blame them for their anger or recriminations. I've failed. Utterly failed.* Marc's self-reproach was significantly more intense than any of the rebukes that had been doled out by those in authority, even as he brooded about how scornful it had been.

He felt satisfied that every conceivable endeavour to root out the reprobates had been conducted thoroughly and even with ingenuity, but with no means of preventing more criminal activity and his failure to solve even one kidnapping case, he felt woefully deficient.

There was but one confidante to whom he could – did – disclose these feelings, but even friend Donan would never be privy to his sense of personal inadequacy and failure. One factor did sustain what little remained of his confidence. He thought that the mayor, the council, and even the bishop realised that if anyone could solve the crimes, it was he – otherwise they long ago would have removed him from office. That single thought emboldened him to hold fast to a tattered fragment of self-worth.

All the same, the wrath that had to date been inflicted on him was wounding, especially when, in his estimation, local officialdom had itself been inept, with no suggestions forthcoming. They sat in judgement vacuous and ignorant, swift to spear searing abuse and caustic jeers with no concept of the difficulties Marc and his deputies faced, let alone appreciation for the arduous and tenacious efforts he and his men engaged in to find the perpetrators of the abductions. That irritated him. Commendation for unstinting zeal, not abuse, in his view would be more appropriate, despite the thus far admittedly ineffectiveness of their efforts.

As he sat in the bishop's antechamber, Marc knew he could expect no support from the bishop on this or on any score. As the sheriff entrusted with safeguarding the people, in this grave instance he acknowledged he had failed miserably. He was consigned to the reality that censure and vituperation were to be his lot. The mayor and council had in fact put him on the rack, so to speak, several times. He expected more of the same from the bishop. He was prepared for a replay of the discomfiture he had only recently endured at the city council meeting. At least, he consoled himself, the insults would emanate from the rants of one man instead of a dozen.

A servant opened the door. 'The bishop will see you now.'

Marc steeled himself, muttering as he stood and walked forwards towards the bishop's office, 'All right, my lad, into the fray.' He was ready for it.

10

INIQUITY

Summer high-spirited behaviour predictably had kept the Magister of Oblates busy in the monastery, but ironically, as the season waned, it was encounters with a newly employed priest – Ankou Trumpière by name – that predominately kept Fidelis disagreeably engaged.

Trumpière was not a Benedictine monk, but that was not unusual. Clergy from many orders who wanted to live and work in monasteries were routinely accepted by abbots to join them. Father Trumpière had expressed to his uncle, Bishop Bernard du Loi, his desire to be appointed Head of Oblate Discipline in the abbey. The bishop acquiesced, and so informed Abbot William, who was confounded, as he had never heard of such a position. William had no choice except to defer to his superior's wishes and without delay sketched an outline of what he thought the priest's duties should encompass, assuring Fidelis would be the priest's superior.

In his first days in the abbey, it immediately became apparent to Fidelis that Trumpière was unsuited to a position of authority over the oblates. Indeterminate snippets of whispers reached his ears that Trumpière was inclined to rage and quick to administer punishments wanting in compassion and proportionality. Fidelis had no direct proof of this, but the frequently overheard and telling muffled talk amongst the oblates that halted the moment his presence became known was a sign of mischief in the air. Fidelis understood boyhood comportment well enough not to expect the oblates to tell him what Trumpière was doing to them, but he was quick to sense that by nature Trumpière was mean-spirited and punitive. Fidelis grew progressively more uneasy about Trumpière's hold over the boys.

With forced patience, Fidelis attempted to guide Trumpière to a better understanding of boyhood conduct in hopes the priest would learn forbearance and restraint. He prompted Trumpière to take to heart the rule of Saint Benedict regarding the treatment of oblates. 'What thou dost not wish to be done to thee, do not thou to another,' Fidelis reminded him, and instructed him Abbot William proscribed harsh punishments as disciplinary tactics. Trumpière listened apathetically, and Fidelis was left with the impression he was not inclined to follow abbey statutes, and, in fact, distained them.

Fidelis communicated his concern to the abbot. 'He is mistreating the oblates, William. I am sure of it.'

Sympathetic to his concerns, William reminded Fidelis that dealing with the matter was problematical. 'The bishop is my superior, and with no actual evidence of abuse, there is no defensible reason to dismiss him from the abbey.'

Fidelis regretfully acknowledged there was indeed no proof of mistreatment, as the oblates were uniformly silent on the matter, no matter how firmly he prodded them.

'Continue your efforts to protect the boys from Trumpière's malevolence as best you are able, and be ever watchful for an incident that will confirm conduct scornful of abbey law. With proof, I can thereafter put forth to the bishop my intent to dismiss him from our abbey.'

Abbot William and Fidelis misguidedly thought the oblates, wary of Trumpière's temper, would avoid situations that would rouse him, and erroneously thought them safe enough. It was not long before they horrifically realised how vulnerable the boys were, and how ignorant they were of Trumpière's impious character.

At first sight, the oblates feared Trumpière. He was a startling figure to behold, with no facial hair, not even eyebrows, and he was completely bald. His perpetual glower conjoined with his abnormal countenance terrified the boys. The consensus that Trumpière was a monster soon was a universal opinion, but dodging encounters with him was difficult if not impossible, as Trumpière sought them out and fabricated cause to punish them.

The exposure of Trumpière's iniquitous nature finally occurred with an incident of unimaginable, unnatural, malevolence.

Michel awoke one night with a need to relieve himself. Guided by a solitary candle that dimly lit the way to the necessarium, he heard stifled but harrowing sounds emanating from Trumpière's room. Michel went to the door and put his ear to it. He heard a boy shrieking, begging mercy. He thrust open the door and, to his horror and disgust, saw Trumpière mounted on the back of the new oblate, Ronan, pounding rhythmically, indifferent to anguished pleas. Incensed, Michel vaulted into the room, forcefully took hold of Trumpière, and yanked him to the floor. He was revolted to see Trumpière's erected member. 'Run, Ronan. Get Fidelis!'

Trumpière got up from the floor and shoved Michel across the room in a crazed assault, striking him with powerful fists and knee blows to his groin. Just as Michel collapsed, Fidelis rushed into the room. He shoved Trumpière to the wall with one arm, leaving a combative right fist to pummel him unconscious. Lucien and the abbot arrived, with several monks in tow. The abbot approached Fidelis and took him firmly but gently, by his right arm. 'Fidelis. Desist. It is over.'

'The bishop intends to do nothing.' Abbot William fumed as he told Fidelis and Lucien about his meeting with the prelate. The monks were incredulous. Irate. 'I described cleanly and fully the bestial assault on a ten-year old child and the brutal beating of another. By God's Holy Rood, the bishop's demeanour signified complete indifference. Think on it! He remained mute about a grave and mortal sin against God and man. He espied me silently, walked to the window, where, back to me, he remained for a long time before he turned and said he would take charge of the matter. He also admonished me to say not a word to anyone, and especially not to anyone superior to him. I was stunned and asked if he would expel Trumpière from the priesthood – for I surely supposed he would, as the offence was so heinous. The bishop curtly dismissed me, saying what he intended to do was none of my affair.'

Fidelis and Lucien smouldered. 'Does this mean what I reason it to, William?' Fidelis asked.

William nodded and sighed resignedly. 'My dear friend, I believe as you must, that the bishop does not intend to punish him or do anything that will hinder his nephew's advancement in the Church.'

'That is shameful – wicked. May the lord's wrath fall on him!' Lucien blustered. William glanced at him, chastisement in his expression, agreement in his thoughts.

Fidelis shook his head in revulsion. 'You may well thus say, Lucien, for verily an ignominious sin against God and nature has been committed – and I must add likewise unlawful in the secular world!'

'I pose to you both. What should I – nay – what can I do? Leave the Abbey? Leave the Church?' William, agitated, strode about, quaking with fury. 'He is my superior, and I must obey him or be excommunicated, my vocation abandoned, my sacred work dedicated to God's service forsaken. I am not willing to pay that penalty. Are you?'

Lucien noted, 'He has us all locked in a vise. We are chattel to this injustice.'

The abbot bashed his hand with his fist. 'If I thought I could appeal to a higher church authority, I would take to the air and ascend with this grievance to the throne of God if necessary! If indeed I thought I could go to a secular authority, I would seize the chance and race with word of this wickedness to the Duke of Brittany himself! To what end? No authority will oppose the will of the bishop. It is I who would be sacrificed on the altar,' he murmured despairingly. 'We have no sway in this.'

'And I no faith in Church righteousness' Lucien wailed.

Silence ensued as each reflected on the implications of what William had told them. William was the first to speak. 'I feel unclean.'

'Betrayed! Of everything you and we have believed in and lived by,' Lucien said.

Fidelis carefully weighed Lucien's pronounce-ment. With conviction, he shook his head. 'No. Pray God allow me to differ. In addition to being men of the cloth we understand the ways of the world and the failings of men. We know Church hierarchy is a corrupt body and has been for centuries. Be that not why Saints Benedict, Francis, Clare – others – founded abbeys? Indeed, so that men and women might truly dedicate themselves to God's work on earth, shun the politics of church and state and reject the evils ambition spawns.'

William and Lucien could but nod agreement. 'We know, of course, even in abbeys vice is found.' He paused and then roared, 'Not in Saint Benedict! By God's precious heart, not in our abbey! We are true to our vows and resolute with our prayerful work to serve the poor and care for the infirm. We pray for the salvation of all and, let me remind you, we leave judgement to God. Go no further than study of the painting that hangs in our abbey of the *Danse Macabre*. It represents death as the great leveler. Everyone, be it pope, cardinal, priest – and yes, even bishop – at their deaths, have to make an accounting.' He jutted his chin in defiance and concluded, 'I believe we can – and must – lay aside the bishop's infamous dishonour and carry on with our avowed stewardship as we always have.' He paused for effect. 'That is what I intend to do.'

William ruefully smiled. 'Fidelis, your passion perforce compels me to say *Amen* to that.' He looked at Lucien. 'And you? What say you, Lucien.'

Lucien stood, stewing with rage. He remained silent, obdurate and unforgiving before he sighed resignation, and reluctantly nodded assent. A sudden thought gave utterance, 'Ronan and Michel! Their defiled beings require all our wit to help them recover, and I for one must seek God's wisdom and strength for the task. I must go to them now.'

Ronan and Michel spent weeks in the Hôtel Dieu. Their physical trauma was easy enough to treat with healing balms and poultices. Ministering to their psychic shock taxed even Lucien's formidable skills. He sorrowfully expected months – years – would pass before the boys expunged from their minds memory of the base assault both had endured. All within the abbey prayed for guidance on how to soothe their souls. They feared the boys might be forever blighted, unable to recapture a sense of their innocence or trust in their fellow human being.

The formidable challenge seemed insuperable, but efforts to heal their souls were divined in consultations between the abbot and his ministers. To impress upon the boys the monastery exemplified all that was good on earth and governed by the practice of virtue to bring all within it closer to God, the monks executed an exorcism to rid the abbey of evil.

At a solemn High Mass, Abbot William read Saint Matthew's gospel about the Holy Innocents and spoke eloquently on the subject in his homily, highlighting his belief that within the abbey such innocence resided in all their oblates.

'What more can we do? I am at a loss,' bemoaned Abbot William to Fidelis and Lucien.

Fidelis lamented neither boy would talk about their ordeal. 'I have tried with as much delicacy as is meet to encourage them to discuss what happened that frightful night but am received with silence.'

'Woeful tidings, Fidelis. Reckoning what befell them would be salutary,' Lucien sighed. 'Pray let us continue to tweak them to exonerate from their minds all perturbations, though it be against their wishes. I will do what I can. I believe Michel owns some regard for me that I can make use of to coax him to relieve his anguish.'

'And Ronan?' Fidelis asked. 'He is new to the abbey, and I for one have not yet grasped what endeavours might distract him from the suffering that gnaws his soul.'

'Send him to me, Fidelis.' William said. 'Let me know him better. It may be I can deduce the means to alleviate his damaged spirit.' He sadly shook his head. 'Such a woeful state of affairs. Beyond these feeble efforts there seems little else to do but pray.'

Lucien observed, 'Tincture of time, my Lord. Only time will heal these blameless boys.'

Michel silently grappled to suppress distressful images of the night he rescued Ronan. At first without success. Even at prayer before his parents' grave, thoughts of that foul night haunted him. The daily routine that commanded time and attention helped numb disquieting thoughts. Lucien ploddingly encouraged him to describe details of that night that most disturbed him. It was, Michel told him, the disbelief that a priest could be so depraved.

He and Lucien discussed the issue at length. 'It bespeaks an unnatural life form Michel. I am sorely tested to fathom it. But so unnatural be it, we must suppose – hope – it is a rare transgression.' Lucien's thoughts turned to the bishop. In an acrid tone he said without elaboration, 'More damning are the measures made to protect the transgressor – a grievous mortal sin.'

Michel was quick to wonder at the implication. 'What mean you?'

'Just that there are those who would shield such violators of natural law from the consequences of their actions.' Michel looked horrified. Lucien was quick to realise he had told the boy more than was seemly. He tried to deflect his attention from the remarks with a comment about how Fidelis had reacted with such degree of righteous rage. 'Of course, it must be considered,' he said mischievously, 'You both breached Saint Benedict's sacred interdiction against violence, but given the circumstance, I for one, bless you for saving Ronan. And I thought the thrashing Fidelis gave that beast quite merciful, given the offence.'

Michel confessed that Fidelis' rescue had earned eternal gratitude and respect from all the oblates. 'I don't think he did wrong. Am I errant to think that?'

Lucien smiled. 'Just between you and me, Michel, I am in accord with you, God forgive me – us!' He added, 'In fact, it pleased me that Fidelis trounced him so. 'Twas a fit censure, and I declared as much to my confessor. You can but imagine how proud I was when the abbot on the instant expelled that vile being from the abbey and dragged him before the bishop.'

Lucien omitted the reprehensible details of the outcome of that encounter.

Michel brightened, knowing Brother Lucien shared his own mind-set and told him so. 'Yet I cannot leave off images of that awful night. I do not know what to name what he did, but it assails my mind daily.' He cringed. 'How could such evil be?'

'Come boy. You know evil exists, and what he did was certainly wicked, but, with God's grace, this will be the only example of it in your life you will ever have experienced. It troubles me still such malevolence despoiled you and Ronan in our sanctuary! We must be vigilant it never more happens. But think on it, Michel. We purged it immediately, cleansed our house and restored it to its natural goodness and righteousness. It is the most any of us in this life can do – in and out of the monastery. My dear boy, in time I pray – we all pray – you rid your mind of the odious memory that weighs heavily on you now and be free to feel joy and tranquility. Know I am here to help you to those ends in any way I am able.'

'Your very presence, Magister, is a great comfort. And Fidelis! Methinks him a hero. Ronan does too. There are times we do tell ourselves we are blessed – and try to feel so.'

'And endowed with courage. I know few your age who would show such bravery.'

'Anger more than bravery, sir.'

'There is righteous anger, Michel, and bless you, you gave it forceful expression!'

Gradually there were at first faint positive signs. Michel focused on duties, prayed more, and spent more time caring for the sick in the Hôtel Dieu. The monks monitored both boys for any shift from rage and sorrow to acceptance. William, Fidelis and Lucien kept an especially prodigious watch, pining to see progress. Steadily, slowly, still tinged with melancholy, Michel exhibited improvement. Ronan remained depressed and brooding. The abbot persevered with kindness and nurture, with devoted attempts to pilot him to a safe harbour.

When his mentors detected Michel truly had returned to normalcy, gauged by how he re-engaged with fellow oblates, behaved with cheerful equanimity, joined in games and sports, and re-established warm relationships with monks, they discreetly withdrew attendance on him to allow the boy to complete the restorative process on his own.

It was gratifying that the alliances he had forged were with oblates of good character, rather than with a few renegades whose antics from time to time intruded on peaceful monastic life. Fidelis and Lucien cheered when Michel's enthusiasm for studies and work returned. It was most notable to Lucien when once again he was beset with incessant questions on medical matters, a sure sign the boy's interminable curiously had displaced melancholy. When it was obvious Michel had evolved into the model oblate Abbot William had once prophesised, Fidelis praised God and the saints for the transformation.

Ronan's state of mind was another matter. His return to normalcy remained a challenge. William had been unable to coerce Ronan to confront his internalised anguish. He worried the damage resided in a core so deep an eternity would transpire before memories of his ordeal would be rent from his soul.

Fidelis, head bowed, with a hand stroking his chin in pensive mode, observed to William, 'For all our prayers, patience, and attentions, it is troubling there has been no surcease from that child's distress, but I have hope. I do believe the coming season's rituals will provide a channel that guides him from this morass to a high ground where he can flex his wings.'

'How so? What inspiration have you in that regard?'

'The inspiration of the festival! With God's grace, Ronan will be filled with the enchantment of the wonder of the Nativity, and therein experience his own rebirth. I shall enlist Michel's aide in this.'

11

ADVENT

A rude westerly wind that conveyed frosted air across the sea to Saint Petroc-sur-lac heralded a change of season, first noted in an inspired autumnal splash of radiant colour on the leaves on trees and bushes transmuted to hues of ginger, auburn, crimson, and gold. Only late daylight of a raking sun dappled the cloister, offering patches of inviting warmth for monks in meditation.

In short order, leaves, now brown with desiccated foliage, succumbed to a gradual, but inevitable, undulating spill to the ground, engendering a swift undressing of the landscape of resplendently colourful scenes that yielded to wintry blasts. The earth conceded cold winter's power soon would reign as nature's bleakest season.

The first Christmas market in Advent proclaimed the arrival of the holy season of *Nedeleg* — Christmas elsewhere in Europe. By any name, the joyful spirit that permeated the air blunted discomfort from the cold and defied the rigid rules of fasting and abstinence mandated by the Church. Its efforts to temper the heathen customs that still informed several aspects of Christmas traditions were in most instances ignored by the people. Merriment and good cheer prevailed throughout the community despite the season's proscriptions imposed by Church dictum.

Advent rituals involved solemn devotions as well as four celebratory Sundays that anticipated the feast of the birth of

Christ. The community and all in the monastery processed to the cathedral to worship at four ceremonial masses of the season. There were many new oblates in the monastery and Fidelis deemed it proper to rehearse a procession with the boys on the Saturday before the first Sunday of Advent. The older oblates took the exercise in their stride. The novitiates exuded animated excitement, well contained as they marched into the cathedral to find workmen on a scaffold in the west transept attending to water damage from torrential summer rains.

Labourers paused to observe the parade from their perch at the top of the cathedral, and, as the oblates approached the choir stall, amused themselves with vulgar gestures as a greeting. These were received with muffled sniggers and a stealthy exchange of insulting pantomime – not unnoticed, but ignored, by Fidelis.

First the hoarfrost, then a moderate, gentle snowfall embellished the yuletide atmosphere at the weekly markets. The town square, glutted with people, left little space to maneuver from stall to stall, but the tantalising jumble of seasonal ornaments, sweet-meats, spices, cakes, and puddings enticed them to press on in pursuit of favourite edibles.

As was the custom, people walked from miles around to bargain for a farrago of coveted wares. Shoppers nibbled ensnaring samples and bought many delicacies that enriched their feasts. Hot cider was freely given as a token of Nedeleg cheer. The mood was lighthearted and convivial and contributed to a merry hubbub.

The multitudes that gathered made Marc Gervais nervous and jittery. He increased the number of men in his constabulary, hoping to forestall skullduggery and worse. His men also were raw with nervous dread after, at the end of November, once again a child went missing in the town. Left but for a moment, Marc was told, as the mother dashed to a shop to buy sweetmeats. Soon thereafter, country folk reported three of their children had been taken from their cottage after they had gone to the communal well. Once more Marc's band of deputies took to the field in a painstaking expedition throughout the countryside, at first close by where the abductions had occurred, then in ever broadening distances from the sites of the crimes. As in the past their efforts were futile, but the troop remained dogged in their persistence with bafflement and frustration trumped by deter-mination.

A lead, however minuscule, spurred them to search on foot and horseback, accompanied by trained dogs. When the bloodhounds tracked scents for significant distances only to have promising trails vapourise, Marc spurred morale. 'It may be that fording the stream dissipated the scent. We may pick it up again further north – upstream. Follow me!' When all reached a consensus there was no point in continuing, the search party mutely steered back towards St. Petroc-sur-lac with a reignited despair incapable of expression.

The four Christmas markets were perfect chaotic scenes for a clandestine seizure of a child – or, God forbid, more than one. Marc told his men to aim for an inconspicuous presence and instructed them to don ordinary clothing - as did he, by leaving his chain of office dangling from a peg in his office. He ordered his men to disperse and stand guard in a wide range of sectors in the square, and at each entrance to it keep scrutiny with optimum visual advantage. He admonished them to take heed of the slightest deviation from expected appearance or behaviour. Satisfied the scheme was well thought out and rehearsed, the deputies took their posts.

Marc, intense by nature, and, after months of dis-appointment and strain, stood agitated as well as vigilant in the centre of the square. Of a sudden, he saw a man wholly atypical of the region and held his breath. He sharpened his inspection to register an indelible imprint of the man. He was of average proportions and unusually finely dressed – hardly the garb of persons seen at Christmas markets. *Such men send their underlings to shop.* Marc's heart began to pound, and riveted, he maintained close surveillance of the stranger's every move. When he penetrated deeper into the crowd, Marc unobtrusively snaked his way through it, following his quarry, alert to his every step. As Marc moved closer towards him, the man stopped, and Marc nimbly backed into the shadow of a stall, keeping a watchful eye. Momentarily, he was perplexed.

The man stood inert, staring forwards with glacial blue eyes. Marc moved slightly forwards for a glimpse of the man's focus. His stomach began to churn. He saw a small boy standing at a honeybee stall with a crude homemade hobby horse. The child stood next to a woman with an infant not three months old in her arms.

She had selected an item to purchase when the boy said, 'I am going to ride my horse.'

The woman called out to him, 'No, Ives. Wait for me.' The child blithely ignored her and left the square as the vendor wrapped the honey pot the woman had chosen. He had her money with change to be given back to her. She hesitated and decided to conclude the transaction before pursuing her child.

Marc saw that the man was on the move. He saw him approach, then pass the stall and exit the square. Marc sprang after him, barreling forwards through the crowd, and ran out of the square where he saw the man with his hand on the boy's shoulder, whispering to him. Marc dashed towards them just as the boy abandoned his hobby horse and took the hand offered to him by the stranger. Marc was upon them now. 'You, sir!' He yelled.

Releasing the boy's hand, the man turned sharply Haughtily, he surveyed Marc. 'Just what is it you want?'

Marc ignored the brazenness of his posture and shouted 'I am the sheriff of this jurisdiction, sir, and I want to know what you are about with this child. Is he your son?'

At that moment the boy's mother, infant in her arms, ran towards them calling, 'Ives! Ives!'

Marc demanded the man identify himself. The stranger spat at him portentously, 'I am not accountable to you.'

Marc moved towards him with menacing steps. He spoke to him commandingly. 'You, sir, are indeed so! I ask you again. What are you doing with this child?'

The woman had reached her son and drew him close to her, leaving the honey pot to crash to the ground. She looked intently at the man with frightened eyes. The man ignored the sheriff's question and addressed the boy's mother. He spoke to her in a fawning tone. 'Madame, I noted the child playing on his little horse and merely asked him if he wanted to see a real horse. Is that not so, my child?'

Ives nodded. 'He told me I could ride his horse, Mamá.'

The woman and Marc exchanged insightful expressions. Neither was persuaded the man had innocent intentions. Marc decreed, 'You, sir, are coming with me.' He turned to the woman and asked if she would kindly accompany them to the prison to give a deposition. Indignant, the man protested forcefully, and vainly struggled to wrest his arm free from the rigid hold Marc had on him.

The altercation had attracted several people's attention, including that of Mayor Serrigond who, promenading towards the square, had witnessed the *fracas*. 'Gervais!' he bellowed. 'Unhand him! What are you about, you boorish cur!' Without loosening his grip, Marc explained the circumstances to the mayor.

'Nonsense. Yaldson! Do you know who this man is? Let go. Let go, I say.' Marc dutifully released his hold of the man's arm, chagrined and perturbed. The mayor continued, 'André Buchet is well known to me and to Bishop du Loi. He is the master of the choir of the Duke of Brittany.' The mayor turned and bowed obsequiously. 'I beg your pardon for the abuse of this fool, Master Buchet.'

Marc never took his eyes off the man. He saw immutable cruelty in his eyes and an arrogant sneer on his face that convinced Marc he had indeed had malevolent intentions to abduct the boy.

The mayor barked at Marc. 'Go to my office at once. Await me there.' To the woman he said, 'You, Madam, take greater heed of your children!'

He turned to Buchet and offered to escort him to his horse as he engaged in conversation. 'Tell me, sir, what brings you to our humble city on this day?'

'I come with an invitation to dine with the bishop later this evening, Monsieur le mayor . . . .'

Marc stood amidst a small assembly of snickering folk for whom the incident had been but a dumb show. The mother of the children, however, touched his hand and gazed at him with gratitude. She was quivering. 'I care not what that man said. I believe truly I am in your debt today, sir. I do not think I can ever thank you enough.'

Grateful for her approbation, Marc bowed and thanked her for her confidence. Softly he said, 'Madam, we all must take heed of one point of which the mayor spoke. In these perilous times it is truly meet to be ever attentive to our children. That is not to give you blame. I saw what happened. But I think we both now know that not an instant of one's guard is possible.'

The woman said ruefully, 'And all for a honey pot.'

Marc entreated her, 'Come, let me get you another. It would greatly please me.'

The woman blushed but demurred. 'I am already in your debt, sir, more than I can ever repay.'

He did not insist, bowed, and bade her farewell. 'I wish thee God's grace. I am happy your son is safe.' As she walked away, Marc wondered who this creature was. 'Happy man to have her for wife,' he muttered. Then he trod wearily towards the mayor's office.

The spiritual rituals of Christmas snapped the effects of austere wintry gusts in the abbey, replacing them with glowing warmth. As town folk prepared for revelries, festivities, feasts and merriment, Luke's gospel about the birth of Christ fashioned its own atmosphere of joy amongst the clerics. Temporal revels were mostly eschewed, but ecclesiastic traditions and rituals that had evolved over centuries imbued an enduring gladness in the monastic community.

Monks, lay brothers, and oblates worked diligently to construct the large crèche annually placed adjacent to the cathedral pulpit. In and around it were the superb polychrome figures associated with Christ's birth in a stable that had been sculpted centuries before. None was more beautiful than the Madonna, but all – Saint Joseph, angels, shepherds, livestock, the three kings and their camels – were as exquisitely formed.

Michel assisted in the endeavour, assuring Ronan was ever at his side and equally engaged in arranging the familiar and moving representation. To everyone's delight, Ronan demonstrated artistic skills not even he knew he possessed. Astonishment and commendation met each detail as Ronan fashioned a large hillside scene that featured a strategically sited large cave that dramatically directed to it the eye of the viewer. The crèche, with all the principals, was assembled there. Shrubbery, trees, and flowers embellished the hillside composition, considerably enhancing the creation's beauty.

The praise Ronan received from all, and especially from the abbot who had been summoned specifically to admire the construction, uplifted his spirits, and endowed him with a newfound sense of dignity and self-worth. 'Truly, Ronan, you have produced a wonder that will enrapture all who see it. The abbot called out for parchment, ink, and pen. 'I want you to sign your work so that all may know the name of the master who made this.' Ronan muttered humble thanks for the abbot's effusive tributes, giddy with pleasure and pride.

Fidelis encouraged Michel to further explore the wonders of the cathedral with Ronan. 'Me thinks within this holy place lies the true secret of his deliverance.'

Uncertain how he might accomplish that end, Michel nevertheless welcomed duties inside the cathedral and the time spent with Ronan. The boys placed fresh linens in repositories, stored candles in bins and kept supplies of wafers and wines for use at Mass. They scurried to finish their chores so they could spy on workman who had inundated the space, there to complete the cathedral ambulatory before Christmas.

Each day labourers climbed wooden scaffolds that circled the heights and remained until dusk, since the ascent and descent posed unnecessary risks and consumed half an hour of precious time. Michel and Ronan watched at every opportunity as, creaking and moaning, a great multi-pulley winch powered by two men who walked inside a large turning wheel hoisted stones to the heights.

They hooted when workmen groused and cursed when a hammer fell on toes or a stone didn't fit a space because of a miscalculated measurement. They tittered when workers relieved themselves into pots of clay, and laughed outright when the men speared vulgar gestures at them in retribution.

Duties and distractions vied with Michel's observa-tions of architectural detail that impressed him. 'Look at those soaring arches, Ronan. They look as delicate as lace. I wonder that they were carved from stone. And the stained-glass windows. Is it not beautiful the way they glint in the afternoon sun? Come. I want to show you the figures of the *misericords*. They are beautifully carved from wood.'

The artistic intricacies of the reliefs depicted everyday follies of imperfect man preoccupied with earthly matters. Fantastical bestial and commonplace animals were represented in complexly fashioned figures. Michel mused that their artistry was unappreciated by most of the oblates when they walked in procession on feast days past the stalls. 'But pray look at this one.' He showed Ronan the figure of a wife beating her husband with a broom. 'Is it not jolly? It's always good for a smile. And look at this one.' It was an image of a stonemason gesticulating wildly with a pained expression, apparently from having dropped a piece of limestone on his foot. Ronan uttered a hoot, much to Michel's satisfaction. As they walked forward, Michel said, pointing to a stall, 'These ones are not at all mirthful.' One panel showed a teacher caning a lad. Both boys winced. On the other side of the stall, a panel depicted a group of monks gathered in a death vigil at the bedside of a dying cleric. Michel observed, 'Sad, that one . . . but even the grim carvings are beautifully wrought.' Ronan nodded as he studied the complexity of the artist's work. He examined several of the misericords with intense appreciation of the artistry.

Michel strode with him and took note. 'You have that kind of talent Ronan . . . just as my father did. I think you should pursue the craft.' Ronan beamed.

Just then, one of the lay brothers called out to the boys. 'We need more straw for the crèche, lads.' Ronan was the first to volunteer. 'I shall get some from the stable.' Michel, buoyed by Ronan's enthusiastic response and pleased by his enjoyment of the cathedral's wonders, without delay called out, 'Wait for me!'

Brother Cook always surpassed his culinary talent in preparing the *Nedeleg* feast. No sovereign king could hope for a more delectable banquet. As Christmas Day approached, Brother Cook presented his menu to the abbot. William exuded animated approval. 'Brother Cook, you exceed all past triumphs. My thanks are especially profuse for the roasted swan. My personal favourite!

'There will be duck, quail and partridge as well, my Lord. And I thought fish in a special wine sauce of my own creation! Naturally, there will be a medley of vegetables, fruit and cheeses. The sweets, with your permission, will be a surprise.'

'You have planned a veritable cornucopia of delights. I prophesy all will acclaim this your greatest achievement, and I count the days until the feast. Bless you, Brother, and praise God for your culinary genius,' William said, aware of the pleasure his enthusiasm emitted. Brother Cook bowed and smiled, feigning humility as he withdrew.

Thomas turned to an issue that annually caused consternation – the Festival of the Boy Bishop. He glanced at the directive sent by the bishop who, with great ceremony had announced the names of those chosen for the annual event. He sighed. *Episcopus puerorum. God save me what impiety might we expect this year.* He shook his head.

The occasion of the Boy Bishop was a traditional seasonal highlight throughout Europe and the British Isles that had been inspired by the gospels of Matthew and Luke, in which Christ pronounced the innocence and purity of children the criteria for admission to heaven. Over centuries bishops and their councils linked this celestial model to the Church by establishing the role of a Boy Bishop as the ideal Christ had in mird.

During Advent, the assembly led processions in the town and in close by hamlets to collect money for the church and local parishes and to participate in religious services of the entire community. The Boy Bishop's sovereignty culminated in a spectacular, greatly anticipated pageant in the cathedral that took place on the feast of the Holy Innocents. The religious nature of the event had long devolved into an excuse for an annual disquieting bacchanalia celebrated with plays, music, dancing, and banquets, accompanied by boisterous and rowdy conduct. As in other parts of the continent, many of the clergy and the sheriff in Saint Petroc-sur-lac were not enthusiasts of the long-established ritual. The clergy were offended by the disrespect and vulgar excess, and distained the spectacle of a boy in performance as an ecclesiastical patriarch with a band of youths in clerical garb in attendance. They complained it was a sacrilegious travesty that detracted from the solemnity of the commemoration of the Murder of the Innocents. Abbot William concurred with all in the monastic community the event was profane and disruptive of the spirit of the season.

The sheriff shared his views, and Marc rued the occasion's invariable drunken behaviour and disruptive ructions that demanded a full complement of his men on guard throughout the town. For the laity, the festival challenged the forbidding authority of the church that regulated all aspects of their lives, and that alone made the Boy Bishop festival a welcome occasion. More and more vociferously the clergy frowned upon the fête in Brittany and elsewhere, but its popularity made it difficult to abolish. Church authorities felt compelled to allow the pageant to prevail despite their loss of control of public conduct, sensing resentment and revolt were they to suppress a greatly heralded and much anticipated occasion.

'A boy chosen to be a bishop? How so, Magister Lucien? How can *that* be?' Michel asked.

Lucien kept to his task as he told Michel that on the sixth December, the Feast of Saint Ran,' he hesitated and commented, 'The patron saint of Brittany is known as Saint Nicholas in other European countries, as you may know.'

'Ah,' Michel absorbed the information that was in fact new to him.

'Youths are chosen from the ranks of students and choristers for just one day, mind, to assume the offices of the bishop and his clerics.'

Michel's eyes widened in astonishment. 'What do they do?'

'Too much if you ask me!' He thought a moment. 'Hmm. Let me see . . . they preen about during Advent, and after Nedeleg. Imagine this. The miniature clerics have the authority to perform all liturgical duties, save for the priestly privilege of celebrating the mass.' Michel looked aghast but also intrigued. 'The apogee of his 'reign' begins with much pageantry on the eve of Childermas.'

'Childermas?'

'The feast of the Holy Innocents. There is a ritual in which the bishop assists in putting bishopric robes on the Boy Bishop on the eve of the feast, and the next day he and his subordinates prance down the nave of the cathedral. The Boy Bishop preaches, usually on the topic of the slaughter of all male children under two as decreed by Herod, the governor of Judea at the time of Christ.

'When is this feast?' Michel asked, baring his excitement.

'On the twenty-seventh and twenty-eighth of December.' Lucien noted Michel's elation and added, 'You will be pleased to know, Michel, oblates participate in procession, and are in attendance for both ceremonies, seated in the choir stalls. A most favourable place to observe the spectacle.' He shook his head before continuing. 'The problem is after the ceremony on the feast day there usually is much drunkenness and riotous behaviour in the town. '

'That sounds most unseemly, Magister. All the same I wish oblates could go into town and celebrate – without the drink, of course.'

'Michel. I am surprised. I would have thought that prayer and fasting in the monastery boosted your dedication to do God's work and to rejoice in the Saviour's birth,' Lucien teased. 'Now, would you be so kind as to hand me that crock?' Lucien laughed at Michel's deflated expression. 'Do not look so child! Even in a monastery there is much merriment. Why even now our musicians rehearse, playing joyful music to entertain us. And a truly wonderful – memorable – Nedeleg feast is being prepared by Brother Cook. It will be a very happy festival for us all. You will not be wanting, I promise you.'

Michel smiled. He in fact anticipated marking the holiday with spiritual benedictions as well as with gaiety. Accompanied by much joyfulness, the observance of church ceremonies had always been the custom in his home, and this year more than any other he felt the need for repose and grace to bear the void he sometimes felt, as often he yearned for his mother and father and longed to be back in his homestead. Abbey rituals helped dispel the sense of loss when the feeling came upon him, and the solemnity of Christmas, he was sure, would give him a vibrant sensation of his parents' presence within him.

Two more children had been kidnapped from a hamlet just under a mile from Saint Petroc-sur-lac. Marc Gervais knew the place – Aldrien – but not well. There was only a small cluster of cottages bordered by grazing meadows, vegetable and herb gardens and a small population dependent on itinerant merchants for their household necessities, not that they could afford much. Peddlers wandered throughout the countryside with wares – gloves, fabrics, farm tools, pots, and kitchen ware. In this hamlet there generally were few buyers. It was a poor as well as isolated area.

The only information Donan had relayed to Marc was that the children were a six and four-year-old brother and sister. When Marc arrived in Aldrien, he went immediately to the cottage of Lysona and Bernez Lefevre to interview them.

'They were close by, in the field, playing in the snow. I could see them from the window,' Lysona told the sheriff.

'Where were you, sir?' Marc enquired.

'A cow had gone astray down a small ravine to the stream. I went to fetch it.'

'You were gone a long time?'

'No, sheriff. Not at all. No more than twenty minutes.'

Marc turned his attention to his wife. 'Madame, you say you could see the children through the window. Were you watchful?'

Lysona confessed she had been distracted by the wails of her infant. She had attended to his needs. 'It took no longer than mere minutes to clean and swaddle him.'

Marc was dismayed to hear neither saw nor heard anything. Lysona told the sheriff she went to the window immediately after putting her infant into the cradle, vaguely aware of silence that had displaced the laughter of playing children. The snow had begun to fall more heavily, and visibility was poor. She left the cottage just as her husband approached, cow in tow.

When she saw he was alone, panic ensued. She returned to the cottage, scooped up her infant and took her to the cottage of Madame Hilard to mind whilst she and her husband looked for the missing children. 'We searched until dark,' she wailed. 'My husband deemed it wise to ask for help. He walked into Saint Petroc despite the storm.'

Marc nodded noncommittally, but apologised for his delay. 'I was on a mission with my posse, and my deputy was alone last night, unable to return with you, sir. I am sore aggrieved by your loss,' he said feebly. He hedged a moment before asking, 'The snow on the ground. . . did you note any tracks, footsteps or horse prints?' *Sounds are muffled by snow*, and Marc did not bother to ask if the woman had heard any noise.

'Yes!' Bernez exclaimed. 'I remember now. There were. And wheel prints. But the snowfall had become a blizzard and the tracks were hard to follow. Finally, they were gone.'

'Can you tell me the direction?'

'North. They were to the north.'

'How can you be sure?' Marc pressed.

'I have lived here all my life. I know the pathway to Dinan.'

Marc left the desolate parents with assurance a search party would scour the area north of the hamlet, beginning at dawn. It was much the message he routinely gave in these matters. He knew it reflected the feckless efforts of his investigations, and he felt embarrassed, but there was little else to say. He wanted to leave hope for another day. 'Pray for your children's deliverance. I shall do what I can.'

Before returning to town, he visited each house in the hamlet to incorporate whatever he learned into his strategy and intention to implement a sweeping, thorough search. At one cottage, Marc was astonished when the woman from the Christmas market answered his knock. She too was surprised. In her arms she held her infant daughter. He introduced himself by name.

'My name is Nolwenn Hilard, Sheriff. Please. Come in from the cold.'

Her son, Ives, seated near the hearth, beamed recognition when he saw Marc. Marc teased him with pleasantries in a playful banter. Nolwenn approved the exchange with a smile.

There was an awkward pause. 'Your husband, Madame. He is not here?'

'My husband died in January, Sheriff. An accident.' She averted her eyes from him.

Inexplicably, he referred to his own bereavement and said empathetically, 'My wife died in childbirth. The infant was still born. It would have been a son.' His voice trailed off. He recovered a semblance of deportment and added, 'I am deeply sorry for your loss, Madame.'

'And I, yours,' said Nolwenn. 'We have a common sorrow, Sheriff.' He nodded. She sighed. 'You are here about the children, are you not? Please. Sit down. Give me a moment to put Genviev in her cot.' Satisfied the baby was drifting off to sleep, she approached Marc and sat on a bench beside him.

She paused and said plaintively, 'I had ventured out to collect fresh snow for drinking water. So much snow. It is difficult to go to the well when it snows – and needless. The snow was not falling too heavily at that time. I paused to watch the Lefevre children playing. They were rolling around in the snow, making merry. I called out to them to go closer to their cottage so their mother could be better watchful. They did as I asked, and I returned to my cottage satisfied they were safe. They were no more than a few paces from their front door. I know Madame Lefevre well. She is very mindful of her children.' Her voice faltered as the realisation of their abduction clearly refuted the assertion. Her eyes welled with tears and she dabbed them with her apron. 'I am sorry, sir. When I think of those dear children, and how I might have lost Ives. He would have been outdoors as well, save for a mild fever.'

She got up and walked over to the hearth and bent down to kiss her son gently. When she stood, she remained motionless, back to Marc. She tightened her lips to contain her emotions. Her mouth trembled. She turned and said, 'Forgive me. Jeanne and Edwane Lefevre are such delightful children. Always happy and obedient. Always of good cheer and playful. Their parents are devoted to them and to their baby, Vivienne. Everyone in the hamlet loves them.' The tears flowed freely now.

Marc said nothing but thought her compassion appealing. He had questioned countless numbers of people in the past, and not one had demonstrated such dismay or sorrow. Most gave brisk, perfunctory statements, and many were disinterested and worse, they were often evasive. He was moved by her kindheartedness and sweetness.

With these thoughts, he observed her more closely. He thought her lovely, with shining russet hair beneath her kerchief. She was not tall, but slender and fair, and her brown eyes were luminescent, despite the well of tears. All her features were fine and, compounded, formed a beautiful face. He saw she look puzzled, and he shook his thoughts and cleared his throat. 'Yes . . . such a tragedy. You can be sure my men and I shall do all we can.' He tried to sound convincing.

'I know you will, sir. That is all one might wish.'

'Pray tell me, what did you when you came back into the house?'

She shrugged. 'I was busy with the pots of snow, placing them close to the hearth to melt faster. I did look at the children from the window. They still were near their cottage. That was the last I saw of them.' She put her head down to maintain composure.

'Bernez Lefevre said he saw traces of horses' hooves leading north.'

She nodded. 'His wife told me that. But – I am sorry – I saw nothing. My thoughts were about the children and I did not notice anything else.'

'No strange noise?' he prodded.

She shook her head. 'I was so occupied I didn't even note when I no longer heard the children at play.'

Marc sighed 'It is late. I had better leave for town. I must assemble a search party. I . . . I want to tell you, despite these tragic circumstances, it is a pleasure for me to see you again – oh, and your children, of course.'

'Must you go immediately? I have brewed *Ypocras* for Nedeleg to give as gifts. There's a pot steaming on the hearth. It will fortify you on your cold jaunt back to town. Please, will you not sip a cup?'

Based on the modest home she lived in, Marc surmised this widow had very few worldly goods to spare. He was touched that she should offer to share the spiced wine with him, a relative stranger. To refuse would be discourteous. 'That would please me very much, Madame. But only if you will drink with me.'

She laughed and protested she herself was not much of a wine drinker. 'But I shall,' she said merrily, 'have a cup in good fellowship.'

He studied her as she ladled out a portion for him. *Why does my mouth feel so dry*? He was transfixed by her, gazed steadily at her, and smiled readily when she handed him the cup of mulled wine and placed her cup on the table.

Nolwenn called to Ives, 'Come, my dear, and have some honey cake with us.' She laughed as Ives bounced across the room and climbed onto a bench. Marc declined to have any, with more charm than was necessary, and he laughed with her as Ives greedily scarfed his treat.

They talked about their lives. He learned that her husband had owned some land which she now leased that provided her with a steady, if small, income. They both confessed to missing their spouses.

Nolwenn told him, 'We have known more than sorrow Sheriff, surely. We have our joyful memories, do we not?'

Marc nodded, and wondered at the ease and comfort he felt in her presence. She was warm, good natured, wise, and gracious. He knew he had to see her again.

As he took his leave, he told her he would return with a report of his investigation.

'And perhaps we shall meet in town. I shall go to Mass in the cathedral on Nedeleg,' she said, smiling. Marc was silent for a moment as he thought, then dared to say, 'Madame, forgive me. I don't wish to presume – I too shall be at the cathedral for the Mass, and thereafter I host a dinner for close friends, Donan Cadoret, and his wife,

Anne-Gaël and their two children, Oliver and Barbara. They are twins, and much the same age as Ives. Dare I ask you for the honour of dining with us?'

Nolwenn, surprised, was momentarily speechless. 'Oh, but I could not possibly presume on your kindness,' she protested.

'But of course not. I should not have asked. I beg your forgiveness.'

Nolwenn blushed faintly, 'It is just that, well, it's too much of a presumption on your hospitality.'

Marc's face brightened. 'Oh, but I assure you of the contrary! I am an excellent cook, and it would be a great pleasure to have you join us at a holiday feast. Donan is my deputy and a great friend. His wife is charming.'

A dazzling smile radiated across Nolwenn's face. 'Sheriff, I have been friends with Anne-Gaël!' We grew up in the same village. We were at school together. Oh, it's so long a time since we have seen each other!' She paused for a moment before speaking. 'Lysona Lefevre tells me she and Bernez have decided to go with the baby to her parents for Nedeleg and make their home there. Such a sad time for them,' she looked away as her mind raced with thoughts of how she might accept the invitation. She turned and smiled. 'My neighbours, Catherine and Adrienne, also intend to go to town with their daughters – Cecilie and Marion – to be with family. Other neighbours go to family in other villages. It means I have nothing binding here.' She bit her lip and raised her eyebrows with excitement as she stood. 'Yes!' She laughed, surprised at her own boldness. 'Yes. I should like to dine with you all. Very much.'

Marc laughed as well, pleased at the prospect of seeing her again soon. 'Good! Wonderful. After Mass, then.' Having given her directions to his home, Marc departed feeling more gladness than he had known for a long time.

12

A CHRISTMAS TO REMEMBER

Awakened on Christmas morning by the cathedral bells, Michel lay for a moment thinking of past holidays with his mother and father. The memories dulled his good temper. The continually tolling cathedral bells in jubilant tones of exaltation coaxed him into a more joyful humour despite himself. 'Nedeleg!' he exclaimed – quite against the rule of silence – and leapt out of bed to ready himself for Prime.

Christmas day was the climactic moment of an Advent season that had begun forty days before with prayer and fasting. Having known hunger more than half his life, fasting had not been a trial for Michel, but during Advent it struck him it was the first time since entering the monastery he had not had his appetite satisfied.

Each year, the citizens of Saint Petroc also grudgingly submitted to Church dictums to fast and attend mandated liturgical devotions of the season. A reprieve from fasting on Sundays was permitted, and the faithful with gusto took advantage and indulged in large festive meals and revelries. Not even the Church could thwart the exuberance that prevailed from Advent's four Sundays before Christmas to Epiphany on the sixth of January.

In many places the season extended to *la Chandeleur* – Candlemas Day – on the second of February. It was the feast of Christ's presentation to the temple when folk processed to mass and gave a *denier* and a candle to the cathedral. The candles were blessed and returned to the faithful as comfort for a time when they were sick or lay dying. Luminosity as consolation and fortitude to endure life's inexorable vicissitudes.

None of the oblates felt deprived by the secular excesses outside of their community. Or, if they did, they accepted the disparity without complaint. It helped that the restrained, pious atmosphere and the spiritually inspired rejoicing were offset by the delicious Sunday meals of the holiday season that Brother Cook prepared. For Michel and for most of the other oblates the monastery Christmas season's banquets gratifyingly far surpassed any they had ever had.

Mass on Christmas day was a dazzling display of church ritual in which the bishop and several priests from the town's parishes, arrayed in rich and colourful clerical garb, processed into the cathedral followed by the monastery community, including oblates, and an overflow multitude of the faithful who spilled out onto the cathedral grounds.

Once back in the monastery, solemnity and piety were displaced by the ecstatic reaction to the feast Brother Cook and his staff had prepared. It was a visual and gastronomic sensation that elicited muted awes from the monks and oblates. A cloth covered trestle table had been placed in the middle of the refectory. The promised swan had been stuffed, cook, and reassembled, its feathers and elongated neck restored. It rested on the middle of the table surrounded by an ornamental display of vegetables and fruits styled to look like flowers. Several species of fowl and fish that had been baked, sautéed, and broiled were artfully arranged. Savouries, sweetmeats and nuts filled the table, completing the gastronomic excess. Uncut wine was plentiful and contributed to an unusually gleeful assembly, with few listening to the lector's droning voice throughout the meal.

An equally joyful, if not as resplendent, celebration took place in the domicile of Sheriff Marc Gervais on Christmas day. The reunion between Nolwenn and Anne-Gaël on the instant rekindled their friendship of the past to Marc's and Donan's delight. The children were unreserved in the pleasure of new companions. Marc had chosen special treats for each of the children, designed to entertain them as well as keep them engaged as their elders indulged in Marc's culinary endeavours. The day passed swiftly in a relaxed and jovial atmosphere, and ended with arrangements for their next rendezvous before the long Christmas holiday season ended. There was neither a thought nor mention of civic woes.

On the evening before *Childermas*, the monastic community assembled once more for the procession to the cathedral that would introduce to the community the Boy Bishop and his retinue. The oblates gulped with delight when they passed through the portals. The cathedral had been transformed into a resplendent and magical cosmos. A radiant shimmer from innumerable glimmering candles bedazzled everyone's senses. The reverberations from the organ and the sonorous voices of the choir rebounded off pillars and echoed throughout.

As he slowly made his way forwards in the procession, Michel absorbed what seemed to be a fantasy world. The air hung heavy with the disparate scents of lit candles, incense, and evergreens. He took his seat alongside the choristers, exultant to be in so excellent a position from which to behold the pageantry.

When the fanfare began, all eyes converged on the entrance to the nave. Awe-struck mutterings could be heard above the stentorian timbre of the organ's music and choral refrain as the bishop and his council in full regalia entered. They were followed by, in equally grand appointments, the Boy Bishop and his richly robed attendants.

In slow, steady paces the cavalcade glided towards the altar. Michel shivered with exhilaration. A twinge of envy passed through him as he admired the robes of the Boy Bishop that were as fine as those for a pope. He was bedazzled by the princely floor length embroidered silk and flowing cloak, the rich silk mitre worn by the Boy Bishop and the gilded crosier he deftly handled to mark each step. Throughout the ceremony in which the bishop bestowed on the Boy Bishop and his attendants all the prerogatives of ecclesiastical office for the day to follow, Michel, spellbound, was inclined to believe that what he saw was an illusion and one he never wanted to fade.

A great disappointment swept over him as booming strains of the organ marked the end of the ceremony, shattering the magic, and the principals in the drama assembled for a stately recessional. Dispensing blessings and dignified acknowledgements to the congregation that bowed before him, the Boy Bishop and his canons marched down the aisle of the nave towards the doors of the church with the Bishop and his council trailing them, followed by choristers, the monastery community and oblates.

On the following morning, Michel hurriedly prepared for the *Childermas* pageant that would replicate the splendour of the night before. With elation, he joined the cavalcade that processed from the monastery. Once inside the cathedral Michel and Paol Eric smiled at each other in silent agreement it appeared more splendid than the night before. The sun shone through the stained-glass windows, and created an illusionary sparkle of radiant clusters of mottled gems. The glittering candles were a mere complement in the morning to the bright natural light. Throngs once again overflowed, as enthusiastic as the oblates to witness the stirring grandeur of the occasion and to hear the Boy Bishop's sermon.

After the magnificence of the prior evening's ritual, Michel's expectations were unbridled. When the Boy Bishop and his followers appeared and began to parade down the aisle of the cathedral, their bearing confounded, then shocked him and all in the congregation. Michel and Ronan looked at each other with stupefaction. They watched, as unsteady on their feet, boys pranced pompously in their ecclesiastic attire with leering smirks, sniggering. Scandalised worshippers murmured disapproval.

As the Boy Bishop began his sermon, disapproving murmurs could be heard throughout the cathedral. He slurred words in rambling incoherence, strangely muttered, and he wobbled at the lectern. The immeasurable regard Michel transformed into dis-enchantment and disgust. Shocked, scornful grumbles throughout the cathedral conveyed the general revulsion.

As the oblates left the cathedral with Fidelis leading the way back to the monastery, Michel saw some of the so-called clerics just outside the great doors, noisily distributing memorial coins with no monetary value to children who had attended the event.

The sound of Fidelis shouting, his voice booming with indignation, startlingly drew his attention to several boy-priests trampling the rose bushes and flower beds, defiling the sanctity of the garden. Fidelis was left behind as several oblates dashed past him in pursuit of the vandals. Henri reached the garden before anyone else, with Padraig, Paol Eric and Adrian close behind. The delinquent boys turned on them maliciously. Adrian delivered solid punches to an adversary. Padraig's blows routed two of the boys who bolted from the premises. Enraged, Michel rushed forwards to wrest Paol Eric from the grip of one scalawag, sending him flying, and wrested Henri from the clutches of a lout, flogging him repeatedly with powerful blows until Fidelis pulled him up by the scruff, leaving his arms flailing, aiming for a target.

The bishop and the abbot witnessed the mêlée, appalled by the brawl and the damage done to the garden. The bishop commanded the drunken ruffians be rounded up and taken to the sheriff, and ordered the oblates back to the monastery accompanied by the monks – Michel still held fast by Fidelis.

Disheveled and bloodied, chastened, and full of trepidation, Padraig, Michel, Paol Eric, Adrian and Henri waited for

Fidelis in the prior's chancery – and the punishment he was sure to deliver.

When Fidelis entered the room, he asked the boys quietly to sit down. He spoke in a civil manner, but in a distinctly admonishing tone. 'Such violence in no circumstance is excusable in our monastery. You have committed an offense against one of God's – and Saint Benedict's – precepts.'

Tears ran down the face of Michel's bowed head.

'I do not seek nor wish an explanation from any of you. I saw the provocation, and I am certain you, Henri, and you, Ronan are gratified to have been delivered from the fists of those ragged castaways.' Fidelis sighed. 'Padraig, as a senior oblate I would have hoped for greater restraint, but you acquitted yourself well in defending the garden. This I cannot deny. Michel, you exhibited daring, and it was commendable of you to aid your fellow oblates.'

He paused and paced. 'But! Despite the wicked and destructive misdeeds of that riffraff, there must be a consequence for you all for breaking a fundamental principle of our abbey that admits no use of force.'

Agitated, he sat down. 'You should know those churls are to appear before the bishop for assault and destruction of the garden – Church property, mind you – and account for their drunken state inside the cathedral that blasphemously degraded that holy place. Their punishment will be severe.' He looked at each oblate steadily before adding, 'My authority is to consider the consequence for your transgression.'

The oblates worriedly looked at each other, each wondering what that portended for them.

Fidelis silently recalled his own savage lapse of restraint when he assaulted Trumpière. He empathised with the boys' just anger, but could not entirely condone it, mindful of Saint Benedict's edict to which he too was bound. He had uncomplainingly submitted to the punishment given him at the time of his disobedience of the Rule, and continued to atone for his violent attack on Trumpière, however well-deserved it had been.

What should I do? Loving Mary help me. How can I punish them when I too have been guilty of just such aggression against another? When he finally spoke, there was a tone of humility in his voice. 'Michel, your assault was the most violent. During recreation tomorrow, you are to walk the labyrinth in the cathedral that traces man's journey through life to eternity twelve times, meditating on Christ's dictum to turn the other cheek. Also, replace the cloths over whatever remains of the rose bushes to protect them from the frost. Come Spring, it will be your task to restore the garden.' He was silent for some minutes.

Ronan was the first to speak. 'Please, Magister, may I have permission to assist Michel?' Each of the oblates echoed the request. Fidelis suppressed a smile before giving nodding assent, commending their loyalty to their friend. 'Yes. You may all consider it your penance as well.' He looked at each one carefully before telling them, 'I myself shall work with you all. That is, I shall supervise the work.'

The tone of his voice lightened. 'Remember, lads, Saint Benedict taught us that gardens are signs of God's glory on earth – a laudation of beauty where serenity and peace reflect God's presence. It is a sacred obligation to return our garden to its former splendour.'

The boys, taken aback by the mild rebuke, bowed, and turned to leave. Michel wondered why Fidelis had not asked him if he was sorry for the offence. He was glad he did not, because he was not sorry for what he had done, or at least not as sorry as he was supposed to be. Fidelis surprised them further when he remarked pleasantly, 'I believe your fellow oblates are reveling in some festive games in celebration of the feast. You have my permission to join them. You also have my blessing. Now go.'

13

A TITHE AND A DEPARTURE

Le Maréchal Baron Gilles de Rais and his consorts were at the Château de Merlin for Christmastide. Now January, the baron signaled his intention to depart from the region with a request to deliver a tithe to Bishop Bernard du Loi, a long-standing Church tradition

As an august member of a rich aristocratic family born in Champtocé-sur-Loire, a castle near Angers, the baron had several estates, lodging for a few months in one before moving on to another. He had several favourites, including castles in Tiffauges and Machecoul, both close to Nantes. He resided in one or the other several months longer than in others of his properties.

The citizens of Nantes boasted they had so prestigious a resident nearby, although his reclusive nature disappointed them. He was rarely seen outside the gates of his estates. This also held true when he was in residence in the Château de Merlin near Tréhorenteuc. His presence there was sensed by all, nonetheless, and most notably by the bishop, since the estate was in his province, and the annual tithe would be delivered to him.

Having been advised of the baron's intentions, Bishop du Loi conspired to mark his departure with a dramatic show of tribute to the aristocrat, whom all thought to be pious and renowned for his generosity to the Church. Bernard du Lois remembered the revenues Gilles de Rais gifted for the construction of a cathedral and several regional churches. That stimulated du Loi's rapacious nature, and he conjectured a sumptuous gala with great ceremony, pomp and feasting in honour of the famous hero of Orléans would incline him to reciprocate with a contribution to the bishopric of more than usual extravagance.

The bishop's keeper of the treasury, Monsignor Carric, stood nervously as the bishop attended to his attire. He was impatient to speak of administrative matters to him.

The bishop placed his gold chain of office over his soutane, a gown with thirty-three perfectly spaced buttons of amaranth red silk – more purple than red – from the collar to the hem. His dresser encircled his waist with a sash of the same colour and fabric that reached his shoes and gave the bishop a moment to admire himself. 'Impeccable,' he declared. He reached out with one hand and Carric rushed to fetch the *zucchetto* that lay on a table. He dutifully placed it dead centre on the bishop's head. The bishop fingered his well-trimmed goatee and asked Carric to give him the small gold comb he used to groom it. His vanity satisfied, he moved to a throne-like damask silk armchair and asked Carric what he wanted to discuss.

'Your Grace. This costly banquet will greatly reduce our coffers.'

'To be sure. Ah, but Carric, we shall be feeding the baron's ego as well as his stomach,' he said, smiling avariciously. 'The lavish occasion will undoubtedly puff up his pomposity as well as his gift to us . . . that is to say, his gift to the Church. This gala will pay for itself and then some.'

Bernard du Loi's intuition proved predictive. The rich, famous – and egotistical – baron donated a profligate sum that considerably depleted his wealth and increased that of the bishop.

The evening of the fête was unseasonably pleasant, emulating it seemed, the spirit of the occasion. The bishop's palace doors were opened to the elite of Saint Petroc-sur-lac eager to be presented to the legendary baron, who was as close to the peoples' hearts as was Yann the fifth, Brittany's ducal ruler.

Curious about this hero of Brittany, the numbers keen for a coveted invitation exceeded that which the bishop's ballroom could accommodate, and one of the timeless rituals of such affairs was the degree to which people wheedled whatever influence they had to guarantee their names be on the list of the chosen ones.

La Comtesse Sara Marie de Rennes was heard to say it was well known and much gossiped about, that the baron was as erudite as he was handsome. 'He has an extensive library, and is an impassioned patron of literary endeavours, my dears.'

'Indeed,' added Madame Maria de Paimpont, and told a small group, 'He is a patron of music, and has even founded a music school for children.' As they chattered, it was revealed the Baron de Rais was an enthusiast of the stage as well, esteemed as an author and even as an actor, and had spent a fortune on one of his theatrical productions which left him in great debt. 'A condition, *le Marquis de Dinan* commented, 'he foolishly ignores, I'm told.'

The assembly stood, hushed, when the baron summoned forth pages who carried an elaborately carved chest and lay it at the feet of Bernard du Loi. The bishop feigned surprise before expressing a puffery of gratitude that, to those with a fine-tuned ear, sounded suspiciously prepared in advance.

Conjuring modesty, the baron said with self-effacing humility as he presented the tithe to the bishop, 'This is but a gesture of thanks for the great honour you do me on this occasion. I am bereft of praise sufficient to your beneficence.' He smiled and bowed obsequiously, fully conscious of the number of guests who strained to hear his comments. 'I am and shall always remain your most humble and obedient servant.'

The bishop bowed and gestured with his arm. 'Pray accompany me, Baron, to the balcony. I have arranged a unique entertainment. An Italian company has come to present a fiery pageant, an art that originated in ancient China.' Murmuring delighted approval, the invitees followed the baron and the bishop onto the balcony where the evening's finale burst into the evening sky in an astonishing display, startling many of the guests and enchanting others, the baron among them.

On the rampart viewed from the bishop's palace, was an immeasurable row of packed fireworks encased in parchment that, when exploded, stridently propelled towers of glowing sparks into the air forty metres high. The illusion of fountains of fire emitted awed gasps. A dragon fashioned from paper over a wooden framework stuffed with fireworks hissed noisily, spewing fire and smoke from its orifices as it glided on a virtually invisible wire from the top of the rampart towards the balcony, creating a phantasm of an animate fiery attack that produced frightened screams.

Plebeians in the town and peasants for miles around were terrified by the abrupt sound and sight of explosive roars and flashes of light from rockets that torpedoed into the air, rupturing the familiar natural order of stillness and black night. They evoked fear in many that evil spirits had overtaken the heavens.

The oblates were awakened by the cataclysmic sounds, and dared leave their beds to determine the source of the booming explosions and flashes of bright light. With trepidation as they breached a strict monastery rule, they rushed from their dormitory to the highest point of the monastery where they could see an unearthly sky that had a blazing fire that gradually dissipated into a smoky nebula. The noise was deafening as whistling rockets blasted into the air, shrilly bursting into flashes and sparks of yellow and orange light that jetted across the sky.

Entranced, they were uncertain they should be enthralled or alarmed. They were certainly mesmerised, and did not notice the appearance of Fidelis. He stood, watching the fireworks, but his presence augured a mission. He waited patiently until the spectacle ended before confronting the boys about their disregard of the Rule. The oblates were abashed to see him, and stood stupefied, uneasy in their guilt. They girded themselves for the consequences of their audacity, still not knowing if a dangerous enemy or witchcraft had invaded the world.

Fidelis told them what he knew about the phenomenon of fireworks, relieving their anxiety, and left them to contemplate the marvels they had seen. The wondrous experience had a far greater impact than the discomfiture of having been found out, and Fidelis was satisfied they would willingly accept the penalty to follow.

The baron left the region the next day to travel to his most palatial residence, Champtocé sur Loire. He passed through Rennes to call upon the bishop there before heading southeast, with squires, heralds, servants, and choirboys, thereby once again sparing Marc Gervais and Saint Petroc-sur-lac civic disruption.

By the end of March, Marc Gervais was mystified, but relieved. The succession of kidnappings had ceased. The level of tension he felt had not, despite there not having been any disappearances since December. *Had the malefactors moved on to another, unfortunate, faraway province leaving his region safe and in peace?* He had asked himself that question in the past and had been jolted when further abductions occurred. He would not succumb to false hope again.

Haunted by the year's tragic events in which, despite Herculean efforts, not one kidnapper had been apprehended or one child rescued, his confidence was in tatters. He was depressed and riddled with guilt when he thought of the families in perpetual grief and a community continually apprehensive other children would disappear. He felt the dishonour of failure. He sought refuge from despair in visits to Aldrien and Nolwenn Hilard, knowing her company would relieve his dejection. Occasional visits became regular ones, then constant. Days became normal again –

even peaceful, and Nolwenn's sweet nature and the charm of family life gradually lifted his spirits.

Their friendship was inevitable. They shared innumerable interests and values that intensified their regard for one another, and their relationship showed promise of enduring – evolving. Nolwenn comforted him, and soothed his soul until the remorse that burdened him diminished, replaced with cheerfulness and pleasure in her company.

The affinity between them advanced in mere months into an attachment just short of love. Trust and empathy were adhesives that drew them ever closer. They were easy, comfortable, and playful with each other, and Nolwenn glowed with appreciation at the demonstrable affection between Marc and her children. Marc enjoyed being with Ives and Genviev, with a growing sense they were the children he had always longed for. He gave them treats, played with them, applauded their interests, and delighted when they received him with expressions of fondness, even love.

Nolwenn's regard for Marc reached beyond what had been mounting attraction. Importantly, the warm and mutual affection between him and the children had further endeared him to her. He had become an integral part of her world. Each visit was spiced by his special touch of kindness and thoughtfulness. His attention to her children moved her deeply – his eagerness to teach Ives to ride a pony, the gentleness with which he held Genviev in his arms on horseback, the stories he recited, the songs he sang, his playful diversions with both children. He became a part of family life as it once had been for Nolwenn.

As each week and month passed, happiness etched into Marc's core, suppressing thoughts of the calamitous past. When he began to bring flowers to Nolwenn, it signaled a shift from social calls to a courtship. As their relationship evolved into romance, they were shy about expressing their ardour. The shadow of Nolwenn's husband lingered in both their minds and checked any show of the passion that had begun to swell in them. Nolwenn's memories of her contented life with her husband uncomfortably intruded on the happy days she spent with Marc, and she struggled guiltily with conflicted feelings. Marc sensed her reserve, but sensed too, time and patience on his part would eventually resolve the impasse, and he was temperate enough to wait, mindful of his own feelings after his wife died.

His exemplary demeanour served both well for but a brief while, as for both it became increasingly apparent their time together was insubstantial, lacking a significant element. Neither knew how to move beyond this hindrance and go forwards until one day, as Marc arrived, Ives ran from the house joyfully calling out, 'Papá! Papá!' Nolwenn stood at the doorway, glowing, her welcoming smile intermingled with an unmistakable expression of love.

The day passed happily enough, but indoors, as a steady rain had begun that kept them close to the hearth. By nightfall, the children were comfortably abed in their room as the drenching rain persisted. 'You should stay the night,' Nolwenn said quietly. A surge of longing deposed discretion, and Marc gently drew Nolwenn near to him. With hands tenderly holding her face, he searched her eyes for an invitation. She moved closer to him and lifted her mouth to his. The lingering kiss progressed to impassioned lingual discovery as Marc's hands explored her body, the contours of her hips, her breasts. Nolwenn moved still closer, felt his pulsating tumescence, and released a moan of pleasure. She broke away from his embrace, her bosom heaving with desire. She took his hand and led him to her bed. The steady rain could still be heard, but the damp chill was no longer felt.

The days began to lengthen with the coming of spring, and the dreary winter landscape yielded to the fresh and tender green sprouts and buds that presaged nature's reawakening. Michel knelt at the grave site of his parents on the anniversary of the day he entered the monastery.

He remembered it as the day of his birthday because it was the feast of Saint Isidore. The annual commemoration of the saint ensured associations of family life before he became an oblate that would forever be remembered. The events of the fifteenth of May and all that followed had been a transformational year in which he had suffered desolation, tragedy, anger, and he had labored tenaciously to reclaim a sense of what it was to love.

He had found peace and love, different from that which he had known in the comfort of his parental home, but in the benevolent presence of paternal monks, a soulful love he sensed was unconditional, God given. He had learned to value a spiritual life of commitment to the principles espoused by Saint Benedict, and lived up to assiduously by the Benedictine priests and friars who had so enriched his life. Michel had come to value monastic life above all else, and gave thanks to God for his good fortune to be in such a blessed place.

Life in Saint Benedict's monastery was nothing he had imagined it to be, and he had had adventures beyond his wildest dreams. The canonical bells that structured the rhythm and cadence of the routines of life symbolised the fulfillment of Michel's needs and desires, and he no longer looked beyond the abbey walls for happiness or personal gratification. The rituals of prayer, the joy derived from learning, and rewarding work contributed to a happy mind and soul. It pleased him to think how gladdened his parents must be to know of his contentment.

Michel vowed an annual pilgrimage to his parents' grave on the feast day, even though the date would always trigger the memory of the last time he saw Marie and Yann Dunard, and thoughts of their sickness and death would always sadden him anew. He knew he could never avoid the incongruent feelings of loving, happy memories and melancholy and longing that would always mark this day of remembrance. Each sensation was a part of his recollection of the precepts his parents taught him. They were legacies he cherished, and he wished always to swear allegiance to them and treasure them.

Michel finished his prayers and rose from his knees. He gasped when he saw the beauty of the sky at sunset that welcomed his gaze. It was as if the heavens were sending him acclamation and approval by filling the sky with glorious colours such as he never could have imagined that filled the landscape for as far as he could see.

As the sun descended beneath the horizon, clinging to its fading brilliance, its burnished power produced an interminable strand across the sky, mirrored in the lake, of pallid blue that blended with a luscious stretch of sea foam green. Above it was a wide, breathtakingly bold swath of radiant magenta, undaunted by a seamless margin of black clouds that hovered over, obfuscating the sky above. He stood, enchanted by the majesty of the site until chapel bells cut short his rapture. *Vespers. I'm late. Oh, dear Lord, not again!* The eleven-year-old oblate raced towards the monastery

PART TWO

14

THE BLACK POTION

'The black potion has lost its potency. We must act to prepare a fresh supply.'

'Lucien, I implore you do not plague me with this on this perfectly beautiful spring morning,' Abbot William responded unhappily. They sat in the cloister garden surrounded by early April blossoms that had not yet declared their identities. The abbot and his dean often discussed abbey business there in seclusion on temperate days, especially at times when momentous affairs, with critical decisions to be made, tested their judgement. The garden's beauty and serenity alleviated the burdensome weight of such weighty discussions. Communication between the two reflected the ease of their relationship, and their discourse was often peppered with wry humour and spirited dialogue in the relaxed environment.

'Plague me! Do you say plague me? Why, William, such rapier wit!' Lucien laughed, and added mischievously, 'It is indeed a perfect day to 'plague' you with this, as I am sure to find you in a cheery temper. And singularly apt, as it happens. We face danger from a plague.' He paused for effect. 'The pestilence.'

Lucien had William's full attention now. The abbot looked alarmed. 'Pestilence? Pray God, no. Explain yourself, Lucien.'

'A report from Brindisi informs me ten thousand have died, with many times that number expected. We call it the Great Mortality with reason, and know the disease cannot be contained and will travel. I am filled with foreboding. We may be on its path and must be prepared.' He clenched his hands and added, 'A goodly amount remains of the potion prepared three years ago, thank God not spent for want of any threat of an epidemic, but . . .' He leaned towards the abbot to emphasise, '. . .wiser men than we, William, have affirmed the potion's efficacy wanes with time. In just a little time. Should *la peste* make its way here, and I have good reason to surmise it will, a large quantity of doses of the *miraculum potionem* at hand is requisite. Freshly prepared. We have long deferred doing this.'

' Cause to surmise it will reach Saint Petroc, Lucien?' The abbot asked uneasily.

Lucien soberly recounted how he had studied the trajectory of the disease and predicted that, once it had swamped all of Italy, it would beset France, then Brittany.

William leaped from his chair and paced as he absorbed Lucien's disquieting – frightening – message. When he sat down and faced him, he said petulantly, 'You want *me* to dispatch our men to embark on this quest?' He looked sternly at Lucien. 'Be mindful the community is sure to resist.'

Lucien countered. 'Resist – certainly. But for sure, obey.'

'So, I am to be the sacrificial lamb who announces the news, am I?'

'Who better, my Lord Abbot . . . for who has the greatest authority?'

Abbot William's head began to throb as he silently and worriedly evaluated the ominous implications of Lucien's contention. At length he resignedly nodded assent and sighed, 'I shall inform the community this day.'

The medical faculty of the University of Paris had been commissioned by King Philip VI in 1348 to study the origin of the plague that had ravaged the continent the year before, annihilating sixty percent of the population of the western world. The faculty concluded that the pestilence had begun when a conjunction of Saturn, Jupiter, and Mars in the constellation of Aquarius produced a wet, sultry atmosphere that caused the soil to exude poisonous vapours.

When the deadly disease showed signs of waning, with fewer victims, the nature of the study shifted to consider the convergence of planets that would explain how and why that phenomenon was so. All were befuddled when the pestilence vanished, since their astrological studies gave no sign that would happen.

It had been demonstrably and widely known in the region for centuries that the abbey's secret potion mysteriously protected those exposed to the plague from the deadly disease. Verifiable too was the fact it was ineffective once symptoms of the plague appeared. Importantly, its immunity was not long lasting. Should exposure to the deadly disease be ongoing, repeated doses of the serum were crucial.

The potion's formula had been passed down from prior generations of abbots and consigned to a hidden place known only to the abbots and his deans. At the first sign of an epidemic of the Black Death, the abbey would share, as it had done in the past, the preventive tonic with communities and abbeys near and far.

The story of how the potion made its way to the Abbey of Saint Benedict is worth recounting. Around 1272, a wounded knight of the Holy Sepulchre, returning from the ninth and last crusade, travelled from Jerusalem across Italy and France and took respite at the Abbey of Saint Benedict for what was to be a brief postponement of the long odyssey home.

When his wound festered, the knight, sometimes delirious with fever, languished in the Hôtel Dieu for months. Given willow bark to lower his fever, the monks patiently bathed the raw cavity in his thigh with wine and rosewater. They diligently dressed the wound with mustard poultices and other trusted remedies until, gradually, the fever abated, and the lesion slowly granulated and finally healed. By that time, the knight – Michiel de Dunkerque – had successfully petitioned the Abbot – Blaez by name – to make the abbey his home. Michiel thereafter lived long and peacefully in the place he had come to love and, in the cloister beside the soothing sounds from the flowing fountain, he passed into eternal tranquility, entombed *ad sanctos* in the cathedral crypt.

Before his death, he revealed to the abbot an astounding account of a preparation that prevented the plague. The catalyst for the revelation was the rumour of a virulent epidemic in Constantinople. The knight worried great suffering would ensue should such a calamity occur in their midst. By then old and wasted, the knight summoned the abbot and confided to him the secret formula he said had originated in Upper Egypt more than a millennium before. It did not cure the pestilence once it took hold, he admonished. For those who only had been exposed to the disease, however, the potion protected them from infection on condition a mere half walnut shell of the brew was ingested for seven days.

Michiel de Dunkerque pulled the abbot close to him and in a frail whisper, murmured, 'This I bequeath to you, my dear friend, in gratitude for the care, shelter and love provided me these many years. There, look there in my pack.'

The abbot retrieved a nine paneled folded square of dusty parchment that had a faded Cross of Jerusalem painted on one side. Unfolded, each of the nine panels, written in Hieratic, Greek, and Latin, described one step of the potion's formula:

Square 1: *In the name of Amon, Isis, and Imhoptep soak, ht-w3 wood # in 20 pods of water salted with one pi of natron and a pod of honey.*

Square 2: *Remove the wood and set aside the soaked water. Grind the wood into chips; grind the chips into dust. Soak the dust in the water.*

Square 3: *Add a pi of crocodile dung. Add two pi of camel dung. Add a pi of unicorn horn. Add a pod of a pregnant woman's urine.*

Square 4: *Place the mix in a covered clay vessel and put it on the belly of a feverish male child for the passing of one sun.*

Square 5: *Pour the mix through sheets of coarse linen; take the elution and once more pour through a fine sheet of linen.*

Square 6: *Pour the elution onto a glazed dish, and let the sun drink of the water until dry.*

Square 7: *Scrape the black dust from the dish into a vial. Seal the vial with wax of bees.*

Square 8: *When the pestilence threatens, open the vial and pour the white of one Ibis egg into it. Agitate.*

Square 9: *Add two pods of water to the vial and drink the black potion. This you must do for seven suns.*

Michiel de Dunkerque had so convinced Abbot Blaez of the efficacy of the arcane formula the abbot became driven with wonder about the legitimacy of its claims. He gave the task of deciphering the formula written on fragile ancient papyrus fragments to his learned fellow monk, the renowned physician Watkin.

Brother Watkin assiduously studied all the works of Pliny, Herodotus, Dioscorides, Galen, Soranus, and even Paulus Aegineta, hoping to garner insight on effective substitutions to replace the perplexing and murky ingredients set down in the ancient formula. He examined the writings of Ibn bin Azzar, looking for references to the Egyptian formula, but met with no success. He tweaked the likely proportions of the Egyptian recipe using ingredients commonplace in the Western world. It took years and many trying but promising experiments, to produce, with equal effectiveness, the miraculous Egyptian preparation.

Brother Watkin determined *ht-w3* wood # referred to rotten, moldy locust tree wood. A *pod* was one tablespoon. A *pi* was the equivalent of a pinch. Carp dung successfully approximated crocodile excreta, as did sheep droppings for camel chips, goat hoof for unicorn horn, and the white of a brown stork egg for that of an ibis egg. Simmering the contents in a pot until only its residue remained eliminated the nonsense of putting a clay vessel baking in the sun on top of a howling feverish infant.

The urine of a pregnant woman remained an essential ingredient, and an adequate quantity was sometimes the most difficult component to obtain, dependent, as it was, on the cooperation of practitioners of urinoscopy who examine the urine of pregnant women and make prognostications based on their analysis. They had to be approached with tactful and clandestine negotiations that usually entailed a bribe of some kind before the physicians agreed to deliver the indispensable commodity.

The formula referred to treatment for only one person. Multiplying all the ingredients enough for multitudes was the supreme challenge, requiring the efforts and cooperation of many.

The decision to keep the potion secret had been reached more than one hundred and fifty years before. The then Abbot of Saint Benedict, Abbot Raphael, after long debate with his advisors, rejected sharing the formula. Raphael feared, in the hands of the iniquitous, it could be used for unthinkable evil purposes, with the capacity to cause catastrophic destruction. He and his counselors recalled how a marauder once had seized the prescription to use for malevolent purposes. Fortunately, he had been apprehended by vigilant guards at the gates of the town, and the formula had been returned to the abbey. The incident further convinced the monastic hierarchy of the potential for the potion's nefarious use.

Hypothetically, in the event of an outbreak of the Black Death, even a small army of men, having taken the potion as protection from the sickness, could seize infected and dying plague victims and deliberately expose them to the general populace, thus ensuring the total annihilation of the population. The idea of apocalyptic warfare was not beyond belief. It only took one malevolent faction to formulate enough of the elixir to obliterate an enemy or enemies and the population of entire countries.

With solemn pledges to distribute the potion readily to all in need, the good monks of Saint Benedict unanimously vouchsafed to keep its formula forever secret and unattainable except to trusted guardians in the abbey. The then Abbot Raphael hid Brother Watkin's prescription and the ancient Egyptian scroll in what he hoped – and proved to be – an undetectable place. Its site was passed down from abbot to abbot and, in this year of 1439, only Abbot William and Brother Lucien knew the location.

When Lucien first arrived at the abbey, the abbot charged him caretaker of the ancient parchment and the formula Brother Watkin had so astutely adapted from it. Watkin had referred to the prescription as 'the black potion' and the sobriquet endured. Its secret location had been inscribed in code on a small piece of parchment and hidden in a wax sealed Byzantine *encolpion* gifted to the abbey by a well-travelled monk. The bronze cross-shaped and decorated enamel icon opened like a hollow clamshell. Like his predecessors, William wore it perpetually as a pendent. Upon his death, his successor would inherit it and be told of the miraculous properties of the black potion and its ancient roots.

Lucien enlisted every monk, lay brother and oblate to participate in the taxing undertaking to forage the countryside for the ingredients required to concoct the recipe in vast quantities. He was circumspect about the kind and amount of information he gave to the monastic community collectively. Small groups were each taken into confidence to find ingredients for the formula, but in isolation of each other, and each group, sworn to secrecy, knew but a fraction of the ingredients that comprised the entire prescription. Lucien had selected his associates judiciously and trusted them, grateful for the tiresome and often odious work involved in the preparation of the mixture. The odour of rotting wood, animal excrement and urine were particularly loathsome but indispensable, and no one complained – outwardly, in any case.

Lucien scoffed at physicians who examined the colour of urine poured into a *matula* to evaluate signs of inflammation, convinced it had no diagnostic purpose, but he appreciated the widely practiced procedure, for it served his objective, and he had some time ago contracted with the urinoscopist, Dragonet – an honest man – to deliver urine from pregnant women to use in making the potion in exchange for a corrody of abbey wine, cheeses and fresh produce.

Dragonet in turn distained Lucien's professional skills and was derisive of his medical treatments, convinced the celibate cleric employed the art of witchcraft, not science. He thought him completely deficient in iatric skills. Dragonet had not a jot of curiosity regarding what Lucien did with the piss of pregnancy. He was content to accept the offerings Lucien gave him in exchange for urine he would in any case normally discard, satisfied he had the better of the bargain between them.

Dragonet knew, as did many physicians, about the black potion the abbey brewed, and derided its efficacious claim. He and his colleagues before him relied on conventional precautionary measures in times of crisis: protective gear of a leather tunic, gloves and a bird beaked mask packed with vinegar, cinnamon and cloves, the fumes of which, it was believed, forestalled contagion. None grasped the correlation between the futility of these observances and the instances of deaths amongst those physicians who valiantly administered to plague victims.

Indifferent to Dragonet's opinions, Lucien reserved a voluminous amount of urine residue for future use and obtained fresh supplies whenever possible to use in the preparation of the only prescription that prevented the plague.

Sun streamed through the slender, long windows on the south side of the refectory. When Abbot William entered, he appeared preoccupied, distracted. He took his place at table, bowed his head, and intoned the grace before meals written by the fourth century poet and ascetic, Prudentius.

In nomine Patris, et Filii, et Spiritus Sancti, Te sine dulce nihil, Domine, nec iuvat ore quid adpetere, pocula ni prius atque cibos, Christe, tuus favor inbuerit, omnia sanctificante fide. Amen.

William nodded to the members of the monastic community and to the lector and sat down. Benches scraped in unison as all sat. A door on the west side of the refectory opened and nine lay brothers wearing spattered aprons entered with large clay bowls, and began to ladle a generous portion of a thick grain and vegetable soup into each of the monks' wooden porringers. Eight more brothers brought platters of crusty, coarse brown bread to be passed along the tables, and pitchers of *justitia* – watery wine the color of wound washings.

The congregation ate and drank silently as the lector's voice echoed in the hall accompanied by the muffled movements of the kitchen staff, the sounds of scuffing spoons in laden bowls, and the dull rap of cups placed on the tables. The oblates also slurped soup, flavoured for them with pieces of beef. They ate their bread washed down with milk. Several oblates, Michel included, surreptitiously put chucks of bread in their sleeves for a late evening nibble.

Once the meal had ended and the monotonous hum of the lector's voice ceased, the throng placed spoons in their bowls, rose and bowed their heads for the ritual blessing. When Abbot William rose from his chair and began to speak to them, all eyes turned to him and they sat down to listen.

'Brothers, I have something of great import to disclose to you. Our reserve of the black potion has diminished potency. It will no longer protect one from being infected by the pestilence.'

There was an audible groan throughout the room, testimony that the monks, to a man, abhorred the drudgery involved in gathering the ingredients for the serum. They cheerlessly but dutifully listened to the abbot's directives. 'Tomorrow you will begin to search the forests for as much mouldy locust wood as can be found. Those of you with practice in this will instruct novices. We have been delivered from an eruption of the pestilence in recent years, but . . .' He paused and continued with a sigh, as he told them of the reports from Brindisi of the number of fatalities from the disease. He ignored the murmur that coursed through the refectory. He cloaked his apprehension concerning the potential for an outbreak of epidemic magnitude in Saint Petroc-sur-lac and the suffering and panic that would transpire, and beckoned Lucien to continue as he sat down meditatively.

'Brothers, most of you have helped me in past labours to gather the wood that is essential for making the potion,' Lucien said to them, urgency in his voice. 'It is the key ingredient, and I am gratified by your cooperation and' – he suppressed an impish smile before continuing – 'your zeal as you take on this disagreeable task.'

Lucien scanned the room and, assured all were attentive, added, 'Given the tidings from Brindisi, we need to prepare as much of the draught as we are able. We keep to the undertaking as in the past and go to the moist areas of the forest where little sunlight enters. That is where the black fungus grows. Find clusters of locust trees, but with care. As you know, there is a great deal of bramble and thorny brush in the thicket, so be wary. Look for fallen branches that are buried in rotten leaves. Mark well the decayed, reeking black slime. Assuredly, your noses will be your guides,' he quipped. 'Feel the rot. It should be wet, soft, and gummy to touch – but with no beetles or signs of worms. Daily I hope for piles of the substance under the roofed yard outside the dispensary. We shall begin at first light.'

He called out, 'Brothers St. Jean, Becket, and Colin, kindly form your companies and report them to me. Brother Richard, please make a list of the names in each company. Brother Robert, pray come see me. I have instructions specifically for you.' After a brief pause, satisfied he had given thorough directives, Lucien concluded, 'I have nothing more to tell you for the moment. Once we have enough of the rot, I shall send forth consorts to search for other ingredients.' Lucien faced the abbot, who nodded supportively.

William stood. All followed his example and bowed their heads to recite the ritual *deo gratias*. The abbot and his staff led the procession of monks, lay brothers, and oblates from the refectory into the glow of an early spring evening. The congregation dispersed, free to pursue recreational activities. The monks headed to the common house and the lay brothers to their cells, all to speculate about the possibility of a new epidemic of the plague and to grouse about the planned hunt for the foul wood for the black potion.

Anton, an oblate new to the abbey, broke the rule of silence as they walked from the refectory towards the dormitory. *Sotto voce*, he peppered Michel with questions. 'Why do they have to have rotten wood? What is the black potion? What is it used for?'

'Shhh,' snapped Michel. 'Be patient. We can talk in the dormitory.'

Brother Audren, always swift to catch out misconduct amongst the monks and oblates, heard Michel speak and summoned him, sneering crossly. 'Tomorrow morning you will give an account to Prior Fidelis of this infringement of the Rule.'

Michel gloomily continued on his way to the dormitory, irritated that once again he would be punished for breaking a rule, but comforted he at least still had a goodly portion of bread as a treat for later. Anton awaited him and apologised. 'It is my fault. I shall go with you to Fidelis.'

Michel shook his head. 'Nay, it seems I am always being chastised for some wrongdoing. You are new to the monastery. It takes time to comply to the rules. It seems even after five years I have not been able to!'

Anton smiled his thanks. He was a small and frail boy who had been born with a harelip. He had told Michel that an itinerant surgeon who had learned harelip repair from a *Talmudic* Spanish Jew corrected the defect when he was one year of age. Now, at nearly fifteen years old, he was noticeably undersized, malnourished in his first year, unable to adequately suck. Michel had befriended Anton in his first few days as an oblate, just as he had been befriended by a senior oblate five years before to help ameliorate the adjustment to abbey life.

Normally during recreation, the oblates sat at small tables playing chess or knuckle or pebbles games, but such diversions were ignored in favour of discussing the news told them at supper. The older, experienced boys patiently explained what they knew of how the black potion was formulated and its vital importance in preventing plague.

Henri, Paol Eric, Christopher, Adrian, Ronan, and Michel sequestered themselves in the quiet corner by Michel's bed and invited Anton and two other new oblates, George and Tristyn, to join them. 'We all helped find rotten wood the last time Brother Lucien made the black potion,' Michel said. 'We don't know what the slime does, and many other ingredients are added to it, but no one knows what they all are. It is a big secret – the biggest secret in the abbey. Brother Lucien knows, of course. For five years I've helped mash, boil and sift plants, mushrooms, berries, herbs, and the like for his use in the Hôtel Dieu. Some, I think, may be for the potion, but everything he uses becomes medicines for all kinds of sicknesses, not just for the black potion.'

Anton thoughtfully asked, 'Do you think I can go with you tomorrow?'

Michel assured him they all would be inducted into service. 'After prime we shall be given our assignments. Mind, it's unpleasant work. The rotten wood stinks.'

Teams of sixty-two monks and lay brothers, twenty oblates and twelve horse drawn carts laden with barrel sized straw baskets set forth in every direction the following morning to collect the rotten locust wood. Michel was in Lucien's company headed north towards the forest. It was the longest distance from the abbey.

The group passed the monastery's extensive wheat fields before they arrived at a fork in the road where they veered right until, just before noon, they reached dense, thicketed woodland. 'Let's get those horses out of the sun and give them water. Over here, off the path,' Lucien instructed. 'We shall begin our work close to the pathway. 'Twill be less wearisome to drag a full basket to the cart. Later, as we go deeper into the woods, we can form a row and pass the baskets to each other to unload into the casks.' The crew quickly ate the midday meal Brother Cook had prepared and, with no further delay, they wedged through the dense thicket to search for the prized rot.

It wasn't long before Lucien spotted promising spoil. The forest floor was thick with decaying fetid wood ideal for the purpose, and he and his team efficiently gathered samples for their large baskets.

The time passed quickly. At one point they heard the thumps of several galloping hoofs pass by on the main road and felt the ground vibrate as the horses sped by. Lucien commented, 'Well, *there* are some fellows in haste,' and he bent down to hoist more of the rotted wood into a basket.

By late afternoon, Michel observed with relief his and Lucien's basket was nearly full. He put aside thoughts of the thicket's fusty smell, and stole a moment to stretch an aching body when he heard a sound – a shriek – somewhat far away, but distinctly a scream. He paused, perplexed, and looked around him. 'What was that noise?'

Brother Deniel, just a short distance away, answered he had not heard anything.

Michel said, 'It was afar, but I heard it clearly – from over there.'

Oblate George glanced in the direction Michel had pointed to but saw nothing but dense woods. 'An owl, perhaps.'

'No. Owls sleep in the day.'

Lucien stood erect and peered through the trees. He put his hand on Michel's shoulder. 'Over there, well far afield, up and to the left over the trees. Can you see the tip of that turret of Baron de Rais' château? That might be where the sound came from – probably the squeal of a pig being slaughtered for roasting. The baron must be back in residence.' Michel nodded, satisfied with the explanation. Lucien continued, 'Did I ever tell you I know him . . . well, knew him? The baron, I mean.' Michel looked surprised. 'We both were at Orléans with Jeanne.'

'I saw him once. The day I entered the monastery. In a pageant when he made his way through Saint Petroc. I remember he smiled at me, and I felt very proud,' Michel acknowledged. 'What is he like, Magister?'

'Hmm. He is valiant, as they say.' Julian looked at Michel and said, 'But I fear to stain your esteem for him, for I thought him vain, arrogant and cruel.' Lucien thought before adding. 'I remember he seemed to . . . how can I say it?' He reflected but a moment before telling Michel, 'He was quite ruthless. He gave the distinct impression he truly enjoyed the killing. In one instance, I witnessed him tormenting and inflicting non-lethal wounds on a soldier before he slit his throat.' Lucien shook his head in disgust. 'He laughed like a madman, leering at the blood spurting from the wound as the hapless fellow slowly expired. It was wicked.' He shook his head again in a shudder. Michel was disconcerted. His long-held regard for the baron instantly vapourised. Silently, both turned to the task at hand and talked no more.

They were deep in the woods. They had worked seven hours, pleased their efforts had filled all the baskets. 'A good load for a mere day's labour,' Lucien declared. 'We shall continue tomorrow, rotating routes to the south, east and west so that the distance walked by each group will be equitable. We must hurry now. The sun will set soon enough. We shall not get back to the abbey until well after dark.'

It took more than seven weeks before Lucien was satisfied they had accumulated enough of the rotted locust needed for processing. As the decayed wood simmered over a fire in mammoth vats, crews of monks, sworn to secrecy regarding the nature of their assignment, set out to collect other of the required components.

Laden with culinary delicacies and several bottles of vintage wine, Lucien met with the trustworthy Dragonet, pleased to accept samples of urine from women with child and assurances of more within weeks.

Twelve weeks passed before a fresh stock of the black potion was ready to be shelved in the cellar – not as much a supply as Lucien had hoped for, but still a goodly amount, sufficient he hoped, should the need to use it arose. At least they were prepared, and that lessened his concern about continuing reports of widespread instances of the pestilence.

Abbot William led his congregation in prayer, beseeching favourite saints to intercede to God to relieve the suffering of the plague's victims and to give thanks their abbey had been blessed with a remedy to avert the disease should adversity strike the region.

15

A PEACE FRACTURED

Marc and Gwen Gervais celebrated their fifth wedding anniversary in July, an occasion that reflected the success of a happy union.

Nolwenn's gentle, kind and trusting nature enriched Marc and made him less chary. Her sympathy and compassion for others moved him to greater charity. He basked in the household she kept with unfailing good humour and tender devotion, and delighted in her cleverness and intelligence that ensured good company. At night she was a willing and passionate love partner. His abiding love for the children prompted him to formally adopt Ives and Genviev as his own. Life was further complete when twin girls, Madeline and Sarah were born two years after they married.

The couple complemented each other. Nolwenn's patience tempered Marc's restlessness. She was optimistic in contrast to his mistrustful cynicism. She was tranquil, and moderated Marc's occasional agitation after a day scuttling after thieves. They worked well together to create a loving, stable home that brimmed with goodwill and contentment – a home to which Marc was now able to return to each evening from town.

Marc and Donan had reached a mutually satisfactory arrangement in which Marc organised space at the prison where he and Donan could daily conduct official business, and Donan, Anne-Gaël and their children took up residence in Marc's town house. Anne-Gaël enjoyed the bustle of town life, and the children reveled in the number of new friendships they made. For Marc, having a home away from town after a lively day of dealing with petty crimes gave welcome reprieve. Donan was able to deputise other staff to handle night intrusions on civic order, and each were able to have carefree evenings with their families secure in the knowledge a night force would keep the peace. Marc especially felt grateful for uninterrupted escapes from the cares of his occupation that had so beleaguered him in the past.

There had not been a single abduction of a child from Saint Petroc-sur-lac in five years. No longer did Marc feel the fear or desolation that had gripped him with each harrowing incident in which a child had been kidnapped. His now happy life had effaced from his mind memory of past horrors, all of which had faded into a nebulous and hazy shadow land associated with some surreal universe, completely unrelated to his now idyllic world. He brimmed with confidence. This new life assumed a natural, untroubled cadence of domestic happiness and gratifying social relationships. With Donan as his reliable deputy, the sheriff's work was rewarding, interesting, and pleasantly challenging.

On a sun-drenched Sunday, godparents Marc and Nolwenn took the children to town for a baptismal mass and a celebratory feast welcoming Anna Regina, the new addition to the Cadoret family.

There were, in fact, ongoing Sunday occasions, whether in town or in Aldrien. Marc delegated authority rotationally for the duty watch, freeing him and Donan for the day, happily leaving official concerns to others.

Nevertheless, Donan had a report of the morning's activities ready for Marc upon his arrival. 'A brawl that led to an arrest – and much needed sleep for one of our most frequent revelers after many tankards at the tavern last night.'

'Lagu Tatin.'

Donan laughed. 'Of course. Who else! It is always Lagu Tatin. I do believe he has been our guest ten – no – twelve times in the past two months. I think to give him permanent residence!'

'Heaven forefend! All the same, I trust he will be our lone captive.'

'I cannot guarantee that, but I think naught more will disturb the day.'

'Well! To more important matters,' Marc said, jovially. We have a basket full of fresh delectables from our garden for the table. And wine from my vineyard.'

'And Anne-Gaël is not wanting in having prepared goodly savouries and sweets! We shall have a banquet!'

Such lighthearted, relaxing times were a given when the four friends gathered, either in town or in Aldrien, whatever the occasion, Invariably the antics of the spirited children kept them engaged as well as amused, but they could always count on time enough for convivial conversation amongst themselves, much laughter and a hearty meal prepared by expert hands from both households.

Having been spared kidnappings for five years, Marc, Donan and their wives – the general populace, in fact – no longer felt hazards lurked beyond their doors. A need for maintaining tight security gave way to a casual resumption of old practices. In the community, fear had long given way to complacency. People once again felt secure and lived their lives accordingly. Children once more were sent to town for provisions, to the fields to mind the sheep, and to Marcel's slaughter-house with animals for slaughter.

Marcel was a prime beneficiary of the renewed civic harmony. Business in his slaughterhouse flourished. Located on the road to Dinan, it was a long but not prohibitive walk for town folk, and even senior oblates from the abbey were charged to take the occasional steer or sheep there to be butchered.

Some of the meat was used by the monks and lay brothers to make sausages, and large portions of meat were seasoned, dried, and stored until winter for use in stews for the oblates. Fresh meat was distributed to the needy. In the monastery, only two legged animals were prepared for consumption by monks and lay brothers, compliant with Saint Benedict's decree.

The abbey bartered for all the animal skins of no use to Marcel, who welcomed the delicacies and the wine from the monastery cellarer as payment. The skins were processed by lay brothers and oblates who crafted fine leather goods from them as well as parchment and vellum.

Michel and George, on a hot and sunny Wednesday, ambled towards Marcel's slaughterhouse with two cows in tow. George of Carcassonne was a few months older than Michel and a jolly companion, with a freckled face and impish nature. He had striking blue eyes banded by thick black eyelashes the colour of his hair. They were the same height, but George lacked the energy and stamina that came easily to Michel, and now, on the road to the slaughterhouse, he complained of being breathless and tired of walking.

'Patience. Look there. You can see the slaughter-house already. We are nigh. And Marcel is sure to give us cool cider and a bun to refresh us.'

Marcel welcomed the oblates cordially, and, as anticipated, served them several treats. As the boys munched on buns and drank cider, Marcel entertained them with news from the town passed on to him by his customers. Michel and George were avid listeners, eager to relate all the gossip they heard to the oblates on their return.

'The meat will be ready by Friday. It will please me well to see you again.' Michel smiled, knowing Marcel anticipated the cache of wine, cheeses, fruits, and vegetables that would be in the horse drawn cart when they returned to collect the meat and animal skins.

They were old enough for the task: a boy of fifteen and his twelve-year-old sister. At their parents' behest, they took two sheep to Marcel to butcher, and, as was his custom, Marcel rewarded them with refreshments. He told them to return for the meat in two days.

He was annoyed when that same night the children's parents incessantly beat on his door, wanting to know where their children were. His heart sank as he told them they had left his slaughterhouse late afternoon. He expected they had returned home. He knew nothing more. He stared blankly as a recognisable apprehension emerged. He said weakly, 'I fear I cannot help you.' He paused as each communicated to the other the alarm they felt. Marcel told them, grave unease in his voice, '*Monsieur, Madame* Cadoc, I think it wise you hasten to Saint Petroc-sur-lac and speak with the sheriff.' They bolted out of the slaughterhouse, leaving Marcel crestfallen and full of trepidation.

Marc and Donan were in the sheriff's office when Galaren and Charlotte Cadoc arrived, hysterical, to tell them their children had been abducted. Dumbstruck, both men exchanged looks of anxiety and foreboding.

Donan escorted them to a bench in an outer chamber, wrote down the details of the disappearance and by rote recited what had been five years before the standard assurance addressed to stricken parents that the crime would be thoroughly investigated and the sheriff and his men would do all they could to recover the children. His mouth uttered the words, but his mind rejected their value. He watched them as they left, distraught and disoriented, and wondered who was more upset, the Cadocs or him. He staggered into Marc's office to see him already pouring over kidnapping files from the past. 'I cannot believe this is happening again. We were fools to think it would not betide us once more.' Numbed and apprehensive, he asked, 'Donan, are you as fearful as I the nightmare begins anew?'

'That is assuredly what I fear.'

A niggling disquiet gnawed at them, as each realised the five-year hiatus from evil had ended. Fear of failure surfaced as recollections of past futile efforts engulfed them. Each sensed the town's tribulations would worsen.

'What do you think should be our first act?' Donan asked.

'Do what we always did. Call out the guard and send them scouting. You and I shall go to the slaughterhouse to question Marcel.' Marc hesitated. 'I have seen oblates on the pathway to the slaughterhouse. I think to go to the monastery and give them fair warning of what has happened.'

Having informed a shocked Prior Fidelis what had transpired and received assurances the oblates would not venture forth further, Marc joined Donan and both rode towards Marcel's slaughterhouse.

After Vespers, Fidelis went into the oblates' dormitory and announced, 'The terror is back, my sons. Two children went to the slaughterhouse and thereafter disappeared.' He added curtly, 'Henceforth, four lay brothers will take livestock to the slaughterhouse. No oblates may leave the monastery.' He said no more than that. The oblates knew better than to question Fidelis for additional information.

The boys were abuzz with speculation and fright. Michel and George had conflicted feelings. They confessed to each other to be saddened about the children's kidnapping but were struck with a reprehensible thought it was they who could have been set upon. They felt the guilt of it and quickly said an *Ave*. Michel quietly said, 'Tomorrow at Mass I shall petition Saint Joseph to help find the children.'

George asked Michel, 'Do you think they will find them?'

'Oh, yes. I am sure of it. Have faith,' Michel reassured

him. His thoughts were otherwise. *No one will ever see those children again.*

Some days after, Fidelis went to the Hôtel Dieu, certain he would find him toying with his potions in the infirmary. 'Pray forgive the disturbance, Lucien.'

'Not a bit of it. You are most welcome; I assure you dear friend. Your visit is well timed. I have put aside my experiment for the day. Come. Join me taste the fresh cider just delivered me by Brother Cook!'

They spoke with consternation about the kidnapping, expressing shared fear more children would go missing. Fidelis told him he had assigned lay brothers to guide the oblates to and from the school. 'To be sure, our oblates are protected whilst in the monastery, and the brothers as guards should make them feel safe from harm, yet the younger boys are sore afraid despite my efforts to assuage them.'

'I shall lend my voice to your assurances their protection is secure.'

Fidelis nodded thanks. 'Brother Alexander and his fellow school masters will also endeavour to alleviate the boys' distress.' Fidelis inhaled deeply. 'This is a wretched care brother.'

'Indeed so. We live with fear and uncertainty again.'

The two fell silent. Fidelis quaffed some of the cider and changed the subject. 'There is a matter, a pleasant topic, about which I would like to discuss with you. When I spoke to Brother Alexander, he took leave to inform me of Michel's scholastic standing. It seems the boy has earned the distinction of the title 'scholar.' That moved me to consider the boy's future, and I thought of his work with you. Tell me, Lucien, how goes it with him in your infirmary?'

Lucien's face brightened. 'Forsooth, he is a most amiable colleague and is very dear to me. I have naught but praise. He impresses daily. He is truly gifted, Fidelis. And he works hard. With patients he employs skills efficiently and effectively, with sound judgement and, importantly, with kindness.' He chuckled. 'When he is with me, he is driven by curiosity and eagerness to learn. He nigh exhausts me with interminable questions.' Lucien stopped speaking for but a moment.

'Not only on medical matters, my friend, on life, secular and spiritual. It oft times astounds me to hear profound and wise pronouncements from but a lad. He is on a serious quest to discover life's meaning, impatient to grasp the essence of the human condition and how that relates to his soul.'

Fidelis nodded contentedly. 'I have long noted his devotion to spiritual matters. Surely that informs the dedication in the hospital of which you speak.' He sighed. 'Mind, he persists with infractions of the Rule.'

Lucien raised his eyebrows. Fidelis waved away his concerns. 'Minor breaches. Overall he is faithful to the dictums of Saint Benedict and, given his past woes, I take little heed at what are truly minor infringements. More often he is immersed in silent prayer, and I am ever hopeful the peace, conciliation and soulful nourishment he seeks are granted to him.' After a pause he prodded, 'As to his future, I suspect we are of one mind on this.'

Lucien nodded. 'University.'

Fidelis smiled. 'University! And, God be praised, he has expressed a desire take holy orders. The monastery shall fare well with another physician and priest doing God's will.'

'So, we both are of one accord. Michel should study medicine. How might we proceed?'

'I suggest we approach the abbot on the matter with an aim to receive his commendation.'

Just then the Vespers bell rang. Lucien and Fidelis rose from the benches. 'Let us also pray on the matter, Lucien.'

Unmentioned was Michel's muscular development after years of work in the gardens and fields, an asset when lifting weak patients to cleanse them or change the linens on their cots. Useful as well, when hauling supplies to the infirmary and to the granary or buttery. But neither Fidelis nor Lucien imagined a situation in which Michel would employ his brawn in a fist fight.

The misadventure transpired when the oblates Devi and Samzun overplayed their bullying at a feast day ceremony in the chapel at which, during Vespers, the oblates stood with lit candles in their hands.

'I tell you I saw them, Michel.'

'What? Purposely drip hot wax onto Anton's head? Surely even they could not be so wicked!'

'I tell you I saw them do just that,' Christopher insisted. 'They were standing in front of me, and I saw Devi first whisper to Samzun, then deliberately tilt his candle so that wax drippings fell, searing the top of Anton's head. You know the rest.'

Aghast, Michel leaped from the bench and seethed. 'Demonical. It cries for vengeance.' He rambled for a few minutes. 'Anton still is in the infirmary, and only God knows the degree of the burn.'

'The pain!' Christopher added.

'At last they have gone too far.' Michel looked to the end of the room where the offending rogues sat, laughing.

'What are you going to do? Michel, wait! You'll get into trouble.'

Fuming, Michel careened towards the errant oblates with clenched fists. He rushed Samzun with a whack so strong the oblate fell to the floor. Devi warily backed away as Michel menacingly said, 'Those who do harm to others warrant the force of a bruising clout. I am about show you what that feels like.'

Devi taunted him and said, 'I defy you.'

At that, Michel delivered several bruising blows. Once Devi was on the ground, he turned to Samzun, now on his feet. 'Make ready for the flogging you have earned these past years!'

'I shall tell Magister Fidelis. Then we shall see how brave you are.'

'No matter,' and Michel lunged into Samzun with powerful punches that left him bloody and dazed. 'This is but a sample should you mistreat any oblate again. Out of my sight. Scum!'

The miscreants cowered as they rose from the floor and quickly took refuge in the *necessarium* as the oblates cheered Michel. Paol Eric, however, was quick to observe apprehensively, 'You are sure to be punished for this, Michel.'

Michel told him he would welcome whatever censure Magister Fidelis might deliver. 'But I doubt the cowardly vermin will relate to him what happened. They would place themselves in jeopardy.' He laughed. 'It was a well-deserved beating, as you well know. They have been tyrants far too long. You can trust they will not dare further harm anyone more.'

After Compline, Michel sought out Fidelis. 'Magister, I wish to confess.' Michel followed Fidelis to his cell where Michel told him, 'I sought retribution for the wrong done to Anton, Magister. I struck two oblates with all my might until they bled. I looked to Saint Adrian Aquinas' precepts regarding a just war to justify my action.'

'Oh? War was it?' Fidelis constrained to restrain his amusement of Michel's donnish assessment of what had occurred. 'And what, pray, has become of Christ's precept to turn the other cheek?'

Michel squirmed. He lowered his head. 'I sought vengeance, Magister, on two oblates who have tormented oblates for years.'

'Does that justify an offence against the Rule?' Michel looked contrite. 'Who are they?'

'Please, sir. I do not wish to say. I don't want them to get into trouble.'

'Yet you place yourself in jeopardy. And what if I were to tell you I already know their identities?' He fell silent. Fidelis believed it had been a just rebuke, but one he could not condone. 'I need not remind you what you did was illicit and absolutely forbidden. This is not the first time you have broken the Rule of Saint Benedict in this fashion.'

Michel pleaded forgiveness. 'I am sorry for the trespass, Magister. Truly. But I confess I am not sorry I assaulted them, for I am assured they will no longer taunt young oblates, sir.'

Fidelis sighed, dismayed he was of the same opinion. He made a note to profess this to his confessor. 'Hmm. You may be right, my son, but there must be a consequence. What you did cannot be excused. Am I to believe you are sorry for the offense?'

Michel thought for a moment and muttered, 'If you say so sir.'

Fidelis chose not to challenge the qualified statement of remorse, and instructed Michel to trace the labyrinth in atonement for the sin of violence against another.

'How many times, Magister?'

'Hmm? Eh . . . just once. Twice! Now. Let us dismiss the matter. *Te obsolvo en nomine Padre. . . .*'

Michel shakily stood, incredulous to have received so light a penance. He politely asked if he could leave. Fidelis shook his head and said, 'Allow me to take advantage whilst you are with me, Michel. I want to speak about your wish to study medicine.'

Surprised by the shift to the unrelated topic, Michel welcomed it. 'Do I aspire too highly, Magister?'

Fidelis told him, 'I think our lord abbot will make that decision for you.' He put his arm on Michel's shoulder. 'Brother Lucien and I spoke to him on the matter, as it is time for you to proceed to university should you want it. We both highly recommended this. Brother Lucien considers you a competent aide in the dispensary and a skilled and compassionate nurse to the infirm. I attested to my satisfaction regarding your character and spiritual commitment, despite, shall we say, occasional lapses, and

Magister Alexander attests to your scholarship. In sum we recommended to the abbot that you be sent to the great school of medicine at Padua where you will learn all that is known of the art of healing.'

Michel looked stunned. 'Magister I am humbled. That would be a distinction beyond any dream I might conjure.'

Fidelis patted his arm and said, 'Dream, Michel, but leave others be the judge of it. Meanwhile, keep to your duties and studies. The matter is in God's hands. And as for *you*, henceforth keep *your* hands to yourself!'

16

THE PLAY'S THE THING

The feast of the Assumption of Mary into heaven on 15 August was first granted public recognition by Pope Sergius I in the eighth century and made official by Pope Leo IV in the ninth. People in the town of Saint Petroc-sur-lac marked the feast each year with great fanfare and spent weeks preparing for it. To no lesser degree, so did the sheriff, who painstakingly reviewed security plans and practiced simulated drills. He pushed himself to an extreme, fraught with worry there would be more abductions.

'Marc, you have overreached yourself to ensure naught happens on the day of the feast. You are completely spent from your toil. Let me keep the watch, stand in your stead on the feast day.'

Marc shook his head. 'I would have greater trepidation were I not in command.'

'That says little of your trust in me!'

'Not so. My dependence on you is infinite, Donan, but I think of swarms of people who will gather and remember tumults and tragedies of the past, and I am troubled to the quick.'

'That is what troubles me! You are so anguished. I think you need rest. Your men are proficient, and I would think myself well able to lead them and safely keep the peace'

'Surely every man is needed.' He turned a worn-out face towards Donan. 'I tremble, I tell you, for fear of wicked happenings.'

'As do we all. Our bailiffs are well apprised of the danger and well able to conduct our business,' he said impatiently. 'There has not been an attempt to seize a child in the town for five years.'

'Yea, but farther afield . . .'

'In the town, I say! Methinks it is well known how keenly our men are trained to keep the watch. You must have greater faith in their ability. Look you, if it's your absence that concerns you, come with your family to relax, have a holiday. You will be close at hand should you be needed – which is doubtful. It would rightly please Nolwenn, Anne-Gaël and the children to be here for the merrymaking.'

Marc was tempted, and finally acquiesced after he and Donan reviewed all the tactics they had devised, leaving Marc confident Donan was as astute in his instincts as was he, and as capable to command. Almost immediately he wanted to retract the decision. 'I am not certain it is wise, Donan. It will be a chaotic day and there are many uncertainties . . .'

'Nothing any of us have not witnessed. Marc. All will be well.'

Nolwenn was more than happy with Marc's news. She was exultant. 'How wonderful! You are always on duty on festival days and we can never go.' She hugged him happily. 'I shall ask Siobhan Delón to mind the twins – such a good neighbour. I'm sure she won't mind. And I shall prepare a large basketful of savouries and sweets for us all. Oh, Marc. It will be such a lark.'

Nolwenn's enthusiasm fortified in Marc's mind Donan's idea was a good one, and on the feast day he was at the reins of the horse drawn cart with Nolwenn and the children dressed in their finery, prepared to depart for town. They arrived in time for the procession that proceeded from the cathedral to the Place d'Aszhur where, to the side of an altar, stood a living tableau of the Virgin Mary and Christ's disciples depicting the ascension into heaven. A mammoth crowd filled the square and respectfully focused on the Mass celebrated by the bishop. The vast number of people caused Marc unease, and he instinctively assumed the professional awareness to which he was so accustomed.

After the mass, festival entertainment usurped pious devotions. There were performers from every region in Brittany to dazzle the crowds that surged in number. Distracted by tumblers, acrobats, jugglers, fire eaters and jesters, Marc put aside lingering misgivings, pleased by his family's excitement. Clowns performing sportive tricks received rollicking bellows of laughter that contributed to a jovial commotion. 'Pick the Pea' for cock sure gamblers who thought themselves quick eyed was one of the many attractions. Fortune tellers moved amidst the revelers, luring patrons with promises of good health and good fortune. There were edifying morality plays and comic theatre for those with bawdy taste. Marc and Nolwenn joined Anne-Gaël and her two oldest children, and sought amusement with the children's pleasure in mind, laughing with them as they giggled at a gaudily dressed jester in a folk show on a caravan stage.

It was a unique sensation for Marc to have no responsibility except to enjoy the amusement of a partying crowd. He had just eased into the novelty of it when his instinct for chicanery noticed something untoward. He warned Nolwenn in a whisper before he loped over to an unsuspecting man amongst those watching the comic capers, whose pouch would otherwise have been severed had not Marc ensnared a thief just as he reached out with his knife. There was a scuffle, and all attention turned to Marc as he hurried the felon out of the square towards the prison.

'Note the time, Bailiff. I shall deal with this on the morrow.' He named the offence and left the thief arrested before scurrying back to the square and Nolwenn's side. He found her and the children where he had left them and returned his attention to the show.

Michel was playing chess with Tristyn whilst several oblates played a game of knuckles. Both boys shared the aspiration to be a priest in the Benedictine order and had forged a deep friendship. They were companions at work and play and avid listeners to the latest gossip Paol Eric, Christopher, Adrian and George copiously provided.

The report this day was unsettling. Henri had raced into the dormitory and uncharacteristically had babbled at race speed. 'Did you hear the news? Two children are missing. I heard the abbot tell Magister Fidelis. At the fair. A boy and a girl from the same family.'

Alarmed, all stopped playing their games. *Two more missing?* It had been years since they had heard of such terrorising news, and now, in just a short while four had disappeared. They listened avidly as Henri described the details of what he had heard. Michel wondered, 'How old were they?'

'Don't know.' Henri answered, scratching his head, emitting a dusting of dandruff. 'What difference does it make?'

'None, I suppose. It is only that I have oft times wondered why only children go missing. I think it curious. And threatening. Why children? What happens to them?'

The question was not intended as rhetorical, but Michel received no replies. Henri just shrugged. An uncomfortable silence followed, broken by Tristyn, who looked at the chess board and asked, 'Whose move is it?'

Donan stood at the door of Marc's home. Distressed that the worst had happened on his watch, he was anxious to report to Marc, dreading his reaction. He had ridden from

Saint Petroc with alacrity to tell him of the two children who had vanished.

Marc blanched, unsettled by the news. As Donan expounded on what had occurred and where, an ominous premonition beset Marc. 'What time did it happen?'

'I'm not sure. I would say about two o'clock.'

Marc winced. 'Two o'clock? Two you say?'

Donan looked perplexed but continued his story. 'The father had been threatened by a thief who was snatched in the act by one of our men. All attention had been on the seizure. Only after did the parents notice the children were gone. They searched everywhere. There was no trace of them, and apparently no one who had seen them. They came to me . . .'

Marc swayed. Nausea overwhelmed him. He lurched outdoors and vomited.

Aghast, Donan rocketed to his side and helped him to his feet.

'Donan,' Marc sputtered, weeping. '*I* made that arrest. I saw the cutpurse reach for the man's pouch and tussled with him. People were mumbling. All was confusion. The father asked me what had happened, and I assured him nothing had been taken. I held the thief steadfast and dragged him to the prison. Christ in Heaven! Those children were taken as I stood watching a fool on a stage.'

Donan remained by Marc's side, but all efforts to console him were rebuffed. He finally rose to leave, telling Nolwenn, 'Tomorrow the investigation begins. I must prepare tonight. I pray Marc will fend off his present state. We are going to need him.'

Nolwenn nodded. 'Oh, would he not grieve so. It were not his fault. We both know that.'

Donan nodded wanly. 'Yet it was I who persuaded him to take pleasure in the day.'

'Give off feeling blame. It is to no avail. Nolwenn sighed. 'Go in peace, Donan. I shall abide with him.'

Marc was listless, depressed. Forlornly, his head bent, he told Nolwenn, 'Tomorrow it will fall to me to set to the chase when I am the one who caused this abduction. How can I pretend to have the wiles to lead when I am so wanting?'

'You do yourself great injustice. This was not your doing. I beg you, leave off, my dearest Marc!'

Marc ignored her pronouncements, and sighing, Nolwenn quietly listened as Marc berated himself. It was as if the one incident had released a bottomless wellspring of self-recrimination. He despaired over and over about the years of failure to apprehend those who had abducted children, and grieved for the parents who had lost their babes.

'Why do you punish yourself so? It is foolhardy to think of the past. Now it is rest you need, for tomorrow you will have much need of vigour and a clear mind for all you must do. Your men are counting on you.'

'To what end, Nolwenn? Nothing will come of it.'

'Oh, Marc. Why say that? I remember well you were the first and only person parents turned to when children disappeared, such was their confidence in you. And please think on this. You were only one of many in pursuit of those monsters. Yet you say only you are found wanting. Why, pray? You are not God endowed with supreme power and thereby more able than lesser men. My dearest one, you have naught but compassion for others and their failures but leave none for yourself. Be that wise or useful? And now you think yourself blameworthy because those two children vanished. Why think you so? You witnessed a crime and did well in catching that thief. You could not know there was evil about. I understand your feelings, but you are wrong to think what happened is because of your negligence. All your men were in the town. On guard! Yet they saw nothing untoward. You rightly do not blame them, and they will not blame you. They only look to you for leadership. You must provide that, remembering they praise your wits, rely on you, and follow your command. Husband, you do yourself wrong in this and do harm to those who look to you for guidance. Please shake off this sullen humour for everyone's sake.'

She held him soothingly in her arms as he emptied his soul with a cascade of tears. When he seemed spent, Nolwenn gently raised his head and kissed him. 'I am for bed, Marc. There are babes who are expectant of me each morning to arise and greet them lively with good cheer for the new day and whate'er it brings. I would bid you do the same for your men. Do not abandon Donan and others who follow you with trust. Remember how much they need you.' She kissed him tenderly and said, 'And remember too, I esteem you more than anyone else. I hope you think on it.' She kissed him again. 'Good be to you, my love.'

Nolwenn's rebuke had stung, but Marc thought hard on her faith and optimism in his abilities. After some pensive moments, he rose and abjectly followed her to their bed, hopeful rest would arouse a rekindled glint of spirit to confront the task that awaited him.

Donan sat across from Marc in the sheriff's and spoke to him of the organised launch he had formulated the night before. He told him that four teams awaited his orders to dispatch in all directions. One man was deputed to the family's home with a well-rehearsed message of hope. 'Several men are doing a house to house search in town. The performers are forbidden to leave town and await interrogation. Each of their caravans has been searched. Nothing untoward was found, but they will be held until you are satisfied they are blameless.'

'Well done, Donan. I thank you. I . . . I cannot think of any more that might be considered. The fact is, I have not been able to think at all, save about those missing children.'

'Listen well, Marc. You must shake this choleric humour. This is naught but insipience. Folly! We all have been found wanting in the past, and, since then, who among us imagined this evil would again come upon us – certainly not the wracked parents who sent their children to Marcel's or those who went to the festival. Five years without incident quelled all our fears. We felt safe, for good and all, believing the devils were gone forever! Leave off guilt – as I have forced myself to do.'

Marc looked at him. 'Why say you that?'

'Because of me you were a reveler, not a sheriff.' He looked forlornly at his colleague. 'But it does no good to dwell upon that thought.'

'None. Whatsoever. I made the decision, my friend. Not you.'

'And what decision will you make now, pray? We must act, and we await you to command us. If we succeed in routing out these fiends, it will be because of you. Only you, Marc.'

'You hearten me, surely. As does Nolwenn, my sweet Nolwenn.'

'There you have it! Surely you agree there is merit in our hope you will, as always, guide us.'

'With your help, Donan.'

'I thank you . . . and anticipated your need of me.' Marc guffawed at the feigned conceit. 'Now, it came to me . . .what think you to further examine old investigations?' Donan set files of papers on the table in front of Marc. 'For sure they'll spark fresh insight.'

Marc looked intently at the stack of old cases before him as if they were new minted coins dropped into his lap. After a moment's thought he said with enthusiasm, 'Ay. To study the past is prelude to our present tune. I think this a logical pursuit – however painful. 'Twill indeed inspire us with new perceptions.'

Marc began to peruse the documents. As he kept his eye fixed on Marc's face, Donan could see glimmers of curiosity intensify and the embers of despair expire. He waited with gratified patience for Marc to comment.

Marc exclaimed. 'Indeed, a worthy undertaking. Well done! I am remiss in not having considered it myself.'

He took a deep breath. 'Truly you have roused me from dark and useless melancholy, my friend.'

'No matter, Marc, if you are now right ready for the chase.'

'Indeed so. And this time I do not intend to fall short of the prize!' He embraced his deputy. 'Now to begin.' He grinned mischievously. 'I commend you on making this proposition. *You* can toil through the records and deliver me a summary report.'

'What? Go through all those stale papers!? I object!'

Marc laughed. 'A jest, no more. I need you for more important matters. I shall assign the task to a subordinate – one who dares not complain. Just now I want you close to me. I shall need your counsel.' He rubbed his hands vigorously and declared, 'Let us question each of the bands of performers. Round them all up. I am impatient to hear their stories, as well you must be too. They, after all, had the best view of the people in the square and from the best vantage point!'

The minstrels, troubadours, jugglers, jesters, actors, and gamesmen were not in a compliant mood. Each hour wasted in Saint Petroc-sur-lac affected their livelihood. Mostly, they fretted they would be blamed for the disappearances. When the sheriff and his deputy began to interrogate them, it became apparent none was a suspect. Relief coursed through them all, and, no longer wary, they eagerly endeavoured to help.

'Mind, I did not see anyone near,' said one of the actors from the morality play, 'But at the port into the square there were three horses held in the shadows by a man. I paid him no heed at the time.'

The fire-eater said he had seen several men wandering about, weaving in and out of the crowds. 'I wondered they were not interested in my or anyone else's sport. Why else were they there?'

'I saw them too,' said a juggler. 'One of them rudely brushed me as he ran by. I and all my balls landed on the ground. Blessed be the saints I had forsaken juggling knives! Other than that, the man seemed harmless enough – save his attire. 'Twas not at all in keeping with that of folk seen at fairs or festivals. I wondered what he was about, but lost sight of him, and so resumed tossing my balls and collecting coins for my troubles.'

The jester recalled seeing some men also well-dressed wandering about. 'Aimless like. At the time I took no heed, but after what has happened their purpose is surely suspect. Be it likely *they* made off with the children?'

'Can you describe them?' Marc asked.

'Sorely, I cannot. I gave them but a moment's thought at the time.'

A troubadour said, 'We have wended throughout the whole of Brittany for years to all the major towns and many a village and hamlet.' The members of his company nodded accord. He continued, 'We know stories of many children taken – and n'er found.' A stream of corroborative murmur confirmed his statement. Several from the various groups spoke out in accord. One said, 'Aye, 'tis so. And mind, all this year we have also heard tales of children seized. As newly as this spring.'

Aghast, Marc asked sharply, 'Where was it in spring you heard this? How many?'

A minstrel answered, 'In truth, I heard of five that had gone missing – all boys. Our troop was in Nantes.' He signaled to a fellow singer. 'Here. You tell him. It was you who told me.'

'Aye, that be true enough, but there be little to tell. The father of one of the boys asked me if I had seen a child of six alone along the pathway. I was sorry to tell him I saw no such a thing and wished him well in finding his infant. Then he told me that four others were missing.'

'Did he say anything further?' Marc asked, masking his distress.

'That he did, sir. He told me, in all, his son was the eleventh child that had disappeared since January.'

Marc began to sweat. He glanced at Donan who looked stricken. 'Had they no knowledge of those responsible for the disappearances?'

'They were very wary. It seemed to me they did know something but were afraid to speak out. One of the servants of Baron Gilles de Rais I talked to in a pub told me a Scotsman took a child from the baron's house in La Suze.'

Marc flinched. *What was a child doing in the baron's household?*

Another actor spoke out. 'Our players were in Machecoul last November. There was much uproar about six children gone in the few days we were there. In that year, told was I, thirty had vanished without a trace.' He turned to his fellow thespians to validate his account. Affirmative mutters and nods expressed verification. Marc shook inwardly, but maintained an impassive expression, and dared to ask if anyone knew anything more. An actor from the bawdy play recalled an incident in Vannes. 'I saw a man outside an inn put a little boy – beautiful he was – on his horse and ride off. He was wearing fine garments. The boy was a peasant in rags. Curious, I told what I saw to the innkeeper. He said it could have been the duke's master of the choir, as he had only just left the inn, but he knew nothing about any boy.'

An acrobat said, 'Mind ye, sheriff, every town we have visited have their tales. Vannes, Nantes, Machecoul, Saint-Etienne-de-Montluc, Champtocé, Tiffauges. I believe I can say none here can tell you the number of children we've heard gone missing, but there were many, and the people were very fearful. Were I to guess on it, I would tell you that, in the past five years, hundreds of children were disappeared.'

'When you detained us, we were afeared you would suspect us,' called out one of the men.

Donan and Marc registered the information with horror. Both sensed this year, as five years before, Saint Petroc-sur-lac was to be the victimised town. Suppressing his distress, Marc asked imploringly, 'Were none of the children found?'

The manager of the mystery play troupe shook his head. 'Not as we know, sir. And neither did we hear of any caught for the crimes. Unnatural it is, very sorrowful, mind, but we never were troubled, since it seemed only children went missing. But like I said, very sad indeed – sinister in fact.'

Marc listened despairingly, but, though deeply troubled, he was satisfied the itinerants had told all they knew, and granted them permission to leave Saint Petroc-sur-lac with assurances any further incidents of missing children would be reported to him. 'Ay, sir, that we shall do,' said the manager of the comic players. 'Satan be at work, to be sure. We wish God's grace you find success in ending these wicked deeds.'

Marc and Donan gloomily sat in their office. They resisted the inclination to dwell on the anxiety they felt, and instead strained to develop fresh strategies. 'Donan, I want you to send deputies to the towns mentioned by the itinerants to determine what happened in each. I want to know the breadth of the investigations by the chief deputy in each region – dates of disappearances and the numbers lost each year. Good God, surely one of them found a missing child!'

'Once I have the mayor's permission, I shall go to Nantes and Machecoul. God willing, we all shall learn much we can apply to our own efforts here. I am right uneasy. I think an unspeakable terror is being visited on us once more. Me thinks the children lost to us lately is just the beginning. And God my saviour help me, at this moment I have not the least idea how to prevent their seizure.' Donan's expression reflected Marc's views. 'There is much to do. I want you to take command in Saint Petroc whilst I'm gone. You and the men are sore needed to prevent what I fear may fall on us.'

As Marc and Donan confer, an abduction is about to take place. A freckled lad, with the fine sculptured face of the Celtic people, Flann Fitzcathal walks absent-mindedly along the forested path on his way to town with a large, empty sack tossed over his shoulder. He inhales the

succulent aroma of late blooming osmanthus that sweetens the afternoon air.

As he nears the edge of the woods contiguous to the abbey fields, he sees a man through the trees on horseback riding in his direction – not unusual on this frequently traversed main road.

The boy arrives at a partial clearing in the woods where afternoon sunlight speckles the road and warms his face, but dims his vision. When he is but steps from the edge of the forest, he breathes in the floral scent one more time before stepping on to the main road towards town. He squints as he sees the rider approaching, noting his blue cape fluttering rhythmically in the breeze.

When the rider sees Flann, he reins in his horse to a loud nickering halt. Fleetingly looking around him, and satisfied no one is about, he spurs his horse into a full gallop, confusing and alarming Flann, who trembles as the snorting animal thunders towards him. He quickly backs off the road, ceding the road to the horse and its rider. To his shock, the horse heads directly towards him. Paralysed by fear, he stands, mouth agape, as the rider tugs hard on the horse's reins, triggering the grunting horse to rear. One of its fore hoofs crushing weight plummets on Flann's chest, and he drops to the ground screaming in pain.

The attacker draws the horse backwards to an agitated standstill. The boy, sprawled and unconscious on the ground, is now easy quarry. The man dismounts to pick up the limp body and throws it across his saddle. Remounting, he clips the horse into a gallop and races north. The sack, stained with fresh blood, and one of Flann's shoes lay abandoned, the only evidence he has been there.

By early the following morning, deputies to several towns had been dispatched. As Marc and Donan reviewed the particulars of Marc's planned excursion to Machecoul, a distraught Brennan Fitzcathal charged into the office and begged help. Marc feigned calm to soften the father's agitation. 'Please sir. What has befallen?'

'My son has disappeared. My wife and I spent a sleepless night. At dawn I took to the path that led to the main pathway to town. At that juncture I saw Flann's shoe and bag. It has dried blood on it. There are marks of horses at the site. He is lost to us; I am certain of it.' He tearfully gave the items he had to the sheriff.

Perturbed to hear of yet another disappearance, Marc asked Donan to fetch a horse. He said to Brennan. 'When my deputy returns, we three shall ride with hounds to the location. The dogs are sure to find the scent from the shoe and bag and even from the ground, and shall follow their lead us. We must hope they take us to the villains. Do not despair.'

As they waited for Donan to return, Marc made idle chatter. 'Forgive me, you are not Breton born. Have you been in this region long?'

Brennan shook his head. 'My family and I left Ireland this year to escape English tyranny, and settled just north of Saint Petroc-sur-lac. I keep a carpenter's shop. Flann is my apprentice, and skilled in tooling wood.' He took a laboured breath. I sent him to town for some supplies.'

Marc nodded, his head full of speculative thoughts. 'Where is your domicile?'

In the forest at the juncture that leads to Dinan and to Tréhorenteuc.'

'Tréhorenteuc!' Marc exclaimed. *Close to the Baron's chateau.*

Brennan looked perplexed. Just then Donan arrived with horses and hounds and the three men set off on a questionable rescue mission.

When they arrived at the point where Flann had been brutally assaulted, they alighted from their horses. Marc scrutinised the ground carefully, noting the scuffed earth, shattered leaves from trees, and stomach-turning patches of dried blood. He turned to Donan and noted he too had caught the implications.

Marc urged the boy's father to return to his home. 'We shall search for your son. Truly, sir, there is nothing you can do. We are trained to this. Take the horse and go to your wife. You are needed for solace. As difficult as it is for you, I beg your patience to wait for our report. I promise you one later this day. You best be at home with hope and prayers our quest will reap the reward of your son's return.' Reluctantly, with sorrow etched in the furrows of his face, Brennan nodded, and wordlessly turned the horse to the path that led to his cottage.

Marc brought forwards the dogs to sniff the shoe, bag and the earth that marked the place of the assault on Flann. The canine pack enthusiastically snouted about, bayed loudly, impatient for the hunt. They took command, and Marc and Donan, respecting their instincts, followed as they led them to a path into the forest. Frequent snuffles of the ground followed by grating yaps indicated the soil continued to deliver evidence. The sheriff and undersheriff were unmistakably on the trail where the horse and its unfortunate cargo had traversed. The animals abruptly veered right at a secondary road. Donan spoke nervously, 'Marc, this is the path that leads to the baron's château.'

'Aye, Marc said calmly. A territory forbidden us by the bishop.' Defiantly he said, 'I am not turning away, Donan.' Nodding to the dogs, he added, 'They are onto something, and we are following as far as they take us.'

They waited outside the keep after sounding the château bells. When a servant opened the grate of an average sized door incised from the carriage sized entrance gate, they asked to speak with persons of authority. Sometime after, a man stepped through the gate. 'My name is Poitou. I am the head of this household. What is it you want?'

'I am Marc Gervais, the sheriff of Saint Petroc-sur-lac. This is my deputy, Donan Cadoret. A boy went missing yesterday. Our dogs have the scent from the boy's shoe and bag. They led us to this place. I am here to interrogate your staff about this grave matter.'

The man called Poitou told him haughtily, 'What do you deduce? One of us has the boy? The baron will be sorely nettled by this impudent intrusion, and is sure to complain to the bishop.'

'Be that as it may, you will do as I say.'

Poitou looked disdainfully at Marc and Donan, hesitated, then said, 'I shall assemble the servants. There are many. It will take time. Wait. Here, outside the gate.'

Marc and Donan agreed the man's hostile attitude was but a prelude to the baron's reaction to their enquiry. Marc commented, 'The bishop to be sure will be told, and I am certain to be summoned. No matter. We are here with cause.'

When all the staff convened outside the gate, a lengthy enquiry ensued. Questions were forcefully put to the servants, with hopes an unguarded flicker of inconsistency in responses would reveal treachery. To no purpose. Not a scrap. Two of the servants said from time to time they gave food to orphan children and sent them on their way. All insisted they knew nothing about a missing boy. When all had been interrogated, the man Poitou stepped forwards and said contemptuously, 'Why ever would you suppose wrongdoing here? Please leave our property, Sheriff. Now!'

Dispirited nothing had been accomplished by their expedition, Donan was perplexed, for the hounds had been steadfast and confident as they stalked the scent. Marc was less so. 'Donan my suspicions increase. More than ever I think to go to Machecoul. There is nothing more to do now save hobble to Brennan's house.' They fell silent as Marc devised fabrications to relate to the family that would stave off despair.

Marc and Donan arrived at their headquarters to find a

courier from the bishop with a message that demanded Marc's immediate presence. A knowing glance transpired between them before Marc set off to the bishop's palace.

A biting reprimand ensued the moment Marc was in the bishop's presence. 'Vile wretch to infringe upon the baron's demesne! Singular knave to disobey a manifest prohibition. You not only disobeyed that interdiction, but brazenly all but accused his subordinates of monstrous deeds.'

Mark detailed the solid grounds he had to investigate at the castle, and moreover boldly declared he was not satisfied the servants told him with veracity what they knew of the matter.

'You will be told this just one more time.' fumed the bishop. You will *never* more go near the baron, his household, or his land in any manner. Insolence! Outrage! Gilles de Rais is known throughout the Duchy and all of France to be a devout and estimable servant of the Church who is favoured by the Holy See. Your trespass on his land is damnable! There is to be no further intrusion from you, Gervais. I warn you. Be prudent in this or suffer removal from office – and more. Prison!' Scornfully, he brandished a curt dismissal.

Marc had years ago been inured to angry tirades from the bishop, the mayor and the council, and was not surprised or intimidated by the rebuke. He was baffled on two accounts, however, and confided as much to Donan when he returned to his office. 'The bishop was informed of our enquiry at the château apace. I would deign to say he had been informed of it before we arrived in town. I have no doubt of it. That is suspicious.' He shook his head before continuing. 'And why is he so intent to prohibit the baron's demesne to us? It inclines me to greater qualms.' He conceded, however, that they would have to search elsewhere. 'We shall all the same set a watch at the border to the baron's land and question any persons who go beyond it. For the moment, I want to interview folk in town of what they know of the matter.'

Doggedly they pushed on, questioning and probing throughout the area – merchants, town folk and innkeepers, even passersby. All shook their heads and disallowed they had seen anyone suspicious. Marc believed many seemed evasive and uneasy. He wondered about that.

The deputies had not yet returned from Vannes or Montluc, but reports given to Marc from Tiffauges and Champtocé indicated, in the prior five years, more than forty children had been seized from each area. *The baron has castles there*, Marc thought unsettlingly.

His deputies had conferred with city authorities and had interrogated scores of people, but had learned nothing of substance beyond the fact those towns had suffered the loss of many children.

Marc prodded his men to describe the reactions of people whom they interrogated. The deputies cited exhibitions of reticence and taciturn reserve, confirming Marc's own impressions.

When the men returned from Vannes and Saint Etienne de Montluc, the senior deputy told Marc, 'Some of the merchants in Montluc mentioned something worthy to consider. They told me beggar children in the past had been a plague, snatching their wares and escaping 'ere the merchants knew what they were about. He told me that each year the numbers of these children and their thefts decreased until, as of last year, they ceased to be an annoyance. It baffled them the young robbers were all gone.'

Marc turned to another deputy. 'Did you hear this in Vannes?'

'In a manner of speaking, sir. We did ask two merchants if they knew of any children other than those who had been reported missing. They told us that beggars and orphans were no longer a nuisance. They did not know why this should be.'

Marc and Donan, speechless, considered the inferences and how they might apply to Saint Petroc-sur-lac.

Marc plunked two tankards of ale on a table in a quiet corner at the Herblain Inn and sat beside Donan on a bench. Shaking his head, he moaned. 'How could we have not considered beggars?' Donan nodded agreement such children would be the easiest to be kidnapped. 'That should have weighed heavily in our deliberations. By God's holy bones there must be innumerable missing children who have never been tallied.'

'A frightful thought, but, God's body, a sound one based on the reports from other provinces.'

'Would you agree the number of destitute children equal to those known missing?'

'Alas, very like. Such children make for easy prey.'

'Yes. Easy marks for the taking. Were there, five years ago, fifty-six seized by force from Saint Petroc, not twenty-eight as we had supposed?'

'Jesus' skin! Pray God, no.' Donan paused. 'But as I think on't – possible.' Donan responded lifelessly, struck dumb by the prospect. 'Holy Mary . . . .'

'And the numbers reported from Tiffauges and Machecoul! Jesu. Double *those* numbers too?' Marc leaped up and paced, and wrung his hands in anxious supposition. 'What in the holy name of Christ is the manner of evil that confronts us?'

'And confounds us!'

'Think this, Donan, we must assume such is likely to happen once again. Now. This year. Here in Saint Petroc.'

A momentary wave of lightheadedness washed over Donan. 'I quake to think it.'

''Tis cause for trembling indeed.' Marc paused to collect his thoughts as he sat down facing his deputy. 'I ask you, have you ever studied people's countenances when we question them?'

Donan shook his head. 'What mean you?'

'Looking over records, I recalled peoples' reactions, and of a sudden remembered that oft many seemed circumspect, wary. At the time I had assumed they were but affrighted. Now, five years on, I think they kept information from us. I saw fear in their eyes. In these last few days I have noted it again, as have several of the officers in other towns. What could it mean?'

'They are peasants, Marc, and we well know a fearful and superstitious lot by nature. It could be no more than that.'

'True. But think further. Suppose their mien reflects fright should they reveal what they know – fear of retribution?' Marc stood and paced the room. 'The fools! Were they to have trust, we might long ago have found those accountable. It boils my blood when I think of the hindrance their silence probably has been.' He signaled Aubert to replenish the tankards. 'How in Holy Writ could they think hiding information would keep them safe or help them recover their children? Damn them. They exposed all their children to harm.'

'Neighbours' children as well,' Donan exclaimed.

'Yea.' Marc washed his hand over his face nervously. 'Without their cooperation, I am without compass. I tread on quicksand.'

Marc visibly jolted as a galling thought crossed his mind. 'Sweet Christ. Should the mayor know I now seek information about missing beggars, he would have my head. Still, I am unmoved in what I intend. I must proceed with haste to Machecoul. You can be of great use to me, Donan.'

'Name the order.'

'Here is my thought. The stories told us by those wandering players blister my soul, but they are of inestimable value. Whilst I am gone I want you and a few carefully chosen deputies unknown to the town chatter with folk and gain familiarity – trust. I shall do the same in Machecoul. Merchants, innkeepers, men in taverns – especially men in taverns.'

'What you propose will take time. Folk do not readily welcome strangers. They will be wary should they be questioned.'

Marc shrugged. 'You give little credit to the power of flattery, Donan – and the enticement of coinage. We shall aim for newfound amity with money and bottomless drink. They will have persuasion on two counts – we shall be thought of as benefactors and the drink will slacken tongues and yield hearsay of great profit.'

Donan shook his head in doubt, but said, 'As you wish, Marc,' and added dryly, 'At least 'twill be a welcome change from forays through the countryside. Bless you for that.' He grinned. 'So. What would you have *me* do?'

'Supervise deputies unknown in Saint Petroc – and keep the peace in the town is all. Are we agreed?' Donan nodded. 'Good. I am full of foreboding.' Marc mused. 'Fearful evil is afoot nearby. We need guile and wit and more imagination than any of us singly possess to eke benefit. But together! Surely, we are crafty enough to trap folk who know more than they wish *us* to know. We *must* do! Tell the men to be most mindful of looks that mean to belie.' Marc clasped Donan's hand. 'Well . . . I leave it to you. As for me, as soon as Serrigond gives me permission, I swiftly go to Machecoul.'

17

A BLOODY INCURSION

Disturbing reports a large company of defectors from the French Valois army in Rennes heading southwest with Petroc-sur-lac in their direct path forced Marc to scuttle his design to leave town.

The dreaded *écorcheurs*. Their butchery was legendary. They had scorched and plundered the Norman and Breton countryside for years, robbing, raping women and young girls, stealing food and farm animals, and even fleecing victims' clothes. They were swift, thorough, and illusive, constantly on the run.

When first sighted in the vicinity of Saint Petroc-sur-lac, church bells throughout the area pealed a general alarm. The abbey ushered in citizens from the town to capacity before securing its gates, hopeful the scoundrels would fear the wrath of God were they to profane sanctified grounds.

An intervention to restore a semblance of control of the panicked multitudes who tried to escape from town was the first order of the day for the sheriff and his crew. That accomplished, the mayor delegated Marc Gervais, as a former soldier at arms, to direct the municipal and military guards and the many who volunteered to defend the town. Marc decided it was crucial to move his forces, armed for combat, into the fields surrounding the region in hopes of containing them there, away from Saint Petroc-sur-lac.

Bloody encounters left several of the detail dead and wounded, but a greater number of the *écorcheurs* became carrion for vultures that patiently circled in an aerial ballet over the dying and the dead. After days of fighting, the remaining marauders, like the vultures, picked clean many innocent victims who lived on the northern outskirts of town, leaving many households wasted and denuded. The troops of Saint Petroc-sur-lac fought hard and relentlessly. Each day's skirmish aimed to drive the invaders from the region towards another ill-fated locale. After having endured a great number of casualties, their numbers greatly diminished, Marc and his company contented themselves with the full retreat of the remaining band from the Saint Petroc-sur lac area.

As Saint Petroc's troops under Marc Gervais' leadership defended the region, cholera infected hundreds in the town. The stricken had fever, vomiting, diarrhea, and pallor. Town physicians treated their patients with the customary method of bleeding. Fifteen of those patients died. The abbey hospital overflowed with the sick. At Brother Lucien's instructions, aids administered hyoscyamus and poppy to quiet the bowels, willow for fever, and profuse amounts of liquids. All of those nursed in this manner recovered.

Lucien went to the neighbourhood that had the greatest number of people who were sick. He observed there was one source of water there and all who had fallen ill had drunk from that well. In contrast, those who drank water from other wells in town and the monks who drank from the abbey well did not succumb to the sickness. Lucien concluded the one specific well had been infected by some unknown *animaculae*.

He approached the municipal council with an appeal to close the well. The council examined the evidence Lucien set before them, and, although skeptical, conceded the one well might have foul water and agreed to seal it. . . in due course. There was no time for Lucien to speculate further on the matter, as casualties from the battlefield arrived at the Hôtel Dieu for treatment on the hour. Many injuries were blessedly minor, and responded quickly to poultices and poppy. Many of those savagely wounded died or suffered amputations of limbs and gross disfigurement.

Amongst the injured was Marc Gervais, who had been struck by an arrow in his shoulder. The injury was not grave, and Lucien attended to it before conscripting Michel to change dressings, cleanse the wound, apply healing ointments, and take him nourishment.

'I did not expect to meet again with you, Michel. How grown you are!' exclaimed the sheriff.

'I am Brother Lucien's apprentice, sir, and am thought to be competent.'

'That bodes well for me. I know your skill in ferreting out wrong doers, and now, to my surprise, I find you gifted in the healing arts,' Marc teased.

Michel refused the bait but smiled. 'I trust you will not find me wanting, sir,' he said modestly, and proceeded to treat Marc's wound in a professional manner as Marc told him about the battles in which he had been so recently engaged.

'A cruel waste, Michel. Mindless and tragic. We had no choice in the matter.' He mused sadly, 'Never have I gone to battle by choice. Men killing men. Senseless. Against God and nature.' He gritted his jaw as he thought of the carnage of war. 'A rotten lot, the *écorcheurs*. I sometimes fear the world never will be rid of them. Our hamlet, Aldrien, and my family were not disturbed, but a large area of the countryside is despoiled. They killed many of our combatants and innocent inhabitants as well. They were out for blood and spoil. I thank God we were able to fend off the bastards from the town, but . . .' He grimly shook his head as he thought of the carnage.

'Brother Lucien told me they have been overthrown and are in flight, sir.'

'Just so, but only to move towards other luckless provinces to violate them. Me thinks the Duke should gather his mighty forces against them.'

Michel's eyes widened. 'Do you think that will happen, sir?'

Marc sighed. 'Not likely, Michel. Not until they menace the Duke and his treasure directly. Power and money are what some in the world are after. You are well to be out of it here in the monastery!'

Nolwenn Gervais entered and happily embraced Marc. Her relief to see him healing well was evident. She took a moment to thank Michel for his devotion to the care of her husband, and offered him a basket of fruits and sweets as thanks for his pains. Michel blushed and demurred. 'Perhaps Brother Lucien can portion the gift to our patients, my lady.' He smiled and bowed a retreat to leave Marc and Nolwenn to a private reunion.

As he left, Michel heard Marc tell his wife that Brother Lucien had given him leave to return home the following day.

'Yea, but you must swear to rest until the wound is completely healed, lest I bid him detain you here further!' Nolwenn chided.

The mob of *écorcheurs* having been repelled, the people of Saint Petroc-sur-lac rejoiced. But just two days after what had been assumed to be a complete rout from the area, unbeknownst to anyone, three stragglers penetrated the barricade of the walled town and strayed stealthily through narrow lanes.

In just one day they broke into a wine shop, stole food from a store house and, as they wandered, looked for trouble. Looked for women. They raped three before Marc's deputies became alerted to their presence and formed a brigade to track them down.

The renegades quenched their thirst at the well marked for closure, and they drank wine until saturated. Their drunken meandering took them to a road that led to the cathedral. The vandals whooped when they saw a girl, who, turning to see them darting towards her, ran fast into the cathedral.

Michel was at the main altar collecting hardened wax drippings from candles that would be liquefied and made into candles again when the stamping of running feet broke the silence. He turned to see Claire race down the nave and heard yelling and cursing close behind her outside the cathedral door. He grasped a threat to her and ran from the altar to her side, took her hand, and pulled her to the steps that led to the crypt just as the three *écorcheurs* surged into the nave, stumbling and swearing.

Michel and Claire hurtled down into the shadowy gloom with only dim filtered light that penetrated through glass blocks placed years ago in the ceiling. They could hear boisterous shouts and the tramp of boots echoing above. Michel whispered, 'I know a tomb that is empty, and its cover is partially open. Hurry.' They reached the tomb and, with effort, squeezed into it. Echoes of stone grating against stone resounded throughout as they struggled to slide the stone lid shut. Still vulnerable to detection with a sliver of an opening, they pressed their bodies as far as from the gap as they could, and prayed. There was a momentary spine-chilling silence in the catacomb until raucous stomping down the steps that led to the chamber announced the presence of the scoundrels in the crypt.

Claire began to pant in panic. Michel reached over and gently placed a hand over her mouth. They remained quiet, but nothing could subdue the sounds in their heads of their pounding hearts. The piercing squeal of metal that suddenly grated across the lid of the vault that sheathed them stilled their hearts as, frozen, they feared discovery. No attempt to open the tomb allayed their dread, and they presumed an idle, frustrated scrape of a blade was all it had been... enough to inform them the men were close upon them.

'God's spleen! She stirs my blood!' One of the sleazes drooled.

'Shut up you whoremongering lump! Be still and listen. She's down here. We know that. We shall have her yet.'

A lengthy silence ensued. Claire and Michel did not move. They barely breathed. They could not be certain whether the men were still searching for them, had left, or had fallen asleep from alcoholic excess.

In the darkness, their sense of each other's presence grew more pronounced. Michel leaned over Claire's body to scour what could be seen from the not entirely closed tomb. In a far corner there were shadowy outlines of three men on the floor. They appeared torpid, for whatever reason he did not know, but he could not be sure they were unconscious or about to become so.

Michel whispered what he had seen. 'We must wait.' The growing awareness of Claire's warmth and breath aroused forbidden stirrings, and Michel realised Claire responded to them.

She felt Michel growing against her, and she began to breathe with anticipation new to her. In that black space they momentarily yielded to a passion that relieved their anxiety. Michel gently fondled her breasts and Claire felt Michel's throbbing member against her thigh. Aroused, she reached down to stroke it. Michel glided his hand inside her dress to explore her erect nipples. Claire elicited a restrained moan as Michel let his hand drift down until his fingers reached a furry down to explore. A moist, soft, private place.

A sudden awareness of wrongdoing simultaneously moved them to separate. Silently each considered the feelings they knew were inconsistent with principles they had been taught and believed. Their consciences aborted a moment of discovery and promise of ecstasy, and left them gutted with remorse. Awkwardly they waited in silence, with guilt as well as hope the peril that menacingly lurked in the crypt would retreat.

A sudden mêlée jolted them with fearful conjecture. They listened as shouts of several men rebounded off the walls. Michel peered through the opening in the slab and excitedly told Claire that the men were sentinels carrying torches. They battled – no, subdued – the varlets. The sheriff was there. They were safe. They shouted and hammered the lid of the tomb with their fists. It did not take long to be released from the tomb.

Marc listened raptly to their story, extolling their good sense. He explained the presence of his men and himself. 'Two women saw the blackguards reel towards the cathedral and reported them,' Marc told them 'We came immediately. I think you know you have been most fortunate.'

'Aye, sir, we are beholden to you. You saved our lives,' Claire whimpered as tears streamed.

'Be assuaged, child. You are no longer in danger. You can safely go home to your mother. One of my men will escort you. The *écorcheurs* all have gone, heading east and south. God help those who find themselves in their path. As for these three, they will regret not to have gone with their fellow outlaws. They will be charged with grievous crimes and will hang.'

To Michel, he smiled and said teasingly, 'Although it pleases me to see you again, Michel, it would appear I meet you in the most unlikely places. And so soon after your kind ministrations to me in the Hôtel Dieu. You must tell the abbot of this latest of your adventures. And pray give my salutations to all in the monastery.'

Michel fielded the chaff by saying with admonish-ment, 'Sir. Me thought you had been delivered from your sick bed on the promise you would rest easy at home!'

'Now, Michel, do not you be crabbed with me. My wife shares your view and has not been so polite in her rebuke. Truth be told lad, I feel fine . . . and, judging by today's events, I am sore needed here in town.'

'God knows, sir, I am ever thankful you *are* here.' Michel bowed low with a deep sigh of relief. 'I am ever at your service.'

Marc laughed at the solemnity. 'And I, sir, at yours!'

Bells chimed without surcease to announce a Mass of thanksgiving and comfort to victimized families as the three captured *écorcheurs* languished in the prison awaiting their trial. Not long after having been arrested, they became sick and, desiccated by extreme dehydration and unrelenting diarrhea, and further weakened by a physician's bloodletting ministrations, they died. Many called it divine retribution for the evil they had done.

Claire and Michel were relieved they were unharmed, but their moments of ardour left them penitent. Michel confessed to his mentor and priest he had violated his vow of chastity. He tearfully described to Fidelis in the confessional what had transpired in the sarcophagus, and professed contrition

Fidelis absolved him in the traditional manner of the sacrament, but took great pains to discuss with him the import of what had transpired. 'It was an occasion of sin, Michel – and an impulsive indulgence to feelings that are natural to all men, as the great philosopher, Abelard, noted. And yea, feelings natural to boys your age! You are now absolved from any wrongdoing by the sacrament of confession, but I think it provident that you meditate further upon the matter. You are but fifteen years of age, and have several years before you must decide your future path, but it may be meet to ask yourself now whether your vocation is to live a celibate, monastic life, or one centered on a wife and family. Perhaps that is what God wants for you when you are no longer bound to the monastery. You should pray on it. You have sufficient time to come to a determination on this crucial matter.'

Michel shook his head, quick to tell Fidelis, 'No, Magister. Before seeking you out to confess what happened, I did meditate, and thought and prayed hard on the matter. I have taken vows of chastity freely and willingly, and I am truly sorry for my transgression. I am certain. I have no doubts. I wish to dedicate myself to monastic life. I yearn for nothing more than to serve God by serving humankind.' He elected not to tell Fidelis that what he had experienced with Claire would always be a unique and welcome memory. He also realised that their presence together in school would never be the same.

Once the town had been saved from the *écorcheurs*, Marc faced another crisis. The parents of four boys, ages ten to sixteen, reported them missing. They told the sheriff the boys had gone to a nearby quarry to swim. 'The day was warm and sunny, and we saw no harm in it.'

The parents became apprehensive as night fell and none of the boys returned home. They and several neighbours searched the area, fearing they had drowned. The hamlet where they lived was under Marc's jurisdiction, and he went to the quarry with several deputies, where it was apparent the concern they drowned was unfounded, as there was no trace of their clothes or shoes. Marc concluded they were victims of an all too familiar crime.

He sent one of his team back to Saint Petroc-sur-lac to fetch the hounds. The dogs explored the area, and only tentatively nudged their masters to follow a trail to the north road. At some point it became clear the scent had vapourised, leaving yowling hunters aimlessly sniffing the ground, snaking around without purpose, whimpering in perturbation. Shy of any clues, Marc called off the chase, leaving him with nothing positive to report to the boys' parents. It was an undertaking he loathed, and he noticeably wailed. *Nine children under seventeen, two of them under five, vanished in a month. A fine accounting it will be for Serrigond.* He scoffed. *He'll not be inclined to grant any favours.*

When Marc met with the mayor, he related to him the order he had given his deputies to continue their investigations in town and in the surrounding region. He did not mention the bishop's interdiction regarding the baron's estate. He broached the proposition to investigate in Nantes, concealing his design to go Machecoul. He thought it prudent to omit his intended destination, the site of one of the castles of Gilles de Rais, since Marc now was convinced the authorities were protecting the baron, and the less they knew of his objective, the better.

'What do you mean you want to go to Nantes?' the mayor demanded.

'Your Excellency, the company of players who were here on the feast of the Assumption told us about children who disappeared within the last five years we had not considered. They also attested hundreds throughout Brittany have gone missing in the past nine years.'

Serrigond blanched. 'What are you saying? Hundreds? Impossible. *Nine* years? What are you talking about?'

'I come to that. First you must know that my men have gone to many towns. Authorities in each jurisdiction reported the number of children missing since that time. Including Saint Petroc-Sur-Lac, the number adds up to at least four hundred children.'

Serrigond blanched. Then bellowed. 'Impossible.'

'No. A certainty! The itinerant players at the festival told us that since March this year they know of many children who had disappeared from every Breton town they visited.' He paused and acknowledged, 'My report tallies eleven children reported missing from Saint Petroc so far this year.'

He paused to allow time for Serrigond to absorb the data. 'Truly you understand the importance of meeting with the sheriff in Nantes to discuss what has transpired there. It is a great city, and based on the information given us by a number of sheriffs in other towns, I am sure I will learn much that will help me in my quest here.'

Mayor Serrigond sat, visibly shaken. He said nothing as he worriedly sifted the information Marc had given him. Perspiration appeared on his brow. He looked frightened.

Marc dared to tell the mayor about the children gone who had never been reported. 'We know now beggars, gypsies and orphans also vanished. The roaming players informed us it was general knowledge in all the places where they performed that homeless and gypsy children were no longer seen, when in the past they were a persistent nuisance. We must suppose, as do the town merchants in those quarters, they were all abducted.' He added, 'And that would also have been the case here five years ago.'

'We shall assume no such thing, Gervais! What care I about riffraff and whelps? If they are gone, good riddance to them! My interest is only about children reported missing by their parents.' His voice resonated with anger, but his face registered terror.

Marc reluctantly confessed to the mayor that, as in the past, his investigations had been to date futile. 'I need to seek counsel in this. I must go to Nantes post haste.'

The mayor scoffed and taunted him with a familiar refrain of denunciations. 'This is not the first time you have made us look like imbeciles in this province. I remember well the incident years ago when you detained a nobleman. I shall repeat to you the bishop's warnings – tread very carefully, Gervais. I do not want to hear more of your recklessness.' Marc stood, endeavouring to appear contrite and penitent, allowing the mayor time to recover his composure. Jittery, Serrigond asked, 'How long will you be gone?'

Marc answered deferentially, 'Ten days, My Lord – perhaps a fortnight.'

'Two weeks, no more,' the mayor said grudgingly. 'Report to me as soon as you are back.' For want of an additional slur, Serrigond waved the sheriff out the door, left to cower from the information Marc had given him.

Marc arrived in Machecoul, located southwest of Nantes, and took lodgings at a local inn. He informed the innkeeper he was a sheriff, and was astonished, as the innkeeper gave him a key to a room, to hear someone behind him say sardonically, 'Welcome to Machecoul, the town where children get eaten.' He turned to see three men sitting on benches, tankards of beer in their hands, laughing.

Marc blanched. One man called out, 'You go to the castle? You won't find children there – the baron be long gone.'

'Why do you assume you I am going to a castle? What castle?' The man merely turned his back to Marc and laughed again.

The innkeeper said, 'You will get no cooperation here, Sheriff. We keep to ourselves in Machecoul. And we keep quiet.'

'Yet he mentioned a castle. Is it the Baron de Rais' castle? Will *you* tell me where I would find it?' The innkeeper thought a moment. Drawing Marc close to him, he whispered directions. Marc felt giddy. *Surely the innkeeper and his patrons associate the baron with children who have disappeared.* He swayed out of the inn. *As I thought! The baron!* He had little time to indulge in feelings of satisfaction for having found further inferences about Gilles de Rais' villainy. He giddily anticipated finding the evidence he needed to charge him and his cohorts at the castle, and he quickened his pace.

As he made his way there, he stopped to interview merchants and passersby to test his newfound suppositions. His chain of office attested to his authority, and all who answered his questions without exception exhibited a by now familiar unease and tension but avoided compromising or informative disclosures. Disappointed, Marc discontinued his attempt to interrogate anyone, and focused instead on finding the baron's castle.

The remote citadel was a good distance from the town, isolated and surrounded by forest. At the gate he unrelentingly tugged on a rope to activate the bells. The peals echoed dissonantly as did thuds when he hammered the entrance door with his fist. A toothless hag appeared behind him, seemingly from nowhere.

'You'll not find anyone inside. All gone, they be.'

'Who are you? Marc asked. 'How do you know there is no one here?'

'I live here, don't I? Not in the castle, but there, deep in the woods. Left to my own, I be.'

'You live on the castle grounds?'

'Aye, that I do. On castle grounds. They never find me. I be well hidden in the forest.' Her darting eyes and idiosyncratic behaviour unnerved him. She smacked her lips and wrung her hands constantly. She laughed – a cackle more than a laugh. She clutched one of Marc's hands and pulled him towards her. 'I know what happens here,' she crowed. 'Come. I'll show you.'

Marc thought the woman mad, but he was not going to miss a word she had for him. He hoped something of value would come from the encounter no matter how deranged he thought she was. She led him through the woods to a sizeable glade. 'There, there it be,' she said. 'There be where the goings on take place,' pointing to the clearing's treeless ground. She kindled Marc's interest further as she told him of children's agonized screams she had heard. 'Many times, I can tell ye.'

'What cries? What screams?' Marc demanded anxiously.

She beckoned him look at the dell. She pointed to the sky and then to the ground and said, 'I first saw it when the new moon appeared and the stones and stars were one. That's when it began.' She rocked, as in a trance, and crooned, 'When the night sky shone bright, with full beams of moonlight, aye, that's when the children cried – like wolves, they did, baying and howling at the moon. It feared me and I hid away. When it was quiet, I waited – a long time I waited. But I went back to see, careful like. I saw the stones – like I told you – on the ground. Five-pointed stars they were. And there were blood on the ground everywhere. Terrible it was. And eerie, I thought it – the stillness, when only a while back there had been but outcry.'

'Did you see anything else?' Mark asked hopefully.

'That I did. I went to a place at the edge of the wood

where the ground were broken, like plowing. Come. Follow me,' she chortled.

Marc saw nothing unusual at the site. The hag told him, 'When it were newly dug you could see it. Nature has hidden it, you see.'

She squinted. Her dull eyes were circled by yellow arcs of senility. 'Doubt me, do you?' she challenged.

Marc shook his head but was speechless. In truth, he was stunned by what she had told him. Stones, five-pointed stars. He was not sure what they inferred other than satanic rituals. Blood. Its mention revolted him. But he wanted to know more.

'I was great afeared and ran from the place,' she said. 'I went many times before I swore not to go there more. Don't you tell . . . don't you tell!' And she ran into the woods, leaving Marc aghast, bewildered, and perturbed. Marc analysed what the mad woman had told him. Who would believe her babble? Yet there *was* physical evidence in the clearing of manmade disturbance of the earth. It was hardly compelling or indicting, but suspicious enough to be pursued. He realised a visit to the town's sheriff was overdue. He wanted to give an account of the encounters he had had in the town and at the castle, and to listen to what the sheriff knew regarding Machecoul's missing children.

Sheriff Eadric Herán was cynically casual about telling Marc specifics of kidnappings in Machecoul. 'Twenty boys and six girls went missing last year. In five years, in sporadic incidences,' he surmised, 'a hundred – a hundred and fifty? I lost count.'

Marc's mouth went dry. 'Have you accounted for the disappearance of beggar children?'

'Oh, then double the number.' Herán smiled sneeringly.

'The hag in the forest told me she heard children

scream. How was that not detected by those in the castle or heard by others in the area?'

Herán shrugged. 'No one lives in that area, and it is very like the baron sent his household ahead of him.' Marc reflected on the logic of Herán's explanation, but insisted people in the town must have had suspicions.

'It be idle to hope for hearsay in this town. Anywhere, for that matter. No one will talk, not even those who had children taken from them. They be enfeebled from fear.'

'They fear the wrath of Gilles de Rais, don't they?'

Herán raised his eyebrows expressively but said nothing.

Marc asked him pointedly, 'Where is the baron and his entourage now? I know they are not in Machecoul. I thought for a time he was at his castle near Tréhorenteuc, but I found only a handful of his vassals there.'

Herán paused. 'It is rumoured he be at Tiffauges. He has not been here for a long time.' he said pointedly, 'Or he could be in Tréhorenteuc despite what you think.'

'Why do you say that?' Marc was horrified at the thought.

'He is cunning. He has the protection of those in power, not to mention bootlickers. I would not put anything past him.'

Marc's head spun with the impact of Herán's confirmation that Baron Gilles de Rais was the kidnapper and murderer he had been pursuing for years. He was incredulous the sheriff behaved with casual detachment about so gruesome a matter. He controlled wild emotions and calmly asked, 'I take it no more children have disappeared here for some time.'

Herán hesitated but admitted that was the case. He smiled acidly and added, 'Not since the last time the baron was in residence.'

Marc was crestfallen. He outlined to Herán all the information he had amassed from the many jurisdictions his deputies had visited. Conjoined with what Marc had uncovered, the Baron Gilles de Rais was irrefutably guilty of crimes beyond scope and imagination. Marc said, 'I can show you a site on the castle grounds where I believe many of these children are interred.'

'There is nothing there. Gone years ago. We had long been aware of the baron's, shall we say . . . irregular ways. Hah!' He spat contemptuously. 'There was much lively rumour at the time you see, and we scouted the area thoroughly. Dug up forty bodies at one point. Found evidence of fires where bodies probably were burned. We shall never know how many.' He let the information sink into Marc's mind. It mildly amused him to see the disturbing effect it had on him. 'That is when we were forbidden to enter the baron's property.' Herán shook his head in disgust. 'So, you must understand, I cannot now go with you even if there were new evidence. The interdict stands.'

'Incredible! You discovered countless murdered children's bodies on the baron's land and higher authorities, civil and ecclesiastic, did nothing?'

'I did not say that Sheriff. I told those who rule over us what I knew and was censured for my efforts, is all,' he said sullenly. 'And you? Have you not encountered – shall we say – impediments?'

'Aye. To be sure. The local bishop has warned me keep off the baron's lands. Look you! These bishops *know* the baron is implicated in these crimes. Why do they protect him? This flies in the face of justice. Are they all so corrupt?'

Herán shrugged. 'Say what you will. There's nothing to be done. I've given up trying.'

'So. You will not come with me to the castle to unearth evidence.'

'No. I told you. I cannot. And should you try, my instructions from higher-ups would mandate I arrest you – although I am disinclined to do so.' Herán said tartly, 'You must accept it. Neither one of us can defy the bishops.'

Marc stood, confounded and mystified. When he regained his composure he said resentfully, 'It would appear I have no choice then to bid you farewell and return to Saint Petroc-sur-lac. I will tell you this – I scorn the bishop's interdiction. I shall search for burial sites at the baron's château near my town. From what you say, there will be absolute proof of the baron's guilt. They may arrest me, but I *shall* do this.'

'Do as you like, and I wish you well, good fortune, and God Speed! I think you ask for great trouble in this for yourself. I hope I am wrong. One thing: be there evidence such as I have told you that does sway your bishop, be assured of my support. Should you be chastised, as was I, hope you will keep my name out of it.'

18

PILGRIMAGE DISRUPTED

The monastic community of the Abbey of Saint Benedict in
Saint Petroc-sur-lac accepted an invitation from Abbot
Sebastian of the Abbey of Saint Sulpice near Dinan, a
repository for a precious first-class relic of Saint Benedict
of Narsia in the form of a gold palm frond with a crystal
windowed case that contained what was believed to be his
carpal bones. In their refectory hung a life-sized mural of
Saint Benedict holding a cracked flacon of wine. The
painting's theme recalled the legend that Benedict had
blessed a cup of wine and instantly detected poison in its
contents. The flacon cracked, and the contaminated liquid
spilled harmlessly to the floor.

Prepared for a five-day pilgrimage, the monastic community assembled at dawn in the cloister. Abbot William
surveyed his monks and said. 'We shall go by way of the
north gate from town onto the main pathway towards Dinan
at a steady, but easy pace. Brother Cook and his staff have
filled a cart with victuals and skins full of wine, beer and
cider.'
    The tallest of the oblates, Michel stood at the head of the
procession holding a stanchion that boasted the abbey's
standard. Two acolytes and a cross bearer were directly
behind him. The abbot and his dean followed and, behind
them in a paired column, were monks, and finally Prior

Fidelis, followed by the oblates. Oblate Tristyn trailed the entourage, appointed to guide the carted horse.

The day was warm with a bright sun that shone in a Tiepolo sky. Trees bore signs of seasonal change, and occasional zephyrs animated leaves with a flutter that produced melodic crooning. The pilgrims intoned hymns of praise to God as they ambled northwards. When they reached the fork in the road, Michel recalled that the right fork led to the heavily forested land of the Baron Gilles de Rais where the rotted wood for the black potion had been collected, and he thought of Brother Lucien's damning indictment of the baron that had so disturbed him.

The procession branched left, and passed Marcel's slaughterhouse. He, his wife Marilu, and three daughters, Felicia, Eileen, and Fenella, had assembled to greet the sojourners with freshly baked buns and cider. The pilgrims lingered a while to enjoy the treat and the welcome respite and, buoyed by waves and cheers, they continued onwards. After several hours of walking, a cool, shady glade beside a waterfall that spilled into a gamboling stream invited the entourage to rest and slake their thirst. Brother Cook's tasty morsels were consumed in an agreeably festive atmosphere in which, with permission to converse, animated banter reflected lighthearted humour.

The wayfarers reached the Abbey of Saint Sulpice in time for Vespers, then supper, followed by recreation. Despite their fatigue, they reveled in the camaraderie of their *confrères,* who mingled convivially as if with old friends. The oblates spent the time comparing the quality of life in their respective monasteries until bells heralded Compline. After selected prayers and antiphons in the cathedral, all retired for a well desired rest.

The following day was observed by all in quiet meditation, save for the observation of the Divine Office during the day in the chapel and the familiar routine of silent meals.

A solemn feast day procession through the town took place the next morning. The people of the town lined the main thoroughfare as priests, monks, and oblates chanted litanies to Mary and Saint Benedict, and crowds responded with the melodic strains of *Ora pro nobis*. As the last oblate passed them by, the revelers joined the procession to the cathedral for the solemn High Mass and after, a final ritualistic homage to the relic of Saint Benedict in a solemn forward moving cavalcade, as the organ's sonorous strains reverberated throughout the resplendent candlelit Gothic edifice. The congregation passed by the holy relic mumbling prayers, making the sign of the cross, and genuflecting.

When the ceremonies ended, leaving the cathedral to its silence, the monastic group retired to the monastery where the two abbots presided over a sumptuous meal followed by a recreational period in which all lauded the events of the awe-inspiring day.

An interim day of repose before heading back to Saint Petroc-sur-lac, though restful, did not restore the pilgrims' energy. The older monks especially felt sapped after the long trek and the activities of their celebratory visit. Nevertheless, the reluctant retinue, after customary expressions of civil niceties that expressed gratitude for the exceptional hospitality given them, took their leave of Saint Sulpice and began to process slowly south. Taking refuge at midday in a grove was a welcome relief. They gathered beside a brook, where the sweet murmur of the water that glided over smoothed stones lulled all into a drowsy tranquility, and languidly, they munched on rustic bread, cheeses, and fruit, drank refreshing beverages, and savoured the sojourn from the wearying march. Time passed, and Brother Simeon worriedly approached Abbot William with his sundial. 'Our homeward pace should continue at a quickened step, for we are sure to meet the night well before we reach the abbey.'

William nodded and signaled a continuation of the walk to their abbey. As the day progressed, the gait of the monastic flock slackened, their energy depleted by what felt like an interminable hike so soon after the pilgrimage had begun. Tristyn, with the now empty cart and horse, trailed the group, and, imperceptibly but consistently, the distance between him and the others increased. By the time they reached the fork in the road that led to Saint Petroc-sur-lac, Tristyn was so far behind, his appeals to slow down could not be heard, but merely echoed off boulders on the side of the road.

Dark, in a quarter moon sky, the ebbing light of day had long petered out and the pilgrims were only at the abbey's fields. The town and its mighty wall could only hazily be seen in the distance.

Finally, the procession ended in the refectory where the kitchen staff that had volunteered to stay behind to cook them a welcoming meal was presented as a more than usual exemplary treat. The voluminous evening repast was devoured, not eaten, by the grateful travellers. The lector's reading was the entire Rule of Saint Benedict.

Michel's spirits were buoyant even amid the community's silence until he realised Tristyn was not at the oblates' table. He scanned the entire refectory on the unlikely chance he was in another area. When certain Tristyn was not there, he approached Fidelis.

'Magister. I have something of import to tell you. Tristyn is missing.'

Abbot William and Prior Fidelis considered the possibility Tristyn had simply fallen behind and would soon arrive at the abbey. As they debated the point, apprehension encroached upon them. William dispatched two monks north to look for Tristyn. When they returned, their report bode ill. 'We rode to the fork of the pathway, but there was no sign of the boy. We went beyond, to Marcel's abattoir, but he had not seen him. We made a hasty return to tell you this.'

William blanched at the news, and sent mounted monks to the sheriff's headquarters to request a search party, resisting what he knew would be a futile gesture to himself tread the darkness on the north road in search of the oblate.

Hours later Michel, still awake and alert in his cot with diminishing hope Tristyn would be found, prayed fervently. Sleep finally triumphed over anxious watchfulness, and soon thereafter the bells for Prime jarred him awake. Fidelis entered the dormitory and told the oblates that Tristyn had not been found. Neither was there a sign of the horse or cart.

The entire day in the abbey was chaotic; the quotidian routine of monastic life completely disrupted. Sheriff Marc Gervais had not yet returned from Machecoul, and Donan and two others assumed the duty to question the monks and oblates. The hope was that, however slight, information helpful to the enquiry would surface.

The chapel was full of monks in prayer. There were continual appeals to Mary the Mother of God, to Saint Joseph, and to Saint Ran. Rhythmic clicks of rosary beads and voices that intoned litanies to the Virgin resonated throughout the chapel the entire day.

By nightfall, Michel's distress mounted to torment. The haunting awareness that not one child who had disappeared from the region had ever been found advanced his fear to a frenzy.

He concentrated on the details of the prior evening – most particularly that moment, now indelible in his mind, when he last saw Tristyn. He was able to envisage clearly that had been at the fork of the road, when he had casually turned around to see Tristyn well to the rear of the procession.

A chance hoot of a night owl reminded him of a debate about a muted shriek he had thought was a scream when his crew foraged for rotted wood in the forest. Satisfied at the time by Lucien's theory it was a squeal of a pig being slaughtered at the baron's castle, Michel now inferred a much more sinister explanation. *The fork way close to Baron de Rais' chateau!*

He tried to reconstruct the conversation that had taken place about the baron Gilles de Rais. *What was it Lucien told me about the baron when both were at Orléans?* It had soundly and pejoratively affected his opinion of Brittany's hero. *What was it Lucien had said? Vain . . . ruthless and – he strove to get it right – 'He truly enjoyed the killing.'* Lucien had shaken his head and shuddered.

Michel began to sweat. Unsettlingly, He recalled the number of times the north road had been cited as the last place children kidnapped had been seen. The baron's castle was to the north. *'He truly enjoyed the killing.'* Whenever Gilles de Rais was not in the region, no children had been abducted. When he and his men were in residence at his château, talk about abductions became widespread. Michel was shaking with premonition. *The baron. But of course.* Michel was sure of it. He leaped out of his bed to seek Lucien to tell him his qualms and halted, aware of the infraction it was to leave the dormitory without permission. He reasoned that, in any case, no one believed what a mere boy had to say. He could not, however, contain his anxiety, and decided this was a dire emergency.

He ran to Lucien's cell to rouse him with his suppositions. As coherently as he could in his distressed state, he told Lucien of his suspicions. Lucien stared, motionless, and sifted the information carefully, incorporating it with conclusions of his own. 'I believe you are right. I *would* have told you that. Your argument is compelling.' Lucien and Michel looked at each other with trepidation. Lucien concluded there was nothing to be done for the moment. 'The deputy will arrive after Prime, and you can tell him your theory. I shall stand at your side to support you.'

Donan was disturbed by the boy's assertions and the monk's corroboration. He said edgily, 'You are talking about the most famous of men in Brittany.'

'Surely that is not pertinent,' Lucien answered.

'Oh, but it is. The bishop has forbidden any intrusion on the baron's privacy.' Donan hesitated before telling them, 'The sheriff and I face excommunication should we disobey his interdiction.' He sighed and wiped his sweat drenched face. *I wish Marc were here to deal with this!*

He paused before confessing he and the sheriff had had just such misgivings despite having found nothing untoward at the castle. 'It is conjecture only. Without proof, I cannot act on this, as much as I wish to. The bishop would destroy me.' He touched Michel's hand. 'I am sorry, lad. I know you fear for your friend.' He tried to give Lucien and the boy assurance the search would be steadfast and thorough. 'At this moment there are men and hounds in the field, resolute in their commitment. When we finish our work here, we shall join them. I promise you we are doing all we can to find the oblate.'

As they walked away, Michel and Lucien agreed Donan's pledge lacked substance. 'Brother, what can we do?'

Lucien looked plaintively at Michel and answered, 'It appears we can do nothing.'

19

SUBTERFUGE

Flustered and anxious, Michel conceived a plan of action he knew would be a mortal sin in the mind of the monks – and God. He would go to the baron's château.   The illicit nature of this resolution challenged his conscience to the core but certain the posse's efforts would be fruitless as had always been the case, and having been told of the bishop's edict that forbade access to the baron's property, he felt it was left to him to attempt a rescue.

He dejectedly was mindful what he intended was the gravest breach of abbey rule that would place his soul in peril, but he worried more about the peril Tristyn faced. He grappled with the conflict of obedience to Benedictine rule and the love for a friend, and hoped he might annul the gravity of his sin with confession and absolution – but only after the deed was done.

He was tempted to confide in Lucien and Fidelis but feared they would forbid him to go. *Better to go without an injunction.* This resolve weighed heavily, for he knew he would lose what he most valued – the trust Lucien and Fidelis had in him. He trembled at the thought they would revile his violation of the vows he had taken. Miserable in a quagmire of duplicity, he nevertheless resolutely kept to his decision. He prayed Blessed Mary would intercede for him and help him find Tristyn and, praying for courage and fortitude as well, he calmly resigned himself to accept the consequences of disobedience to abbey rule, mindful of the compounded disappointment there would be from past misdemeanors he had committed. *This will cost me any hope of medical studies in Padua I might have had.*

One of Michel's duties was to take the remains of the unspoken for dead to the common pit outside the abbey, inter them, and cover the bodies with lime. The following morning presented him this chore and offered him opportunity for action. The occasion chanced on the feast of the birth of the Virgin Mary.

Michel thought it a good omen to set about his quest on Mary's day, and fortuitous, since the abbot, Fidelis, and Lucien would be busily engaged in the annual ritual related to Our Lady of the Grape Harvest in which winegrowers brought their best grapes to be blessed and placed grape clusters in Mary's hands and around the base of her statue.

Just before dawn Michel dragged a cart with two bodies in it towards the pit. On the horizon he saw the black of night progressively blend with an ever-intensifying orange hue of a new day. He was quick to his task, but in his haste to retreat from the abbey, he neglected to cover the bodies with lime. It was too late to go back, and Michel hoped the lapse would not be noticed.

He stayed to the backfields. Moisture that clung to early morning grass and leaves evaporated from the heat of the now bright sun in a cloudless sky by the time he arrived at the fork in the road where he last saw Tristyn.

Certain no one was in view, he took to the thicket, noiselessly sidling parallel to the path that led to the baron's château. He pricked a finger on a sharp twig in the dense darkness of the forest and stemmed the flow of blood with his scapular, regretting it instantly, as the image of Mary was now stained with his blood.

He stumbled in the underbrush over a stump of burnt wood, and saw another small piece that had a faint etching. Michel picked it up and identified it as a charred piece of the monastery's cart. The Abbey of Saint Benedict that had been carved into the wood had been blistered away, leaving a scrap with an enigmatic 'Sa . . . c' engraved on it. He put it in the pocket of his habit. It was evidence Tristyn had been there. The chilling possibility he too had been burned to ashes enveloped Michel with anguish. He rummaged around the site, and sighed relief there were no signs of human remains.

He heard horses' hoofbeats, and zipped behind a tree with an eye to the road some distance beyond. As riders passed by, he muffled a startled impulse to yell out when he saw they clasped two small children. Heart thumping, he felt blunt terror. Fear disguised as doubt perturbed him as he wondered what good he could do against grown, armed men. He struggled for breath as his apprehension soared. He was unable to move. He was alone and frightened.

Toughening his nerve, he slowly forced a step further into the thicket. Swallowing hard, he doggedly moved as silently as possible for what seemed like forever until, sheltered from view by the tangle of dense woodland, he was close to the château. He halted when he heard men's voices permeate the atmosphere, chanting disturbing intonations followed by sudden screams – crazed shouts full of pain and dread. He restrained an instinctive impulse to flee, and instead stood motionless.

He subdued a growing panic with controlled breathing and will power. With indescribable trepidation, he steadied himself for his undertaking, remembering that the screech he had heard years ago was exactly what he had come for now. He steeled himself to confront whatever evil that lurked about. He was saturated with perspiration, and thorns insistently snared his habit, impeding his progress. Michel ripped it off and let it fall to the ground.

He moved forwards, shaking, and advanced cautiously until, still in the thicket, he saw a clearing and heard slurred – drunken – voices, like those of the *écorcheurs* who had stalked Claire. He kept close to the trees until he was adjacent to the glade, careful to keep well hidden.

He curbed the impulse to go to the rescue of the piteous whimpering and crying children he heard, ruled by awareness of the futility of doing so. He realised any advantage his presence had would be lost. He remained motionless, well shielded from detection, and scanned the area. He saw opportunity to move safely forwards until he could see into the clearing. He canvassed the site and faltered, his heart pounding, his stomach roiling.

There was a large pentagramme star marked with stones on the ground, and horrified, he saw on each of the five points was a bound, immobilised child's naked body. Behind them were pikes with the decapitated heads of ten children. Michel's revulsion was greater than his incredulity.

The images were too hideous for his mind to absorb, and his body revolted at the sight. He gave way to retching, struggling to mute the sounds that emanated from his body as his stomach continued to contract and spew its odoriferous substance until there was barely anything left.

Desperate to act, he stood concealed behind a tree, aware he could do nothing useful. Horror-stricken, he internally reminded himself of his purpose there, and forced himself to scan the hideous sight, with faint confidence he would see Tristyn. He wondered how he might save him if he did see him. Cringing, petrified, he anxiously assessed the situation, recognising with an ever-escalating sense of certainty there was little hope for rescue of anyone including himself.

He shook with wild fright, but forcefully subdued his body's mutiny until he felt able to move stealthily even closer. Remaining out of sight, he stopped when the men in the clearing, richly dressed, but erratic and stumbling, roughly groped captive children. Michel listened helplessly in silent agony to desolate cries for mercy.

One of the men had a boy by the neck with a dagger pointed to his throat. Another stepped forwards. 'No, no . . . dog of Lucifer. Christ's ballocks! You must prick him lightly. Bah. Out of the way. Poitou! Take the knife. Show him how to do it,' he snarled. He moved on to another of the sacrificial victims and a sodden drunk who stood over the child. 'Out of the way, you piss ant. You killed the last one too soon. You must make the puncture small, just enough to make the body spasm, but not kill.' The man staggered groggily. 'Turd-faced drunken dog. Move aside.' He opened the codpiece of his britches and lay over the child. Deftly, as the boy struggled and screamed, he thrust the dagger into the boy's throat.

The child coughed blood, and foam from the puncture wound gushed from his gullet. The pitiful child urinated and, voiceless, emitted silent screams. The man's seed spattered on the child's belly as more blood and foam spilled from the child's now collapsed larynx, and his body quivered, shook violently and convulsed. Having reached an orgasm, the man laughed demonically, took the knife, and slit the boy's throat.

What had been a terrified, tortured human being was now a limp sack lying in a pool of his own blood. The body quivered one more time and was still. Death had released him from his torment. The killer's flaccid penis protruded from the codpiece as he howled satanically. He severed the boy's head from his body with a knife, and kissed his sad victim's lips with ardour.

Michel recoiled, repulsed by the abomination, and stricken with nausea, gave way once more to a silent expelling of residual vomit that left him drained, stunned, bereft of the capacity for thought and action. Instinct pressed him to remain out of sight as his mind strove to grasp the reality of what he had witnessed.

He laboured to regain his wits, and forced a glance into the diabolical scene in the clearing. He smothered a scream at the sight of the perverted killer. *Giles de Rais*. Michel was near faint from the repugnance of what he had witnessed and the shock of having confirmed the identity of the murderer.

With formidable effort, he remained immobile and hidden, constraining himself to focus his search for Tristyn, with hope thereafter to escape from that vile place. A redoubtable task, as atrocities continued before his eyes. He resisted impulses to race away from the evil by turning his face away from the slaughter. His mind rebuffed further absorption of the ghastly images. With closed eyes, he covered his ears to muffle the sounds of agonised voices, and desperately tried to think of a means to extricate himself from the horror. He exerted every effort to regain a modicum of self-control by repeating over and over in his mind that he must do something, anything to stop the foul and vile defilements transpiring so close by. He wrestled urges to confront the evil with equally powerful resistance to make his presence known, realising that would put him in equally mortal danger and achieve nothing. Longing to cry out, he suppressed the urge by covering his mouth tightly with his hands.

A sudden cessation of children's screams enabled him to recover a semblance of control, and he compelled his eyes to examine the faces of each of the now dead children. Sorrow was greater than the gratitude that none of the victims was Tristyn, and he sobbed voicelessly until there were no tears left.

He once again visually scouted the clearing and its periphery. His heart pounded so violently he feared it was audible and, despite his caution, he suddenly uttered a cry. Incredulously, he saw Tristyn tied to a tree at the edge of the clearing, and prayed it was not a hallucination.

All other thoughts dissolved from his mind as he quickly calculated the distance between them to evaluate if it was possible to dare a rescue. He was relieved to see dense thicket directly behind the tree to which Tristyn was bound. He studied the ropes and dared hope he could loosen them. He looked for other children similarly trussed to trees but saw none. He surmised Tristyn was to be the next – and last – victim and, overwrought, prayed fervently, pleadingly.

He conquered mounting terror with force as he scoured the clearing. He sighted the degenerates on the far side focused on an obscene ritual, and dared to rejoice. It was the opportunity he needed to release Tristyn and retreat from the inferno in which they found themselves. His mouth was dry, and he could scarcely breathe, so great were his excitement and fear. He controlled thoughts of peril and failure and trusted, with another silent prayer, he had the means as well as the will to accomplish the rescue.

He moved furtively through the thick copse until he stood just behind Tristyn, concealed from view. The debauchers were still on the far side of the clearing with only their backs visible, their inebriated voices incanting raucous and weird, dissonant chants.

Although rattled beyond imagining, he whispered into Tristyn's ear to stay still. Tristyn flinched and stiffened, expiring a breath of newfound hope. He strained to remain motionless and hold back the tears that threatened to spurt from his eyes as Michel slowly loosened the ropes.

Michel whispered he would signal him to back away into the shielding density of the woods when he was completely unleashed. He steeled himself, wiping sweat from his brow, and uttered softly, 'Now!' With an understanding his escape depended on silence as well as cunning, Tristyn idled back guardedly into the thicket unnoticed.

Michel counted on avoiding detection long enough to grope through the forest to safety. It was a huge gamble. Michel had determined the direction towards which they should go and silently took Tristyn's hand as a signal to step further back. Once embraced by the shelter of the thicket, Michel rethought his plan. He knew when it was detected Tristyn was gone, men on foot would troll the woods. He was grateful the density was such no horse could enter. He reasoned time had so far been on their side thanks to the drugged and drunken condition of the murderers. The oblates moved furtively but as swiftly as possible through the thicket, putting as much distance between them and the hell they had left behind.

When well away, shouts and enraged curses that Michel had anticipated assailed their ears, and paroxysms of dread coursed through each of the boys, pressing them to greater speed, encumbered as well as protected by the dense vegetation. They could hear distant voices and sounds of feet thumping. Then a shout, 'Christ's nails! It be the habit of an oblate. They go to the monastery. To horse!'

As they heard horses take to the path in a gallop, other sounds grew fainter, and finally could not be heard at all. Less panicked, the escapees shimmied through the forest in an erratic pattern as an evasive maneuver. They could not be sure their pursuers on foot had desisted searching for them. Their course took them daringly close to the main road that led to the town.

Audaciously, they kept it in view, careful to use the thicket as camouflage as they moved forwards. They relied on gestures rather than speech, but Michel finally broke the silence and murmured, 'Rotten chance they found the froccus. Now they know where to look for us.' He shrugged wearily. 'Can't be helped,' and he looked to the sky. 'Soon the sun will be fading. The halfmoon's light could work against us, but we may be able to use the shadows to our profit.'

The boys stumbled upon a small cave near a stream, and hid. It was close to the monastery's open fields. The refuge provided time for Michel to think how they might get to the abbey and safety. Tristyn beside him strained to contain sobs, and Michel put his arms around his shoulders and held him fast. He felt edgy, and lamented no matter what route they chose, the clear advantage was on the side of their iniquitous adversaries on horseback. They waited nervously, each with his own images of the wickedness they had seen, as the late afternoon sun tired and began its slow descent. Birds' chirping as they sought perches on which to roost for the night ceased, replaced by an unnerving silence.

In the distance, monastery bells began to knell, and soon after darkness encroached as Michel tensely formulated a strategy. Some time passed before he whispered, 'Now we can move on. Let me go first to the pathway, and, if there be no horsemen in sight, I shall signal you to follow me. We must quickly cross over to the wheat field, and, with God's grace, the height of the grain will shield us from view. We have to stay crouched, low to the ground and crawl.' Michel swallowed hard. 'It is very risky.' Tristyn nodded, fully understanding the danger.

Prone, the tall wheat waving in the evening breeze sheltered them from view. Michel and Tristyn grated the earth with their hands and feet as they thrust forwards on their stomachs. When they arrived at the edge of the field, they could see the town wall and the rear door to the abbey. Michel gauged the location of the burial pit from where they hid. There was a wide buffer of grass between the wheat stalks, the pit near the main road, and the monastery door well to the right, with only shadows of the wall to provide minimal concealment. Michel lamented it seemed to be a forbidding distance away.

They heard hoof beats striding the city wall, treading slowly as their pursuers scrutinised the area. The oblates stayed low in the wheat field, barely breathing. The thuds of hoofs and squeaks of leather bridle seemed terrifyingly close. They were such a small distance from detection and death or refuge and safety.

The men in pursuit dallied further east to the north road. They moved close to the wall towards the town's gate but kept in the shadows to avoid detection. Two guards and their horses were on duty at the portcullis, closed for the night. Four guards were posted on the battlement.

Michel decided the distance between them and their pursuers gave an opportunity to bolt. 'Tristyn, run quietly but as fast as you can to the monastery door, then pound on it with all your might and scream loud enough to wake the dead. The night watchmen should be close within. If vigilant, they will take action without delay. Should you be detected before the door is opened, I shall zoom forwards with raucous sounds. That will confuse the churls, and perhaps divide their ranks and slow them down, but only for a little time. With luck, and should God will it, the town's guards will react to the disturbance and set upon them, giving me time to join you – hopefully within the monastery.'

Tristyn gasped skeptically, but nodded assent. He silently darted off, keeping to the wall, enveloped by shadows. When he reached the monastery's entry door, he brazenly let out piercing screams and battered the door with his fists. There was no sign of the horsemen, so Michel raced at full speed towards the north wall with hopes he could reach the monastery door as well. With sinking heart, he heard galloping hoofs and knew the assailants were headed in the direction of the monastery door that had not yet opened.

Michel veered course towards the open pit, shrieking and screeching. As he ran, he heard a whiz tease his ear, and saw an arrow strike the ground just paces ahead of him. The hoof beats were fast upon him now. An inspired impulse directed him to the open pit where he prayed he might wedge himself between the two bodies he had placed there in the morning. He guessed where he had deposited them and hoped that, with no lime cover, he would sustain minimal burns to his body.

He arrived at the edge of the foul-smelling pit, and covered his face with his *camisa* when an arrow gashed his left arm that so weakened him, he plummeted into the mound of putrefying bodies. Dizzy from the pain and nauseated by the smell in the pit, he blindly reached for and found the recently dead bodies not yet reeking.

He lay motionless, face to the sky, as he heard revolting fizzing sounds of methane and sulfated gases emanating from decomposing bodies around him. He also heard men tramping around the edge of the pit issuing profane curses, heartened they were foiled by the darkness that protected him. There was a rush of arrows that whistled by him and loud thumps as they found marks in the pit.

He dared to sigh relief when he heard alarmed and incensed voices. *Monks? Pray God they are monks.* When the commanding bellows of men chimed in, Michel dared to hope further. The menacing shouts forced the assailants to recoil and dash a craven escape. He heard galloping hoof beats grow fainter and sounds of concerned voices above. Michel hazily saw the lights of torches and thrust an arm upwards. The lay brothers who held the torches saw shrouds of the dead move.

Michel weakly called out, 'It is I, Michel. Please. Help me.'

20

RESCUED

Once inside the monastery, with frenzied screams, Tristyn stridently indicted the baron and his men the arch-villains of all his torment. One of the monks rushed him to the *Hôtel Dieu*.

Lucien quieted Tristyn's panic with a tonic, and calmly treated the boy's inflamed thorn induced sores, uttering soothing words of comfort whilst begging the oblate to enlighten him of Michel's whereabouts. The abbot and Fidelis appeared at the threshold of one of the infirmary stalls, and quietly assessed the child's distress.

Lucien said, 'Take your time. Tell me what you can.' Tristyn's rants slowly transmuted to tears, and his speech, slurred by the soporific's effects, became incoherent mumblings before he lapsed into merciful sleep. Lucien glanced up and said despairingly, 'I fear Michel is lost to us.'

Not long thereafter, Michel, wounded and barely conscious, was carried into the cubicle, his body covered with burns and sores. 'We took him from the common pit. He seemed to rise from the dead,' said the lay brother Estienn.

'Praise be to God,' Fidelis blurted. 'At least he is alive.'

Lucien issued curt orders to Laurentius and Quimper. 'Take him to the lavorium and remove his camisa. Let water gently stream over his body until his skin is thoroughly cleansed of all lime residue.'

The monks gently showered Michel's limp body before returning him to the infirmary for treatment. Lucien adroitly examined him to assess his wound and the damage to his skin. He sedated him heavily to keep him unconscious and pain free. The arrow lesion, skin irritation, cuts and abrasions from the thorny thicket were attended to and, satisfied both boys were comfortable and asleep, Lucien wearily left their side and joined the abbot and Fidelis.

'The bailiffs are alerted and are in pursuit of the caitiffs,' William said. The abbot looked at his prior and dean, sadness on his face and in his voice. 'I hope the boys will be able to enlighten us of their ordeal when they awaken.'

Lucien shook his head.' I dare not think of their state of mind when they do awake.'

The following morning, Lucien examined Michel's wound and the many abrasions on his body, as Laurentius nursed Tristyn. The boys, now conscious, lay with glazed eyes, listless. Fidelis sat patiently besides them, praying softly, but audibly, with hopes familiar words of spiritual comfort would soothe them. 'And Matthew wrote, Christ said to suffer little children to come unto him: for such is the kingdom of heaven.' Michel began to moan, heartbreak in his voice. 'The children. Oh, Blessed Mother, your children. What they did to your children!' He tried to sit up. 'Did Tristyn tell you?' he cried. 'The Baron! And his damnable men. At the château.' He fell back on the bed and sobbed uncontrollably.

Lucien and Laurentius quickly stepped forward. 'Nay, nay. Be calm. We shall be with you and keep you safe,' Lucien said reassuringly, and administered sleep potions. The oblates resisted the looming drowsiness as if fearful upon awakening they would find themselves back in the hellhole. The power of the drugs proved greater than their trauma, and they slumped once more into a deep sleep. It was a therapy Lucien, with caution, repeated several times, supposing, unconscious, their wounded minds might begin to heal. 'God grant them some peace in sleep,' he sighed. He kept them sedated for days, with faint hope the protracted rest would prove salubrious.

Donan and his men had no information for the monks except to inform them the château had been abandoned.

In their infirmary beds the boys grappled with images for which there seemed no adequate expression. At times, their bodies quavered as horrific images invaded quiet repose. Michel was the first to refer to their ordeal, and the more he described the macabre, sinister perversions incised on his mind, the more intense baleful whimpers from Tristyn filled the echo chambers of the great hall.

Lucien bit his lip to contain his sorrow as Tristyn recounted the lewd, sickening, unnatural acts he had seen committed. 'They were so drunk I think they forgot I was tied to the tree. I was to be the final victim. All the others had been killed.' And he began to cry.

Their fitful bursts of weeping and of fractured narratives of unimaginable depravity bedeviled comprehension. The narrative Tristyn and Michel uttered, repugnant, grisly, hideous, shocked, and immobilized Lucien and Quimper as they stood with contrivances of medical care in their hands mid-air, their mouths agape. All – the abbot, monks, and lay brothers – felt the shame of ineptness in the presence of such troubled minds. Fidelis sat, immobilised, with unrestrained tears spilling onto his scapular. 'Lamentable boys!' He cried out. 'Now we know what hell looks like.'

Michel told Fidelis, 'There were many being desecrated and killed. They would have killed me too had I made my presence known. So I did nothing. Nothing. Oh, God forgive me my cowardice.'

'Nay! Valiant, courageous, intrepid in danger. You are all those things, Michel! Your decision has sense and merit. You would have been unable to save Tristyn and you too would have been slaughtered. You must believe that and forgive yourself.' He reached out and took hold of Michel's hand. 'Those children are now saints with God. They are safe in heaven.' As he said it, Fidelis fought tears as his mind told him they should have been safe on earth.

Michel was hot with fever from his wound's exposure to lime and the contamination from decaying bodies. His arm was swollen and red, painfully full of pus. When awake, agonizing memories haunted him which he obsessively recounted to Lucien and Fidelis. Neither of the boys felt satisfied they had adequately expressed the evil they had seen. Sudden strident and perturbed screams rebounded off the infirmary walls when the depraved images that plagued the boys surfaced. The soporifics relieved them in sleep from recalled horrors, but neither Lucien nor Laurentius knew how to abate the repellent nightmares that intruded on their souls.

Marc Gervais returned home, anxious to unburden himself to Nolwenn of all he had seen and heard in Machecoul. Aghast by all he told her, she held him close to her, caressed and comforted him. 'Despite all, your homecoming gives me such joy, my dearest love.' She wanted to ask him many questions, but sensed sleep was essential. 'Bid thee rest, Marc. You need all your strength to face the ordeal your report will incite.'

'I cannot do else wise, my sweet girl. I am spent to the core.' He fell into a profound sleep as she cradled him in her arms.

Late the following day, refreshed, Marc rode to town to the militia's office. He rushed to tell a confounded Donan what he had heard and seen in Machecoul, unmindful of Donan's fruitless attempts to gain his attention. Marc's astounding news distracted Donan from the urgency of his own. 'The baron! And the bishop. He protected him with orders not to intrude on the baron's property. He knew of the baron's offences.'

'For sure you can believe he knew. I aim to write a thorough account of this . . . this monstrous affair so contrary to natural law, and present it to the mayor and, yea, to the bishop. Force them to act.'

Donan interrupted him. 'Marc. I beg you listen. I have news of prime import that has transpired. The abbot several days ago implored my presence at the Hôtel Dieu post haste where tales of indescribable evil were recounted to me by two oblates. What happened to them confirms all you have reported to me.' Donan gave Marc a full accounting. 'The boys are in safe hands, but the murderers escaped. The chateau is empty and silent. They are all gone.'

Stunned, Marc leaped up. 'I shall away to the abbey!'

Abbot William described how Michel had discovered the baron's den and had saved the oblate Tristyn from the unimaginable. 'We weep for the lads and truly know not how to help them, the which grieves us mightily, for indeed we fear their souls may be irreparably rent. They have obscene tales so heinous, the mind recoils.'

Marc followed the abbot to the Hôtel Dieu and encountered Lucien. 'I pray telling you of their ordeal may help relieve their tormented minds. You must hear what they have suffered, poor troubled souls, if your mind can bear the horror.'

Marc's arrival was heralded as a hero's welcome. He was the law, with authority to punish their tormentors. Both boys brightened, impassioned to tell him about their Calvary.

Marc shuddered with disgust, and groaned with pity as the boys described the sordid details of the carriage and bestial acts they had seen. Their expressions reflected the ordeal it was to talk about what had happened.

Paradoxically, the oblates felt an urgent need to describe their experience in detail, despite the heightened distress they endured with the telling. Their voices at times ruptured into convulsive sobs. Michel implored, 'How can there be such evil?' He thrashed about, his mind overcome with images of atrocities. 'Children. Some no older than four years. Holy Mother of sweet Jesu!'

Marc listened, more saddened than he had ever been. The stark contrast between evil and good had never been so manifest. He praised the boys for their bravery and daring. 'Truly, I doubt I or any other could have met such terror and triumph with such valour.' He looked to the abbot and Brother Lucien besides him in the cubicle for affirmation. 'They will be arrested, and you can be assured your testimony will bring them to ruin.'

'I could but save Tristyn,' Michel wailed.

'Absent your mind awhile from what you could not do, and dwell on what you did. And this. Think on the numbers you have saved. Hundreds of children's lives. None more will suffer at those monsters' hands. Now the world knows of it, for all time children will be protected from such perversion. Be sure of it. Pray be consoled and strengthened with that thought and know how great is the gratitude of all in Brittany.'

As Marc left the Hôtel Dieu, the Abbot and Lucien at his side, he summarised the information he had amassed in Machecoul. 'With no delay, my deputies and I now hasten to the baron's citadel in search of evidence. We shall ransack the land, sure to find proof to hang the baron and his damnable associates. My report to the mayor and the bishop will tell of outrages in every quarter of the land. The fiends at last are in our grasp. I am impatient to have them condemned.'

With a full complement, Marc defiantly rode north to the demesne of Baron Gilles de Rais, and as expected, the place stood abandoned. Marc and his men on foot followed the trail Michel had described, and arrived at the clearing forthwith. They found no traces of geomancy. No stones.

No bodies. There was only an unnerving stillness, and the imaginings in Marc's mind of what had happened there. There were obvious signs the earth had been disturbed, and roughly. There were vestiges everywhere of chafed soil, and just beneath it, Marc was certain there was dried blood that had been spilt. He and his deputies split ranks and searched the thicket that surrounded the clearing. Marc found Michel's habit. Inside the pocket was a curious piece of burnt wood. He thought to return both to the boy.

The search for evidence of a burial site was unproductive, but as they tracked the grounds, they found unmistakable signs of a recent fire. They raked and sifted the mound of ashes and found numerous bits of bones. *These are all that remain of those lamentable innocents.* Marc checked tears that flooded his eyes. There was no more to be done there. He and his deputies silently collected the evidence that denounced those responsible for hitherto inconceivable evil.

Mayor Serrigond, having digested Marc's damning account of iniquities committed by Gilles de Rais, summoned Marc Gervais to his office, to be there by noon. Seated behind his desk, Serrigond heard the cathedral bells mark the hour just as boot steps sounded outside his door. Marc was admitted and stood impatiently before the mayor, waiting for him to speak.

The mayor appeared tense. His head was down, eyes focused on Marc's indicting report. 'I met with the bishop yesterday, Gervais. You realise your account will be suppressed,' he said without looking up.

Marc's reaction was swift and incensed. 'Suppressed? How so? There can be no doubt of the crimes committed by the baron and his confederates. From 1432 to the present they have tortured and killed hundreds in the most abominable and heinous manner. There is testimony from victimised parents and eyewitness accounts,' he screamed.

Mayor Serrigond deliberated fretfully before he spoke. His voice faltered when he did speak. 'You are a fool, Gervais. An idiot, I tell you! These are but allegations. Who would believe the word of an oblate who illicitly took flight from the abbey? The tales of itinerant tinkers and peasants? The crazed ravings of a lunatic hag?'

Marc protested with no attempt to restrain his rage. He took a sack from his pouch and emptied it onto the desk. 'Look closely upon these bones found at the baron's château, Serrigond. Found in the ashes of the fire that consumed their bodies.'

'They could be animal bones, Gervais. Animal. Get them out of my sight. You present no evidence that supports these charges, I tell you.'

Marc stood, smouldering. 'Not so! You conspire against justice to disclaim the evidence. They are children's bones, and you know it. Many more in Machecoul. Forty bodies were exhumed on the baron's lands last year. I can get confirmation of that and more – two townsfolk reported they saw servants of Baron Gilles de Rais remove forty skeletons from one of Champtocé's towers last year. These bones, ashes, and eyewitness accounts of the slaughter are proof enough the baron and several of his courtiers murdered many children, probably more than we shall ever know of, and did so in the most unspeakably depraved manner.'

His fury threatened to overwhelm him. He was closer to physically attacking the mayor than in any other situation in his life. He controlled his actions with more effort at his command than he knew he had, but continued to roar venom. 'What exactly is it you fear, Serrigond? Disfavour? Perchance discharge from your office as mayor? Or are you also given to corrupt ribaldry! God's wound! Tell me, Serrigond, what must happen before you concede the devil de Rais is the transgressor of *all* the tragedies our community has suffered? Pray tell me what must he do before authorities arrest him and his evil disciples and bring them to trial?'

'The bishop in the past has told you, as he told me yesterday,' the mayor answered uneasily, 'There must be evidence of an offence against ecclesiastic law. And there is none.'

'A shameful lie. Murder not an offence against God! Tell that to Moses and the fifth commandment given him! An ecclesiastic offence? By Jesus' precious blood and Holy Mary's blue mantle, Serrigond. Why . . . tell me why the bishop protects the baron? Why do *you* reject the evidence before you? You who have been most eager to capture these demons.'

The mayor avoided a direct look. There was shame etched on his face. 'The only assurance I am able to give you is that no further harm will come to children in the Saint Petroc-sur-lac region. The baron will not return more. You must be satisfied with that.'

'That sounds like a disclosure you know the bishop is complicit. God give me strength!' Marc exclaimed, 'Be satisfied? The baron must hang, I tell you! If I must go to the Pope with this, I will see him on the gibbet!'

The mayor sighed wearily. 'What you say will not happen. The pope! A fantasy. He and the bishops control all law, church and civil. This is beyond my jurisdiction, Gervais. I swear it. Would that it were not so.' He paused, appearing genuinely troubled. He fidgeted with a quill, avoiding Marc's glaring eyes that were afire with outrage. 'Unhappily, you and I,' he said feebly, 'must be content no harm will come to any of our children hereafter.'

'Nay, Serrigond! I shall rouse the people against this bawdry.'

'Bold words, Gervais. Tell me what you propose to do to alter the sovereignty of higher authority?'

Marc digested the challenge and it left him lame. His powerful body, so full of anger and indignation, suddenly looked flaccid and defeated. He knew the mayor was right. The two men stared at each other in silence. There was nothing more to say on the matter. Marc turned and stumbled out of the room, eager to find refuge for his mangled soul.

He went to the militia office and told Donan to instruct their posse to stand down for the time being. 'However despicable the pronouncement, the mayor's argument has merit. It would serve naught but ill to go to the bishop.'

'Nevertheless, Marc, you will go. I know you. You *will* go, is that not so?'

Marc perked up. 'Ha! Indeed you know me well, Donan. Aye. By Christ's holy blood, I shall. I cannot let this stand.' He sighed. 'I could not live with myself – or face Nolwenn if I did nothing. The bishop will have to tell me through lips false to the precepts of Christ before I leave off!' He managed a smile. 'I shall return to inform you of the results of our parley.'

Resolute, with a pugnacious step, he went directly to the bishop's palace to confront the highest authority in the region.

Bishop Bernard du Loi, ever inscrutable, listened apathetically to Marc Gervais' charges. The report was on the bishop's desk, but he did not refer to it. He stood and faced Marc with a scowl that complemented the distain in his voice. 'Gervais, you have been warned to leave off enquiries about the baron. We consider the report you submitted a malicious slander.'

Livid, Marc shot back, barely able to maintain civility, 'Your Grace, you don't believe that. I know not why you shield him and his men, but that report shows I have amassed enough evidence to commit the baron and his men to the hangman twenty times over. The eyewitness accounts told by the oblates who saw inhuman acts, the bones found at the Château de Merlin, and witnesses to the removal of skeletons from Champtocé are substantive proof of their guilt.' He paused and insolently asked, 'Knowing this, I ask you,' he cried, 'how can you live with yourself?'

The bishop erupted. 'You dare say that to me!' He rushed forward and whacked Marc's face with such force he reeled. 'Men have been put to the wrack for lesser offences, Gervais. You flout my authority and insult me? You are nothing. Nobody, I tell you.' He paused to regain his composure and, with a faintly sinister smile said, 'The entire matter is irrelevant in any case. As you know, the arraignment of the baron can only take place were there an ecclesiastic offence. Since he is known to be devout and a well-beloved benefactor of the church, that is a remote likelihood.'

Marc gasped. 'By Mary's virgin skin, Serrigond said that to me. How in God's name can *you* say it? A man of the cloth. Are not the violation, mutilation, and murder of children offences against God? Rank, vile, unnatural, devilish offences.'

Coolly the bishop sneered, 'Perhaps against God, but not offences against the Church – the only authority I am authorised to protect and to ensure its laws are obeyed.'

'This is filth. You make me ashamed to be part of such a church.'

'You can always quit it, sheriff. We can ease the way for you and order a writ of excommunication.'

Marc spoke up sharply and with disgust 'You think to frighten me? It is not I who am damned to eternal fire.' He paused until he forced control of himself. 'You say it is not an ecclesiastic matter. The mayor says he must defer to your authority. Who in God's blood must I address to have this demon arrested to prevent more murders of innocents?'

The bishop archly told him, 'No one!' he shouted. 'Will you not understand? There is no one. Moreover, we shall communicate with Rome about your slanderous accusations. You have attempted to under-mine church law. Gervais. You could burn at the stake for this!'

Marc's eyes blazed. Defiantly he thundered, 'You before me, bishop. I shall go to Rome myself with these facts, not accusations.'

'Go if you will, Gervais,' the bishop said and derisively added, 'My nephew, Cardinal Trumpière, is now a member of the Curia. He will be happy to enlighten you about church law.'

'There is no authority on earth to turn to,' Marc concluded. Abbot William, Prior Fidelis and Dean Lucien sat in numbed silence, each inwardly wrestling with the implications the news bore that Marc had brought them.

Abbot William looked at his colleagues and then at Marc and lamented, 'Detestable. Detestable. Shame on the bishop and on the Church. Where is Christ in this?' He shook his head in sorrow.

Fidelis asked woefully, 'God almighty, is there no way to bring these demons to justice?'

'Fidelis,' Lucien interjected cynically. 'You miss the mark. There *is* no justice on earth.'

'How so?' Marc implored. Can it be possible there be no resort? It is ignominious to let fall this evidence, without . . .' His voice faltered. 'I have no words to describe this tyranny.' He guffawed. 'So. At last we have our murderers, and we are told they are above the law.'

'An ecclesiastic conspiracy,' Lucien opined. 'Who would have supposed it? I feel despoiled.' His face disclosed distress. 'Those boys! I must away to Michel and Tristyn. They must not know there will be no action taken – no justice for the unclean acts they witnessed or for others' suffering. They would not understand. By God's holy rood, *I* do not understand!'.' He thought momentarily. 'Yet I cannot to lie to them,' he said despondently.' The room fell silent.

Marc asked, 'Surely they will find out?

The abbot said with confidence, 'This abbey is a world unto itself, Sheriff. Here we can guard and protect the oblates from the wickedness in the world – yea, even though it comes from authorities within the Church itself.'

Marc clasped the abbot's hand. 'I hold you and your brethren in highest esteem, My Lord. You all are truly Christ's vicars on earth.' He sighed. 'As for me, I have civic duties to attend to.'

William said. 'We are sore aggrieved your years of dedication to put God's earth back on a rightful path is so defiled. We in the abbey bless you for all you have done. You have our prayers that your just cause will in time prevail. I believe I may speak for all when I say we shall continue to trust in God's providence.'

Marc scoffed at the notion. 'I wish I had your faith, my friend.' He reached into his pouch and handed Lucien an oblate's habit. 'I forgot to give this to Michel. There is something in the pocket – a charred piece of wood with letters on it. He may want it.'

Marc rode home slowly, nursing disillusionment and wrath, wanting to seek the consolation he could be sure to find in the company of Nolwenn and his children. Their goodness and innocence would be a comfort to him, and their loving hearts would ease the bitterness and disenchantment he felt.

21

ABRADED SOULS

The laceration in Michel's arm became infected. He was delirious with fever. Lucien changed dressings several times a day with alternating poultices of hot vinegar, natron, egg white and honey. He covered the wound with cerate of wax and chalk. To no avail. By the third day, the odour of putrid tissue became pronounced. The black gangrene was not yet evident, but should it become discernible, Lucien feared he would have to amputate.

He decided to cut the sutures and reopen the wound to let it dehisce. Pus and acrid drippings oozed from it all day, and Lucien tirelessly cleansed the area with wine, after which he poured a mixture of honey with copper and silver filings on the wound. He patiently repeated the procedure frequently.

By the fifth day, he saw no more pus. With satisfaction, the wound responded well to dressings of myrrh, wine, and diluted honey, and slowly it began to granulate until eventually, it closed. The fever lessened and then ceased. The blisters on his skin healed. Michel began to feel hunger and vigour. He was mending well, but the distress of what he had witnessed persisted.

Although Tristyn had long been released from the infirmary, the spirits of both oblates remained torpid, with gruesome flashbacks of what they had seen. The monks prayers and fond attentions did little to condole the oblates' psyches.

There were fitful nights of disturbed sleep, and with the night came horrific nightmares. Shrieks of terror awoke them as lurid images of menace and death stalked them. Tristyn told Fidelis of mesh that entangled him, and traps that imprisoned him, and described nightmares in which children ran hysterically, naked, in circles, with bestial men with sinister claws and weapons in pursuit.

Michel had a reoccurring dream in which he was in a black cave in which sporadic bolts of light revealed children's grimacing, still bleeding bodiless heads staring at him. He felt sticky blood as he fingered the walls in search of an exit. He told Lucien about a dream in which he was walking outside the walls of the town where he saw men jovially tearing the skin off dead children and lining the walls of the town with their hide. He often cried for no apparent reason, whether alone or when Lucien attended him, helpless to soothe him.

Tristyn visited Michel often in the Hôtel Dieu. They talked endlessly about their common woes, as if infinitely repeating the defamations would wash away the memories in the inevitable flood of tears that accompanied their recollections. 'Tristyn, how did you survive that infernal ordeal for three days?'

Tristyn's response fueled tears as well as images he wanted to suppress. 'I cannot describe the horror. There were thirty or more of us in a dungeon. In darkness. Some of the boys were beggars who had gone to the château in hopes of food. Others were from families in town and nearby hamlets. We expected death would be our lot, and soon. We prayed, but wailed more. They began to kill the day you arrived. We were taken to that clearing. I need not tell you more. You saw all.' Tristyn cried.

'Oh, Tristyn, The nightmares . . .'

Tristyn nodded. 'Yea. It is painful to be awake and more so to sleep.' They clung to each other, bound by fearsome recollections. They spoke constantly of what they had witnessed, and prayed fervently, unaware that, in doing so, they were unburdening their abraded souls and slowly healing their scarred psyches.

Lucien felt strongly that their return to wellbeing greatly depended on the conviction of Gilles de Rais and his associates. Fury consumed him when he thought about the authorities who shielded the baron. He thought they abetted the wicked acts that were offences against humanity itself.

He remained silent on the matter with Michel. Whenever asked, Lucien gave evasive answers, with firm expressions of reassurance the hoped-for justice would come to pass. 'News travels slowly, Michel. I am not sure that it is known where the baron and his men are. But they will reveal themselves and, God willing, be arrested and taken to trial. Meanwhile, we must rejoice! You exposed him and his foul crimes, and now communities close and wide know him for his corrupt nature. He is finished. There will be no more unholy crimes against children. Be assured, when he is brought down and imprisoned, I will be the first to tell you of it.'

Michel and Tristyn's *travail* continued for several months. Fidelis' and Lucien's benevolent ministrations to the boys were unwavering, and their compassion and soothing assurances generally had a calming effect, but only temporarily. There were no tonics to relieve their inner demons, and both boys had unexpected episodes of overwrought outbursts. Fidelis expressed worry they never would recover from their ordeal.

Their fellow oblates, ignorant of the details of what had transpired, were perplexed by their behaviour. The boys evaded the convivial company of Paol Eric, Adrian, Christopher and others during recreation, and lay silently on their beds, or went to the chapel to pray.

When pressed, Michel and Tristyn were circumspect in what they said. They did not want to burden their friends with the sordid details of what had happened. They thought it enough they know that Tristyn had been a captive of the baron and Michel saved him and both escaped. 'It was a miracle we escaped. Michel was brave, and brilliantly planned my rescue,' Tristyn allowed.

'You're a hero, Michel!' George declared.

'Tell us more,' Anton begged.

Michel demurred, as guilt wracked him for not having saved others.

Fidelis intervened to some degree. He explained to the oblates that Michel and Tristyn were recovering from an ordeal that went beyond surface wounds. 'You can be of help only with kindness and patience. And silence on the matter. You can do little else.'

The abbot, Fidelis and Lucien discussed measures that might distract the oblates from their wretchedness. Fidelis inventively proposed mental concentration as a ploy to divert the boys' minds. 'I have spoken to Brother Rafe. He will set them to copy scripture, and, in so doing, encourage their minds to think about the grace therein.'

'Indeed, an uplifting activity for their sad dispositions,' the abbot agreed.

'He also wants to teach them how to make the black ink used to write on parchment. You know the passion he has about his work. In fact, there would be much for them to learn and much to do to keep their minds occupied.'

The abbot nodded. 'Make the arrangements, Fidelis. Pray God, the boys find consolation in this endeavour.'

Lucien added, 'Your idea has merit, Fidelis. And I shall keep Michel's mind diverted in the dispensary and assign him daily to the infirmary to see to the needs of the ailing and dying.'

The Christmas season gave another opportunity to remind the boys that peace, love, and decency far surpassed worldly malevolence. The monks encouraged the boys to participate in the abbey's Christmas rituals and revels, urging them to muster some of Christmas tide's joyful spirit.

Fidelis wisely understood it was impossible to put aside the lingering thoughts they had of those butchered children, and suggested they and all in the monastery dedicate the season to the children who had been murdered. Abbot William added the victims to the roster of the Holy Innocents.

'We must pray to those children who suffered and died, for surely they are in heaven and favoured by God as innocent martyrs,' Fidelis told Michel and Tristyn. 'How they must rejoice you both are with us still to do God's work on earth.'

The Boy Bishop still reigned on Childermas day, but Michel now recognised the event was a shallow vanity that detracted from the true value of spiritual matters. He and Tristyn asked to be excused from participating.

Tristyn spent a great deal of time in the scriptorium, and Michel could be found in the snow garnished cloister, unmindful of the cold, deep in prayerful meditation.

Disturbing dreams no longer constantly troubled the boys, and eventually they began to mingle with their fellow oblates and join them in quiet diversions. Both became skilled at playing chess. The game required concentration that kept away all other thoughts, save to check the king!

Tristyn worked tirelessly in his role as an apprentice to Magister Rafe in the scriptorium. By January 1440, in that austere, peaceful environment he felt protected and safe, and began to feel peace as he copied inspiring messages from holy books.

Michel continued to work with Lucien in the infirmary. Each day's discovery further excited his interest in medicine and dulled the memory of horrors he had witnessed. Each day, with prayer and meditation, he felt cleansed by God's grace and less haunted by evils he had seen. He continued to wonder when he would hear word that the Baron Gilles de Rais and the other ogres had been apprehended.

22

JUSTICE

Marc was at home with his family in September 1440 when Donan delivered a letter to him. 'It is from the sheriff of Machecoul, Marc. I knew you would want to read it immediately.' Eadric Herán had written with astounding news. After Marc eagerly read the letter to Nolwenn and Donan, he said excitedly, 'I make haste to the abbey.'

Both rode into town and parted ways as Donan went to the constabulary and Marc went to the monastery, impatient for all to hear the news. He waited in the reception room, and when the abbot and his senior monks entered, he grinned and said simply, 'He has been arraigned,'

William, Fidelis and Lucien were momentarily incredulous. 'It is so. He is accused by the Bishop of Nantes of sacrilege and the violation of Church immunity for having committed an ecclesiastic offence for which the Church pounced on him!'

'Humph. It took a year since you laid bare his crimes.' Lucien remarked contemptuously.

'Yea 'tis as you say. But the baron is arrested. I am content enough with that for the time being.' Marc summarised the information in Herán's letter.

He told the monks that the arrogant, perhaps drunk, or drugged baron and several of his company broke into the Church of Saint Etienne in Mermorte near Tiffauges in the middle of High Mass. He and his men attacked a prelate by the name of Jean le Ferron, threatened him, towed him from the church, and rode off with him.

'The quarrel was about a claim on one of de Rais' properties. Geoffroy le Ferron had been charged by the Duke of Brittany to occupy one of the baron's castles in lieu of vast sums owed him by de Rais.' Excitedly he added, 'Know this, Geoffroy is the Treasurer for the Duke of Brittany! He had settled his brother, Jean to reside in De Rais' castle in his stead. You can believe de Rais' offence against ducal authority will ensure the baron now cannot escape the wrath of Church *or* State.'

Marc glibly remarked to the abbot, 'God's providence, My Lord?'

'When did all this happen?' William asked.

Marc scanned the letter and grimaced, 'It has taken four months to arrest him.' He related to the monks that the assault had taken place in May, and in July the baron de Rais met with the Duke of Brittany in Josselin to discuss a 50,000 écus fine imposed on him for seizing Le Ferron that had not been paid. He paused and looked at each of the monks. 'Can you believe it? They favoured money instead of criminal charges!'

Abbot William speculated numbly, 'Thus, had de Rais paid the fine, the duke would have dropped the charges against him.' The supposition shocked them all.

Josselin!' gasped Fidelis. 'So close to Saint Petroc and the baron's château.'

Lucien spoke up. 'Just so. The baron was bargaining with the duke near the very place where he had slaughtered children.' He shook his head in disgust.

'What does the letter say about an indictment for the murder of the children?' Fidelis wanted to know.

Marc told him that appeared to be a separate matter. 'The letter says that, also in July, the Bishop of Nantes, Jean de Malestroit, visited several churches in his parish to make enquiries about children rumoured to have disappeared. Mind you, the bishop did so only as a favour for his nephew whose friend had suffered an offence at the hands of the baron.'

'Then . . . the bishop never would have begun to investigate except for his nephew!' Lucien opined.

Marc nodded. 'Aye, you can believe just so.'

He related how Herán wrote that the bishop met with many parents who, certain they had church protection, eagerly told him their children had disappeared. All implicated the baron as being responsible, but said they had been afraid to speak out against him for fear of his wrath. Marc interjected proudly, 'The proof linking the baron to the abductions was forthcoming from the just Sheriff Herán of Machecoul. The bishop determined his was convincing evidence that warranted a civil trial.'

'A civil trial?' Fidelis wondered what the implication was.

Marc explained there would be two trials – ecclesiastic and civil. Lucien derisively speculated the civil trial would not have been decreed but for the arraignment on the ecclesiastic matter.

'All this in July! They all knew in July. How many children were murdered as the hierarchy was dilatory, scheming about damning evidence, and doing nothing about it.' The abbot complained. 'They too will be answerable to God.'

Marc said, 'De Rais is a nobleman, and subject to a different standard of law than we mere impotent mortals. Moreover, you might conjecture with good reason the duke covets de Rais' properties and treasures, and has spent much of the time since July seizing them for himself.'

'Money. It's always about money, 'Lucien sneered.

Fidelis noted, 'At least the baron is in custody.' He asked Marc, 'Who else with him?'

'Woefully, but two others.'

General disbelief echoed Fidelis' reaction. 'Two? But two? How can that be so? There are a multitude of those fiends. Michel told us he saw many men at the chateau.'

'Many fled – his cousins Gilles de Sillé and Roger de Brequeville among them. Several of de Rais' confederates to the crimes agreed to give testimony in exchange for immunity. André Buchet, the duke's master of the choir, is one of them.'

Marc interjected, 'André Buchet. I remember him well from a suspicious encounter five years ago! Now I know he had been commissioned by de Rais to find boys – *pretty boys* – for the baron. None of those brigands will be arrested or go to trial, though by God's right, they will be condemned by the world.'

'Not enough. Not enough.' Lucien said. 'Who are the others arrested?'

'A servant known as Poitou – I talked with him at the château last year – and another body servant, Henriet.'

'This is blasphemy. All those murderers unpunished for their hellish deeds! I mourn this disgrace,' the abbot said heatedly.

'The most heinous of men faces judge and jury,' Fidelis pointed out. 'I thank God for that, but lament the injustice most of the offenders have escaped retribution. This cannot be justified.'

Marc commented, 'We can at least revel the baron's evil web is at last unraveled.' He shook his head dejectedly and mused, 'Still, it is completely beyond my ken how the others will have escaped the noose.'

'The others will know the people's justice, God willing,' Lucien offered. He turned and told Marc, 'We bid thanks to the bearer of this news. It is more than we had come to expect, though it be less than deserved.' He turned to the abbot. 'With your permission, My Lord?'

'Aye. You will be impatient to tell Michel and Tristyn. Go, and with my blessing.'

This is but the beginning.' Lucien told Tristyn and Michel. 'We have need of patience. It may be months before all the testimony is compiled against them, for the law moves slowly. For now, we can be gladdened that the wheel of justice has finally begun to turn in the right direction. By the time the jurors issue judgement, all their evil deeds will have been disclosed and they will pay mightily for their crimes, mark me!'

Lucien's words proved only partially prophetic. The anticipated wait was brief. The civil trial convened on the eighteenth of September and the canonical tribunal, on the nineteenth of September at the Tour Neuve in Nantes.

Relief coursed through the citizenry of all Brittany, for all now believed without doubt their children were safe. It was also safe for people to come forwards with their stories without fear of retaliation, and they went to court in droves.

Herán wrote in a second letter the canonical court conducted by church hierarchy curiously appeared to be only concerned with evidence of heresy and sacrilege. Sodomy was considered a sacrilegious transgression. Marc read aloud:

'They made no mention of the murders. It has been left to the civil court to hear testimony from the families of victims and from witnesses who saw children being seized. Each day there are stories from wretches who have suffered at the baron's hand. They sicken the soul.

Many children who were debauched in diabolic ribaldries had been purchased from peasants who were desperate from want. There are depositions that state some children were sold for the price of a loaf of bread or a new dress. Abandoned urchins were snatched from town streets and alleys. Beggars who sought alms at the very doors of the baron's various castles were swallowed up in his devilish lair. There were also children who had been entrusted to de Rais' protection seemingly for service in his choir or as pages. False promises. Their parents never saw them again. Some were told they died; others, they had been sent to other nobles' castles.

Troubling is the fact that the court will only admit testimony from select classes of citizens - the gentry who have accusations that can be substantiated. Peasants' stories will be discounted. That suggests that, when de Rais is found guilty, nameless children will not be among those counted. It will affect the numbers who fell victim to his villainy. There are rumours that six hundred children fell prey to his wickedness. That figure will never be officially calculated by this court, of that you can be certain. Proof of the vast numbers went up in smoke, and lies with the many who were burned to ashes and thrown into cisterns.

I myself have been summoned to give testimony to the civil court. I have decided thereafter to stay on in Nantes until the trials have concluded. You shall be the first to know the rulings of the canonical tribunal and that of the civil court. Whatever the number for which he is found guilty, he will undoubtedly be condemned. That much we can at least predict.

This will interest you. The baron's behaviour in court has been outlandish. He not only at first denied the charges, but declared the judges were not competent to try the case. It is laughable to impugn the authority of the bishop of Nantes and Jean Bloyn, Vicar of the Inquisitor of the tribunal, but that is exactly what he did.'

The proceedings were in Latin, with interpreters for those, like Herán, not proficient in the language. Additionally, the sheriff of Machecoul had contacts who were able to explicate subtle legal details he otherwise would have missed. He passed on all the information he had to Marc Gervais, who shared Herán's missives with Donan, the abbot, Fidelis and Lucien:

'For his insolence, the tribunal excommunicated de Rais, and he responded with impudence. He told them they had not the authority to do so.

Another day, he completely reversed course and begged forgiveness, confessed his crimes, and asked to be redeemed into the Church's good graces.

He claims eight hundred murders!

Mind, I have it on good authority he has not been tortured, and his confession was freely given – undoubtedly, in his mind, to save himself from eternal damnation as well as dismemberment once he has been hanged, as hanged he will be.'

Lucien contemptuously said, 'As if the Almighty would forgive a desperate man's contrition. God knows as do we the fiend still would be butchering innocents had he not been accused and arrested. There can be no absolution in his so-called confession or forgiveness from a just God!'

Another letter described an abomination even more execrable than all others that had been exposed. No one thought that possible despite what they already knew:

'A priest named Prelati, who had vilely been granted immunity, told the court he had promised de Rais he could summon a devil called Barron who would transform lead into gold should he sacrifice the hand, heart, eyes and blood of an infant – the which de Rais did – witnessed by Prelati. The remains were kept on display under glass in his private chamber.'

Lucien wondered, 'Be there no limit to his turpitude?'

Lucien told Michel and Tristyn much of what he knew, but selectively, ensuring they learned only details of the trials that would be uplifting. The oblates felt most gratified to know the children of Brittany were at last safe from harm. 'People everywhere are telling the court details of how their children disappeared, lost to them forever. In each instance, the baron and his band are indicted as the wicked ogres responsible.'

Peevishly, Michel remarked to Lucien, 'It took them a long time to accept the truth of the accusations.' Lucien did not comment. Nor did he tell him or Tristyn that only three were on trial.

23

Pestilence and Death

The arrest of Baron Gilles de Rais, Poitou, and Henriet, servants and accomplices of the baron, coincided in September with a visitation in Saint Petroc-sur-lac of the Black Death that had caused great numbers of deaths in Italy the prior year.

The threat the disease would reach Saint Petroc had never been far from Lucien's mind. He had marked its path attentively and with precision, keeping the abbot informed with specific details of the numbers stricken and the numbers of deaths in each locale. A network of monks communicated details of the course of the sickness as the deadly peril struck each of their regions.

When Lucien received word that gave the numbers of those who had the pestilence in Dinan, he realised the disease would soon reach Saint Petroc-sur-lac. He was only minimally encouraged that those who had become ill and died were not of epidemic proportions. It was a small – but legitimate – reassurance that the scourge was not as widespread or as virulent as it had been in the past. He thought that little comfort for those who had been infected and had died. And he worried that the abbey's supply of the black potion would not be sufficient to the need when the plague reached Saint Petroc-sur-lac.

Lucien gathered the monastic community to announce their region was but days away from the pestilence in their midst. 'We are prepared to care for the stricken in the Hôtel Dieu, and hopefully we have enough of the black potion for our use and to portion with others.' He paced as he continued, 'I call you together today to ensure you all know your assignments and are ready to meet this crisis. Those who nurse the sick – and I shall require many volunteers – will be given the black potion for protection from infection. You will be housed apart, adjacent to the infirmary, and meals, cleansing and use of the necessarium will take place there. Daily Mass and the Divine Office will be observed in the infirmary. School will be suspended. Oblates will keep to their dormitory, the cloister, the refectory, and the chapel. All patients in the hospital at the present time will be moved to a cluster of beds absented by those who will be assisting with plague victims.' He sighed. 'I am ready for your questions.'

'Brother. Many of us will have direct contact with those who are afflicted with the scourge, but we all have heard that the sickness is in the air – a kind of vapour. Why, pray, are we all not to have the black potion?'

'It is a good question, Brother. There are many hypotheses of the cause of the plague. A miasma is but one of them. I dismiss that idea. The fact is no one knows what causes the disease, although it is certainly a contagious disease, and caution must be taken to absent oneself from others who may be infected. But I am certain there is nothing in the atmosphere within the abbey that is harmful, so I beg you be as assured of your safety as I am. Remember, patients with plague will go directly to the Hôtel Dieu. None in the monastery will be threatened by them or the disease that afflicts them.'

Abbot William stepped forwards. 'I would like lists of those who will serve as infirmarians and cooks. Almoners and their assistants will be given the black potion and quarantined. Distributions to the poor will be uninterrupted, but donations of any sort will no longer be accepted from anyone outside abbey walls.' As he finished, the bells for

Compline tolled. The abbot gave his blessing, and the monastic congregation made their way to the chapel.

As predictable as the coming of the dark of night on a moonless night, rumour spread that the plague was about to reach Saint Petroc-sur-lac. Many town folks panicked and fled to relatives in other parts of Brittany. Those who stayed in town barred their doors, and having stored large supplies of foodstuffs and water, waited, prayed and like Odysseus in *The Odyssey*, burned sulfur in their houses hoping to purify the air. Travellers were banned entrance to the municipality, and stragglers infected with plague fell dead on roads and in the streets, consigned to a mass grave. Following Acron's command during the plague of Athens in ancient Greece, civic authorities ordered bonfires lit to forestall the disease. That tactic did not save its ruler Pericles from expiring, nor did it save citizens of Saint Petroc-sur-lac.

Lucien issued doses of the black potion to all the caretakers with assurances it shielded them from contagion. 'Be mindful the preventive effect lasts but a few weeks. Should there be epidemic proportions of plague victims that occur beyond that time, it will be meet to repeat doses of the potion. Pray God it does not come to that, for we have but a finite supply.

The first patients with plague that arrived at the Hôtel Dieu were two sons of the town butcher. Lucien and Quimper burned their clothes before attending them. They cleansed the boys' bodies with cool fresh rose water mixed with vinegar, and Lucien gave them essence of poppy for pain. Michel fetched treatment supplies, and sat with the children through the night, following Lucien's instructions to administer a brew of coriander and rose water with a touch of tartar and willow juice to treat the pitiless headaches, muscle pains and fevers.

When groin swellings appeared, Lucien applied plasters and poultices of herbs mixed with mercury, to no effect. Lucien then cleansed and drained the painful buboes, explaining the benefits to Michel. 'It is our last hope, Michel.'

The black potion had carelessly not been distributed to all the members of the boys' family, and the father, mother and two sisters became ill. They were admitted to the hospital just as the boys' conditions became grave. Pus filled buboes under their arms and in their groin caused unbearable pain, and did not respond to treatment. Despite all efforts, the boys died just as their parents and sisters progressed to this critical, life threatening stage. Lucien and infirmarians, with Michel at their side, doctored them night and day. To no avail. Only the mother recovered. Her grief was a mournful sight to behold.

The afflicted grew in number, and the hospital was overflowing with the sick. Isolation precautions were no longer possible. Pain induced groans and screams throughout the Hôtel Dieu were relentless as monks and infirmarians vigilantly nursed the suffering hoards, working exhaustively days and nights. White aprons worn over monks' habits stained with dried blood and pus were the visual evidence of their labours.

As a bed became available either because of a recovery or a death, the sheet and the victims' clothing were removed. The clothes were burned. Cots with fresh linen boiled in lye soap were readied to receive another poor wretch. When deaths occurred, bodies were unceremoniously consigned to the burial pit, typically with no surviving family members to mourn them. Giving succor to the sick and dying with prayer was the priority of the priests, and consequently there was no clergy available to pray over the dead put to rest in the common pit.

Michel was singularly most useful to Lucien when he treated those poor souls who knew they were about to die. He administered anodynes that blunted pain, and equally valuable were his gentle manner and his compassion.

Prayers were soothing, and, as men and women reached the abyss, the strength derived from Michel's loving care transmuted fear and despair into serenity and peace.

Lucien's faith in the competence of his apprentice and his awe at the effect the boy had on patients allowed him and his workers to treat those who had a good chance of survival. Secure in the knowledge Michel had faithfully taken all the doses of the black potion, Lucien rested easy he was safe from infection.

Of one hundred who contracted the disease, fifty to seventy died. Of two hundred stricken, one hundred thirty died. Michel lamented, 'It is doleful to see such suffering, Magister. I look for God's hand in this and find it wanting.'

'Trust in God only to give you and those poor wretches courage and strength, boy. Pray for that. Desist from superstitious thoughts of God punishing mankind or coming to anyone's aid. I have heard just such talk these last days. It is foolish to believe the deity regulates what happens to us for either good or bad. I have told you that before. Something we know nothing of causes not only plague but other diseases. It is beyond our cunning to know how that occurs. He paused a moment and added reflectively, 'Perhaps one day . . .'

Michel pondered Lucien's words and told him, 'I shall pray all the same, Brother, that God protect the people in our town and spare those from death who come to us afflicted.'

Lucien inwardly disavowed the idea prayer would save anyone, but responded, 'Such faith can only be of great benefit.'

A month after the Black Death first visited the citizens of Saint Petroc-sur-lac, in diminishing numbers, fewer and fewer became plague-ridden. When no instances of the pestilence had been reported for six days, normalcy seemed a possibility and hope began to supplant dread, considerably lessening the terror that had gripped the populace. Lucien, however encouraged, remained warily anxious. He confided to Michel that the stock of the black potion had been totally depleted. 'There is only one portion left, and no time to prepare more. I want you to have this should it be needed, Michel.'

Michel protested, 'Why me, Brother? We all have already had taken two vials of the potion.'

'You among us have been least exposed to the disease, and the young are more susceptive to infection.'

Lucien took Michel's hand and spoke with an intensity of purpose that was unusual to emphasise his concern. 'Listen to me now. Should one plague victim enter these doors, I order you to begin the potion for seven days. Is that understood?' Michel nodded and put the vial in the pocket of his habit.

Neither thought there would be the need for it. Lucien met with his crew of caregivers and gave instructions to begin maneuvers to return the hospital to its pre-crisis norm. 'All the cots must be thoroughly scoured with limewater and vinegar, and surplus beds taken to the storehouse. The chairs, tables, walls, floors – all must be thoroughly cleansed. Everything contaminated by the plague must be purged. We begin tomorrow. Thereafter we will terminate the quarantine.'

A day later, however, a boy of eight, carried to the door of the Hôtel Dieu by a girl, was taken to a cubicle where Michel was working and placed on a cot. Jolted, Michel saw Claire enter the room. She and Michel had avoided each other since that day in the cathedral vault, and when she saw Michel, she looked startled and, embarrassed, turned her attention to the boy. Michel too averted his gaze. He looked at the child, and a glance revealed the nature of his illness. *The pestilence, and Claire is sure to be afflicted!* Overcome with desolation, Michel's shoulders sagged. *The black potion. She needs to have it.* He reached into his pocket and grasped the vial. *I have had many doses. I surely am safeguarded from becoming infected notwithstanding Lucien's warning.* He bit his lip. *What if I'm wrong?* Michel stared at Claire, anxiety rising. He thought of the implications for himself if he gave the vial of the black potion to her. *I might die.* He began to sweat and could feel his heart race. A moment passed. He took a deep breath and relaxed his body. *But Claire would live. She must live.*

Lucien entered. He paled when he looked at the child. Reluctant to utter the words, he turned to Claire and said sympathetically, 'I am sorry, child. It is the pestilence. Do I presume this is your brother?'

She nodded. 'His name is Alain.'

'When did he become ill?'

Claire answered that just the day before he was well. 'Only this morning did he begin to speak of headache and to the touch was very hot.'

'That bodes well, lass.' Lucien told her in an optimistic tone. 'You brought him here in the earliest state of the sickness. I am hopeful. Trust we shall do all we can for him.' With no more vials of the black potion at his disposal, Lucien could only offer solace. 'Now   you must go and quickly. I pray Christ, Mary and Saint Benedict give you health and peace. I shall keep you advised on how your brother fares.'

Michel left the cubicle with Claire, accompanying her to the door of the Hôtel Dieu. He asked her apprehensively 'Are you well, Claire?' She nodded.

'Are you certain – no cough, fever, headache?'

'Yes Michel, truly. Only Alain is ill.' Tears filled her eyes. 'My mother and father and two sisters are dead these past three days.'

Stunned, Michel stood, weighing the implications. He reached into his pocket. Taking her by the hand, he put the vial of the black potion in it. 'Mix this with water and take a small mouthful daily for seven days. It will protect you from the pestilence.'

'Michel, is this not meant for you?' Claire objected.

There was a second of hesitation before he lied, 'I have more.'

'Can I give it to my brother instead?' she supplicated.

He shook his head. 'If only you could. The potion must be taken before symptoms appear. Be hopeful. Alain has only just shown signs of the sickness. Brother Lucien has had many favourable outcomings with such patients. I am confident he will be made well.' He looked at Claire affectionately and added, 'I rest easy knowing this remedy will keep you from harm. I mourn the loss of your family and will pray for them as well as for Alain. Fare thee well, Claire. May God's blessings go with you.'

Michel asked Lucien if he could attend Claire's brother. Hesitant, Lucien asked, 'You have begun to take the potion, have you not, Michel?' Michel nodded, with no trace of the lie on his face. Lucien looked relieved and nodded assent. 'Then you have my permission.' He gave Michel his blessing, and the oblate rushed to his patient's side.

For two days and nights, confident in the skills he had acquired, Michel cared for the boy and barely noticed Lucien's silent presence as he proudly observed Michel's expertise.

He was quick to reassure him as Michel became alarmed when buboes appeared. 'Calm yourself. It is a critical stage, but the child is strong, and I have confidence he will survive this. I shall lance these to drain the blood and pus before they grow larger and burst. Note how I do it.' Michel nervously watched as Lucien performed the procedure. He barely flinched at the rank smell of the infected matter that filled the room. Lucien applied a poultice and sighed. 'There is naught to do now except treat each new symptom as it appears.'

'I shall pray, Brother.'

Lucien smiled and said with irony, 'A good idea, Michel, and faithful to the mandate of our profession that we *first, do no harm.*'

Michel dismissed the jibe, certain prayers are heard and answered.

'Be of good cheer, boy. What we are doing is all that can be done. Keep in mind, Michel, you have witnessed how such treatment has saved many, and this lad is young and had been in good health before this infection. I remain certain he will recover.'

Consoled by Lucien's assurances, Michel remained at Alain's bedside, giving him potions, sponging his body, moistening his lips, and praying – aloud and silently. He watched closely, drained with fatigue, as Alain slept after having been given poppy for the pain, and his breathing was deep and regular for a while. Then, expelling air from his body, he stopped inhaling. Michel frantically shouted for Lucien, lifted Alain to his chest and held him tightly. He burst into tears and prayed to God to spare Claire's brother just as Lucien rushed into the stall and seized the boy from Michel's arms. He laid him flat on the bed and pounded his chest with his fist. There was a loud wheeze and an intake of air and then another, until the child resumed normal breathing. 'He is asleep. It is like a miracle, Michel.'

Lucien wiped his sweaty brow and felt the tension leave his body. He looked at his apprentice, bothered by his appearance. 'You look exhausted, Michel. You must rest. I shall keep the watch. Go. Do not worry. The boy's condition will not worsen.'

Michel immediately fell into a deep sleep, but when the bells for Prime rang, he felt wasted. He dragged himself out of the bed. *I am ill*, he thought. *I must not be ill. Alain needs me.* He slowly walked to the child's bedchamber. Breath did not come easily. Lucien, as promised, was there. At the sound of Michel's voice, he said, 'The buboes are free of pus. The fever is gone. He is going to recover, Michel.'

Relieved to hear Lucien's pronouncement, Michel suddenly felt very weak and swayed unsteadily. His head was pounding. He begged leave to sit down. Lucien looked at him and rushed to his side, his face sapped of colour. 'Blessed Mother. Please, for God's sake tell me you have been taking the potion as you avowed.' Michel slowly shook his head. Lucien took Michel into his arms. 'By all that is holy, what have you done?'

Claire, elated by a message sent from Lucien that informed her that her brother would survive, immediately went to the Hôtel Dieu. Brother Iohannes told her she could not enter.

When she persisted, he said crankily, 'Wait but a moment.'

Lucien appeared at the gate and told her, 'He will be well enough to go home in two days. You cannot come in. You must wait.' Lucien said simply.

Disappointed, she asked, 'Is Michel about? 'I want to thank him for his help.

Lucien fought back tears. 'Michel is very sick.' Claire was stunned to hear it. 'It is the pestilence.' Claire begged to see him but was dissuaded by Lucien. 'You are in danger of infection, child. I cannot allow it.'

'No, Brother. Michel gave me a vial of the black potion, and I have been taking daily doses. Michel assured me I would be protected. Please, please, let me see him.'

Thunderstruck, Lucien looked blankly at the girl. With a despairing sigh, he stepped aside and motioned her forwards to the chamber where Michel lay.

The sight of Michel shocked her. Pain was evident on his sallow face. His breathing was laboured. Laurentius sat by his side. Claire asked him, 'May I stay a while? And before I go I must thank Brother Lucien for all he has done.'

Brother Lucien had quietly entered the room and stood at its threshold. 'Not I, child – Michel. He never left your brother's side for days, and then only when Alain began to get well.'

The sounds of voices aroused Michel's awareness. He opened his eyes. 'Claire. You are safe. And Alain will get well. I . . . I am content.' He studied her tear-stained face and said weakly, 'Do not worry. I too shall recover. Brother Lucien will see to it. Come visit me in a few days. You will see.' He smiled faintly and whispered, 'Safe. You are safe, Claire. That is what matters.'

Claire whimpered, 'Oh, Michel, it grieves me to see you so.' She composed herself. 'I shall never forget what you have done for my brother. And your sacrifice for me!' Her face glistened from the flow of tears. Michel shakily reached for her hand. She kissed it and declared, 'I shall raise Alain as if I were his mother. . . and he will know you saved his life – and my life as well!'

'Nay. 'Twas God's will, Claire. I am merely His instrument.'

Claire clenched Michel's hand. 'When Alain is old enough, I shall take holy orders as thanks for this deliverance.'

'It pleases me to hear you say it,' Michel said softly. He cringed with pain and coughed uncontrollably. Bloody sputum eructed from his mouth. Claire, aghast, turned to Lucien, who rushed to Michel's side and cleaned his mouth. When the coughs subsided, he gave Michel a soporific. When Michel lapsed into sleep, without looking at her, Lucien whispered to Claire that the disease had progressed to the lungs. 'It is an ominous sign. You should say your farewell.' He swallowed hard. 'And then please leave. I shall continue to do all I can.' Claire kissed Michel's cheek as he slept, and with a heavy heart, sobbing, left the Hôtel Dieu.

Increased pain, coughs, and bloody mucous roused Michel. He looked at Lucien and smiled weakly. 'The black potion indeed has miraculous powers, Brother, but for a shorter space of time than I had supposed. The Great Mortality has me in its grip.'

'Would it were not so,' Lucien lamented. He gave him more of the opiate and, with a moist cloth wiped Michel's brow. 'Sleep, Michel. I shall stay by your side'. By nightfall, his condition further deteriorated. Lucien felt numb from the realisation he was powerless to save him. He prayed for acceptance that he could not heal the boy he had come to love as a son.

In the morning, Lucien at his bedside, Michel opened his eyes and murmured, 'I must make confession, Brother. Magister Fidelis, will you bid him come?'

Of course. I had forgot. Stricken with sorrow, Lucien feigned levity. 'And I think I know what that confession will be, Michel. Disobedience! Falsehoods – lies! They have long been flaws in your character, my boy!' The words were harsh, but there was tenderness in his voice.

Michel looked at him lovingly. 'Dearest Lucien. Be comfited. I am content. It is right and just I join my mother and father in the manner in which they entered heaven.' His voice weakened. He rasped, 'Will you lay me to rest besides them?'

Lucien dared not respond lest a flood of tears betray his grief. He kissed Michel's forehead and gave him his blessing, murmuring, 'I love you dearly, my son.' Then he went from the Hôtel Dieu to look for Fidelis.

As his life force ebbed, Michel made a last confession and received the sacrament of Extreme Unction. Fidelis told him 'I shall give you a special blessing, my son, but I think you go to God without blemish. The choirs of angels will be jubilant to receive you.'

Lucien entered the alcove and sat by the bed, stroking his hand. 'Michel, can you hear me?' Michel nodded, without opening his eyes. 'I have only just heard. Gilles de Rais is to be hanged.'

'God have mercy on his soul.'

'If you say so, dear boy,' Lucien said, barely able to disguise his rancour. He took Michel's hand and whispered, 'Your work on earth has been truly faithful to God's design, and I am confident your just reward award awaits you. Intercede with Him for me, I beg you, my dearest boy. I shall need that. I shall need your intercession.'

Michel tried to speak. Lucien drew close to him as Michel whispered, 'Do not fear. Be assured God and his holy mother will attend to my petitions.'

Lucien held him in his arms as Michel gave up the struggle it was to breathe.

Michel's bier lay in the nave of the great cathedral. The abbot, attended by Fidelis, Lucien, Laurentius and Quimper, celebrated a High Mass, after which a grave next to Marie and Yann Dunard received Michel's remains on 26th October 1440, the day Baron Gilles de Rais was hanged in Nantes.

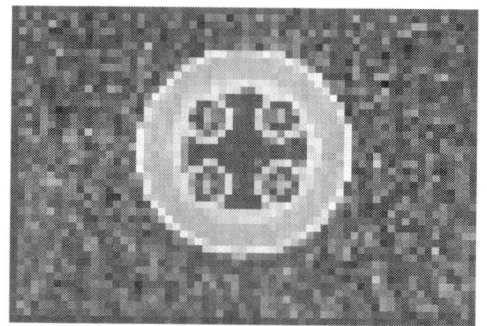

EPILOGUE

The Year of Our Lord 1490

Lucien sat alone, basking in a comfortable *chaise* in the cloister languidly stroking a feline companion by his side, both made drowsy by the warmth of the springtime sun. His eyes brightened as Abbot Tristyn approached him with a grin on his face and a document. Lucien raised his eyebrows with curiosity, and extended his hand as he took the parchment proffered him. 'A papal decree,' he muttered with wonder. Intrigued, he began to read it, befuddled, then surprised, and then elated. 'Blessed. And now this! I am overwhelmed.' He began to stutter with excitement. 'A . . . a . . . saint.' Excited, he struggled to rise from the chaise but abandoned the effort in favour of a prideful sigh.

'Yes. Yes! And here is the invitation to the canonisation ceremony. For me, Prior Gaetan and, naturally, you. First and foremost, you. The senior surviving monk in the abbey who personally knew Michel.'

Radiating delight, Lucien said quietly 'Saint Michel de Pobrér. My Michel. It is too remarkable. Too wonderful. Hard to believe.' He shook his head and silently savoured the news. 'Rome. A canonisation. He looked at the invitation and then the abbot with regret. 'Well, of course I cannot go . . . but it is a great honour of course to have been invited.' He paused, frustrated. 'Too old . . . too old.' He smiled. 'Ah, but you and Gaetan will be my eyes and ears, and will tell me each detail of this . . . this monumental occasion.'

'A wise decision, I think, Lucien. But a lamentable one.'

'A rational decision! Oh, I shall be content enough to await your full account of the ceremony on your return.'

Tristyn smiled indulgently. 'I brought you these to read as well. The Declaration of Canonisation and the Papal Council for Sainthood's summary of their findings and conclusions.'

Lucien virtually lurched for the documents as he bade farewell to the abbot, eager to study the canonisation process, hopeful it would controvert his habitual derisive judgement of such proceedings.

Several readings of the declaration instead confirmed his longstanding opinion of that body. Their findings in fact elicited guffaws. 'Drivel pure and simple.' *Ah, but Michel! Your character and moral fiber indeed were those of an extraordinary – saintly – human being.* 'No doubt about that,' he said audibly. 'The greatest honour of the Church, flawed though it may be, is apposite.'

It pleased Lucien to know the world would venerate Michel. Pray to him. Do him homage on his name day. 'Yes! The feast of Saint Michel l'Archange.' He smacked his lips in satisfaction and again said aloud, 'What matter, Michel, how they made their decision? What matter, *Saint* Michel. The important thing is you are being given your due!' And he chuckled as he thought of the ludicrous deductions that prompted the committee on sainthood to recommend the tribute.

Lucien continued to read the decree, interested that it confirmed that which all Bretons long had concluded: Michel was the protector of children throughout the land. 'Right and just . . . right and just.' Lucien whispered. He thought lovingly of the boy who risked his life to save a fellow oblate, remembered how he nursed those sickened by the pestilence with no regard for his own vulnerability and, finally, the sacrifice of his life to save a friend. 'The black potion,' he muttered. *Apportioned for his use only . . . Still, there might not be a Blessed Claire if he had not given the potion to the girl. Hmm. God's providence?'*

A final reading taxed his patience, and Lucien said forcefully, 'Never in my ninety-eight years have I read such folly,' The cat raised its head and looked quizzically at him before resuming its nap.

I told you, Michel, this world is ruled by fools and filled with superstitious twaddle. How I wish I could hear your laughter, share your amusement. He put the documents aside and read again a long letter from his old and esteemed friend, Philippe Lyçon, a Benedictine monk who had on several occasions in recent years been a guest at the abbey. Lyçon had presided over the downfall and excommunication of the erstwhile Cardinal Trumpière, and was himself a cardinal and a member of the Vatican Curia. He routinely kept Lucien abreast of the inner workings of that mysterious body, a generally reprehensibly shady lot in Lucien's view.

The letter from Cardinal Lyçon described in detail testimonies by parents to church authorities about the restoration to health of their children through their prayerful petitions to Blessed Michel de Pobrér. Their assertions they were miracles were presented to the Vatican for its perusal, '*And, upon exhaustive examination, the Church concurred,*' wrote the Cardinal. Lucien shook his head in disbelief. 'Daft! The rulings are preposterous, based on faulty, wild suppose-tions.'

He took up the panel's summary and looked for the case that exemplified his thinking, such as the parents who reported their child had an abnormally large head. '*It were possessed. And none of the remedies returned our child to us,*' the parents attested. The committee subscribed to the prevailing interpretation it was a sign the baby was bedeviled, and the baby had been transformed into a fairy child, a changeling.

Pure superstition. An 'exchange' to oust a 'fairy' and return a baby to normal? Magical thinking – as are all the shibboleths desperate people resort to. Lucien didn't wonder the so-called remedies failed. *The child had hydrocephaly, fully described by Leonidas in the second century and Oribasius in the fourth.*

Lucien noted that the parents prayed to Blessed Michel whilst a physician gave the infant lily of the valley, anise, parsley, and burdock root. *That*, Lucien concluded triumphantly, caused the fluid on the brain to drain and restored the child's head to normal size. *No surprise the Church prefers the drama of a miracle. The Church relies on such notions. The power of inter-cessory prayers of saints at the right hand of God reinforces belief as well as ritual – to the Church's benefit.*

Lucien read another 'proof' of a miracle in a narrative about a six-year-old boy who fell through the ice on a lake. The parents retrieved the limp child from the water, who was, to all appearances, drowned, lifeless. They wrapped him in thick woolen blankets and rubbed his body briskly as they prayed to Blessed Michel.

He was never dead! Look to the writings of Paulus Aegineta in the seventh century. The warmth from the blanket and the massage that stimulated the boy's body animated consciousness. Lucien murmured vocally, 'Yet, it was loving kind of them to attribute their child's recovery to Michel, my little Saint Michel – and credit him with a second miracle!'

Lucien reviewed yet another 'miracle.' A little girl lay close to death with a high fever. A great believer in the popular superstition of the times, the mother measured her daughter with a string, cut it to the exact length of her child's body, and embedded the string into a handmade candle. She lit the candle in the cathedral in Saint Petroc, and knelt on the stone floor where Blessed Michel's coffin had laid after his death. In just three days, the fever was gone, and the child awoke. The mother attested she was cured of all disease and ascribed the cure to Blessed Michel. The Church agreed. Lucien shook his head and roared with laughter. Exasperated, Lucien sputtered, 'A candle and a prayer cured her? Dull wits. The lot of them! God, give me patience!' *The Tribunal might have referred to ancient Hippocrates On Fevers and their progression and regression.*

Lucien did believe it remarkable – and even wonderful – people travelled from all over with their children to the cathedral and the place Michel had lain in funereal repose because they believed he performed miraculous cures. He had for years observed that phenomenon in the cathedral, and was impressed to read that all those who wrote in support of Michel's candidacy for sainthood had followed the exact ritual. They went on their knees, carrying their children, placed their babes on the funeral site, and intoned prayerful appeals to their young saint to intercede to God and his blessed mother that their children might be cured. Several affidavits professed cures through Blessed Michel' intercession. *Such faith*, Lucien mused silently, *such simple faith.*

He wistfully recalled his own supplication to Michel as he lay dying to intercede to God on his behalf. Does God in fact answer these prayers? *I didn't think so then. Now I am not so sure.* He sighed as he recalled that moment so long ago, wiped a tear, and returned to Cardinal Lyçon's letter.

'*The Papal Council for Sainthood certified Michel had intervened on behalf of countless numbers of children, having studied, often with awe and wonder, official documentation of the miracles wrought and ascribed to Michel de Pobrér's intercession.*

They reviewed records decades old when Blessed Michel had been declared Venerable, in which glowing testimonials related to the oblate's life and death written by the Blessed Claire and Abbot William, Prior Fidelis, and Dean Lucien of the Abby of Saint Benedict in Saint Petroc-sur-lac, Sheriff Marc Gervais from the town, and a letter that attested to the accuracy of their accounts written by the bishop of the time, Bernard du Loi.'

'Bernard du Loi. Hmph. Well at least he confirmed the merits of the testimonials,' Lucien sneered aloud, and tried to shake the memory of him from his mind, summoning instead loving images of the revered William, Fidelis and the gallant Marc Gervais before returning to the cardinal's missive.

'*After months of deliberations, careful consideration of all testaments of miracles submitted by sworn witnesses, and prayers for guidance, the testimonials and three salient factors swayed the committee to reach the unanimous decision that Blessed Michel de Pobrér is a saint, and should be canonised:*

I: The biography of Blessed Michel de Pobrér written by his close friend, Blessed Abbess Claire of Saint Petroc-sur-lac. The book documented several miracles performed by the saintly candidate. Blessed Claire avowed that Blessed Michel saved her life on two occasions, and that it was his influence that inspired her to become a nun. Following Blessed Michel's example, she dedicated her life to the care of the sick. She founded the Benedictine order of Sisters of Caritas and established five abbeys. She wrote that in her youth the saintly Blessed Michel rescued her from menacing brigands, protected her from the Black Death, and successfully treated her brother who had been afflicted with the plague, and in fact had brought him back to life after he had ceased to breathe. As a direct consequence of his selfless dedication, Blessed Michel was stricken by the disease, and died.

II: The archives of the abbey of Saint Benedict of Saint Petroc-sur-lac chronicled Blessed Michel de Pobrér's demonstrable and exceptional courage in times of jeopardy, most notably when he saved the life of oblate Tristyn de Vannes – now abbot of the Abbey of Saint Benedict – from the iniquitous baron Giles de Rais. Blessed Michel's testimony to the constabulary was a crucial element in the capture and conviction of said baron, whose wicked crimes against children have been well documented.

III: In addition to the required, infallible evidence of three miracles attributed to the candidate, Blessed Michel had in his possession several items deemed to be sacred:

1. A scapular with an image of Mary, the mother of God, with dried blood of the Virgin on it. It has been declared a second-class relic.

2. A record of two sworn written accounts by two lay brothers who witnessed Blessed Michel rise from the dead where he had been buried in a common pit of shrouded corpses.

3. At the time of his death, Blessed Michel had a small piece of wood engraved with the letters 'Sa... c...' – Sanctae Crucis – on his person. The committee agreed only a saint would be worthy to possess a fragment of the true and holy cross.

Lucien could barely contain his amusement. *Infallible evidence, indeed.* It never ceased to astound him how the Church arrived at fallacious – outlandish – conclusions.

Had he been asked, Lucien could have elucidated the facts. How Michel's blood from a cut had stained the scapular; how he had sought refuge in the open pit and was wounded by an arrow – no more than that. *No resurrection* The fragment of wood was from the burned abbey's cart marked Abbey of Saint Benedict. He recalled Marc Gervais had found the charred scrap of wood in the forest, and remembered the fragment had 'Sa . . . c . . .' incised in it. He mumbled, 'It takes great imagination to stretch that to *Sanctae crucis*!' And he laughed again.

He inwardly fumed when he thought how the Church deferred to the evil baron's rank despite the depraved crimes of which he had been convicted, angrily recalling how de Rais had been buried *ad Sanctus* in the church of the Monastery of Notre-Dames des Carmes in Nantes. *Profanity. Fawning hypocrites!* 'I must not think on it,' he blustered. *Think of Michel . . . canonised a saint! So. For once the Church got something right!* Lucien smiled. It didn't matter how they had arrived at the truth of it.

On the fifteenth of May 1490, the Pope in Rome presided over the canonisation of Blessed Michel de Pobrér in a resplendent ceremony in the Vatican's Saint Peter's Basilica, built in the fourth century and much in need of repair – or demolition. A prestigious location had been reserved for Abbot Tristyn and Prior Gaetan of the Abbey of Saint Benedict in Saint Petroc-sur-lac in honour of the monastery that had sheltered Blessed Michel in life.

After the canonisation and attendant festivities, the abbot and prior returned *post haste* to the abbey, and made their way to the cloister with a banquet – savouries, sweets and wine to account to Lucien the marvels of the occasion.

They feasted as they described in detail the ceremony and the basilica in which it was held. Abbot Tristyn told him, 'It was erected on the very site where Saint Peter is buried. We knelt at his tomb in the crypt located under the altar! In the basilica, there is a large, much venerated bronze statue of Saint Peter sculpted by – who was it they said? – Arnolfo di Cambio I believe . . .

Prior Gaetan said, 'The statue is greater than life size. Very imposing. It depicts Saint Peter holding the keys to the kingdom in one hand and giving a blessing with the other.'

The abbot interjected, 'Travellers from all over the world for one hundred and ninety years have knelt before that statue to appeal to Saint Peter they be granted entry into heaven should they die in Rome on their pilgrimage. The toes are smoothed and polished from the touch and kiss of so many people.'

Lucien nodded approval. 'Yes, yes. Wonderful. Do please continue. Tell me about the canonisation.

'Oh, very solemn,' said the abbot. 'And dazzling to the senses. The basilica accommodated more than four thousand people from all over Europe, there to honour our Michel. The air was heavy with light and smoke from the candles. And the sounds! Angelic voices of choristers, and thundering music played on the organ resounded throughout the cavernous space. The pope delivered a homily so full of praise about the life of our little saint it left me in tears. How I wish you had been there.' Lucien smiled and nodded his appreciation.

Prior Gaetan handed Lucien a copy of the pope's sermon, and spoke animatedly about the accolades and homage given by the pope. Tristyn continued, 'Once the rituals of canonisation ended – it all seemed too short – the pope was elevated onto a throne and carried through the crowds inside the basilica and then outside to the cloister and beyond where hordes of people filled the site and cheered. He gave his blessing with one hand and in the other held aloft a first-class relic of Blessed – that is – Saint Michel l'Archange de Pobrér . . .'

'A first-class relic, you say?' Lucien asked, perplexed. What mean you?'

Abbot Tristyn responded. 'Rome requested a relic, and ordered Michel's body exhumed. I had no choice except obey, and sent a finger-bone from his right hand to Rome.'

Lucien remained silent for a moment, irate to hear Michel's remains had been desecrated. He finally spoke as if to himself, silently setting aside his indignation. 'You stir memories of the last time I saw his peaceful body, dressed in the robes of a Boy Bishop. Michel loved pageantry, is that not so, Tristyn?'

'Tis true, Lucien. He was in awe of the spectacle and the apparel of the feast of Childermas. So. That is why the monks dressed him in the regalia of a Boy Bishop!'

Lucien nodded. 'He looked very regal as you may remember, and. from all you say of the canonisation *extravagantem*, such a grand occasion would greatly please him. You will recall there was a streak of vanity in him.'

Abbot Tristyn smiled uncomfortably, but said nothing. Prior Gaetan looked askance at the implication the newly minted saint had human frailties, but foreswore comment, attributing the indiscretion to his fellow monk's old age.

Gaetan continued with his account of the procession. 'There were thousands of people in the cloister, on the steps leading up to it, and in the area surrounding the basilica. Oh, if you could have but seen it! You cannot imagine the acclaim. The abbot and I stood at the portals to the basilica, and rejoiced to see such a gathering and to hear the roaring ovation that greeted the pontiff. Thundering, truly thundering. Families and children were everywhere. So many children! We were told some were those who had been cured by our Saint Michel. I can never forget the magnificence of it all.'

The abbot smiled and added, 'Truly, the splendour of the day is sadly incapable of description that does it justice, but surely it must gladden your heart to hear our poor account of it.'

Lucien nodded, smiled broadly, and took the abbot's ring to kiss it. 'Indeed, my heart rejoices, My Lord.'

'I have a letter from the pope to give you.'

Lucien carefully opened the seal and unrolled the parchment. He shook his head in a gesture his confrères interpreted as humility. 'I am most undeserving,' he said, and offered the letter to Tristyn to read.

'Justly full of praise for you and the role you had in moulding the character of M . . . eh, Saint Michel. He turned to Gaetan and said, 'It says in part . . . *for surely your guidance and instruction formed much of the goodness and sanctity of his soul.*'

'Nay, nay, not I. Not I alone. So many others. But it is most satisfactory to receive such tribute from the pope.'

The lavish description about the canonisation ceremony that honoured the young man so dear to his heart imbued Lucien with pride, and euphoria informed his being every day thereafter. Thoughts about the canonisation filled his mind. He re-read the pope's letter to him many times, and tried to fully grasp the extraordinary fact the name of his intern in the Hôtel Dieu – his cherished friend - had been added to the Church's Litany of the Saints. He spent many hours in the cloister resting on the *chaise* made expressly for him, lulled by the warm rays of the sun into reverie. His mind drifted back to treasured memories of young Michel and his lively companions, beloved colleagues, and all the members of the monastic community.

Abbot Tristyn approached Lucien on a mild May morning to present a visitor to the abbey. 'Brother Francis has come from Lyons to stay with us for the summer. No doubt you will become fast friends.'

Lucien bid him welcome and encouraged him to bide awhile with him.

Brother Francis sat on a bench beside Lucien and commented, 'You seem particularly happy today, Brother.'

Lucien nodded jovially, and handed him a copy of the pope's proclamation. 'I confess I have read it over and over,' he said, and shook his head with amazement and pride. 'Saint Michel . . . from our abbey!' He turned to the visitor and informed him, 'Only just canonised, you know.'

'Abbot Tristyn has told me of your close relationship with the newly canonised saint and tells me you – and he – knew him well.'

Lucien brightened and said, Indeed, we both knew him. Michel came to our monastery as an oblate just ten years old. Thereafter, he was my apprentice in the Hôtel Dieu. My protégé. Tristyn arrived five years later. Michel saved the abbot's life!'

'Saved his life? Your protégé did that?'

'Indeed, he did so.' Lucien narrated in detail how Michel rescued Tristyn, exulting in the impression it had.

'Astonishing. It fills my heart with wonder to hear of such valour. He truly was singularly heroic. Please, tell me more about him,' Brother Francis implored.

Lucien surmised the friar expected to hear about sound character traits. and, however true, he recited a somewhat prosaic account: 'He was decent, loyal and true, intellectually talented, curious, quick to learn, hard working. Had he lived a long life, he would have been an accomplished and compassionate physician.' His voice wavered with sadness as he speculated what might have been.

Brother Francis confided, 'All that? So young and yet so gifted.' He shook his head in awe.

Lucien ruminated a long while. 'To all appearances, he was much like any other lad his age – full of mischief, loved to play, have fun. He was strong and athletic. Excellent at chess.' He paused. 'Mind, he got bored in chapel and rarely listened to the lector in the refectory. And he told lies with the best of them, and on more than one occasion. The infractions of monastery rules – Saint Benedict's rules – continually frustrated Prior Fidelis' hopes for reform.' He laughed. 'Boys *will* be boys, Brother. And Michel!' Lucien shook his head in remembrance. 'He was stubbornly independent and given to decisions that conflicted with monastic dictums. At times we thought him completely unruly. He must have walked the labyrinth in penance hundreds of times in a mere five years.' Francis looked shocked.

'I have written an account about him. Wrote it some years ago. I have never shown it to anyone. Now I think it a good time to make copies for others to read. We have one of those newfangled printing presses. It would break the heart of our old Master of the Scriptorium,' he said as an aside. 'When they are printed, I shall give you a copy.'

He closed his eyes and envisaged Michel as if he were a living presence, and silently summoned memories of his apprentice. 'He was everything you have heard about him – humble, kind, devout, concerned for others, good humoured, and loved by all in the abbey. He was even a special friend of the town sheriff! And the poor who came for alms had great affection for him. He was a great help to me in the infirmary and, thinking back, I probably gave him more responsibility for caring for patients than is seemly for one so young. But he was exceptionally bright and able, with a passion to learn, and devoted to serve others.'

He thought a moment and said, 'Courage! Courage was his greatest attribute. He faced fear boldly – like Saint Michael the Archangel crossing swords with the devil. He ignored dire peril to himself when he saved Tristyn from the hands of the Satan of our age, Gilles de Rais is but the greatest example of his spirit.'

Lucien studied Brother Francis's mien and then laughed heartily. 'Yea, though he may have seemed outwardly ordinary, he was anything but and, especially when tested, he was stout-hearted.' Lucien paused, remembering that, in any crisis, Michel thought only of others. That sparked recall of his rescue of Ronan from Trumpière, the into the fray battles with aberrant boys. . . . and the fateful day he emphatically ordered Michel to take the black potion at the first hint the plague was a threat, and how Michel broke the vow he would do so in order to save his friend, Claire. Wanly, Lucien murmured, '*Greater love hath no man than this, that a man lay down his life for his friend.*' He looked at Brother Francis, who appeared perplexed. 'From the new testament, Brother. John, Chapter I. Courage and love. More than anything, those qualities defined Michel.'

Tears surfaced as he dwelled on the magnanimity of Michel's sacrifice of his life and the greatness of his soul. After a brief time, he recovered his composure, and with vexation as well as affection, said, 'Mind you, for all that, confound the boy, he was nothing but trouble and the most disobedient oblate in the history of the monastery!'

THE END

Acknowledgements

My best friend and lifelong partner, Angel Colón, has throughout this project been of inestimable help. His insightful suggestions, inexhaustible fact checking of my mediaeval medical research, technical support, graceful patience, and unfailing encouragement have been the *sine qua non* to bringing this historical novel to fruition. It is truly as much his work as mine, as both of us have had an enduring interest in the story of Gilles de Rais, in mediaeval life, the history of the Roman Catholic Church, and the lives of children in past centuries, and Angel sustained an active and avid interest in the progress of my work. Endless thanks to Aisling Colón, who has an editor's instinct and a proofreader's ruthless pen, and whose unremitting work, artistic contributions, support, and commendation made all the difference. In equal measure, my thanks to St. John Colón for his tireless artistic efforts to please, and especially, but not solely, for the cover page that so beautifully captures the substance of the novel. Thanks to Madie Livesey, my first reader who encouraged me unstintingly, to Alex Packer whose accolades sustained my confidence. His and Raoul Wientzen's advice about and insights into the publishing world have been an education. John Petruccione's scholarship on the early Christian poet, Prudentius, provided an appreciated authentic touch in the monastic setting. The insights into Breton life and history from Jacqueline and Anne Gaël Le Conte and Patrick Cooper have been invaluable. Special thanks to Patrick for the gifts of his works of art I knew from the outset I wanted incorporated into the book. Grateful acknowledgement to

Bobbie and Joe di Gaetano, Sisters Catherine Joan, SND and Deirdre Doyle, SSH, to whom I am much indebted.

Additional reading of interest include the 1440 transcripts of the trials of Gilles de Rais: *Laughter for the Devil*, translated from Latin and French into English by Reginald Hyatte (Rutherford, N.J.: Fairleigh Dicken-son Associated University Presses, c. 1984).

A History of Children: A Social-Cultural Survey Across Millennia, Colón, A. R. and P. A. Colón, Westport, Connecticut: Greenwood Press, 2001 is available for those interested in the history of oblation, of changelings, and mediaeval superstitions.

Nurturing Children: A History of Pediatrics, A. R., and P. A. Colón. Westport, Connecticut: Greenwood Press, 1999 and *Tincture of Time: A Concise History of Medicine, Colón, A. R. and P. A.,* Amazon Press, 2020 survey mediaeval medicine and medical practices.

There are innumerable sources about the plague, but, in my opinion, the most readable are: *Plague and the Poor in Renaissance Florence,* Carmichael, A.G., Cambridge: Cambridge University Press, 1986 and Gottfried, R. S. *The Black Death.* London: Free Press, 1983. Academic treatises of general medieval life can be found in *Medieval Households*, Herlihy, D., Cambridge: Harvard University Press, 1985, Herlihy, D., 'Medieval Children.' *Walter Prescott Webb Memorial Lectures.* Austin: University of Texas Press, 1978, *The Domestic Life of a Medieval City.* Ran, D., Lincoln: University of Nebraska Press, 1985, and 'Childhood in Medieval Europe,' Ran, D., *Children in Historical and Comparative Perspective.* Ed.: Hawes, J.M., Hiner, N.R. New York: Greenwood Press, 1991. *Life in Medieval France,* Joan Evans, New York, Phaidon, 1925, and *A Distant Mirror,* Barbara Tuchman, New York: Ballantine, 1978, the most interesting and pleasurable reads about life in medieval Europe.

Author's note

Although Michel de Pobrér, the monastery and its inhabitants, the sheriff and his associates live in a fictional world in fifteenth century Brittany, Gilles de Rais and his followers are actual persons guilty of the unspeakable crimes described in *The Oblate*. The continually referenced extant transcripts of de Rais' trials provided me the facts to arrive at the novel's historic truth.

The black potion is a fabrication, although not the chimera it might seem. One of its properties yields the antibiotic tetracycline, confirmed by traces of streptomyces, a mould that fluoresces with tetracycline crystals that have been found in bones 1200 years old. (Larson, Clark Spencer. *Bioarchaeology*. Cambridge University Press, 1997, p. 92). A species of rotten wood, deciphered from hieroglyphics as *ht-w3* containing these streptomyces, commonly ingested as beer in ancient Egypt, are still found in wood in over 70% of Sudan and southern Egypt. Thanks to Angel Colón for that!

The Rule of Saint Benedict, the oblation of children, the dedication of Benedictines to prayer, to labour and care for the poor, the medical care and the *material medica* of the 15th century, the superstitions, the *processus canonisationis,* and even the menace of the *ecorcheurs* are authentic to the period, as are the verbal exchanges amongst the novel's personae.

The canonical tribunal in Nantes officially concluded one hundred and forty children had been abused, tortured, mutilated, and killed by Gilles de Rais and his malefactors. The civil court adjusted the number to greater than two hundred victims on the strength of strong testimony from witnesses. Many experts believe hundreds more – all cremated – may reasonably be added to those numbers. Some allege as many as six hundred innocent children were killed by de Rais' and his nefarious band.

The trial was swift and conviction certain. On the twenty-sixth of October 1440, Gilles de Rais was hanged. Only two of his many associates were hanged -and burned at the stake - on the same day, the others having fled or, having cooperated with the courts, were granted clemency. Having expressed contrition for his deeds, the authorities, in consideration of de Rais' aristocratic heritage, spared him the ultimate dishonour of disembowelment by flames, and permitted his body to be buried in a casket and entombed in the abbey of Notre-Dame-des-Carmes in Nantes, Brittany, where it remained until the monastery and its church were destroyed by Napoleon's army in the eighteenth century.

The innumerable instances of paedophila and child abuse that dominated much of the news in the late 20th and early 21st centuries inspired the narrative of the novel.

P.A. Colón, Dublin, Ireland

la peste   p. 143

Made in the USA
Columbia, SC
19 March 2021

34016930R00176